V

VOLCANO

Richard Swanson

SWAN

A R.W. SWANSON & ASSOC., INC. BOOK
Littleton, CO U.S.A.

VEGAS VOLCANO

A Swan Book
Published by R.W. Swanson & Associates, Inc.
9227 East Lincoln Avenue #200
Littleton, CO 80124

Email: swan05@sprynet.com

SWAN is an imprint of R.W. Swanson & Associates, Inc.
Cover art and design by Richard Swanson
Cover layout and typography by Cynthia Swanson Fisher

ISBN: 0-9673271-5-6

First mass market edition: June 2004

Printed in the United States of America

10 9 8 7 6 5 4 3 2 1

VEGAS VOLCANO

If a city were measured by
how many prayers were offered up
within a 24-hour period,
Las Vegas would be the holiest place on earth.
Everyone prays that the next card,
the next roll of the dice
or spin of the wheel,
will be the one to change their life.
It is a city of both hope and broken dreams.
In spite of its attempts to pass itself off
as just a normal, growing community,
it remains the Sin City of the world.
Oh, there are other places
where the sin is more real.
But, Las Vegas is not about reality,
it is about perception.
Big men with even bigger egos
have built huge pleasure palaces
where fantasy reigns.
Any whim will be indulged,
if you dare to bet big enough.
After dark, millions of lights turn the city
into a pulsating, vibrant world.
On the surface, it is all glitz and glamour,
but there is a darker, less desirable underside
that threatens to erupt at any second.

ACKNOWLEDGEMENTS

This book could never have happened without the love, inspiration and support of my wife, Delia, and my family and friends. They all contributed. Their editing, research and suggestions were beyond value.

An extra special thanks has to be extended to David Fisher and the crew at Continuous Printing Corporation. Their professionalism shows on every page.

This book is dedicated with love to my parents,
Dick and Elaine Swanson.
I am eternally grateful for their
innumerable sacrifices.

PROLOGUE

1946

With a deadly, high-pitched whine, the .30-.30 bullet punched a perfectly round hole in the horse's left ear before speeding off into the Nevada desert.

The rider stared transfixed as the edges of the hole slowly turned crimson with blood. At the sound of the far off report, he spun in the saddle.

The terrified horse shied as the pain made its way to his brain. He instinctively reared up on his hind legs and pawed desperately at the air with his hoofs.

The rider reacted to the panicked animal with a skill acquired from long hours in the saddle. "Whoa!" he ordered as he yanked on the reins to prevent the horse from bolting.

No sooner had the front legs of the quarterhorse hit

the ground than another bullet hit it directly in the heart with a sickening thud. By the time the second report was heard, the horse was already dead. It dropped awkwardly to its knees and fell over onto its left side, trapping the rider under its eleven hundred pound weight.

Buck Anders, a twenty-five year-old deputy sheriff, had found his fugitive!

The fall knocked the wind out of Buck and it took a few gasps before he could reinflate his lungs and take stock of what had happened. He had heard, more than felt, his right leg snap with a sound that reminded him of a large branch being broken.

With panic rising in his throat, he realized that the gunman would try to confirm his kill. He reached for his Winchester Model 94 rifle still in the saddle scabbard and then let out an involuntary scream as excruciating pain shot through his body. He tried three more times to reach the elusive rifle, only to be beaten back each time by waves of pain.

Finally, giving up on retrieving the rifle he attempted to remove his broken leg from beneath the dead horse. Through stabs of pain, he gingerly pulled on the wounded leg, but it was hopelessly caught. He tried to turn to a more comfortable position and watched in horror as his leg rotated to an awkward angle. He knew the femur had been broken completely in two.

The sound of the approaching rider momentarily distracted Buck from his predicament and he turned to see the longhaired Indian rein his lathered horse to a sudden stop.

"Wahoo, Wahoo!" The rider shouted as he waved

his short-barreled Winchester carbine over his head in his clenched fist.

"Dammit!" shouted Buck. "Why did you shoot my horse?"

"Wahoo!" The rider cried again, ignoring the question.

"Piute Bill, you crazy Indian. You're drunk as a skunk!"

"Wahoo!" came the reply.

"Shut up and pull this horse off of me! My leg's broke!"

The whooping rider ignored the order and instead bent over in the saddle and with the barrel of his carbine slipped it under the strap of the water canteen hanging from the saddle horn on the downed animal. Once he had tied the canteen to his own saddle he levered the Winchester and without aiming fired toward the helpless figure underneath the horse. Crack! The shot reverberated across the desert and the dirt next to Buck's face erupted into a small geyser of dust.

"What in the hell are you doing?" shouted Buck completely surprised by the Indian's action. "Jeez Bill, you ain't in any real trouble yet! I only want you for kicking the crap out of that barber ... and now of course for shooting my horse!"

The rider levered the carbine and again shot at the protesting figure, missing by inches.

"You drunk son-of-a-bitch, put up that rifle before you hurt somebody!" Buck ordered at the top of his voice. "You're starting to piss me off!"

With another loud whoop, the renegade turned his horse, spurred it violently, and galloped away.

"Damn that was close," said Buck just starting to appreciate how unpredictable the situation had been.

Suddenly, the Indian reined his frothy horse to a stop and turning toward Buck, again raised his rifle and fired. The slug from the 30-30 shattered the saddle horn on the downed animal and ricocheted into the temple of Buck Anders.

———·———

It was nearly noon when Buck regained consciousness. He had been out for nearly three hours. His pounding head prompted him to raise his hand to his temple. He was not surprised when he felt a warm, sticky substance. Instinctively he tried to stand, but the violent pain in his leg snapped him back to the reality of his situation. At least he was not dead, thanks in no small measure to the fact that drunk or sober Piute Bill was a lousy shot.

It had to be nearly 110 degrees on the desert floor and Buck knew that if he did not get help, or do something himself, he would quickly die of exposure. He really was in deep trouble. In spite of his pounding headache, he was relieved to find that he was only bleeding slightly from the wound. But, he also realized that his broken leg trapped beneath the dead horse was the major problem to be dealt with. Now that he was conscious, it seemed every movement caused excruciating pain. Through grunts and curses, he turned and fished the Barlow folding knife out of his Levi's front pocket.

Opening the knife, he tested the blade instinctively with his thumb and found it to be, as expected, razor sharp. By ignoring the unnatural angle of the broken leg he was finally able to pull himself upright into a sitting position. He carefully sliced the coarse denim material of his pants from just below his pocket to the top of what he could see of his boot. He laid the fabric back, surprised to find only an angry red bump where the bone had broken. "At least I'm not bleeding," he said as he gingerly poked and prodded trying to find the exact spot of the break. He confirmed it was about five inches below his knee.

He stared at the leg and tried pulling on it to see if he could pull his foot out of the boot. It was hopeless! The spurs he had on pulled the boot too tight across his instep. "Damn," he cursed. "I'm going to be done in by my favorite spurs." He had won the engraved silver with gold, inlaid spurs as his prize for winning first place in Saddle Bronc Riding at the Helldorado Days Rodeo.

He was aggravatingly thirsty and he cursed Piute Bill again for taking his water. He found a marble-sized pebble on the desert floor and started to suck on it. It was an old Indian trick that was a remarkably effective way to keep the mouth moist.

Buck knew that he would not last more than a couple of days if he stayed where he was. The desert, seventy miles north of Las Vegas, was a very inhospitable place. Other than a fugitive like Piute Bill, or an occasional desert rat prospector, there was no reason for human beings to venture into its wilderness. Buck knew that help was unlikely to come along. No, he had to do something himself. He knew what that was, but he could not allow his brain to contemplate it. It was too horrible!

His splitting headache, the sharp stabbing pain in his leg, the awful thirst and now the sudden realization that he had lost his hat during the fall and was sun burning, were having their effect. He could feel his strength slowly draining off. He had to do it, and he had to do it now! He had to cut off his leg!

Buck had field-dressed deer and elk, and heaven only knew how many cattle he had butchered, so he knew how to do it. But, it had been a lot easier to separate the legs from animal carcasses than it would be to cut off his own limb!

He sliced off one of the reins from the bridle and then cut off his remnants of his pant leg from the pocket down. Wrapping the bridle around the leg about five inches above the knee, he began to twist it tightly. Each turn on the tourniquet caused almost unbearable pain. But, he continued. After fifteen minutes, his lower leg had turned a light blue and the stabbing pain had turned to a dull ache. Tying the bridle into a knot to hold the twist, he lay back on the scorching desert floor and rehearsed in his mind what he had to do. He had to do it quick otherwise, the shock might knock him out and it was possible, if that happened, he would never wake up. He knew he had to have the artery pinched off effectively enough to hold the pressure of his blood. If the tourniquet did not hold pressure, he would bleed to death.

He thought about suicide, maybe it would be an easier way out. It sounded corny when he thought about it—-but he had been raised a Catholic and suicide was definitely against his religion. As close as he was to death, by some means, he thought it did not make sense to take a chance that he would be journeying to the wrong place in the afterlife!

He spat out the pebble, sat back up and took a long look around and in every direction. He needed to be sure no one else was happening along. With no help on the horizon, he resigned himself to what he had to do. He prodded at his numb leg to locate the exact spot where he would begin cutting.

It felt as if his leg was being seared by a branding iron as the cold steel of the knife started slicing through his leg tissue. He screamed in agony. It took all his will not to stop! The whole thing was surreal. It was as if he were operating on another person. He knew he was screaming but somehow he just kept cutting. The bone had broken cleanly and he was able to slice through the soft tissue of the leg in a matter of only a few seconds. It seemed like an eternity.

Suddenly, he was completely free of his trapped leg! His first instinct was to try to stand and he awkwardly tied it before falling back. His brain was in a fog and it took a minute for him recall where he was and what had just happened.

Regaining some equilibrium, he scooted over to his Stetson and almost wept with delight at the cool shade provided by the dirty, sweat stained hat. Then he passed out.

The desert floor was scorching and the midday sun was merciless. The temperature had climbed to 120 degrees in the shade, if there had been any. The heat proved to be a blessing to Buck. It kept him from going into deep shock.

He was still semi-delirious when he awoke and

propped himself up on his elbow and looked around. A hideous looking vulture was perched on the remnants of the saddle horn and studying him cautiously. When he moved the vulture hopped away about twenty yards, stopped and spread its huge wings menacingly.

Buck scooted over to the rifle scabbard, swept the Winchester out, and levered a round into the chamber. Unlike Piute Bill, Buck was a crack shot and the vulture's head simply disappeared as he squeezed the trigger. "I hate those son-of-a-bitches," he said aloud, ignoring the fact that no one could hear him.

He looked down at what had been, only hours before, the finest roping horse in the county. He ran the back of his hand over its soft jaw. "It weren't your fault pardner, but you left me in a helluva fix."

He looked at the stump of his leg. He could have sworn his missing foot was itching and he instinctively reached to scratch it. He was surprised that so suddenly he would experience the phantom pain associated with an amputated limb. It was damn disconcerting to have an itch you could not scratch.

It was nearly fifteen miles back to his truck and horse trailer the way he had come. However, he had been tracking the Piute and the Indian had wandered all over the place. Due in no small part because he was drunk out of his mind.

Buck knew that he could not make it that far. He would have to find help closer. The nearest road to civilization was Highway 95, which was probably no more than five miles as the crow flies. Unfortunately, Buck was not a crow. In order to reach the highway he would have to cross some very inhospitable and rugged terrain. However, he had no choice!

Using the Winchester as a makeshift crutch, he tried to stand. He fell twice before he mastered it. Then he slowly hobbled off toward the rugged foothills between him and the highway.

The rifle made a terrible crutch and caused excruciating pain in his armpit. But, what the hell, everything about him hurt anyway. By the time, that the blistering sun had settled below the horizon he had made nearly two miles. The full moon rose and bathed the desert in moonlight. "That's a break," he muttered to himself, realizing that it meant he could try and keep going throughout the night. Maybe as the desert cooled off he would not be so damned thirsty! Recalling the image of Piute Bill stealing his canteen and riding off made him so angry he picked up his pathetic pace.

It was about three o'clock in the morning when he realized that the moonlight was fading. Looking upward, he could see a cloud front forming. Then without warning it started to rain

It was not raining a little bit; it was raining buckets! So violent was the rain that Buck began to laugh aloud. "A hour ago I was about to die of thirst, now I'll just as likely drown." Where there had been no shelter from the sun, now there was no protection from the rain. The ground was turning to mud from the rain and each time Buck pushed on the barrel of the rifle it would sink. It was now useless as a crutch. He collapsed onto the muddy ground and sat there hopelessly.

The pathetic figure sitting in the rain was only vaguely aware of the far off rumbling sound. In his semi-delirious state, he thought for sure that a train was coming. "Toot, toot," he laughed. "All aboard for Vegas." His brain knew that there was no train, but the roaring was getting louder.

Suddenly he was sitting in a fast rising puddle and he watched mesmerized as the water swirled about him. Then, without warning, a huge wall of water nearly six feet high was upon him. The flash flood picked him up like a cork and he was swept along in the torrent being tossed and turned mercilessly. He struggled with all his remaining strength to keep his head above the filthy, debris-laden water.

The flood carried Buck across the desert floor and into a canyon in the surrounding hills. In the canyon, the rain stopped and the canyon walls were bathed in surrealistic moonlight as the sky cleared. The torrent of murky water continued unabated however, and he was being scraped along the volcanic walls. Each outcropping served only to punish him without mercy. At a sharp turn in the canyon, he was momentarily caught in an eddy and he somehow managed to pull himself up onto a small rocky shelf. He lay there dazed, nearly dead, vomiting the contents of the putrid flash flood.

It was as if he was in a terrible nightmare and he passed in and out of consciousness. He did not remember if he saw or just imagined shadowy figures dancing along the canyon. When he turned and looked up at the canyon wall he was shocked to see the cold eye of a giant reptile with huge teeth staring at him. Instinctively he tried to protect himself by clawing with his right hand at the hideous face.

He was still clawing at it frantically when upstream

a temporary dam of debris broke. The resulting flood plucked him off his low shelf and washed him along again in the raging current.

Buck washed nearly three miles down the stream before he was deposited unceremoniously at the dispersion of the alluvial plain at the mouth the canyon. Half buried in mud, it was nearly an hour before his delirium subsided enough for him to move. He crawled his way forward. He had no set direction, he just moved because his survival instinct demanded it.

It was nearly five o'clock in the morning before he realized that he was crawling along a different surface than the course desert floor. It was the highway!

When he understood that he had made it, he collapsed and again passed into unconsciousness. When he finally came to, he was shocked to see what was happening. There, directly in front of his face was a diamondback rattlesnake completing its defensive coil and working its menacing rattle. He stared at the serpent transfixed, unable to muster the strength to move.

It was common for rattlesnakes to seek the residual warmth of a highway during the cool morning hours in the desert. It was unfortunate that Buck had chosen this exact spot out of hundreds of miles of asphalt to share with one of the deadliest creatures of the desert.

Buck could not move and watched helplessly as the snake poised its triangular shaped head to strike. A blinding flash of light suddenly illuminated the scene just as the snake struck directly at Buck's head. With a loud roar, the deadly serpent simply disappeared in mid-strike.

Buck was completely oblivious to the screeching tires as the white Cadillac convertible with the pink flamingo on the door came to a stop. He was unconscious when the driver ran to him and turned him over.

"Who is it Ben?" asked the leggy, brunette passenger as she opened her door.

"I don't know Virginia," answered the driver with a heavy New York accent. "Give me a hand, he needs a doctor right away."

———·———

In only his second year of medical practice, Doc Prentice had never seen anything like what the snappy dressed motorist had brought in. It was barely recognizable as a human being. Even his petite but battle-hardened nurse, Vera, had nearly passed out when she first saw the pathetic creature.

Doc worked on Buck for over three hours and in spite of his best efforts, he had to admit to himself that it looked hopeless. "I'm going home to take a shower and get something to eat," he told Vera. "I'll be back around noon to check on him. As soon as possible, we will need to get him to Las Vegas. If we don't lose him over the next four hours, he might be able to handle the forty mile ambulance ride."

"He's awfully strong Doc," said the nurse trying to convince herself that there was hope.

"Even if he makes it, with all the trauma he's experienced, I'm afraid his mind is gone," he cautioned.

It was a few minutes after noon when Doc returned to his little clinic. "How's he doing?" he asked.

"He keeps mumbling something," Vera replied. "But, I can't make any sense of it."

"You go ahead and get some lunch and I'll keep up the vigil," Doc ordered. When he reentered the small combination examining and operating room, he was shocked to see Buck sitting upright on the table. "What the...?" he shouted, as he ran to the upright figure.

Buck grabbed the lapels of Doc's coat and with a catatonic stare shouted, "The lizard stared at me and winked. The shadows played the flute…but I plucked its eye and he blinked." With that, he released his grip and fell back onto the table and into unconsciousness. His right hand slowly opened and something fell out onto the floor with clatter. Doc Prentice bent over and picked it up. It was a perfectly clear stone about the size of a hen's egg.

1961

Doc Prentice had not given the rock that the unfortunate Buck Anders had dropped on his clinic's operating floor another thought. In fact, for nearly ten years, it served only as a paperweight on his ancient rolltop desk. He did not even recall when he first noticed its unusual properties. One day as he sat alone in the office, an afternoon sunray entered the cluttered office and illuminated the egg-sized object. Doc stared in amazement as the sun reflected off the stone prism and dispersed into a display of iridescence unlike anything he had seen or imagined. The room seemed to dance in a kaleidoscope of colors.

Overcome with excitement, he examined the crudely shaped stone in the direct sunlight. He could not imagine how it was possible, but he could not stop his heart from soaring. He ran to the alcove Vera used for making the morning coffee and found a water glass. Holding his breath from his excitement, he ran an edge of the stone over the glass. It left a perfect line inscribed permanently into the surface. He could not believe it! It had to be a diamond…a diamond as big as a hen's egg!

He slumped into the worn leather chair and stared for nearly an hour at his incredible discovery. Then he pulled open a small door behind the clutter of papers on the desk and after rummaging through its contents produced a small brass key. The key opened the lower right hand drawer in the desk. After carefully placing his newfound discovery into a manila envelope and sealing it, he reached into the back recesses of the drawer and pulled out the bottle of bottled-in-bond bourbon. Leaving the envelope in the drawer, he locked it and placed the key into his right pants pocket. He drank nearly half of the bottle of bourbon before passing out in his chair. He was desperately trying to remember what the phrase was that Buck had ranted for hours in his delirium.

Life had not been good to Dr. Fred Prentice. It had started out promisingly enough, good schools, high grades in class, and an internship at one of the best eastern hospitals. Things started sliding when his gold digging, teenage girlfriend came up pregnant. He repeatedly offered to abort the baby, but she would have none of it. She was convinced that this would be the ultimate trap to insure that she would indeed end up as a doctor's wife.

She was three months pregnant and had just turned eighteen when they were married in front of an aging justice of the peace. Four days after the wedding she miscarried. She was secretly ecstatic, but grieved appropriately in public. She now had everything she wanted, a great future and no maternal obligations.

When Doc crossed swords with the senior resident at the hospital over a petty disagreement, the resident gave him a negative review. Suddenly his pool of job prospects dwindled to only one, a small clinic in Las Vegas. The southern desert of Nevada, overrun with cases due to the boom in the area, was desperate for doctors. Las Vegas was young and bawdy and did not care about the pedigree or the past of anyone. Unfortunately, for the new doctor, the senior partners in the clinic had found that they could supplement their incomes dramatically by selling prescriptions for narcotics.

For the workers building the nearby Nellis Air Base, life was terrible. The workers toiled for sixteen-hour shifts in unimaginable conditions. The heat, danger, and unrelenting pressure from the supervisors took their tolls daily. The United States was desperately trying to produce enough gunnery crews to keep up with the new B29 bombers coming off the production lines. If a worker fell behind or could not perform up to the tortuous pace, they were replaced immediately. For many, a nightly binge of alcohol was just not enough to mask the pain. Those were the clients of Doc Prentice's new employers.

Within six weeks of starting his new job, the clinic was raided by local authorities, who felt that they had been denied their just cut. His short time at the clinic made it politically worthless to prosecute him and he escaped with only a forceful instruction to get out of town. His resume was now certainly nothing to brag about. He spent the next six months working odd jobs and sending letters all over the country trying to solicit job offers. Every time that a promising inquiry came up, the subsequent check of this background quickly eliminated him. At age twenty-six, he was a pariah to the elite medical profession. His wife turned out to be totally worthless in helping him through this time. Indeed, she aggravated the situation with her constant complaining. He was also unpleasantly surprised to find she was addicted to alcohol.

What little luck Doc had during this time, took the form of a job offer to establish a new clinic in the small town of Indian Springs, forty miles north of Las Vegas. The pay was terrible and the practice consisted of treating trauma and delivering babies. It was a desolate, hot, unforgiving place and totally devoid of any intellectual stimulation. He hated it, but he made the best of it, and within a few months, had been accepted by the local residents.

His wife however was a different story. She was totally disillusioned at how her life had turned out. Oh, she had become the doctor's wife all right, but rather than the big house and the elite social circles she had envisioned, she was stuck in a godforsaken hellhole. The residents consisted of cowboys, prospectors, and laborers working on the Indian Springs Air Base. She started drinking to pass the time. It was not long before she would spend the entire day seated on her designated stool in the local tavern. She was still attractive, not beautiful, but in a way that made men desire her—-and besides, to a cowboy in town once a month, or to a desert rat in town once a year, she looked great. It was not long before they had persuaded her to part with her favors for the price of a few drinks.

She was a definite embarrassment, but the locals were so desperate to keep their doctor that they practiced a well-developed charade of treating her civilly and saving their caustic comments for their private conversations. Doc Prentice had seen his wife's love making decline steadily as she sank deeper into the bottle. The discovery that the rock Buck Anders had brought into the clinic was a diamond had given him something else to focus on. He spent every spare moment when he was not at the clinic trying to find the source of the gem. He had spent countless hours scouring the desolate area on both sides of the highway where the motorist had made the gruesome discovery of Buck.

This arrangement continued for sixteen years and probably would have gone on for years more except for one telling event. Quite inexplicably, his wife got pregnant. Considering the number of lovers she had, her total lack of concern for protection and the fact she was now thirty-five, it was indeed a medical anomaly. Doc was, of course, embarrassed and enraged and demanded that she let him abort her. But, some heretofore undeveloped maternal instinct kicked in and once again she forbade him to terminate the pregnancy. He would have divorced her, but to do so would be to admit that everyone was sleeping with her except him. In spite of her age and the ravages of alcohol, she was able to carry the pregnancy full term.

Doc Prentice had successfully delivered hundreds of babies and had no reason to suspect that this delivery would be any different. However, it was obvious at the start of labor that there was trouble. The baby was going to be a breech birth and his wife was in terrible pain. In order to facilitate the birth he decided to use medical forceps. The tong-like instruments had been in use for as far back as the twelfth century. By using tongs to grasp the baby's head, difficult births could be expedited and when applied correctly, the use of forceps was a safe method of delivery. The important phrase was of course "applied correctly."

Whether it was a pure accident or a secret desire to attempt a final abortion on the stranger's baby delivering from his wife's womb, even Doc could not tell. The consequence, whatever the cause, was terrible.

The boy was huge; nearly twelve pounds. The pressure from the forceps had compressed his soft cranium into his brain, which had been permanently damaged. Although not completely paralyzed, the boy was blind in the left eye and suffered from spasms down his entire left side.

Doc handed over the baby to Vera, his nurse, and then returned to his office, stripping off his bloody rubber gloves as he went. When he reached his office, he went directly to the rolltop desk and opened the lower left hand drawer. From the furthest recesses of the drawer, he pulled out the bottle of bourbon. Not bothering to find a glass, he uncorked the bottle and took a long swig of the brownish liquid. The fiery liquid burned his throat, causing his head to give an involuntary shake.

"Doc!" shouted Vera breathlessly as she rounded the corner into his office.

Her sudden intrusion startled him, but before he could ask a question, she exclaimed, "There's a another one!"

———·———

CHAPTER 1

Thirty-seven years later

The red Ferrari Testarossa 512M had completed the four thousand-foot climb north on California Highway 247 out of Palm Springs to Prospect Valley. The outside thermometer dropped twenty degrees before the climb leveled out onto a high desert plateau.

———·———

Thomas Knight adjusted his six foot three frame into a driving position suitable for a long distance, and then snugged down the seatbelt of the Ferrari.

Pulling down his sunglasses from the top of his head, he glanced at the white-faced dial on his Rolex Yachtsman. Nearly noon, he noted, wondering why he was not feeling the least bit hungry. The events of the previous week had evidently upset his body clock. Oh well, he thought, small price to pay for having escaped alive. He was glad to have the whole Palm Springs fiasco behind him.

The call from his secretary, Monica, in his office in L.A., said that the need for him in Vegas was urgent. The speed limit on the sparsely traveled two-lane highway was about a third of the top end speed of the 390 bhp machine he was driving. "I think I'll find out if I can open it up some more," he said to himself as he pressed the send button on the cell phone. The phone automatically dialed the preset number.

"California Highway Patrol," Charlene speaking. "May I help you?" The pleasant voice asked politely.

"Char...Thomas Knight. How's my favorite girl?"

"Favorite girl my foot," came the curt reply. She desperately tried to hide the sudden exhilaration she felt from his unexpected call. The image of the handsome face with the subtle laugh lines at the edges of the cool blue eyes flashed before her. "The only time I ever hear from you is when you want something."

"I've been a little busy, but you know I'm always thinking about you," Knight replied smoothly.

"Yeah…yeah, that's a crock. What do you want?"

"I'm on Highway 247 at Prospect Valley headed north to Barstow. What's ahead?"

"Darn you Thomas! You know that kind of information is classified."

"I swear babe...I'll make it up to you," lied Knight.

"You're already into me for six dinners, two romantic weekends and a week's cruise on your yacht," chided the voice on the phone.

Knight laughed, "I didn't realize you were keeping score."

"You're darn right I am, and I'm going to hold you to every one of them," she threatened mischievously. She imagined herself in the arms of the tanned, dark-haired hunk with the classic swimmer's wide shoulders and narrow waist. "Anyway, the computer shows only one unit. He's working both lanes forty miles south of Barstow." Then before Knight could reply, she continued, "Got to go...official business is picking up. I'll add this one to the list." Then she hung up.

Knight tapped a button on the dash and the console-mounted global positioning satellite system swung into place and transmitted his exact location to the colored display. He was three miles south of the CHP officer. He had to force himself to be patient for the next three minutes. Then he could let the Ferrari loose. He was about to push another button and turn on the CD changer, when he caught a glimpse of the single headlight in his rearview mirror.

Motorcycles were common along this stretch of highway, but for some unknown reason this one looked different. Instinctively, he reached into the leather-covered console between the seats and retrieved the 9mm Glock Model 26 handgun still in its clip-on holster. The Glock 26 was his backup gun. His regular Glock Model 18 machine pistol had taken a beating in the Palm Springs adventure and he had sent it back to Tony Amato, his gunsmith in L.A., for repair. In his business, it was imperative to continually be on guard. If anything did happen, Knight knew from experience that there was no substitute for firepower. Nothing could match the Glock 18's ability to launch 1,300 9mm rounds a minute at full auto. The smaller semi-auto 26 and its ten-round clip was strictly a back up, but it was better than nothing. He placed the pistol on his lap as he watched the headlight move up behind him at what had to be at least a hundred and fifty miles-per-hour. The motorcycle suddenly cut its speed and moved up beside the Ferrari.

Knight looked at the crouching rider; everything was a matching gold; the helmet, the racing leathers, and the bike itself. Sensing no immediate threat from the rider, he looked down at the futuristically styled motorcycle. It was a rare Suzuki Hayabusa. "That's one serious piece of iron," he admired softly.

The rider looked over at Knight and while still crouched over the bars, used the left hand to make an OK gesture followed by a thumbs-up sign. Then the rider pointed down the road. Simultaneously the bike shot forward, then slowed, and moved back beside the red sports car. The invitation to race was obvious.

The Ferrari was one of the fastest production cars ever made, but Knight knew it was no match for the Suzuki. The bike could easily triple their current sixty mile-per-hour speed, in less than four seconds. Knight looked at the rider, paused and then with a mischievous grin made a sweeping gesture indicating an *after you*.

The bike and the car shot forward simultaneously and Knight was congratulating himself on how well his Italian machine was doing. However, the motorcycle was pulling away quite respectably. He glanced first at the speedometer, now creeping toward a hundred and fifty mph and then back to the GPS display. With a mile to go, a shallow hill came up and Knight continued to press the bike until just before its crest. Then with the motorcycle, now nearly a half-mile, ahead, he applied the four-wheel, vented disc brakes and quickly slowed to the speed limit.

When he crested the hill, he broke out laughing as he saw the bubble lights on the CHP cruiser flashing as the officer executed a flawless reverse turn and pursued the gold crotch-rocket. The cruiser had the culprit pulled onto the shoulder of the road by the time Knight arrived at the scene. The rider dismounted from the bike and removed the helmet. Knight drove by slowly, curious as to the identity of his competitor.

With a shake of the rider's head, long, golden-tresses cascaded down her back and fanned out across the matching racing leathers.

Knight continued to stare into his rearview mirror in amazement. She was beautiful! And, she certainly was bold, given her choice of transportation. The image of her standing there, pouting at him, as he passed by stayed with him. He put the Glock back into the console and nudged the speedometer on the Ferrari upward. With the CHP officer occupied, he could keep the wedge shaped car in triple digit speeds until he made Barstow.

Highway 15, east, out of Barstow, to Las Vegas is one hundred and sixty nine miles of monotonous and highly forgettable scenery. For most people the drive is made bearable only by the anticipation of the big score they hope awaits them at the slots or the tables ahead.

For Thomas Knight, it was going to be a sure route to danger.

———·———

Prehistoric southern Nevada was once a virtual marsh of abundant water and vegetation. As the eons passed, the marsh and the rivers disappeared beneath the surface, leaving behind a parched and arid landscape holding only the fossilized remains of the prehistoric inhabitants. The water trapped underground sporadically found its way to the surface creating small oases in the desert.

When the early 16th Century Spanish conquistadors had first ventured into the desert valley, they were looking for the Seven Cities of Cibola, the legendary lost cities of gold. They did not find them, but if they had waited, they would have been amazed at what happened four hundred years later.

On Christmas Day in 1829 a Mexican trader named Armijo led a sixty man party along the Spanish Trail, the trade route between Santa Fe and Los Angeles, camping about a hundred miles northeast of present-day Las Vegas. An experienced young scout, Raphael Rivera rode ahead of the group to the west in search of water. Within two weeks, he discovered Las Vegas Springs. From then on, the abundant artesian spring water would replenish thirsty prospectors using the Spanish Trail during their rush for gold in California.

By 1848, maps began to refer to the springs as Las Vegas, which means "the meadows" in Spanish.

———·———

Crossing the California State Line into Nevada was like going to another planet. Where there had been nothing but featureless desert, there now emerged a world full of billboards proclaiming every imaginable activity. Casinos with large parking lots began to appear at ever increasing intervals, each with a massive sign trying to tempt motorists to pull over and try their luck.

The desert around Las Vegas had been nicknamed the *Gambler's Graveyard*. It was a reference to a local legend that said it was where you ended up if you lost a bundle at the tables, playing on credit, and did not pay up. Occasionally, with all the new construction going on around the city, a contractor's backhoe would indeed rake up some unidentified bones. The casinos made sure that the finds got plenty of press; after all, it was in their best interest to keep the legend alive.

Suddenly, there it was on the horizon! The tops of the gigantic casinos seem to float above the clouds. It looked romantic until you realized that the clouds were actually pollution brought on by a population of over a million people now crowded into the valley. They had moved to one of the most inhospitable places on earth for a million different reasons.

———·———

The Strip" as everyone called Las Vegas Boulevard, the main north south thoroughfare through the city, boasted eight of the nine largest hotels in the world. The hotels in Vegas were not built as monuments. They were not going to stand for thousands of years. Constructed like large Hollywood sets they would be lucky if they were around for a twentieth anniversary. It seemed like every six months or so a less desirable structure was dynamited away to make room for another major resort and someone else's dream.

Las Vegas has its own sense of proportion. It was as if the builders looked at the world's monuments and determined they were too big, too small or otherwise needed to be modified. They had decided that the Great pyramid of Cheops would look much better in black glass rather than in stone. The Sphinx was definitely too small, so Vegas made it fifty percent larger. The Eiffel Tower was too tall and so it was shortened. The New York skyline worked out much better when it was only one-third scale.

In 1966 Caesars Place was the first of the themed hotels to open. It created an atmosphere where reality could be suspended and it did not take much imagination to believe that when you walked through the doors, that you were Caesar. Now, entire Italian towns, King Arthur's Camelot, a pirate village and a gigantic circus all beckoned to the visitor to try their luck. Each hotel was an attraction in and of itself. The hotel had become the entertainment. The hotels combined gambling, entertainment, food and shopping. Once inside there was really no reason to leave. And, they certainly discouraged it. Every hotel had moving walkways to move you from the Strip to the front door but you had to find your own way back. If big was good, then bigger was better and the stakes were being raised every day in a never-ending game of can you top this.

———·———

Knight had the same feeling of anticipation every time he entered the city. When you are away from Las Vegas for a while an inexplicable urge begins to build. You want to see the latest resort, the one they were just starting when you were here last, or you want to see the latest extravaganza. Perhaps you simply want to drop out of your predictable everyday life for a few hedonistic days. It is a powerful magnet.

The bumper-to-bumper traffic, the sidewalk parade of T-shirt and shorts clad hopefuls, and the constant banging of construction noise burst Knight's daydream bubble and caused him to ask aloud, "What in hell was I thinking?" Las Vegas could never live up to expectations, but heaven knows, it tried. Only a U.S. mint could generate money faster than the gambling and tourism in Vegas!

Knight dialed his cellular phone and was rewarded with a pleasant voice asking, "Luciano's men's store at the Colossus resort, may I help you?"

"I would like to talk to Victor Cherenko please," Knight replied.

"May I ask who's calling?" asked the voice with a hint of trepidation.

"Thomas Knight."

"One moment please."

After a short pause, a heavily Russian accented voice asked, "Thomas, how are you?"

"I'm fine," answered Knight. "But I need a new wardrobe." He had left Palm Springs with only the jogging suit on his back.

"Yah, ve vill take goot care of you," came the reassuring reply.

"I'll need at least five outfits; shirts, slacks, shoes, socks, belts, underwear and a swimming suit. And add a couple of sport coats and a tie or two, okay?"

"Yah, ve half everything. Are you coming into to pick them out?"

"I don't have time," answered Knight. "You pick them out, but I don't want to look like Liberace."

Victor laughed, "Ve vill be very tasteful." Then he asked, "Have you been prosperous?"

Knight chuckled at the Russian's tactful question. "I'm still a thirty-four waist." Then he added, "Have the concierge send up a complete toiletries package. I'll be staying in my usual suite." He checked his watch. "I'm still thirty minutes from checking in."

"Yah…yah, I vill personally take care of it, whatever you need. Did you lose your luggage?"

"Let's just say I lost my clothes when things got a little hot last week in Palm Springs." Then, without further explanation or waiting for a response, he hung up. He could imagine that the store was already nearly in a panic as the clerks tried to offer up the perfect combination. Victor had done well with the capital supplied him by his Russian Mafia partners. Knight smiled at the irony of Victor choosing to name his store after Lucky Luciano, the infamous Italian Mafia godfather. The name had been a brilliant marketing decision. When tourists come to Vegas, they want the vicarious thrill of acting as if they were interacting with the mob. They would never imagine that the short, frail, Russian émigré watching the store from his office, behind a one-way mirror, was a real life, modern, Mafia godfather.

———·———

The Colossus resort, the largest in the world, was aptly named. It was huge! Its twin cylindrical towers, each ringed with twelve exterior elevators, seemed to shimmer in the desert sun like solid gold pillars. Las Vegas is for those who dream big and no one was a bigger dreamer than Jack Flynn, the developer of the resort and the current reigning king of the city.

Flynn, by anyone's definition was a real piece of work. At five-foot two, he had a Napoleon complex that approached that of the Emperor himself. He was totally self-indulgent and although not an out and out crook, he certainly had a larcenous nature. He was perfectly suited for Las Vegas and Las Vegas was perfectly suited for him. He had a perpetual frumpy look about him even though his custom-made suits cost five grand apiece. A discreet plastic surgeon had removed the bags from under his eyes. Because of an aversion to treadmills, or any equipment that would have necessitated exercise, he had also opted for liposuction. However, no matter what he tried, he never seemed to get it all altogether. While his appearance always left something to be desired, the same could not be said of his mind. Flynn was as savvy a businessman as ever came down the pike.

He had surrounded himself with the best executive staff money could buy and given the complexity of his deals, even they were challenged. However, it was his reputation of never being topped in a business deal that gave him his greatest protection. Everyone was afraid of the frumpy little character. He had really outdone himself with this latest creation.

The Colossus lived up to its name. Unlike the other major resorts on the Strip, the Colossus did not have a theme. It was just big. Knight suspected that Flynn had been more than a little influenced by his boyhood in Kansas and had created the world's largest "grain elevators."

Even to a casual observer it was easy to see how Flynn had been able to spend over three billion dollars to bring his edifice to fruition. It was not simply a hotel and casino but a complete city in and of itself. The seven thousand rooms comprised a total of over three million square feet of living space. To insure that the windows shimmered like gold, Flynn had used real gold dust in their construction. He had installed a water heating system that insured that even if all seven thousand guests decided to shower simultaneously, that there would not be a single degree difference in water temperature.

In the past, hotels in Vegas had derived sixty percent of their income from gambling and forty percent from the amenities of rooms, food, bar, shops, pools, spa and entertainment. Flynn had turned the equation around. Sixty percent of the Colossus's revenue came from the amenities and forty percent from gambling. Not that Flynn had anything against gambling; his casinos were the largest in Vegas. But, he had been one of the earliest to recognize that gambler or not, he wanted to be sure he was doing everything that he could do to empty the pockets of the one hundred and fifty thousand visitors per day.

There were ten kitchens servicing seven restaurants and providing the banquet facilities to over a hundred meeting rooms. The kitchens served over seven hundred thousand meals per day.

Flynn had added a convention center and an upscale shopping mall. The mall had over two million square feet of tile floors and seventy thousand people a day strolled through, anxious to find a way to spend their money. A buyer could find anything from one hundred flavors of ice cream to a diamond necklace worth fifty million dollars.

The eighty thousand square foot spa provided the facilities to rejuvenate those who had spent the day scouring the shops or the night gambling in the casino.

Once you were picked up at the airport and shuttled to the Colossus, there literally was nothing that you could want or imagine that the resort could not deliver. You simply had to be able to pay.

The Colossus had bucked the trend of trying to be a family friendly resort. Instead, Flynn had concentrated on the aging baby boomers with large amounts of disposable income, and expensive tastes. In spite of the most expensive room prices in Vegas, so far the Colossus had been booked solid. To the chagrin of the skeptics, it looked like Flynn's gamble was going to pay off big. He had opened the first of the two towers to a huge positive reception. In his typical style, he quickly decided to parlay his bet and started building the second tower immediately. It was now complete and only lacked a few final inside touches before it too would be fully occupied.

The ten-story marquee, a heavy contributor to Flynn's one million dollar a month electricity bill, was flashing its digital image trying hard to differentiate itself from the other hotels along the Strip. Beneath the *Now Appearing in the Colossus's Coliseum* the words, *Honey and her Bears* flashed. In much smaller letters under *In the Lounge,* the words *Captain Jack and the Shark Attack* appeared but did not flash. Knight smiled; at least his favorite band had been billed above the buffet.

Captain Jack and the Shark Attack was the best band on the West Coast and in Knight's opinion, the best band anywhere. He had started out as a fan but over the years had become good friends with the nine players. They were one of those bands with real talent that never seemed to break out into the big time. The group wrote their own songs and several big-time artists had made hits out of them. Anyone with an ear for music however much preferred the original performances by the band to the covers by the stars.

A construction crane being removed from the site temporarily blocked the side street that lead to the executive and VIP parking lot. Knight turned at the barricade and guided the Testarossa up the circular driveway to the main porte cochere.

"Welcome back to the Colossus Mr. Knight," said the tall, bronzed parking valet as he opened the door.

"Hi Johnny," answered Knight, as he retrieved the 9mm from the console and slid it and the holster into his jogging suit pocket. "The side street was blocked. See that it gets into the executive parking garage."

"Will do," replied the valet. Then he added, "My offer still stands. I'll give you two hundred thousand for the car."

Knight laughed, "Well at least you're persistent." Only in Las Vegas could a head valet make six figures a year in tips. Johnny Ford had earned enough money parking the big shooter's cars to start his own sizable vintage car collection and had cast a covetous eye on the Ferrari.

"Let's put together a round over at my country club while you're here. Maybe I can win it from you," shouted Johnny as he slid into the tan leather seat.

"Your game couldn't improve that much if Tiger Woods gave you lessons for a year," shot back Knight as the automatic doors opened and he strode into the obscenely opulent, stadium-sized lobby.

The VIP terminal at Las Vegas's McCarran International Airport was more crowded than usual. Susan Strong's white Lear Longhorn jet, with the lightning strike on the tail, had to wait a few minutes before it could be towed out of the scorching sun and into the VIP hangar. The wheel chocks had barely been placed under the wheels before the white, stretch limo with the gold *Colossus* logo arrived. Susan emerged from the sleek cylindrical body of the jet, carefully picking her way down the folding steps to avoid catching the heels of her four-inch Italian pumps. At the bottom of the steps, she paused and looked back through the open doors of the hangar to see a large and rather boisterous crowd.

"It's that Senator, running for President," remarked the tall, gaunt uniformed driver, anticipating her question as he shut the door.

The darkened interior of the limo seemed almost pitch black after the glare of the sun from the outside tarmac. Susan leaned back against the cool leather seat and closed her eyes for a couple of minutes to let them dilate. Then she opened her Coach purse and took out her compact. She fluffed her short-cropped blond hair with her manicured hand and checked the mirror. She looked tired. She really did not know why she had accepted this assignment. Next to her grandfather, she was the largest shareholder in LSI, the world's largest insurance company, and although she loved working as its chief investigator, there were plenty of others to fill in if she wanted to take some time off. Perhaps after this assignment she would go back to Aspen for some R and R. The big mess in Palm Springs had really drained her. The phone on the shelf in the limo startled her when it rang.

"Ms. Strong, this is the LSI Las Vegas office. The office manager asked me to tell you that he's booked you into the Colossus resort."

"Fine. Thank you," answered Susan flatly, wondering if the girl on the other end of the line could possibly be as young as she sounded.

———·———

The main entrance of the Colossus was incredibly busy and Susan was dismayed by the thought of having to make her way through the large crowd of arriving and departing guests. What she really needed was quiet, a good massage and a hot bath. Once in the lobby, she could see there were five lines of people waiting to check into their rooms. The lines snaked back and forth inside red velveteen ropes as they waited for their turn with the clerks behind the massive, white marbled, check-in counters.

She spotted the sign with the raised gold letters to the left of the lobby saying, *VIP Check-in.* She let out a sigh of relief that at least she did not have to wait in those lines.

As the heavy glass door to the suite-like interior of the VIP offices closed noiselessly behind her, she was relieved when the din of the lobby ceased immediately.

The mature, but very well preserved, lady behind the antique desk inquired stiffly, "May I help you?"

"Susan Strong, LSI Insurance, I believe you have a suite for me."

A few taps on the computer in front of the receptionist brought an immediate change in attitude. "Ah...yes, Ms. Strong. Everything is ready for you. Do you have luggage?"

Susan shook her head and sighed, recalling how she had lost her entire traveling wardrobe in the Palm Spring affair. "No. I am afraid I'll have to pick up something while I'm here."

An attractive assistant appeared unobtrusively and announced, "If you will follow me I'll show you to your suite."

Susan shrugged and fell into step behind her guide. Instead of going back into the lobby, they went further into the VIP check-in area, across a large exquisitely appointed lounge area and then proceeded into a small alcove with four elevators. The elevator dinged immediately as the assistant pressed the call button.

Susan smiled to herself. Las Vegas elevators were all like. She was surrounded by glass and mirrors set in brass mountings. The elevator moved effortlessly upward, then suddenly cleared the lower floor structure and continued moving up the outside of the southern tower. The view was fantastic, and Susan could only imagine what it would look like at night when the Strip showed off its full regalia of lights.

The elevator stopped and the assistant led the way down a short hall to a gold trimmed double door with a large, impeccably dressed, security guard seated at an antique desk. The guard stood up as the duo approached.

"This is Gary, he is your private butler and in charge of your personal security. He will accompany you everywhere, anytime you request," instructed the assistant, in a tone that communicated she thought the whole idea was excessive.

"Nice to meet you, Gary. I'm Susan Strong," she said, feeling her hand totally enveloped by just the powerful fingers of the former pro football linebacker. She thought to herself that his size alone would keep any uninvited attention away.

"Yes Ms. Strong. We have been expecting you," he said politely as he opened the doors to the massive VIP suite. He had quickly sized her up as being good for his customary five thousand dollar tip at the end of her stay.

In Las Vegas, every casino went overboard to attract *Whales*, the highest of the high rollers. These were the people who thought nothing of dropping a million dollars in an evening's play. Worldwide, there were probably only a thousand players who could qualify for the designation. The competition between the casinos to attract and keep these players returning to their tables was intense. Like everything else in Vegas, the accommodations for these high rollers had followed the familiar *top this* philosophy. Because the Colossus was the newest kid on the block, it stood to reason that its high roller palaces would be the most outrageous. It took nearly ten minutes for her guide to show Susan all the amenities of the six thousand square foot, seven million dollar suite.

She had to admit that every conceivable luxury and convenience had been incorporated. It was way over the top, but that was the idea. Create an environment that made you suspend reality and stay and play. After all, one bad evening at the tables could easily pay off the entire investment.

Susan turned to Gary and asked, "Can you get a goldsmith to come up after I take a massage and a bath?"

"Will an hour be sufficient? " he inquired.

"Yes, that will be fine. I assume that a masseuse will be available immediately."

The massage had been first-class and the big Swede had been careful not to disturb the bandage on Susan's upper left arm. The gunshot she had received in Palm Springs had done only superficial damage, but she had been admonished by the doctor to keep the wound covered for at least a week. She was glad that it was in a location that could be conveniently covered. It saved her having to explain why she had been shot by her own bullet.

She had thrown on one of the luxurious robes laid out in the dressing area and moved into the outer suite just as Gary escorted the stoop-shouldered, elderly goldsmith in. She opened her purse and extracted an ancient Roman, gold solidus coin. Her late father had always worn it in a ring and she had thought about wearing it the same way. But, she settled on the idea of wearing it in a pendant instead. It would keep the coin directly over her heart.

The white haired goldsmith clucked and assured Susan that he could set the coin into a diamond bezel exactly as she described. The goldsmith rubbernecked the lavish suite thoroughly as Gary escorted him back to the elevator.

Susan smiled and she wondered how he could possibly exaggerate to his friends the decadence of her accommodations.

Gary returned from the elevator with a huge bouquet of fresh cut flowers with a small note attached. The note had the Colossus logo embossed in gold and asked in an obviously hasty scrawl, *Please join me at six o'clock in my office. I hope everything is as it should be.* It was signed, *Jack Flynn.*

———·———

Jack Flynn had started out modestly enough in Vegas. He had been a partner in a small bingo room located nearly a mile from the Strip. He was on his way down the Strip to work one morning when he saw a small real estate sign on a large parcel of undeveloped desert directly adjacent to the second largest casino in Vegas. More curious than serious, he called the number and asked the price. It was outrageous and in no way obtainable. But, as often happens in stories of the accumulation of mega wealth, he asked a seemingly inconsequential question. Would the seller be interested in selling an option to buy the parcel? He had been astounded when he got the call two days later allowing him to make an offer. He offered fifty thousand dollars, all he had and thought he could raise, for a one hundred and twenty-day option. To his utter amazement, his offer was accepted. He did not sleep for nearly four days as he tapped every conceivable source for the fifty large. Finally, with the money in hand, the deal was done.

Then just when things appeared to be going his way, he was shocked when he generated exactly zero interest from anyone in his attempt to clear the option and pay the purchase amount. The option had only sixty days to go when he came up with an outrageous scheme. He pawned his Audermars Piquet chronograph, up until then his only extravagance. Using the four thousand dollars the pawnbroker gave him for the twenty thousand dollar watch, he had a sign painted. The sign boldly proclaimed that a new major resort, bigger and better than anything on the Strip, was to be built within a year. Under the announcement was an artist's rendering of a casino that shocked everyone who saw it.

Paranoia is a way of life in Vegas. No matter what you come up with, it seems someone is waiting in the wings to top it. The sign struck utter terror into the management of the adjacent casino. They called Flynn and offered to buy the parcel, to protect their flanks. Jack sold the parcel two days before his option was to expire and pocketed nearly seven million dollars in profit.

A prudent person would have taken the money and retired. However, the word prudent and Jack Flynn could not possibly be used together. No, instead Flynn took his gains; leveraged them into a senior position in a bankrupt, run-down casino on Fremont Street in the heart of downtown Vegas, in the area known as "Glitter Gulch."

If Jack Flynn was anything, he was lucky. His new casino took off on a general resurgence in the economy. All the big casinos along the Strip had allowed Mexicans with paper fortunes in petrol dollars to run up huge markers. Flynn stayed with the locals and mom-and-pop players who paid as they played. With the dramatic fall in oil prices, the big casinos suddenly found themselves with millions of dollars of worthless markers. The bankruptcy court was blitzed with applications for reorganization.

Meanwhile, Flynn, with real money to spend, started picking up bargains in land owned by the resorts with desperate cash flow needs. Then in a move that was to change the entire face of Las Vegas forever, he was able to obtain mega financing for the development of the properties by selling junk bonds on Wall Street. His new casinos went up, one after another, each bigger and better. Wall Street liked what they saw and everyone got filthy rich. The momentum was tremendous and continued like a steamroller. It did not seem to make any difference what happened to the economy, Las Vegas just kept building and reinventing itself. Flynn rode the crest of the economic tidal wave like a world-class surfer.

Flynn had grown up in a prosperous family of wheat farmers in western Kansas. They farmed for generations before suddenly one day finding that in the ground, under the golden sheaves, was a massive pool of oil. He was a spoiled teenager, use to having things his own way. Hoping to straighten him out, his family had persuaded him, using the threat of cutting off his sizable allowance, to go the University of Denver. Ostensibly, he was enrolled in the Business College, but his true majors were women and gambling. It was not that Flynn was stupid; he simply had another agenda. He finally graduated, dead last in his class.

Thomas Knight, the son of the owner of a successful manufacturing company was also a student at the University, and it was inevitable that their paths would cross. Where Knight was unassuming, tall, good-looking, a serious student and an excellent athlete, Flynn was the exact opposite. He was egotistical, short and prematurely balding. But, in spite of their differences, they became friends.

While Flynn was changing the landscape of Vegas, Knight had steadily built the world's premier security firm headquartered in Los Angeles. Although he specialized in extracting wealthy clients from extraordinary situations, on occasion, he had allowed Flynn to persuade him to serve as a security consultant on his Vegas properties. In fact, Flynn's current Vice President of Security had been employed and trained by Knight. Initially Knight had resented Flynn raiding his company for talent, but time had healed the wound. They still liked and saw each other, but Knight was obviously more cautious in his dealings with Flynn.

Knight was impressed by the selections Victor's clerks had made. Everything in the six complete outfits of clothes was in perfect taste. Furthermore, they could all be mixed and matched. Any combination was dynamite.

Knight always used the same suite at the Colossus when he was in Vegas. He did not like change. Once he found something that he preferred or liked, he would stick with that until he was convinced something else was better. When he was in college, he had found an off-campus restaurant that made a dynamite, hot roast beef sandwich. He ate the same thing every night for nearly a whole quarter before he discovered a Chinese restaurant's beef and broccoli. It was his main staple for the next quarter.

Knight's unassuming nature was at odds with traveling with an entourage. His extraordinarily wealthy clients were well acquainted with his tastes and everything he would need or would want was provided. He rarely found it necessary to visit his office in L.A. Any information he needed was only a call or an email away. His efficient secretary Monica and her trusty computer, the one she called *Ralph,* were an amazing source of knowledge about anything and everyone.

Steve, the personal butler that came with Knight's suite, answered the telephone efficiently after the first ring. After a short conversation he hung up the receiver and then announced, "Mr. Flynn would like you to join him in his office at four o'clock. I took the liberty of saying that you would be there."

Knight did not acknowledge the commitment. Steve had worked as his butler every time he was in Vegas and knew exactly what to do. "Sometimes you sound just like a wife," Knight kidded.

"Not tonight honey, I've got a headache," shot back Steve quickly. He felt comfortable enough with his relationship with Knight to get by with the cheeky comment.

———·———

Promptly at four o'clock, Knight entered the outer office of Jack Flynn. In addition to the small army of secretaries, administrative assistants and manager trainees, there were five others. Knight recognized three of them: Dwight Basham, V.P. of Colossus Security, the Sheriff of Clark County, and the FBI's Assistant Director. The other two had the nondescript look of Secret Service Agents. Before Knight could acknowledge them however, an extremely attractive secretary rushed to his side.

"Mr. Flynn wants to see you immediately," she whispered to him as she guided him quickly through the crowd. She did not bother to knock as she opened the door to Flynn's interoffice and gently pushed him inside.

Flynn's office was appropriate to his top dog status. It was excessive in every regard. The office was nearly circular, offering at least a 180-degree view of the Strip and the surrounding city. In the middle was an elevated island with a circular desk-surrounded by ten chairs. To the left was a large kiosk with twenty large screen television monitors. To the right was a circular, step-down bar with a dozen lushly upholstered swivel chairs.

Jack Flynn was standing in front of the massive desk on the elevated platform with a sheepish expression on his face. Towering over him, bent over with his face nearly touching him was a distinguished looking man in an obviously expensive suit.

"I'm not going to listen to any more of that crap," the tall man shouted, berating his diminutive audience. He poked Flynn in the chest with his finger, forcefully driving his point home.

"Thomas!" shouted Flynn, turning toward the new arrival, and obviously grateful for the intrusion. He left the tall man on the elevated platform and almost ran to Knight with his hand extended. "Thanks for coming. It's good to see you," he said as he pumped Knight's hand vigorously.

"Jack," acknowledged Knight, feeling the familiar clammy handshake. Then moving to the tall man, he extended his hand and said, "Good to see you again Senator." The grip was dry and firm.

Joe Devlin, Nevada's two-term senior Senator, was the perfect prototype of a politician. He was six-foot two with a full head of salt and pepper hair. His tan was flawless. His impeccably tailored suit was English, undoubtedly Saville Row. His shirt and tie was French designer. Everything about him evoked money. He certainly had enough of it, and he had come by it all honestly. He had made his money the old-fashioned way, by inheriting it. He was wildly popular in the state and his charismatic manner made him a popular choice on all the TV and talk shows. His deep baritone voice was perfect for filibustering.

The President had served his full two terms and could not run again for the office. His Vice President, the natural successor, having been diagnosed with cancer had withdrawn from the race. The party scrambled to find someone who was popular enough with the masses to win the election. Everyone had agreed that the Nevada Senator was the best choice.

Even though he was from a lightly populated state with few electoral votes, he was widely known across the country. He was a shoo-in to be nominated at the convention in the fall.

"Glad to have you here Knight, maybe you can talk some sense into this idiot son-in-law of mine," said the Senator.

They all sat down in unison and Knight broke the ice. "What's up?"

"They kidnapped my daughter Isis and this mealy-mouthed half-wit won't do anything about it!" boomed the Senator as he shot a vile look at Flynn. Isis was his only child and although he had been less than enthusiastic about her marriage to Flynn, in the end he had gone along with her wishes and given her away at the wedding.

Flynn ignored the cutting remark and started to explain. "Yesterday I got an email," he said as he stood up and picked a piece of paper off the desk and handed it to Knight.

We have taken your wife and we want $20 million to help fund our cause. We will email instructions Wednesday. Have the money ready. No cops if you want to see your wife again!

Knight looked up at the pair who had been studying him intently as he read the print out. "Who called the cops?"

"I did," said the Senator matter-of-factly.

"He called everybody," snorted Flynn, obviously upset by the decision.

"I saw the FBI, the Clark County Sheriff and what looked like Secret Service outside," said Knight in a tone that implied his own disfavor.

"I want Isis back and we're going to do whatever it takes," said the Senator coldly.

"The money isn't a problem Thomas," interrupted Flynn. "We've got that much in petty cash and besides the casino has kidnap insurance and the insurance company's rep is already here.

"Senator?" asked Knight.

"Because it involves me and my family and I'm under Secret Service protection during the campaign, I had to tell the President. He's the one that suggested that you be brought in. He thinks one person might do better than all those groups, given their petty rivalries," said the Senator with a wave of his hand toward Flynn's outer door.

Knight stood up and walked to the window. "How about the press?"

"Well so far they haven't got hold of the story," answered the Senator.

"No thanks to you and all the people you just had to bring in," spat Flynn.

Knight shook his head and frowned. It was like listening to two third graders arguing. He had been the best man at Jack and Isis's wedding. She was a gorgeous blonde, ex debutante and totally addicted to Flynn's power and money. Knight was concerned that if Flynn ever lost either of them, she would be gone in a heartbeat. Nevertheless, Flynn seemed to be deeply in love with her. Next to his resort empire, she was the most important thing in his life. Given Flynn's reputation, to think that anyone would have the balls to kidnap his wife was unimaginable.

The pina colada scented volcano at the nearby casino erupted for its first performance of the evening. As Knight stared out the window at the show, he knew how the mayor of the ancient Roman resort of Pompeii must have felt when Mount Vesuvius's volcano had started to rumble.

CHAPTER 2

Susan had spent nearly five minutes on the phone detailing exactly what she needed to the Neiman Marcus personal shopper. The accommodating voice on the other end of the line seemed to be delighted with her requests. "Deliver it to me at the Colossus ASAP," she instructed, "and bill it to the Las Vegas LSI office." She hung up after a quick acknowledgment.

She found Gary rearranging one of the massive floral displays that were sprinkled throughout the suite. For such a hulk, it was surprising to see him delicately placing the flowers to correct the florist's presentation. "I'm expecting several packages. Sign for them," she ordered over her shoulder as she turned back to her dressing area. She would take a hot bath and relax before confronting Flynn.

She had selected two conservative outfits from the six that the personal shopper had sent up. Her perfect size six meant that they fit right off the hangar without any tailoring. As she slipped the jacket of the soft blue suit over the white silk blouse, she was aware of the perfect match between the jacket and her eyes. The charcoal hose clipped into her French garter belt and her raven colored, high-heeled pumps completed her outfit. The cut of the jacket completely hid the bandage on her left arm. Just as she completed dressing, the fax machine began to spew forth the information she had requested from her home office.

Ever since her father, the second largest shareholder in the world's largest insurance company, had been killed and left his shares to her she had felt very much alone. Her Grandfather, the company's founder and majority shareholder, had wanted her to take over the reins of the organization. But, she was a highly active person and being confined behind a desk every day, would have eventually become unbearable. Instead, she had given herself the position as the company's head investigator. She sought solace in her work. After her last adventure in Palm Springs, the one that nearly killed her, as evidenced by the still healing wound on her arm, she was tired, not only physically but also emotionally. She had anticipated that finding her father's killer and avenging his death would bring closure to the pain she felt. It did not and now she just felt hollow inside. She felt as if she were watching a movie of herself as she went through her daily routines. Maybe this assignment could get her out of her depression and back to being her old self.

Actually, the assignment sounded simple. LSI, her insurance company, offered a highly specialized executive kidnap and ransom policy. For senior executives in large companies, increasingly at risk in a troubled world, it made sense for them to be prepared in case they were abducted and held for ransom. The company had already paid out two such claims and it appeared might have to do so again, unless Susan could resolve this case without the ransom being paid or at least recovered. The lengthy fax explained her company's legal position and now it was up to her to explain it to Jack Flynn. It was not going to be easy. Regardless of how much clarification the agent gave when he sold the policy, Susan had always found that there were misinterpretations about how the process actually worked. From what she had heard about Jack Flynn and his demanding nature she knew that presenting her position would, at the least, be challenging.

Susan checked her outfit one last time in the full length-dressing mirror in the apartment-sized closet. She looked great, but for a second a question crossed her mind. Was there something about her looks that had caused the enigmatic Thomas Knight to forget her after their recent escapade in Palm Springs? "Damn you Thomas," she swore aloud, "I don't need to be thinking about you at a time like this." As far as she was concerned, it was just as well if she never saw him again. Besides, since he had not contacted her, he probably had moved on. She turned and strode toward the main door of the suite. As she exited, she held up her hand to stop Gary from rising from his desk. "I'll be all right," she said. "I'm just going up to Jack Flynn's office."

Gary nodded and then added with a tone of sarcasm, “Good luck!”

———·———

Knight had spent nearly an hour gaining all the particulars he could about the kidnapping from the Senator and Flynn.

Flynn had started building a private golf course, about a year before, in the desert fifty miles north of the city. It was nearly finished and only needed some minor decorating touches in the ultra luxurious clubhouse. In a clever attempt to kill two birds with one stone, Flynn had assigned the decorating supervision to his wife. He figured that if she was going to spend money shopping anyway, he might as well get some benefit from it. At least this way the money she spent could be written off.

Isis had driven herself in one of the company’s Hummers up to the course in the morning. She had been met at the clubhouse by two members of the staff and everything appeared to be okay. About midmorning, she had saddled an Arabian riding horse. The short ride would take her to an undeveloped area near the outer perimeter of the fenced in deeded property. She was trying to locate a cactus that could be transplanted into the atrium of the Western themed clubhouse. It was the last time that any of the staff members had seen her.

The horse returned, riderless, to the stable about two hours later. The initial supposition was that she had been thrown, but an exhaustive search of the area had turned up nothing. The staff looked for nearly two hours before they gathered up enough courage to notify Flynn. The email ransom note and the call from the golf course telling him that his wife was missing arrived almost simultaneously.

By coincidence, the Senator had called about an hour after the ransom request had been received, just to visit with his daughter. Before Flynn could give instructions to the staff to keep the problem quiet, some secretary spilled the beans. The conversation between Flynn and the Senator had not been pleasant. They did not like each other very much anyway and this had further driven a wedge between them.

Flynn's theory was to keep the incident quiet, pay the ransom, get his wife back, then run down the kidnappers and cut their balls off. The Senator's plan was to call in every agency in the world to find his daughter, pay the ransom only if necessary, apprehend the culprits and then make a public spectacle out of their punishment. It was morbid, but it would be great publicity for his campaign. The only thing they both agreed on was that the only person that they could both trust was Thomas Knight.

The Senator had left, ostensibly to coordinate the search for Isis, leaving Knight and Flynn alone.

"You want a drink?" asked Flynn as he moved to the marble bar and proceeded to make one for himself.

"A light one," replied Knight, realizing that he had not eaten since breakfast and did not like the idea of booze on an empty stomach.

"Canadian Club, bottled water, and no ice," remarked Flynn, confirming what he knew was Knight's preference. "I don't see how anyone can drink that stuff."

"It's a habit," said Knight, not bothering to explain that it derived from not being able to find American whiskey abroad. The no ice was a precaution against the questionable water supplies he encountered as he moved about the world.

Flynn handed Knight his drink and slumped into a leather covered oversized chair. The large chair seemed to make him even smaller, but he was completely oblivious to the image. "You know Thomas, I have been around the block a few times in this city, but I'm telling you managing this damned Colossus is really driving me up a tree," protested Flynn as he took a healthy swig from his straight-up vodka.

"What do you mean?" asked Knight. He was surprised at Flynn's sudden candor. Flynn rarely appeared to lack confidence.

"The problem is that the stakes have gotten so damned high. You know it doesn't make any real difference if the casino makes money or not. It's all about the stock price." Flynn took another drink and continued. "A five dollar swing in the stock means you win or lose maybe two hundred million."

"That's scary all right," sympathized Knight. Even his own portfolio had been wildly fluctuating recently.

"Those little twerps on Wall Street are barely out of MBA School and yet if they recommend your stock you are fine, and if they don't…." Flynn let the sentence trail off. He got up from the chair, and moved to the windows in the office. The sun was starting to set over the purple mountains and soon the lights of the Strip would be shifting into high gear. "There's nothing on the face of the earth like the Las Vegas Strip at night. You know they call this place the Fat Apple," he continued. "New York is the Big Apple, but this is the Fat Apple," he repeated. "You know why they call it that?" he asked over his shoulder.

"No. Why?" asked Knight patronizingly. He knew Flynn was going to tell him anyway.

"It's because every contract, every purchase…hell, every sale includes not only a fair profit but a fat allowance. You have to add it in just to cover all the skimming and petty theft that goes on. Did you know that just this morning I found out someone in the resort stole three hundred bathtubs? Can you believe that? Three hundred frigging bathtubs."

"Bathtubs?" asked Knight curiously.

"Yeah, bathtubs," replied Flynn as he took a swig from his drink. "There are seven thousand rooms in this place and so we bought seven thousand bathtubs. Right?"

"Seems right," replied Knight.

"Well, anyway between the purchase order, the shipping list, the bill of lading, and the receiving ticket, three hundred tubs simply disappeared. And, of course, nobody knows anything about it. This stuff goes on everyday. It drives me absolutely nuts."

"You could retire and play golf on your new private course," replied Knight in a voice that precluded any sympathy.

"You know I've got two thousand security cameras, a thousand digital recorders, a four hundred person police force and fifty plainclothes investigators covering every square inch of this place. Thanks to you and the security systems you set up it's damn near impossible to steal a dollar from the casino floor. But, the place leaks like a sieve out the back. Can you believe it, three hundred bathtubs?" When Knight did not reply, Flynn continued, "You know the idiot that stole them will probably sell them for next to nothing and then come back in here and gamble away the money."

"Well at least you will get something back," chided Knight hoping to change the subject.

Flynn ignored the remark, "I've got every last room rented for the big computer show in the convention center. With the room, the gambling, the food and entertainment we figure each occupied room accounts for close to a thousand dollars a day in revenue. I'm losing nearly three hundred grand a day because some moron thinks he is going to win at gambling!"

Suddenly the telephone rang and Flynn moved to the desk and picked it up. "Flynn," he said authoritatively and then he listened for a full minute without saying anything. Finally he said, "Okay keep me posted, but don't let this get out of control, got it!" With that final admonishment, he hung up, moved back to the bar and poured himself another stiff vodka without bothering to refill Knight. "It seems that some filthy rich software nerd, showed up unannounced and is trying to break the bank at the roulette table. With his money if he has any kind of a winning streak, we may not be able to keep up with him." Flynn paused, took another swallow of his drink, and went back to the window. “I need you to find her Thomas,” he said softly. Then he added, “Can you believe it …bathtubs?”

———·———

Knight had decided that while waiting for the kidnapper or kidnappers to call he could perhaps uncover a clue that would get the jump on them. The obvious place to start would be at the scene of the crime, the golf course. Flynn had placed all of the Colossus’s considerable assets at his disposal. Therefore, Knight could have flown one of the resort’s two helicopters, but instead he decided to drive. He could retrieve the Ferrari from the parking garage and cover the fifty miles to the golf course in about the same time it would take to prepare and fly a chopper there.

The road north of Vegas certainly lacked for any redeemable scenery. The craggy peak of Mount Charleston, visible above the brownish black volcanic foothills was the only real point of interest. The sun was setting behind the peak leaving a spectacularly orange red sunset. The presence of dust in the atmosphere from the surrounding desert made the sun appear to be twice its normal size. Every few miles there were cars stopped along the road, their drivers standing beside them marveling at the view. Knight smiled and remarked to no one, “All the water shows, pirate boat sinking, and perfumed volcanoes are really pathetic when compared to the real thing.”

———·———

The town of Indian Springs was the closest significant habitation to Flynn's golf course. The town consisted of a small Air Force Base and hundreds of trailer houses. The base was used as an alternative landing strip for the "Top Gun" pilots flying their mock air combat drills from Nellis Air Force Base just north of Vegas. Knight thought the town always looked as if it were totally portable. Other than the school, you could almost put wheels under all the houses in town and simply tow it away.

Thirteen miles north of Indian Springs was the last exit for forty miles. Taking the exit and to the right was a paved road that had a very ominous looking sign guarding it proclaiming that there was, *No trespassing by order of the Department of Energy*. To the left and under the highway was another paved road posted with another very ominous looking sign proclaiming, *No trespassing by order of the Flynn Development Company*.

Knight down shifted the Testarossa expertly as he took the left turn and wondered, in truth, which threat had more teeth.

The Colossus's golf course was a real tribute to Flynn's clever and ruthless business methods. Quite by accident, he had seen a map in the County Supervisor's office showing all the private land holdings in southern Nevada. He had been particularly interested in a small parcel located fifty miles north of Vegas just off Highway 95. What made the parcel attractive to Flynn was not only its easy access to the highway but the parcel's neighbors. Flynn's golf course was surrounded on three sides by undeveloped Bureau of Land Management land. On the north, just across the highway lay the huge Nellis bombing and gunnery complex and the Nevada Test Site.

The Nevada Test Site or the NTS, as designated on local maps, is a Rhode Island sized testing ground northwest of Vegas. On a quiet April day in 1953, a B-50 bomber opened its bomb bay doors. An atomic bomb the size of a car dropped from the plane and fell four miles onto a dry lake bed. After a blinding flash of light, its core hotter than the sun, a mushroom shaped cloud soared nearly ten miles into the desert sky.

Gamblers in the casinos in Las Vegas had momentarily been distracted from their slots, cards and dice to watch the awesome display. Over the next decade, one hundred nuclear bombs were detonated in the open air above the newly named Nevada Test Site. Promoters in Vegas, never ones to let this kind of event go by without finding a way to make a buck, started conducting tours to watch the blasts, complete with box lunches.

Eventually the fallout, which drifted unpredictably for hundreds of miles, became a problem resulting in devastating health effects to the "down winders" northeast of the site in Nevada and Utah.

During the Cold War, from its founding in 1951 until 1992, over nine hundred atomic explosives were detonated in this barren desert. In the 1950's, the atomic tests conducted were above ground. Since then, tests had been conducted only underground, resulting in what looked like a pockmarked lunar landscape. The Department of Energy had been forced to open more of its' files recently, generally in response to lawsuits filed by kooks trying to prove any number of conspiracies. In 1992, a moratorium on nuclear testing was signed by the President and stayed in effect, prompting efforts to find a new mission for the test site.

The area that Flynn spotted had not been polluted by the fallout from the atmospheric tests, thus making it habitable. According to the map, a minor silver strike had been made in the area in the '40s and numerous mining claims had been filed literally covering almost every square foot of the parcel. When the government had seized land for the nuclear testing site it had decided that the parcel Flynn discovered was not necessary to their mission. Therefore, it had lain unused and legally in the hands of the mining claimants. All the claims had originally been perfected by a D. R. Prentice. Evidently, the silver strike played out rather quickly because after the early '50s there had not been a single new claim. An exhaustive search by Flynn's attorneys had been unable to find a D. R. Prentice or his heirs. So, Flynn had laid claim to the land under the theory that it had been abandoned. The State had awarded him the land after only a cursory examination and the payment of some modest filing and acquisition fees. Nobody seemed to notice or care that the head of the granting board owed nearly a hundred thousand dollars in markers to one of Flynn's casinos.

Having acquired the land at a negligible cost, Flynn set about developing it into one of the world's premier private golf courses. The contractors of his Vegas resorts had provided the time and materials off the books. Only Jack Flynn could have ended up with such a jewel, virtually free, but with an appraised value of fifty million dollars!

———·———

It was totally dark by the time the bright red car had traveled two miles down the golf course road. Suddenly across the road, there was a black iron gate and a stuccoed air-conditioned guardhouse. The guard looked up, momentarily blinded by the Ferrari's headlights. A look of recognition and relief swept across the guard's face as he looked through the glass window and determined the source of the unexpected visit. "Good evening, Mr. Knight," he said pleasantly. "I didn't have anyone on the list for tonight."

"Evening," answered Knight. "It was a last-minute idea. I should have had Security call you."

"I suppose you're here because of that terrible thing that happened to Mrs. Flynn," conjectured the youthful guard. He knew he was overstepping his bounds but he was so grateful to talk to someone.

"You know anything about it?" asked Knight, dismayed that knowledge of the kidnapping was leaking out. It was only a matter of time before the press would sniff out the story … then the stuff would really hit the fan.

"I'm afraid not. I told the police and my boss Mr. Basham everything I know, which is nothing. I didn't even see her arrive. Evidently she came in when I wasn't on duty." When no further question was forthcoming, the guard said in an unapologetic tone, "I'm afraid I'll have to call it in…because you're not on the list."

"I understand," answered Knight.

It took less than a minute before the guard was off the phone. "I'm sorry sir, I'm just doing my job." He pushed a button and the gate opened.

Knight smiled, signaling that he understood. "Don't talk to anyone else about what happened out here."

The guard nodded as Knight gently accelerated the powerful sports car.

Beyond the gate, it was approximately another two miles to the main clubhouse. Past the guardhouse, the road was pitch black. There was no moon and the clouds, that only an hour ago had provided such a spectacular sunset, now blocked out even the pinpricks of light from the stars.

The guard's statement about Basham had triggered an automatic reflex of resentment in Knight. He had only had his fledgling security company up and running for a short time when an eager young man answered his ad for part-time security guards. Dwight Basham was ambitious as hell, reasonably intelligent, and it was only weeks before Knight felt comfortable enough to promote him to full supervisor.

Dwight Basham had sewn plenty of wild oats before joining Thomas Knight's firm. In fact, he claimed he was burned out from chasing the good life. Knight's ad came along just as he was feeling a need to settle down into some sort of an ongoing career. He and Knight had seemed to hit it off. Dwight recognized that Knight had much to teach him and Knight felt that he was an eager pupil. Dwight had become Knight's Vice President and confidant.

Over the next three years, Knight's business had flourished and the quality of its clientele had steadily increased. Eventually the business had found its niche and Knight Security had become the premier agency for handling the security for the world's rich and famous.

When Jack Flynn asked Knight to set up the security for his newest Las Vegas resort, Basham had been involved from the start. Knight's contract to supply the security elements for the new Colossus resort was a very exciting project for both of them. In fact, Dwight had become almost as knowledgeable about the Colossus's security system as Knight himself. With the project finished and the major security issues solved, Knight felt that he had accomplished what he had set out to do. Therefore, when Jack Flynn had offered him the job as the permanent head of security, Knight had turned him down. It simply was not in his nature to work for someone else.

Although Flynn had known in his heart that Knight would return to other clients after everything was set up, he could not help feeling rebuffed. It was certainly not above his nature to pettily punish Knight by trying to steal one of his employees. He made a surreptitious offer to Basham to become his Vice President of Security. Dwight Basham had eagerly accepted the position. After all, being the security head of the largest hotel in the world would certainly enhance his resume.

Knight had felt betrayed. He knew he really had not been, but it certainly stuck in his craw that his old friend Flynn had gone behind his back. He had not only lost someone in whom he had invested a great deal of training, but he had to go find another pupil and start the process all over again. The relationship between Flynn and Knight continued to be cordial, but it lacked the warmth that it once had.

Dwight Basham had thrown himself eagerly into the role. He had taken to wearing aviator-style dark glasses even in the casino and had clipped his hair into a high and tight Marine Corps cut. When he changed his name from Dwight to what he thought was the more appropriate "Bulldog", the transformation had been complete. He had started acting like he thought a head of security should act. Now that he had been in the job for a while, he had his shtick down cold.

Over the last year, Knight had put his feelings of resentment behind him. In fact, he even enjoyed watching Dwight's overstated attempts to be perceived as the Colossus's bad ass. He had chuckled for a week when he had been told that Dwight was henceforth to be known as "Bulldog". Knight had to admit the name was impressive, but try as he might, he would always see the world's largest resort's Vice President of Security as a young and naive kid named Dwight.

Knight clicked the Ferrari's halogen headlights onto bright. He made a mental note to advise "Bulldog" to install some reflective road stakes along the road. Occasionally dust storms would blow through the area. They could be worse than fog, completely obscuring everything and making it impossible to identify even the most familiar landmarks.

Knight shook his head as he thought about how that safety issue would never occur to Bulldog. He had tried to impress upon his former protégé that security did not involve only protection against the incursions of others, but against anything that had the potential to harm the client. Knight had taught Bulldog everything that he knew but not everything that he, Knight, knew.

The newly paved road produced almost no tire noise from the Ferrari's Pirelli tires as it drove along. The only real sound was the throaty, distinctive exhaust note produced by the flat-12 engine.

Knight barely had time to react! Only his finely tuned reflexes saved the car and himself. The thing had appeared out of nowhere; even the Ferrari's newly installed heads-up display had failed to pick it up and give warning.

The car spun violently, the high-performance tires clawing at the asphalt road. As the rear tires slid off the road and on to the coarse white gravel of the desert, a fine cloud of dust exploded. The dust completely engulfed the car and its startled driver. The red machine had barely stopped before Knight was out of the car, the Glock 26 handgun held in the classic two-handed combat arms grip, with the left thumb pointed towards the target. The halogen headlights looked like Star Wars light sabers as they tried to pierce the darkness and the dust.

He was desperately trying to see through the dust cloud, the Glock still at the ready. The tritium night sights on the gun glowed perfectly. "Damn, I wish I had my Glock 18," he swore under his breath. He not only would have felt more comfortable with that gun's laser sight, but something told him that he very well might need the 18's fully automatic fire and extra magazine capacity.

He stared into the settling dust hoping to see something, and yet secretly hoping he did not find what he thought he had seen.

It had been nearly eight feet tall, walking upright like a human. However, that was all that appeared to be human. It had two immense phosphorescent green eyes protruding from what appeared to be its head. Its skin, or whatever it was, was a shiny gray. It had a large lump on its back as if it had something slung over its shoulders. Large black tentacles crisscrossed and encircled its enormous body.

If he had not seen it with his own eyes, he would never have believed it! The stories about aliens residing in the desert north of Las Vegas were commonplace. Conspiracy theorists and UFO believers for years had claimed that the government had found and sequestered aliens at a secret base north of Vegas. The base, also known as Area 51 or Groom Lake, had been officially denied for years by the government.

The only trouble was, Area 51 was nearly one hundred miles away and on a highly protected military reservation. The creature Knight had seen was on private property leading to a golf course!

The dust had almost completely settled and Knight had seen no further sign of the alien or whatever it was. Still with the Glock at the ready, he advanced slowly into the night grateful that the settling dust was letting the headlights spread out their reassuring light. He returned to the Ferrari and extracted a powerful Maglite flashlight from his roadside emergency kit in the small storage area behind the passenger seat. With the Glock in one hand and the flashlight in the other, he searched up and down the road and into the desert on both sides trying to find any sign to confirm what he had seen. After fifteen minutes, he wrote off the endeavor as fruitless. Marking the location with an unused flare from the emergency kit, he got back into the Ferrari turned it around, and started again toward the clubhouse. He would do a thorough search in the morning.

The massive clubhouse was certainly impressive! Nestled between volcanic hot rock outcroppings it seemed to grow right out of the ground. Considering Flynn's garish taste in his Las Vegas properties, the tasteful architecture of the clubhouse was totally incongruous. Knight was about to credit Flynn with acquiring some style, but then he remembered that the building had been Isis Flynn's project. The thought brought him back to why he was there.

The night butler showed him to a comfortable and tastefully decorated suite. After a light supper and a quick shower, he collapsed on the soft king-sized bed and drifted off immediately. Despite falling asleep easily, it was a fitful night, full of wild, fanciful dreams about aliens and bizarre experiments. He also dreamed about Susan Strong. He found he often dreamed about the blue-eyed blonde he had met in

Palm Springs, but this time it was different. She kept morphing into the honey colored blonde he had seen on the motorcycle.

———·———

The silence of the underground bunker beneath the NTS test site was suddenly broken.

"Sergeant, I have a bogey in sector seven at three one two," the Corporal called out over his shoulder as he continued to stare at the waveforms dancing across his display monitor.

The burly Sergeant, in charge of the bunker, reluctantly put down his coffee cup and plodded over to the Corporal's workstation with absolutely no urgency. "What is it?" he slurred, his lips still tightly clenched on the remaining stub of a cheap cigar.

"I'm not sure Sarge…it's intermittent."

"Dammit son, the US of A government has invested a fortune in your training so that you would be sure."

"Like I said Sarge, it's intermittent. It doesn't have a human or animal profile," protested the Corporal.

"Well son…I see it blipping too. So unless the entire system is FUBAR it has to be something."

"It comes and goes."

"Private!" called out the Sergeant over his shoulder to the other technician manning a computer terminal. "Check sec seven, three one two, on your infrared."

"Nothing Sarge," came the reply. Then, "No…wait…I've got a lite hit!"

The Sergeant moved over to the infrared screen and studied the elusive image for himself. "Probably just background interference," he said in a voice that sounded as if he were trying to reassure himself. He hated to scramble the security guards to the section and have them come up with nothing. The paperwork generated by a false report was a pain in the ass, to say nothing of the mark on his efficiency report.

There was an intense rivalry between the military controlled *Technology Security Group* and the TSG as they were called and the Nevada Test Site's security contractor. They both were convinced that the other was a collection of arrogant idiots. From their underground bunker, the TSGs monitored everything on the surface by using the military's latest technology including; infrared cameras, motion detectors, and surveillance satellite photos. They had a real aversion to bringing in the contractor's security teams unless they were absolutely sure of an intruder. Any sighting that did not pan out was derided and scorned by the contracted surface patrols as further evidence that the "moles", as they labeled the military personnel, were incompetent.

The surface patrols maintained their share of the security by displaying a physical presence whenever an intruder approached or actually transgressed onto the NTS. They drove about the area in white SUV's wearing desert camouflage uniforms. Locals and the other curious who had seen them referred to them as the "camo dudes". Their standard operating procedure was to park on hills well back from an intruder and yet close enough to be clearly seen. Usually this intimidating presence was enough to turn back all but the most committed intruders. Those who did not get the message and turn back were unceremoniously detained and then turned over to the local sheriff after being charged with trespassing.

For years, the rumor of the governmental secret base, known as Area 51, had been like a magnet drawing every kind of conspiracy theorist. Some were convinced that the government had captured alien beings and were forcing them to reveal secrets about extraterrestrial travel. It all made for great speculation. The emergence of the Internet had been like adding gasoline to an already spreading fire. Rumors of all kinds were everywhere. Secret bases, alien encounters, germ warfare, flying saucers, every unexplained phenomenon in the West was laid to Area 51. This curiosity kept both the TSGs and the camo dudes busy.

The underground bunker was again quiet, only the whirring of the fans cooling the computers prevented complete silence. A full minute passed with the screens appearing normal before the Sergeant spoke. "Log it as an intermediate anomaly." Then as if trying to impress the young operators with his vast knowledge of the job he added, "Gentlemen you just had your first encounter with Spook."

"Who?" asked the Corporal, knowing he was feeding the Sergeant's game.

"Well son," came the answer, "back in the '80s when our machines weren't very sophisticated, we relied on seismic sensors exclusively to locate trespassers coming into the area. And, there were a lot of them. Every UFO nut in the world was up here tramping around looking for the supposedly top-secret base."

"I heard about that," the Corporal added. "But wasn't that in Area 51? That's a hundred miles away."

"Son…any area that was posted off-limits by the government is considered to be part of a giant conspiracy." Sensing he had fully captured his audience, the Sergeant continued. "Well, we would locate them and then send out our security teams to scare the hell out of them."

Milking the story for all its worth he paused and discarded the worthless stub of the cigar he had been chewing on for the last two hours. He reached into the desk drawer and selected a new pacifier. He bit off the end and spit it disgustingly into the metal wastebasket. He lit the new cigar, and puffed on it vigorously to bring it to life. With a small cloud of smoke nearly enveloping his head, he leaned back in his chair and put his feet on the desk. He laced his fingers behind his head and then after another pause for effect he continued. "Anyway, there were hits that we kept getting that looked like it was a trespasser. But the sensors would give off an intermittent signal, just like now. So…we would scramble the security and they would come back empty handed. It drove everybody nuts. The sightings would be concentrated in one area for while and then would shift to another. We added some infrared cameras to check the seismic sensors and try to get a cross-reference."

The smoke from the disgusting cigar had wafted over to the Corporal's workstation and he coughed with deliberate exaggeration, hoping the Sergeant would pick up his hint.

The Sergeant was completely oblivious to the subtle suggestion as he was now relishing his role of raconteur. "So, this goes on for years, like I said, driving everyone nuts. We even had teams patrolling the whole area every night, but they all came up empty-handed. After a while, even we began to think that there really were aliens walking around out there. Of course, nobody wanted to admit it but the sightings were starting to spook everyone. Hence the name, "Spook."

"Did you ever find out what it was?" asked the Corporal as he waved his hand in a futile attempt to keep the smoke at bay.

"No son, we never did," answered the Sergeant. "And until today, we haven't had a hit in our area for three months, right before you guys came aboard. I've talked to the other area's NCOs and we've all started reporting these things as nothing but machine anomalies." He then leaned forward, stood up, stretched, and announced, "I'm going to take a whiz."

The Sergeant had been safely out of the room for a few minutes before the Corporal asked tentatively, "Do you believe that story?"

The Private shrugged noncommittally and asked, "What's FUBAR anyway?"

"Fouled up beyond all recognition," said the Sergeant as he reentered the room just catching the question. He thought to himself, what kind of soldiers are these that do not understand basic military language.

———·———

From a distance, if one could replace the two, white, Chevy vans with camels, the tents on the desert floor of the NTS looked like a tribe of Bedouins had set up camp. However, the similarity ended there. Upon closer inspection, the large, round, sand colored tents were full of the latest high-tech seismic measuring devices. Two men in desert fatigues were intently studying the wave patterns shown on the computer monitors.

Professor Eric Aronson was intimately familiar with volcanoes. His native Iceland was literally a mound of them. His people had lived and died with them for centuries. With all the volcano hotbeds around the earth it was highly unusual to find the world's foremost volcanologist running seismic tests in the desert just beyond the lights of Las Vegas.

The email from Jason Fulmar, the young, Assistant Professor of Isotope Geochemistry at the University of Las Vegas, had been persuasive. Professor Aronson had canceled his appearance at a worldwide symposium in London and had hightailed it directly to the desert gambling capital. In geological time, the high desert was fairly old. Volcanic activity in the area had occurred eons before the modern eruptions that were currently active throughout the rest of the globe.

No. It was not volcanic activity that brought him here. It was the series of earthquake anomalies that Fulmar had documented that caught his attention. Earthquakes were often harbingers of volcanoes and Professor Aronson had made his reputation in the volcanic community by being able to predict when the earth would blow.

"I've downloaded the *tornillo,* the screw-shaped signal from the seismograph onto a disk Professor," said Fulmar proudly. It was the key piece of data he needed to prove his theory. He had first noticed the anomalies and had tried to raise the alarm, only to be treated as a Chicken Little. Only in this case, he was not claiming the sky was falling. Quite the opposite, he was claiming that the earth would explode near Las Vegas!

After months of skepticism and outright rejection, he had been at his wit's end. No one was listening, especially to a part-time assistant professor that did not even have a Doctoral Degree. In fact, he had been such a pain-in-the-ass trying to get someone to look at his findings that he was in danger of having his doctoral candidacy revoked altogether.

Finally, in desperation, he had postulated his theory in a brief and sent it to Iceland. There was only one man that had the credentials to make something happen. He had waited patiently for a response to his conclusions and had nearly given up hope that anyone would take him seriously, when the call came.

Professor Aronson had questioned him at length about his findings. Evidently, he had given the right answers because within twenty-four hours the Professor had been able to get the Army's top brass to authorize a series of tests on the NTS test site. For the last three months the two of them had worked together trying to find evidence, that Fulmar's theory, as outrageous as it seemed, was indeed correct.

"There is no doubt about it," the elderly professor said. "You were absolutely right. But now, we only have days, perhaps hours, to act on our conclusions."

"Do you think we can really head it off?" asked Fulmar.

"I wouldn't want it to get out, but I honestly don't know." The Professor could be candid with Fulmar, but he could not show the slightest uncertainty to the powers-that-be. He had learned enough about human nature in his advancing years to realize that something as radical as what they were proposing would be analyzed to death if there were any doubt. They did not have either the time or the luxury of intellectual argument. They had to act and they had to act now! "I'll show the General what we've got," said the Professor waving the gold disk. "You pack up the instruments in the other van and I'll meet you back at the site command center in a couple of hours."

"Yes Professor." Fulmar knew he was being stuck doing the mundane jobs. And when it was all said and done, he would receive only a small part of the credit he was truly due. But what the heck, a little of something was better than all of nothing, which is what he had before the Professor had signed on.

It was nearly dark by the time he loaded the last box of instruments into the van. He wanted a beer and a shower, in that order. Nobody had told him winning a Nobel Prize could be such dirty, lonely work.

As he reached for the driver's door handle on the van, the reflection in the van's mirror of the thing behind him froze him momentarily, and then he spun around.

The large metal claw struck him across the jawbone and neck. Blood gushed from the tear in his carotid artery. He instinctively put his hand to the wound. He pulled it away and stared transfixed at the bloody appendage. He looked up into the phosphorescent green eyes of his giant attacker. Before he could open his mouth to question why, he was slashed again with the claw, this time across the abdomen. The blow ripped away the lower half of his T-shirt. When he looked down at the source of the searing pain he gasped with horror as his intestines slowly started to ooze from the four-inch deep cuts. "Who are you?" he screamed with his dying breath.

CHAPTER 3

The phone ringing on the night table in the clubhouse's suite violently interrupted Knight's erotic dream, and he was still perturbed when he answered with a sleepy, "Yes."

"It is six o'clock sir. You requested a call," said the youthful sounding woman's voice.

"Thank you," replied Knight, as his manners returned. A quick check of his Rolex confirmed that the call had indeed been punctual. He dressed quickly in his swimsuit and headed for the clubhouse pool. The cool water instantly refreshed him and was just the thing to shake off the cobwebs of sleep. He swam his customary three miles, spending the time trying to focus on Isis's kidnapping. It was difficult. No matter how hard he tried to make sense out of the limited facts he had, he seemingly was always lead back to the alien encounter. Perhaps they really are somehow connected, he thought as he toweled off and returned to his suite to dress.

After his shower, his appetite, dormant for the last few days, returned with a vengeance. The clubhouse chef was hard pressed to keep up with his demands and he wolfed down four helpings of eggs benedict before surrendering his plate.

With his appetite slaked, his plan was to retrace Isis's steps right up to the kidnapping. He could not put his finger on it, but his usually reliable instincts told him that a clue as to why and what happened was waiting for him in the desert beyond the golf course. After borrowing a straw Stetson, filling a canteen full of water, checking his digital camera and strapping the Glock 26 in its holster on his hip, he proceeded to the stables.

He could have selected one of the golf courses air-conditioned Hummers, but somehow he felt a horse would be less destructive to the crime scene. Besides, he liked horses. The groom at the stable had been reluctant to saddle Isis's Arabian stallion for him. The big black was certainly spirited and it took Knight, an expert horseman, a few minutes to establish his dominance over the magnificent animal. Horses can sense if the rider knows what he is doing and the black soon realized that Knight was no novice.

The groom had given precise directions and he easily found the crime scene. As he dismounted, he was dismayed at the plethora of tire tracks crisscrossing the area. "Damn!" he swore aloud. "The authorities around here don't have a clue about preserving a scene." He retrieved his digital camera from his saddlebag and walked carefully around the area. It was only nine o'clock and he had wanted to arrive here while the morning shadows were still long. He snapped a dozen pictures of strange depressions in the coarse desert floor. Without the aid of the shadows, they would have been invisible. They appeared to be tracks of some sort. Whatever it was that had made them appeared to be moving on two legs with an enormous stride. Knight, at six-foot three, measured his considerable stride against the tracks and found them to be nearly two feet longer. He whistled softly and then said with admiration, "Whatever made these was a big son-of-a-gun!"

The tracks continued for only twenty yards before the ground became too rocky to hold an impression. Nearly an hour of scouring the area for further evidence produced nothing. He did not know where the tracks had come from and more importantly, where they led. He took a long drink from the canteen and then gave the grateful horse the remainder of the precious fluid before remounting. The sun was already brutal and it was only late morning. By mid-afternoon the desert would be uninhabitable to all but the creatures designed by nature to eke out their living among the rocks and cactus.

Knight turned the big Arabian back toward the desert. About a mile past the abduction site headed north, was a faded rusted sign proclaiming in ominous lettering, *Trespassers will be prosecuted*. Ignoring the obvious NTS boundary, Knight spurred the stallion up a rocky draw. He had gone another half a mile before he saw the dust rising on the ridge to his left. He reined up and watched as the two white SUVs stopped on a knoll about a quarter of a mile in front of him. The desert-camouflaged passengers opened the doors and set up what appeared to be a powerful spotting scope on the hood of the first vehicle.

Knight reached into his saddlebag and without dismounting, retrieved the Bausch and Lomb 7 x 50 wide-angle binoculars. Through the enlarged image, he could see that the camouflaged guards had a camera attached to a long lens and were snapping pictures.

"Overall not a bad response time," he said with grudging admiration. He put the binoculars back in the saddlebag, reined the horse around and headed back to the golf course. As he headed back, he was grateful that the late morning sun was shining on his back. He had left his Mont Blanc sunglasses in the Ferrari and the glare off the desert was severe.

The glint hit him squarely in the eye, almost as if someone was deliberately signaling him. He reined up the horse and again fished the 7 X 50's out of the saddlebag. Even after carefully focusing, he was unable to make out the source of the reflection. "Probably a beer can," he speculated aloud to the completely oblivious horse. Still, it was something, and after all, he was out here investigating. He bagged the binoculars and neck-reined the horse toward the glint.

He was only twenty feet away from the source of the mysterious reflection when he lost it. When he finally arrived at the apparent source, nothing but desert and rocks greeted him. He stopped the horse, dismounted, and tied the reins to a bush with a loose half hitch. He walked around for nearly five minutes before he uncovered the source of the shining signal. There, wedged in between rocks was a silver and gold spur still attached to the weathered remnants of what appeared to be a cowboy boot. Assorted, bright white bones were scattered around throughout the rocks.

Knight rolled back one of the rocks and the spur and the boot fell onto the desert gravel. Only when he bent over to pick it up did he notice the white bones sticking out of what remained of the boot. He carefully lifted the spur up and stared at it closely. He spit on his finger and rubbed it along the highly tarnished surface to remove the fine film of desert dust. As he slowly twisted the artifact in the sunlight, he could just make out the fine engraving. *First-place—Saddle Bronc Riding—Helldorado Days—1944.*

Knight took the bone, boot and spur back to the horse and carefully placed it in his saddlebag. He then went back to the pile of bones. Knight knew bones and could easily tell the difference between human and animal remains.

He picked around at the nearly fossilized remnants and determined that all the bones were equine. No other human bones were among them.

His handheld GPS locator was with his forgotten sunglasses back in his car. Looking around he could find no obvious landmark nearby. Thinking back to his childhood Boy Scout training on how to determine your position, he popped the catch on the band of the gold Rolex Yachtsman and took it off his wrist. The hands showed exactly ten thirty. He held the watch up flat to the horizon and sighted along each watch hand.

He found an alignment with the hour hand and a notch in the outline of the top of the distant Mount Charleston. The minute hand aligned perfectly with a rocky outcropping about a mile away. Without moving the watch, he waited until the sweep second hand crossed an easily identifiable peak of a foothill. With these, three reference points and the watch hands in the same positions, he could easily locate this exact spot on a good topographical map. Perhaps the Sheriff would have an interest in finding the unfortunate soul with one remaining leg.

The early morning sun had found its way under the portico in front of the clubhouse and onto the Ferrari. The inside of the car was like a blast furnace. Red cars really absorbed the heat. A white one would have been more practical for someone living in a sunny climate. But, the car had been a gift from a grateful factory and there was a strong feeling there that all Ferraris were just meant to be red. Even the name Testarossa meant *redhead.* Knight smiled, most wannabe aficionados thought that the name applied to the exterior color, but it had really been used to describe the red-painted, valve covers on the 12-cylinder engine.

He lowered the automatic windows to let the heat escape and turned the air conditioning on max. It took only a quarter mile before he could put the windows up and turn down the fan.

After the hot horse ride into the desert, the air-conditioning in the Ferrari was obscenely comfortable. Indeed, air-conditioning had been the invention that made it possible for Las Vegas to exist on the scale that it did. Other than a few die-hard gamblers, most of the millions of visitors would never have braved the heat without the cool air of the casinos blowing down their backs.

Knight downshifted the Ferrari and spotted the red flare still stuck in the gravel beside the road, just where he left it the night before. He spent nearly twenty minutes scouring the desert with nothing more than a handful of digital pictures of some possible tracks to show for it. He certainly had no proof of his alien encounter. He decided to keep the story to himself; after all, he did not need his clients thinking he had gone off the deep end. The only thing tangible he had to show for the morning's effort was some unfortunate cowboy's antique spur.

"I'll download the pictures to Monica and see if her computer *Ralph* can make any sense out of them," he said aloud. He turned and fished the laptop from behind the passenger's seat. It only took a minute to connect it to the accessory outlet and dialup his email server. A few clicks of the built-in mouse and the pictures were on their way to Monica.

He upshifted the quirky five-speed gearbox on the Ferrari, turned onto the highway and headed south for Las Vegas. As he passed Indian Springs, he failed to notice the gold crotch rocket that passed him headed north in the other lane.

———·———

The three-dialed Patek Philippe watch on Susan's slender wrist showed exactly six o'clock as she opened the weighted glass door to Flynn's outer office. "Susan Strong to see Mr. Flynn," she announced to the very attractive young blonde behind the large reception counter.

Evidently, the blonde had pushed a signal buzzer of some kind because almost instantly another blonde clone appeared and announced in a syrupy voice, "Mr. Flynn is expecting you. Please follow me."

Susan was used to elaborate offices; in New York, they were all the rage. Flynn's was like many others she had been in, but befitting the name of the resort, twice as large. The small man seated at the huge desk stood up quickly as she entered and almost sprinted to her. Susan did not know what she had expected, but she was definitely struggling to equate the frumpy looking character approaching her with Flynn's fearsome reputation.

"Thank you for coming so promptly," Flynn said as he extended his hand.

Susan casually accepted the handshake, somewhat surprised at how clammy it was.

"I hope your suite is sufficient?" he continued.

"It's quite lovely, thank you," answered Susan as she moved toward one of the chairs Flynn was indicating by the massive desk. She sat down, crossed her long legs, and leaned back, with her arms resting on the lush velveteen upholstery.

Flynn remained standing and leaned back against the edifice of the desk. "I trust your office has brought you up to date on what's happened?" he asked.

"Yes, they have," answered Susan. "I'm sorry to hear about it. It must be very hard on you."

"It has been," Flynn replied, with what Susan could see was a touch of moisture in his eyes. "It has been terrible!" The wave of nostalgia vanished quickly and Flynn became all business again. "I understand that my wife, as an executive employee of the company is covered under our kidnapping insurance."

"Yes, that's correct," replied Susan matter-of-factly.

"The policy limit is twenty million...correct?"

"That's right."

"Well that's what the kidnappers are requesting, so I need it now."

"You are very lucky."

"How's that?"

"Well, the policy limit is twenty million and that conveniently is exactly what the kidnappers are requesting."

Flynn suddenly felt his face turning red with anger. "Just what is that supposed to mean?"

"Merely an observation," replied Susan with a subtle hint of sarcasm.

"I don't like your implication," repeated Flynn, feeling the warmth in his face subsiding.

Susan studied Flynn's face without saying anything, preparing herself for what was to follow. She had been dreading this moment, but she strengthened her resolve and said, "Of course you understand that the policy only pays off after we have conducted a full investigation and have proof that you didn't recover the ransom."

Flynn stared at her with his mouth slightly open. He was not used to anyone questioning him. "What is this? Some kind of a sick joke?" he yelled, involuntarily unleashing his combative nature. His face again flushed red with rage. He turned and walked toward the bar obviously trying to control his temper. He paused at the bar and poured a double shot of imported vodka into a baccarat crystal tumbler. He downed the fiery liquid with a shudder and then turned back to Susan. "Why can't I have the money now? I mean…what the hell good is kidnap insurance if you can't pay the kidnappers?"

"Mr. Flynn, I'm sure your attorneys briefed you on all of this before I got here. You know how it works. So let's not play games," she countered.

Flynn put down his glass and looked at the gorgeous blonde investigator, then his eyes went cold and he was all business again, the product of years of self discipline. "The money really isn't the issue. I want my wife back and I want the punks that did this."

"My job is to find the kidnappers, hopefully get your wife back and to prevent you from losing the twenty million that my company would have to reimburse," replied Susan in a no-nonsense tone.

Flynn moved to the desk and barked into the intercom, "Get Bulldog up here!" Then he turned back to Susan and asked, "Want a drink?"

"A small whiskey would be fine," she answered. It might help keep her growing frustration under control.

Flynn ignored her request and poured two double drinks. He handed her one and then once again downed his with a gulp.

Susan sipped the potent fluid. She recognized the taste immediately as that of Canadian Club whiskey. Then without knowing why she announced, "Thomas Knight's drink."

"What?" asked Flynn distractedly, failing to make the connection.

"Nothing," came the reply. She could not believe that she had instinctively blurted out his name.

"I've asked my V.P. of Security to join us," said Flynn as he again moved to the intercom on the desk. "Is Bulldog out there?" he asked gruffly.

"Yes sir," answered the machine politely.

"Well get him in here," ordered Flynn.

Bulldog Basham certainly did not look like his name. He was not quite six-feet tall and with a mellow, almost childlike face. His hair had been carefully cropped and when he offered his hand to Susan, she noticed his nails reflected the care a weekly manicure would produce. She also noticed a recent dark bruise around his right wrist.

Catching her eyes glancing at his wrist, Bulldog quickly pulled down the sleeve of his monogrammed, French-cuffed shirt to cover the area.

"Ms. Strong will be looking into Isis's disappearance," Flynn stated flatly. "Give her anything she wants." Then with a casual wave of the back of his hand he dismissed them both and headed back to the bar.

At the door, Susan stopped and turned back toward the most powerful man in Vegas, who suddenly seemed to be terribly vulnerable, and said. "We will get her back."

Flynn did not reply but simply stared out the window and drained his glass once more.

———·———

Isis Flynn struggled to gain consciousness. As she came to, the first senses her brain were able to process were the awful stench of rotting flesh and the sensation of cold. The effects of the high-powered animal tranquilizer had left her highly confused and dying of thirst. “Water…” she cried meekly, her voice barely more than a whisper. She could not see clearly, everything was a blur, although she was trying desperately to focus her eyes. It took a few seconds before she could begin to make out her surroundings. She tried to sit up but her limbs were like noodles and she could only manage to roll over on her side. “Water!” she cried again, much louder this time, as her strength began to return. She attempted to sit up again, only to find her hands were held back by what felt like handcuffs. She struggled again, stronger this time, but to no avail. She was securely restrained.

She looked around the large, brightly lit room trying to figure out where she was. There was no sign of anyone. It appeared to be some sort of processing facility. In the middle of the room, a dark shape hung from a ceiling mounted conveyor. It looked vaguely familiar. She knew it could not be, but it looked like a naked, eviscerated, human corpse. Through the remaining cobwebs, she heard the movement of something approaching her. Not footsteps exactly, more like a shuffle. Suddenly there was a low rumble from somewhere underneath her followed by a menacing hiss. A putrid smell of rotten eggs engulfed her, overcoming the persistent stench of the place. In spite of her thirst, she felt as if she were going to vomit. She tried to prevent it by swallowing hard.

With no warning, she felt her wrists grabbed in a vice like grip of someone or something from in back of her head. Then came a sharp prick in the cradle of her arm. She struggled but she could feel the liquid entering her bloodstream. The world started spinning and she felt as if she were free falling into a brightly colored vortex. She was barely conscious when she heard the voice.

"You're giving her too much."

There was no reply, merely a grunt, and then an awkward shuffle. Another hiss sounded and the stench of rotten eggs again permeated the air.

———·———

Susan had spent nearly an hour with Bulldog. It had not been particularly productive. He had seemed much more concerned about impressing her with his power and responsibility than supplying any useful information. She could not quite put her finger on it, call it women's intuition, but Bulldog was not reacting the way a security chief should react. She had expected to see more of a sense of urgency. After all, it was his boss's wife that had been kidnapped and he had been responsible for her safety. With his job clearly on the line, you would expect that he would be overturning every rock.

Susan's investigator nose had rarely failed her in the past and she had learned to trust her instincts. Her first inclination had been to head north to the golf course where Isis had been abducted, but her instincts held her back. No, the answer was probably right here in Vegas. Well anyway, it was where she would start.

Money in Vegas was not just the commodity that fueled the casinos but it was the lifeblood of daily commerce. In Vegas, everything could be had, for the right price. She was counting on it!

Years of living and traveling in large cities had made her acutely aware that there were certain portals through which all information flowed. Her plan was simple, find these portals, and buy what information she needed. The Colossus was the obvious place to start. One of the few things of value to come out of her meeting with Bulldog was a list of all five thousand five hundred employees. She knew that only a handful however would conceivably be of any value. She had decided to start with the one person who knew every one of consequence who came into the resort—the head-parking valet.

———·———

Johnny Ford had one of the best jobs in Vegas, head-parking valet at the world's largest hotel. Even an average valet could park and retrieve up to fifteen cars an hour. Although there theoretically was no charge to park, everyone tipped. At five dollars a pop, a valet could make a hundred and fifty thousand dollars a year, in cash! A recent IRS court case had accused one valet of underreporting his income by at least a hundred grand, and this was after he had already reported a hundred!

Yes, Johnny was doing well; well enough to have a golf course frontage home, a large mini-yacht on Lake Mead, a state-of-the-art computer system and a growing automobile collection. Yet, in spite of his large income he was always broke. First, there was the ever-increasing alimony payment, then the substantial losses due to the overestimation of his golfing skills. His daily cocaine habit consumed most of what was left. It was bad enough to have to contend with all this, but then a couple years ago the Russians had showed up.

First, it was just a handful of crude thugs trying to muscle in on the skin trade by using imported Russian girls. The girls had been easily lured to the bright lights by tales of glamour and prosperity. The reality of finding themselves the virtual property of these gangsters, who bought and sold them like slaves, had been terrible.

After a beachhead had been established in the lap dance bars, these new, young and very ruthless, Russians had branched out into almost every area of petty gangsterism. Shaking down the back-of-the-house employees and contractors for the mega-resorts was reaching full stride.

The allure of the cash business of the valets had been an attractive target. Without matching muscle behind them, guys like Johnny eventually had to fall. Now nearly fifty percent of his valets were Russian connected. They were a royal pain in the ass. First, they all smoked like chimneys and secondly they all were crude. Johnny's real challenge was to try to keep them away from the high rollers and whales. So, he had them work the front entrance, while his hand picked crew worked the high roller's entrance. Moreover, the high rollers tipped better. At least those who had class did. Johnny was always surprised at some of the big name visitors who stiffed him and acted as if it was beneath them to acknowledge his existence.

Between his ever-present cash shortage, his extravagant lifestyle, and now this Russian invasion, Johnny needed a large score to solve all of his problems.

———·———

"Hello Johnny, I'm Susan Strong," the beautiful blonde announced in a tone that implied no-nonsense. "Bulldog said you might be able to help me."

"Oh yes, Ms. Strong. Bulldog said to give you whatever I could," Johnny replied in a deliberately condescending voice. It had not done any good to argue with Bulldog about the advisability of talking to a seasoned investigator like Susan Strong. Where Johnny was highly street smart, Bulldog was arrogant and highly chauvinistic. He felt no female was his match regardless of her credentials.

Johnny knew better, and there was definitely something very dangerous about this woman. Beauty and brains, every time Johnny had come across the combination before he had come out the loser. "What can I do for you?" he asked with faked politeness.

"Is there some place we can talk?" asked Susan, obviously annoyed at the confusion surrounding the valet station.

"Certainly, follow me," came the reply as Johnny exited the small, valet building and led the way into the resort, pausing only long enough to tell his second-in-command that he would be back in ten minutes.

The valet's lounge was just inside the main entrance, through a door marked *Employees Only,* and down a short hallway.

"Would you care for a cup of coffee?"

"No, I'm fine, thank you." answered Susan as she took a seat at one of the break room tables. "What can you tell me about extortion?"

The bluntness of the question and its accusatory tone caught Johnny off guard. "Well I…I don't know anything," he stammered.

"C'mon Johnny you and I both know nothing goes on around here that you don't hear about."

"You give me way too much credit," laughed Johnny nervously, still trying to recover from the initial onslaught. "Hey look, I just park cars."

Susan's blue eyes narrowed as she looked into Johnny's and she said flatly, "I've been at this game a long time and my instincts don't lie. Are you involved?"

"No…no of course not. I don't know what you are talking about," stammered Johnny, his mind racing trying to figure out if she really knew something or was just fishing.

Susan continued to look at him coldly. "I intend to get to the bottom of what is going on around here and if I find out you knew something and didn't tell me…well, let's just say you will be finished in this town."

"Is that a threat?" Johnny croaked with panic rising in his throat. He suddenly imagined his lifestyle being swept away like a losing bet at the tables.

"You're damn right it is and it is one you had better take seriously," Susan shot back as she got up from her chair, turned and left.

Johnny stared at the back of the door for a minute. He then reached down, pulled his cell phone from its holster on his hip, and dialed a prestored number. The phone rang four times before the familiar voice answered. "An insurance investigator was just here and I don't like what she is thinking," Johnny said. Then not waiting for a reply he added, "You said there wasn't anything to worry about!" He listened for a minute to the voice on the other end. "It had better be!" he threatened. He had no sooner replaced the phone on his hip than the door to the break room opened and his second-in-command entered.

"Boss we've got a problem. A tourist is complaining that one of the stupid Russians dented the door on her Mercedes."

"Damn!" cursed Johnny as he brushed by the messenger and led the way out of the break room.

———·———

The two thousand spectators in the Colossus's main showroom screamed in terror as the sixteen hundred pound, Kodiak bear charged out of the fog toward the audience. The massive beast suddenly stopped, reared up on his hind legs and let out a bloodcurdling roar. Extending himself to his full fourteen-foot height the monster pawed at the air with his five-inch claws. The Kodiak bear is the largest carnivore on earth and this one was the biggest of them all.

The children and the women in the audience were squealing uncontrollably, while the men struggled not to give in to their own fright. Suddenly from out of the wings of the stage burst a honey-haired woman in a gold sequined leotard twirling a flaming baton. Barely pausing, she tossed the baton into the air only to have it ripped from its flight by the giant brown behemoth.

Then incredibly the bear began to twirl the baton himself and simultaneously began to do a crude shuffling jig. The audience exploded, yelling and whistling at the top of their lungs. Then they stood and applauded as one.

Honey and Her Bears was the hottest act to ever hit Vegas.

In spite of its huge population, there were very few native Nevadans over the age of thirty, but Honey was one of them. Only during the last fifteen years had Vegas developed a semblance of a rounded economy. Before the phenomenal growth spurt of late '80s and early '90s, Vegas was a town centered on gambling. As the fortunes of the casinos went, so went the town. It was natural then that an attractive, impressionable native would find herself drawn into the glitzy world of the casinos.

Unlike her peers, Honey's future was secure. She had come into a sizable trust fund at twenty-one. But as a teenager before she inherited the money, she was impatient and wanted the glamorous life she saw all around her immediately. At sixteen, Honey was working as a topless dancer in a small off-Strip review. Because of her fully developed figure, it had been easy to find a fake ID. As with most dancers, the small salary barely covered the rent and so it was necessary to supplement her income with other activities.

It was not long before she caught the attention of one of the pit bosses. He was the one who had seen to it that she received her formal education in the art of survival in Vegas. He hired a hard-bitten hooker to show her the ropes and teach her all the tricks. How to select the johns, how to give them just enough to leave them wanting more and most importantly, how to always get the money upfront. She was a natural and it was not long before she was a real pro. Honey liked the money, but it was the action and being in control over men that really turned her on. She specialized in domination. She was added to the book of approved prostitutes used by all the pit bosses. Her skill had even warranted an asterisk by her name, reserved only for those considered the prime cuts. This probably would have been her fate until she lost her looks, but for a couple of pieces of blind luck.

The first was when the off-Strip review's headliner, a magician, found his assistant had come down with a raging case of herpes and could not perform. The trick was an easy illusion and so the magician asked Honey, the most attractive dancer, to help him. In less than an hour, she had the movements down cold. It was not long before the magician fell head over heels for her and she became a regular in his act. By the time the romance cooled, Honey had picked up enough inside knowledge of illusions and tricks to be in high demand among the ever-changing crop of erstwhile magicians.

The other piece of luck was for Honey to land her first job in an animal act. Animal acts in Vegas had started to fade from popularity. With audiences raised on television, they simply were not exciting enough. Besides, for the same cost of feeding and caring for the animals one could easily pay for a magician and his props or even an entire troupe of foreign acrobats.

A newcomer to the scene, a swarthy Russian, was different. His ability to make animals perform was phenomenal. He had learned his craft from his family who for over a century had made their living on the steppes of Russia by performing in small circuses at country fairs. When the circus he was working for cut his animal act in a cost saving purge, he decided to try Vegas. With his heavy accent and quite unattractive looks, he knew he was doomed unless he could find someone to front for him. That is why he brought Honey into his act.

The two of them were definitely the odd couple. The Russian was prone to long periods of depression exacerbated by his ability to consume inordinate amounts of vodka. Honey on the other hand was streetwise, but in an apparent dichotomy to others in her former profession, she neither smoked nor drank. In fact, she was a health food nut. Her only vice was her love for honey. She could not get enough of the golden elixir. She put it in her tea, on her toast and even found ways to include it in her specially blended salad dressing. When that did not satisfy her, she would suck it straight from a squeeze bottle. Over the years, she had consumed the output of millions of hard-working bees.

With Honey and her gorgeous figure as the eye candy for the high roller men and the antics of the bears as excitement for the wives and children, the act was an immediate success.

The small black bears in the act were easily trained and did most of the tricks, but the people came to see the real monsters, the two giant Kodiaks, and the two enormous polar bears. The Russian had raised them from birth and as far as possible acclimated them to working on a stage. When they were cubs their antics, which to them were merely play, absolutely delighted the audiences. But, as adults, they were a different story. The fact was, they were just plain dangerous. Unlike acts with lions and tigers, which could be taught to growl and sit on a stool on command, the bears actually did tricks. The small Kodiak rode a motorcycle, the small polar bear did handstands, while the large one rolled a basketball around and then shot it through a hoop. However, the highlight of the act was, without a doubt, the giant Kodiak named *Thor* twirling the flaming baton and dancing.

Training the small bears was done by using the treat-reward method. However, training the large bears required a much stronger hand. For years, animal cruelty organizations had tried to shut down the animal acts. Finally, they had settled for periodic inspections to determine if the animals were being abused. This is where the Russian's genius showed itself. The skilled use of tranquilizers reduced the natural aggressive tendencies of the big bears. The bears were restrained by nearly invisible leg irons, which were camouflaged by the use of a smoke machine that created the effect that the bears were coming out of a fog. The audience did not have a clue that the shackled bears were permitted only limited movement.

Honey moved around the stage among the bears, seemingly oblivious to their presence. In reality, she always stayed within a carefully marked area that was physically outside of the bears' reach.

To insure the bears moved on cue, the Russian had surgically implanted electrodes in the bear's bodies at strategic locations; between the toes, in the neck, the pit of the foreleg and the base of the spine. Using a small hand-held transmitter, he was able to administer a powerful shock to each of these areas on cue. The resulting involuntary movement delighted the audience while causing the poor beasts great pain. So far, no one had been the wiser.

Honey did not have any affection for the bears. To her they were merely props in an act just like handkerchiefs and cards used in her magician's assistant days. The bears' pain was, in a perverse way, actually a turn on.

Early on, the Russian had put the moves on Honey but she was perceptive enough to realize that any physical relationship would put her at a disadvantage. No, it was better to have an arm's length arrangement secured by the threat of blackmail. Honey knew that if the secret of the bears' tricks were revealed, that not only would the act be finished for good, but also jail was a real possibility for the Russian. She made sure that he never forgot that fact.

While the Russian drank and despaired, Honey lived the life of luxury and excess. Whenever she felt wild, she would put on a brunette wig, a revealing leather outfit, and turn a trick. She felt wild a lot.

CHAPTER 4

The Clark County Sheriff was a barrel-chested man with a tanned face: the color of well-broken-in saddle leather. "You're up early," he said sarcastically as he shook hands without enthusiasm.

"Maybe by Vegas standards," teased Knight. "I was out at the country club looking around where the kidnapping took place."

"Dammit! That area is a crime scene! Nobody is supposed to be out there without permission!" scolded the Sheriff as his face flushed with anger. He turned on his heel and strode to his cluttered desk. He yanked the castigated chair from beneath the desk with a bang and then sat down. "If I had my way about it, I would arrest you!" He knew the threat was frivolous. His boss, the Head County Commissioner and in debt to Flynn, had left no doubt that he was to cooperate fully with Knight on the kidnapping.

There was no love lost between the two, going back to the days when Knight was Flynn's security chief. The Sheriff looked at Knight as a big city interloper taking opportunities away from the locals. It had not helped when Knight had failed to support his application for a managerial position at the Colossus. He paused to let his anger cool and then, giving into his curiosity, he asked in an annoyed tone, "Did you find anything?"

"I don't know. I took some photos and I'm having my secretary and her computer do some analysis." Sensing that he was adding fuel to the Sheriff's fire by implying that the county crime scene investigators were not up to the job, Knight added, "Nothing physical…just photos."

"Well I want to see them too," replied the Sheriff, calmer, but still obviously miffed at this usurping of his authority.

"I used a digital camera and it's out in my car. As soon as we're finished you can have one of your investigators download them," said Knight hoping to smooth the Sheriff's feathers. "But I did find something else about a mile from the crime scene."

"What is it?"

Without answering, Knight placed a black garbage bag on the Sheriff's desk and carefully peeled it back to reveal its gristly contents. "I thought you might have a missing limb case that you are trying to clear."

The Sheriff gingerly picked up the chalk white femur with the black remnant of a boot held onto it by the gold and silver spur. He examined the spur carefully and slid his fingers over the heavily tarnished engraving in the silver. Suddenly, he dropped the bone and pulled back as if he had seen a ghost. "Oh my gosh," he shouted, "It can't be!"

"What is it?" Knight asked quickly, caught off guard by the Sheriff's unexpected reaction.

"It's. . . It's. . . Buck Anders's leg," stuttered the Sheriff.

"Whose?"

"Buck Anders."

"Who is Buck Anders," pressed Knight impatiently.

The Sheriff ignored the question, again picked up the gruesome appendage, and carefully reexamined the spur before adding definitively, "Yep! It's his all right!"

"So?" pressed Knight.

"So! It is just probably one of the most important finds in the last sixty years!" admonished the Sheriff. "Everyone around here has been looking for this ever since Buck cut it off."

"What are you talking about?"

"If you were a local you'd know the story!" chided the Sheriff in a tone that left no doubt about his feelings toward Knight sticking his nose into his business.

"Well I'm not! So what's the story?" ordered Knight.

The Sheriff ignored the question and instead walked around his faux walnut desk, bent over and opened the lower left-hand drawer. He rummaged through its contents before exclaiming, "This is what I'm looking for!" as he produced a half-empty bottle of Kentucky whiskey. He then dumped the remnants of his coffee cup into his wastebasket before filling it with two fingers of the light brown bourbon. He took a long swallow and shook his head involuntarily as the fiery liquid burned his throat. He then paused a moment, staring blankly ahead, before he remembered that he had a guest. "Oh I'm sorry. Do you want a drink?"

"It's only eight o'clock in the morning," lectured Knight.

The Sheriff totally missed the cutting remark, sat down in his chair, and took another long swallow. This time instead of a shudder he let out a small cough. Still ignoring Knight, he opened the front desk drawer and produced a half-empty package of cigarettes and a disposable lighter. It took four tries and a couple of hard raps on the desk, before the lighter came to life. He cupped his hands around the flame, as if he was trying to shield it from the wind, as he lit the cigarette. He took a long drag on the cigarette, holding the smoke in his lungs, before exhaling. The whiskey and the nicotine were having the desired effect.

Knight would have interrupted again with his question but he could see the Sheriff was still locked in his own world.

A minute went by before the Sheriff asked distractedly, "Do you know exactly where you found the leg?"

"Yes…but until I know what the significance of it is, I'm not about to tell you or anybody." Knight's tone left little doubt about his resolve to hold onto his secret.

The Sheriff took another long drag on the cigarette, looked up and said, "It's a long story."

"I'm listening," said Knight not attempting to disguise his growing impatience.

"It all started about sixty years ago. Buck Anders was a Deputy Sheriff working out of this office and he was chasing a local nuisance, a drunk with a bad temper, named Piute Bill. He was wanted for beating up a barber who cut his hair too short." The Sheriff took another drag, "Well, it turns out that Piute Bill set up an ambush, but he was such a lousy shot that he shot Buck's horse by mistake and it fell and broke his leg."

"The horse's or Ander's?" asked Knight.

"Buck's…dammit! Do you want to hear the story or not?"

Knight nodded yes without apologizing.

"Well anyway…so Buck's leg was caught under the horse and Piute Bill steals his water, shoots him in the head and leaves him to die." The Sheriff paused for a second to see if he was going to be interrupted again. "Old Buck was in a helluva fix, what with a broke leg, a head wound, no water, and a scorcher of a day. So he did what he had to do…he cut off his own leg."

"No kidding?"

"Yep…cut it off with his pocket knife!" The Sheriff paused again, "Well, anyway, what happened next nobody knows, but the next day Bugsy Siegel and his girlfriend Virginia Hill found him on the highway north of Vegas and took him to a doctor in Indian Springs."

"*The* Bugsy Siegel…the gangster?" asked Knight. "The one that started the big gambling boom with his Flamingo Hotel?"

"The very same. Of course, no one ever called him Bugsy to his face. If you wanted to stay alive you called him Ben."

Knight had heard the story.

Ben Siegel had grown up in Brooklyn where thousands of Irish, Italian and Jewish immigrants all struggled to make a living among the poverty and disease ridden tenements. It was a perfect breeding ground for crime. Ben had formed a childhood friendship with another erstwhile gangster named Meyer Lansky. Because they were Jewish they could never be formal members of the Italian controlled mob, so they worked on the fringes and formed alliances.

Ben and Meyer eventually put together their own mob, primarily based on robbery, street corner gambling and protection rackets. Because of Ben's violent and unpredictable nature, he earned the nickname of Bugsy. He hated the name and anyone using it in his presence risked his considerable wrath.

By the end of World War I, both the Jewish and Italian gangs were going strong. A swarthy Sicilian by the name of Lucky Luciano had ascended to the head of the Italian mob and he realized the advantage of forming alliances with other gangs regardless of their ethnic background.

Bugsy, Meyer and Lucky became literally thick as thieves. The three of them could not have been more different. Lucky was the thoughtful, analytical organizer. Meyer was the businessman and Bugsy was the sociopathic enforcer. Lucky and Meyer tried to avoid the headlines and even incorporate some legitimate businesses in their enterprises. Bugsy however remained a street thug at heart, eager to use force without any thought to consequences. Finally, his temper became such a liability that his friends persuaded him to go to California. He jumped at the opportunity to get out from beneath Meyer's shadow and he moved his wife and two daughters into a rented thirty-five-room mansion in the upscale Hollywood suburb of Holmby Hills. Bugsy loved the Hollywood scene and he both hobnobbed with and extorted the Hollywood stars.

According to legend, following World War II Bugsy had a vision that a run down town in the Nevada desert could be turned into a gangland gambling Mecca. In truth however, Bugsy was primarily interested in Nevada's recent expansion of gambling laws to include off-track betting on horse races. However, Bugsy began to see the potential of large gambling rooms. He tried unsuccessfully to buy into a couple of existing casinos. After he was thwarted in that endeavor he came up with the grand vision of opening his own casino.

He persuaded his old partners Meyer Lansky and Lucky Luciano to bankroll the enterprise he was going to call the *Flamingo*. The project was in trouble from the start. Bugsy was a gangster, not a developer and soon most of his contractors were stealing him blind. The $1.2 million price tag quickly became nearly $6 million and Lucky, Meyer and other gangster investors were becoming worried about his ability to pull off the project. Further complicating matters was a rumor that Bugsy and his newest girlfriend, Virginia Hill, were skimming money from the project and putting it in Swiss bank accounts.

Finally, the Flamingo opened. However, the weather on the opening weekend was foggy and many of the planes that had been chartered to ferry celebrities from Los Angeles to the opening were grounded. The weather continued to refuse to cooperate by raining, further dampening everyone's spirits. By the end of the first two weeks, only handfuls of people were in the casino and the project looked like a massive bust. Lucky and Meyer, ever paranoid about Bugsy bugging out on them with the money he had supposedly squirreled away in Switzerland, decided that they had had enough.

On June 20, 1947, Bugsy Siegel was shot dead by five slugs from a 30-30 rifle in the living room of his Holmby Hills mansion. His killer was never caught.

From what he had heard of the story, Knight was amazed that Siegel and his girlfriend were, uncharacteristically, the good Samaritans that had saved the unfortunate Buck Anders.

The Sheriff stubbed out the remnants of the cigarette and brushed away some ashes that had fallen on his badly ironed uniform. "Where was I?" he asked. Not waiting for an answer he continued, "Oh yeah…anyway by the time Buck got to the doctor his mind was gone and no one could make any sense out of his ramblings. Anyway, that would have been the end of the story but for what happened next."

"Which was…?" prompted Knight.

"Well years later, a rumor got started that all the

while the Doc was trying to pull him through Buck had a rock in his hand."

"A rock?"

"Not exactly any old rock mind you, but a diamond as big as a hen's egg!"

Knight whistled softly, "A diamond? I didn't know there were diamonds around here."

"Neither did anyone else," replied the Sheriff. "And no one has ever found another one…and several have died trying." When Knight failed to interrupt, the Sheriff continued, "I have open case files on at least a dozen victims that have disappeared throughout the years. Some of them were idiots who underestimated the desert and probably died from exposure. But, at least half of the dozen were pretty savvy desert rats known to be actively looking for the source of the diamond."

"I have never heard anything about this."

"Well in the '50s the government started conducting nuclear tests all around the area that Buck had supposedly crawled out of and so they made the whole thing a top-secret military site." The Sheriff held up the bottle of bourbon with a silent gesture to see if Knight had changed his mind about wanting a drink.

Knight made a brushing movement with his hand indicating that it was still too early for him.

"The damned government, by shutting down that area simply provoked everyone into thinking that there was some conspiracy at work. Then a couple of authors really got everyone's shorts in a bunch by claiming that the government was keeping aliens out there. It turns out aliens were a lot more exciting than some rumor of a treasure and so the story about the diamonds just drifted away."

"Are you talking about Area 51?" Knight had definitely heard of that one.

"Area 51, Groom Lake, heck there must be two dozen installations out there going by all kinds of names. And it seems no end of UFO nut cases that are trying to get a firsthand look. There isn't a good fence around most of the area and the borders aren't clearly marked. I think half the time the security guards out there are deliberately trying to lure people in just so they have something to do by arresting them. Anyway, the guards catch them, detain them until I can go out, and pick them up. These numskulls get charged with trespassing and I hold them overnight or however long it takes to scare the hell out of them. The whole thing is a major pain in my butt!" The Sheriff took another drink. "Over the last week the camo dudes have called me twice to come and get trespassers. The government has really stepped up security for some reason."

"Camo dudes?" asked Knight.

"That's what they call the sites' surface patrols," answered the Sheriff, miffed at the interruption. "And, having all those investigators tramping around out there on Flynn's property has made them doubly nervous. The last thing I need right now is to have news of your discovery to get out. Hell's bells, I'd have a stampede of treasure hunters out there that wouldn't quit. Why just this morning I got a report from the Army that some assistant professor of seismology or something had gone missing out there last night."

"Well I'm not going to tell anyone. I don't want any distractions until we get Isis Flynn back alive," Knight agreed.

"I know you are supposed to be this hot shot security expert and you certainly are well-connected, but I don't appreciate your mucking around my crime scene," lectured the Sheriff.

"Trust me. I didn't mess up anything. In fact, I don't think it could be messed up anymore than it already was," answered Knight sarcastically. "Now do you want those photos I took or not?"

"Of course I want them! Have one of my sergeants download them into the computer on your way out," he ordered. Then he added, "It would appear to me that if you care as much as you claim to about Mrs. Flynn that you'd want all the help you could get."

"Well I do," replied Knight sincerely. "I'm sorry we got off on the wrong foot. I will let you know if I find out anything on my end."

The Sheriff drained the last from his coffee mug and placed the brown bottle back into the desk drawer without comment.

Knight got up and started toward the door.

"Where do you think you're going?" ordered the Sheriff.

Knight paused and turned around with a curious look.

"You're not leaving here without your desert pickings." With that, the Sheriff gathered up the remnants of Buck Anders leg in the garbage bag and tossed it to Knight. "See that Buck gets his leg back."

"How am I supposed to do that?" asked Knight impatiently. "I don't know where he is buried."

The Sheriff laughed, "He ain't dead…he's just in a private sanitarium for the insane."

Susan had called her office in New York and had them run a complete financial check on Jack Flynn. After all, he definitely was a suspect. People had been known to put together all sorts of nefarious schemes to defraud her company, and most of them were for a lot less than twenty million dollars.

She had taken a taxi to the LSI office in the bank building on Fourth Street and picked up the fax pages with the information. She had to explain to the junior investigator on the other end why to use fax instead of email. It never ceased to amaze her about how the younger workers appeared to be totally oblivious to the fact that the emails could be read by anyone with cleverness and a computer.

The fax was revealing. The Colossus was not in the best of shape financially. Construction delays had run into tens of millions of dollars and the analysts on Wall Street were nervous. All it would take is for some junior analyst to put a *Do Not Recommend* on the Colossus's stock, which would create a stampede to sell, and Flynn's whole empire could collapse. He had steadily been selling off chunks of stock and now had only a small stake, although he remained the largest single shareholder. He had evidently made a fortune from the stock sales but her people had been unable to run it down. Her investigator's intuition told her he had probably squirreled it away offshore. Still, even as thin as he was, Susan could not see how twenty million dollars would do anything, one way or the other, to really affect the situation. If he paid the ransom, LSI would pay him and so he did not gain anything. The only way he could gain was if the payoff somehow made it back into his pocket.

Twenty million dollars was a lot of money, but given Flynn's profile and reputation it did not appear that he would take such an enormous risk for such a modest reward. In addition, she had felt something in Flynn's office. Either he really did care about getting his wife back or he was an Oscar candidate actor. No, her instincts told her Flynn was not her man.

———·———

Knight could not sleep. He did not know why. Maybe it was just a reaction to the accumulation of the events over the last few weeks. It seemed that he had just gone from one major calamity to the next. Maybe his body was rebelling against constantly being on guard. But, if there was one thing that could be said for Vegas, it was the ideal town for insomniacs. After all, as the publicity said, it never slept. You could have either a prime rib dinner or breakfast at five o'clock in the morning.

Knight gave in to his frustrations and after looking at the luminous hands on his Rolex, decided. "What the heck," he said, as he threw back the black satin bed sheets and started putting his clothes on. He would go gambling until he felt sleepy.

Casino gambling in Vegas is a very simple proposition. In the card games of twenty-one and baccarat, you place a bet, some cards are dealt and your money is taken. In roulette, you place a bet, a ball spins in a slotted wheel and your money is taken. In slots and video poker you put your money into a machine, press a button, some images flash and your money is taken.

By far the majority of people who come to Vegas play the slots or video poker. It is not intimidating to interact with a machine. There is no one to sneer at you when you do not win, or chide you when you make a boneheaded play. It is gambling anonymously, just you and the machine. It is easy to figure out how to play. There are no real tricks, only perceived ones. If you win, the machine is hot, if you lose the machine is cold.

Human beings have always had the capacity to assign human characteristics to inanimate objects. Nowhere is this phenomenon more evident than in the casino slot area. Players talk, plead and even beg the machines they are playing. They try to read the mind of the machine. Some players are thoroughly convinced that they can connect on a metaphysical level with the flashing box in front of them. They claim they can actually feel the machine.

Of all the games in the casino, the craps tables are the big leagues. This is where the show-offs, the extroverts, play. Gambling at craps is not anonymous; everyone at the table can see how you are doing. It is show-off city. It is where the new groom goes to excite his new bride with his knowledge of worldly things. It is where the frat boy goes to impress his buddies. It is where the big loser goes to get even. Very few players really know all the nuances of the game. Most get by making only rudimentary bets. A knowledgeable player on a hot streak can win big. A novice with the same hot streak will have only token winnings.

Craps is played by rolling two red dice on a large, green, felt covered table. The basic rules are simple. The thrower or the "shooter" of the dice wins if on his first try he throws a Seven or an Eleven, referred to as a "natural" or a "pass". He loses if he throws a Two, Three or Twelve, referred to as "craps" or "don't pass". However, he may continue to throw, if on his first throw he rolls a Four, Five, Six, Eight, Nine or Ten. That number then becomes his "point". He continues to throw the dice until, either he duplicates his point, wins, and "passes", or he throws a seven, loses, or "Seven's Out".

Even within these simple rules, there is an infinite variety of "proposition bets" that can be made. A proposition bet is a bet that is made on exactly what the dice will do every time they are thrown. You have to be very knowledgeable or very foolhardy to make proposition bets.

Nevertheless, in the end it is like all the other games. You place a bet, dice are thrown and your money is taken. A gambling sage long ago commented that the best thing in life was playing craps and winning and that the second-best thing was playing craps and losing. Following this advice he undoubtedly died broke, but happy.

Oh, occasionally some lucky patron does win. They have to, to give the others who are not so lucky, hope. Hope that they are going to be the next to defy the odds.

In Vegas, hope is a commodity. It is the foundation that everything is built on; it is why the city exists.

The casino was not as busy as usual, the late show crowd was still in the showrooms and the tables were occupied by a few hard cases. They would probably be there for hours. They were one of two types, the better gambler who could play for hours without getting hit too bad, or the compulsives who would play as long as they could beg, borrow, or steal another bet.

The first crap table to the left of the casino was a high-stakes table with a minimum bet of fifty dollars. As usual, there were only a few players. The real action was at the next five tables where the bets were the more attractive five, ten, and twenty-dollar minimum. Those tables were crowded and there was no rail space.

Knight could have played in the private casino on the thirtieth floor. However, he was just killing time until he felt sleepy and the crowd in the main casino was perfect for the type of play he needed. Somehow, when you are surrounded by a crowd your own concerns seem a lot less important. He moved to the rail of the fifty-dollar table.

The stickman, the dealers, and the boxman looked up quizzically at the tall, dark-haired man who had the audacity to try his luck in their high-stakes game. The other players continued to stare at their own bets and riffle through their stacks of chips, seemingly completely oblivious to the stranger's intrusion into their game.

Knight loved craps, but hated the other casino games. Occasionally he would try the roulette wheel.

However, it was craps that kept his attention. Everything went at the craps table. Safe bets, stupid bets, bets that even longtime players did not completely understand. Every roll was a new challenge. You could be as bold or as timid as you liked. If you hit a winning streak and bet correctly, you could walk away with a bundle. If you bet the same winning streak incorrectly, you would be lucky to be able to afford a bottle of a recent vintage wine in one of the Colossus's obscenely overpriced restaurants.

Knight moved to the end of the table, looked at the boxman and asked, "Change one hundred thousand?"

The dealer on his end of the table, the one with Elvis sideburns, looked up and seemed surprised when no money was placed on the table. He turned toward the boxman quizzically. The boxman looked up and instantly recognized the tall, impeccably tanned new player. He moved the back of his hand nonchalantly across the stack of the table chips toward Knight without saying a word. He then took a note pad from his coat pocket scribbled on it and then held it up over his head. The well dressed, but portly floorman moved from his position behind the walnut lectern and added his initials to the note. The boxman then passed the note to the dealer who handed it to Knight. Knight signed the marker and handed it back to the dealer. The dealer carefully counted out ten stacks of chips and then paused to confirm that the order from the boxman was correct. When the boxman nodded, the dealer turned and pushed the chips in front of Knight.

Knight picked up nine of the stacks and placed them in the groove in the rail in front of him. He then placed the remaining chips between the white lines on the green felt table marked *Pass Line.* He looked at the dealer and asked, "Ten thousand pass line?" He needed permission to exceed the three thousand maximum bet limit confirmed by the brass plaque mounted on the inside of the table.

The dealer looked again at the boxman for authorization and this time the boxman said confidently with a smirk, "You have a bet, Mr. Knight."

Knight smiled back as an acknowledgment that the game was on.

"New shooter coming out, place your bets," called the stickman as he maneuvered the pile of five red dice with his bent wooden stick in front of Knight.

Knight looked at the deadly red cubes and waved his hand over them saying, "Pass".

The stickman, with a slightly annoyed expression moved the dice to the short, balding man to Knight's left. The man selected two dice from the pile and then carefully stacked them so that a four and three were visible on each end. Then, careful so as not to disturb the precise arrangement, he lifted the dice into the air and arched them toward the far end of the table. The dice rebounded softly from the rubber cushion and the stickman called out, "Eight…easy eight …the point is eight."

Suddenly the table came to life as bets were placed almost furiously. Place and buy bets were shouted and stacks of chips transferred almost magically from the grooves in the burnished walnut rail to the white outlined squares on the green felt table.

Knight moved two matching stacks of chips behind the white pass line and behind the stack already on the table, thereby taking the maximum allowable odds behind the ten thousand-dollar pass line bet. The dealer looked up at Knight who quipped, "What's a horse without a jockey."

The dealer smiled while the stickman gathered the dice expertly with his bent stick and placed them again in front of the short balding shooter.

Again, the shooter carefully arranged dice and then expertly tossed them toward the end of the table.

"Six," cried the stickman. "Came easy…no field."

The table again came to life as losing bets were taken and the winning payoffs made. With the throw of the dice, Knight's instinctive ability to spot the unusual had automatically kicked into gear. A tall man in a faded green golf shirt who was standing to the left of the shooter had made a movement with his hand while the dice were in the air. He had unobtrusively picked a hundred-dollar chip from the shooter's stack in the groove on the top of the rail.

In Vegas, this type of cheat was known as a *rail robber*. A quick glance from Knight confirmed that none of the workers at the table had caught the move. The boxman or the dealers should have been looking for it; after all, their jobs were to watch the players while the stickman watched the dice. However, the robber was a real pro and had timed the move perfectly. He would not steal much, maybe five hundred over an hour's play. He would then move to another casino. With any luck, he could make five or six thousand over the weekend.

"Change one thousand," ordered Knight as he flipped a chip toward the dealer.

"Changing one thousand," said the dealer as he counted out nine one hundred dollar chips and four twenty fives and slid them across the table.

Knight carefully arranged a stack of three chips. He put two one hundred dollar chips on the top and bottom of a twenty-five dollar chip, letting the small denomination chip extend slightly. He called this arrangement a *short stack.* When he was setting up the Colossus's security, he had developed this method to alert a game's personnel to a cheat's action with out tipping off the other players. He placed the *short stack* in the field area, but instead of placing it in the relative spot that he occupied at the rail, he put it directly across from the cheat's position.

The sideburned dealer stared at the *short stack* for a second before he realized what Knight had done. Then, without looking at Knight he called out, "How about Field bets gentlemen?" The stickman turned instantly at the coded question signaling that a cheat was in the game, and looked at Knight's bet. Then without lifting his eyes to the players he rested the bent stick on the table casually, but pointing directly at the cheat.

The boxman, also clued in by the coded question, glanced at the bet. Then he lowered his eyes. He knew that he had messed up and should have caught what Knight had seen. Without looking, he knew that the pit boss behind him had also heard the signal and was already dialing the phone to security.

Knight saw everyone was on their toes; the eye in the sky, the vast network of television cameras and recorders covering every square inch of the public area the casino had been tipped to focus in on the cheat. Knight knew that the rail robber's every move was now being reviewed and recorded for evidence. He looked at the sweep hand on his Rolex. If he had trained the staff correctly, it should be no more than twenty seconds before the cheat would be confronted by security and asked to leave. It would be done quickly and quietly.

The second hand had only reached fifteen seconds when the cheat was tapped on the shoulder by a burly but well-dressed man with a visible earpiece attached to a coil of wire extending under his sport coat's collar. The new arrival whispered in the cheat's ear. The cheat then quickly picked up his stack of chips turned and gave up his place at the rail.

The cheat would be interviewed, added to the book of known cheats effectively barring him from ever playing at any Vegas casino, and then escorted out the side door of the casino The security guard had done his job well. No one in the casino had noticed and even the flow of the crap game had proceeded uninterrupted. The pit boss casually approached the player whose chips had been stolen, whispered in his ear what had happened and then told him how the house would make restitution. Flynn's casinos did not use the exaggerated force popularized in the movies. It was much smarter to simply remove the cheat without upsetting the other players.

"Twelve! Craps!" called the stickman as the shooter's dice stopped tumbling. "Pay the field."

Knight smiled, his *short stack* had won! Not only had he won, but also the number twelve covered in the field box paid triple the bet.

The boxman smirked, shrugged his shoulders, and rolled his eyes with a "lucky bastard" look.

Knight never ceased to be amazed at how people attempted to cheat the casino. Every move could be seen by the eye in the sky and every player with more than room temperature IQ knew it. Still it went on, the cheats never seemed to learn. The casinos themselves were incredibly paranoid about cheating. They poured hundreds of millions of dollars into their security systems and yet every year they only caught about five hundred cheats and nearly half of those were employees.

The idiot he had just caught had practiced for months perfecting his technique. Once he was nailed he and everything about him would be loaded into the database linking all the casinos, as a known cheat. If he dared to show up again he would be spotted immediately and if caught a second time, would be prosecuted. If the poor dumb schmuck had bothered to figure out how much he really made with his scheme, he probably would have made more by flipping hamburgers. Whether it was the thrill of the action or just plain stupidity, there seemed to be an inexhaustible supply of cheats.

In a way, Knight was thankful that these dolts never learned. After all, finding ways to thwart their ingenious plans was one of the things that kept him in business.

"Seven!" called the stickman. "Line away. "

The wanna be Elvis took Knight's chips and the boxman looked at him with an expression that implied he had gotten what he deserved. The loss was more than twenty nine thousand over what he had won on the previous throw!

The losing, short, balding shooter silently counted his remaining chips in the groove in the rail and with no emotion moved another stack of chips to the pass line.

"Place your bets. New shooter coming out," called the stickman.

"Fifty thousand pass?" asked Knight, looking for authorization to exceed the maximum bet.

The boxman smirked again and said, "It's your funeral."

"Fifty thousand don't pass!" said a new voice. The entire table turned simultaneously and looked up at the new player.

"Am I down?" demanded the drop dead gorgeous blonde in the long sleeved midnight blue dress with the plunging neckline. The boxman nodded yes and gestured to the skinny dealer to exchange the wad of bills that the blonde had tossed in front of her. The skinny dealer carefully examined the bills, snapped each one for effect and then placed them in five neat lines of ten so that the eye in the sky could get a good look. He then gathered them up and laid them next to the boxman who quickly recounted them. Then using the clear plastic paddle, he pushed them into the slot of the *drop* in the top of the table.

"Changing fifty thousand," said the skinny dealer as he pushed five neat stacks of chips to the new player. "Good luck" he said with a lecherous grin.

Without counting the chips, the blonde bent over the rail and moved them to the small white outlined box on the felt marked *Don't Pass Bar.*

Knight starred at the new player as she bent over. The dress did nothing to disguise her perfectly formed breasts or hide the gold and diamond pendant that swung between them. Knight grinned; he had seen them both before. He was still grinning when the stickman interrupted with, "No more bets!"

The stickman pushed the little pile of five dice to the blonde. She selected two, without bothering to arrange them, shook them in her hand, and tossed them expertly to the far end of the table. Everyone struggled to see what the bright red cubes said.

"Three! Craps!" called the stickman. "Line away. Pay the Don't!"

Knight did not look down as his losing bet disappeared into the pile of chips collected from the pass line. He was still staring at the newcomer.

She smiled back at him with a smug expression as the skinny dealer paid her off. Then without placing a new bet she tossed four, one thousand dollar, chips to the table workers. She did not count her winnings but instead dumped them into a small beaded purse, turned and left the table.

"Take care of this," said Knight as he emptied his rail and pushed his remaining pile of chips toward the dealer. He then, as if not to be outdone by the blonde, tossed four one thousand-dollar chips to the crew.

Knight was already in pursuit of the blonde by the time the stickman called out, "Place your bets. New shooter coming out!"

———·———

Susan did not know what she had expected to happen. She had just been passing through the casino after dinner in the smallest of the resort's ten restaurants. The urban legend about Vegas hotels was that all the food in the restaurants came out of the same kitchen. Her dinner had tasted like the rumor was true. She had made a note to use her unlimited access to the hotel to find out the truth.

It was pure chance that she had seen the tall, perfectly tanned man standing at the craps table. It could not be, but it was. She found herself drawn as if by a magnet to the table. She was only vaguely aware that she had laid the money on the table and had thrown the dice. She had only wanted to wipe the silly grin off Mr. Thomas Knight's face.

———·———

CHAPTER 5

Susan headed for the cashier's cage at the rear of the casino. She was halfway there when the crowd in the main showroom suddenly exited. Immediately the casino floor was awash with a sea of people. The after show crowd at the Colossus was always the same. They were wired up from Honey and Her Bears and they all needed to take a whiz. Susan found herself with the crowd, on the way to the restrooms, in front of her and Thomas Knight behind her. She sure did not want to see him again tonight! With no escape, she looked for a refuge. A few of the crowd, those with the strongest bladders, were making for the main lounge to quench their thirst. She quickened her pace and with a little luck, she could beat them there. She really was not in the mood for lounging. But, what the heck, a nightcap might help calm her down after her encounter with that damnable Thomas Knight.

She selected a small table inside the entrance to the left. The darkened interior of the lounge provided her with a temporary hiding place. It was obvious that the lounge act was preparing to start the show. The front tables were already occupied by the die-hard fans of the band. They had probably been there for over an hour staking their claim to the prime seats.

"Welcome to the Colossus may I help you?" asked the shapely brunette waitress with gold hot pants and a push-up bra desperately trying to contain her surgically enhanced breasts. The bra would be killing her by the end of her shift.

Susan had not thought about what she wanted and more by reflex than by careful consideration she pointed to the plastic holder on the table advertising the drink of the day. "I'll have one of those. Thank you," she said distractedly.

"One Piute Bill coming out," said the waitress as she slid a bar napkin onto the top of the table.

Thomas Knight looked around the casino anxiously trying to locate the elusive blonde that had topped him at the craps table. He finally caught a glimpse of her blonde hair but she was nearly halfway across the casino floor. He was nearly running trying to catch up with her.

Without warning, the exiting crowd from the show room seemed to engulf her. He lost her in the crowd. Given the amount she had won at the craps table it made sense that she would head for the cashier's cage. He picked his way through the crowd to the cage. She had only been a little ways ahead of him and would not have had time to exchange her chips by the time he got there. But, she was nowhere around. He pulled himself up to his full six-foot three and again searched the crowd, finding nothing!

Why was she there in Las Vegas? When he had called her office from Palm Springs, they had said she was headed back to New York. He definitely had not expected to see her again, and yet here she was somewhere in the gigantic Colossus's casino. But where?

Then he saw it! It was the entrance to the lounge. She must have gone in there!

It took a few seconds for Knight's eyes to adjust to the darkened interior of the lounge. It was already half full and the roadie for the featured band, Captain Jack and the Shark Attack, was making the final adjustments to the instruments and microphones on the stage.

Knight worked his way along the right side of lounge searching the crowd for his elusive quarry. He was nearly to the stage when he heard a voice from behind him.

"Thomas Knight!"

He turned around quickly to find the source of the statement.

"Hey, Thomas, whassup?" asked the band's roadie, his hands full of water bottles and his shoulders draped with fresh white towels.

"Hey," answered Knight, disappointed that it was not Susan. He continued to probe the darkness as he asked distractedly, "Is the band ready to start?"

"Just as soon as I get this stuff on the stage. The guys will be surprised to see you. How come you're in Vegas?" asked the roadie as he shifted his hands to get a better grip on the awkward water bottles.

"I'll tell you later," said Knight impatient to continue his search. "Tell the band I'll catch them before I leave town."

"You're not going to stay for the show?"

"Not tonight. I'm tied up, but I'll see you later," answered Knight as he turned back toward the entrance. "Tell the group to have a good set." He was nearly out of the lounge when he saw her. She was sitting alone at the small table to the left of the entrance. A waitress had blocked her from his view when he had walked into the lounge. She was counting the chips from her beaded purse.

"You're one lucky dame," he announced.

The statement froze Susan in mid-count. She felt as if she had been drenched with ice water. She looked up and her heart started racing. Her head had told her she was trying to escape him, but her heart was hoping he would find her. "Luckier than you," she taunted, her blue eyes flashing.

"Are you going to invite me to sit down?" asked Knight.

Susan did not answer. She simply gestured to the open chair by the door.

Knight ignored her command and instead took the seat facing the entrance. He had developed the silly superstition in junior high school. That was when he had first read about Wild Bill Hickok. The West's most famous gun fighter had been shot in the back the first time he had chosen to sit with his back to the door. It was now a deeply ingrained habit.

Knight tried to break the ice. "How's the arm?" he asked after seeing the slight outline of the bandage under the sleeve of the clinging blue dress. She had been wounded in the Palm Springs escapade and the last time he had seen her was when she was being loaded into an ambulance.

Susan instinctively reached up and touched the wound. "It's fine," she said matter-of-factly. As if you really care, she thought.

"I tried to call you from the hospital in Palm Springs," said Knight, hoping it would be possible to melt her icy reception.

"Well if you were at the hospital, why didn't you just come up instead of calling?"

"No. I tried to call you from *my* hospital," corrected Knight seeing she was confused.

"What do you mean *your* hospital?"

"I was in the Kennedy Hospital in Indio and they took you to the Eisenhower Memorial Hospital in Rancho Mirage," Knight explained.

"You were in the hospital?" Susan asked still confused. "What for?"

"I had a concussion," answered Knight.

"From what?"

"I really don't know. But after they took you away, they told me I was hit on the head," Knight paused and then lowered his voice to almost a whisper, "by my own gun."

Susan had leaned nearer to hear Knight's excuse. She leaned back and crossed her arms in defiance. "That is the dumbest…and I mean *the* dumbest… excuse I ever heard."

"Well that's what happened," said Knight defensively.

The two of them had been together at the Golden Oasis resort in Palm Springs when everything had gone to hell. In the chaos, Susan had managed to shoot herself in her arm with her own .380 Colt Mustang while trying to avenge her father's murder.

Knight had been hit in the head by his own Glock 18 handgun when the explosion at the Oasis had thrown it into the air.

Then the two of them had been taken to separate hospitals. The mix-up prevented each of them from being aware of the other's plight. When they did not hear from each other they had each assumed that the other was not interested. They had been thrown together into a life-threatening situation. For some reason they had connected. Whether it was because they had to combine their resources to survive or because of a genuine affection, neither had been able to sort it out before they were violently separated. They both had left Palm Springs with the issue unresolved.

"I need a drink," said Knight as he swiveled around and put his finger in the air to signal the waitress.

The waitress arrived with a tall drink on a tray that was emitting a fog that was flowing down the sides of the gold glass. She placed it on the napkin in front of Susan.

"What kind of a concoction is that?" asked Knight.

"It's a..." Susan picked up the plastic holder. "It's a Piute Bill," she said definitively. "You get to keep the commemorative glass." She handed the holder to Knight so he could see for himself.

"May I help you?" interrupted the waitress.

"Yes, bring me a Canadian Club and bottled water, no ice," ordered Knight instinctively. He was reading the story of Piute Bill. The waitress left and Knight chuckled.

"What's so funny?" asked Susan, still refusing to thaw.

"I heard about this guy this morning! It says here that he was a renegade Indian who was a crack shot. According to this, he killed and scalped a barber just because he gave him a bad hair cut."

Susan took a sip of the foggy concoction. "Well this drink is potent enough to give anyone a bad hair day!" she exclaimed.

"I have it on good authority that Piute Bill was really a lousy shot and only beat up the barber," said Knight hoping to impress her.

"I don't think a lounge drink advertisement was meant to be historically accurate."

"I know that!" said Knight obviously annoyed at her admonishment. "I just thought you might want to know the truth."

"*That* would be nice!" said Susan sarcastically, implying she had not bought any of Knight's story.

The waitress showed up just in time with Knight's drink.

He looked at Susan. "Do you want another Piute Bill?" he asked seeing she had nearly polished off her first one.

"I think one was enough," she answered.

"Well it doesn't seem right to leave without a least a pair of commemorative glasses," he challenged. "Bring us both another one," he ordered without asking her approval.

The Piute Bill was having the desired effect and Susan was starting to thaw. "Were you really hit in your head with your gun?"

"Did you really shoot yourself?" he countered.

They both laughed simultaneously at the ridiculous images that both propositions projected.

"To Piute Bill!" Knight toasted as the waitress delivered the next round.

Susan giggled, "Piute Bill." She looked into Knight eyes. He really was handsome, she thought. He looked like a man should. There was nothing wimpy about Thomas Knight.

He looked into her now soft blue eyes; the drinks had taken the flashing away. "I really did try to call you," he said.

"I waited. I thought maybe you were having second thoughts."

He reached across the small table and carefully fingered the pendant hanging between her ample breasts. "Your father's?" he asked tenderly.

She looked down and nodded without answering.

When he released the pendant the back of his hand brushed against her cleavage.

She felt as if an electric shock had been sent through her body! She was trembling when he reached down and gently squeezed her hand. She looked up into his eyes and prepared for him to lean across and kiss her.

"Is that *the* Thomas Knight?" asked a strange voice.

Knight and Susan both turned and looked up at the interloper.

There were four of them, dressed in matching black suits, white shirts and thin neon blue ties. They were all wearing funky wire rimmed dark glasses.

The tallest one pulled down his glasses with his hand and peered over the top. "Yep…it's Thomas Knight," he confirmed.

The next one mimicked the tall one precisely and said as he pulled down his glasses. “It’s Thomas Knight and a perfect ten.”

The third one took his turn. “It’s Thomas Knight all right, but she is an eleven at least.”

“Thomas Knight and a twelve,” said the fourth.

“Twelve definitely!” the other three chimed in.

“Hello boys,” said Knight. Then turning, “Susan Strong, I’d like you to meet Captain Jack and the Shark Attack’s horn section.”

Susan nodded politely; their timing could not have been worse.

“Our roadie said you were here but we told him it had to be your twin, because we were sure you’d be dead by now,” said the tall one. He then gave Susan a lecherous grin. “And I suppose you’re transporting this innocent young thing across state lines for immoral purposes?”

Knight blushed involuntarily. “She is a business associate,” he protested.

The four musicians pushed their glasses back up in unison, shook their heads in disbelief, turned, and walked toward the stage.

Knight apologized, “Sorry about that.”

“Are all your friends that funky?” asked Susan.

“What can I say…I live in L.A.,” responded Knight, noticing that Susan’s hand was no longer on the table.

“I’ve got to get up early in the morning and I think Piute Bill has done me in,” protested Susan.

“Are you going to be in town for a while?” Knight asked hopefully.

“Just business,” answered Susan and then with a

smirk, added. "I would tell you all about it, but then of course I would have to kill you."

"I want to see you again," pleaded Knight. "How about tomorrow at…?" He did not have a chance to finish the question.

"I was hoping I would see you again!" said a sultry voice from behind him.

Knight turned around and was surprised to see a fully stacked, honey-haired blonde looking straight at him. There was something vaguely familiar about her.

Without warning, she slapped Knight sharply across his right cheek. "That's for that crap you pulled on the highway!"

She was the blonde on the motorcycle! The vivid image of her and the CHP by the side of the road came rushing back. Knight instinctively raised his hand to massage the red handprint that was slowly appearing on his cheek. He started to blush again. He felt his whole face was turning red. Putting up his best front, he looked back at Susan. She was staring at him with her mouth half open in surprise. The flashing had returned to her eyes.

"I'm…I'm sorry about that," he stammered as he turned back to his assailant.

The honey-haired blonde looked at him coldly and said, "I'll expect you to make it up to me." Then she turned and walked away. Knight could not help noticing how she filled out her gold, skin-tight leotard.

Susan saw the once over Knight gave the departing figure and said in a tone dripping with sarcasm, "She is definitely over developed."

Knight blushed again. "I can explain," he protested.

Susan did not reply but stood up and reached into her beaded purse. Without looking, she grabbed a thousand dollar chip and tossed it on the table. The chip was still spinning by the time she was in the casino. She would not let Thomas Knight see the moisture in her eyes.

———·———

"L-a-d-i-e-s and gentlemen, put your hands together for those rock innovators, those soul generators, Captain Jack and the Shark Attack!" boomed the lounge's quarter million dollar, Dolby sound system. The wildly enthusiastic applause was quickly drowned out by the bass player with the vandyke beard and the beret setting the beat. The lead singer leaped onto the stage, ripped the microphone from the stand and lamented in a soulful voice, *"I played the game of love too smart. I took my chance...but didn't gamble with my heart!"*

Was there a message in the song's lyrics? Knight wondered, as he got up from the table. Ignoring Susan's chip he took a fifty-dollar bill from his money clip and laid it on the table. He was emotionally exhausted and needed sleep now! The audience was going wild as he left the lounge.

The band was showing them no mercy, playing from their souls. There was no doubt about it; Captain Jack and the Shark Attack were at the top of their game.

The waitress put the empty glasses on her tray with the fifty. She looked at the thousand-dollar chip, smiled, kissed it, and put in the cleavage between her breasts. Only in Las Vegas could serving a couple of rounds of drinks with sore boobs be worth a thousand dollars!

———·———

It was after midnight when Bulldog Basham rang the doorbell to the suite. He tapped his foot impatiently on the garish custom carpet as he waited for the door to open. When the door finally opened, he burst through it, almost knocking the beautiful woman in the brunette wig and leather bustier off her six- inch heels.

———·———

The phone call from Knight's secretary, Monica, was unexpected. A sleepy glance at the Rolex showed that it had been only twelve hours since he had downloaded the photos taken at the kidnap site.

"Well boss…I found what made your mysterious marks in the desert."

"Please don't tell me it was aliens," pleaded Knight only half facetiously.

"What…What on earth are you talking about?" Monica was obviously confused.

"Never mind! So, what's the scoop?"

"Are you sure you want me to tell you?" asked Monica, milking the moment for all it was worth.

"Yes dammit," snapped Knight. He was in a foul mood after the scene in the lounge. He had just managed to fall asleep and the last thing he needed right now was to play twenty questions.

"Snowshoes!"

"What?"

"Snowshoes! That's what made your tracks."

"You mean like Eskimo's snowshoes?" asked Knight incredulously.

"The very same. Well not the *very* same...but snowshoes."

"We're talking about the things the Eskimos use to walk on loose snow? The things that look like tennis racquets...right?" pleaded Knight.

"Well...they are modern snowshoes. They don't look like tennis rackets anymore. But more like...well...kinda like swim fins!" answered Monica, obviously pleased to have found a comparison. "They're made of plastic now."

Knight was still not sure what Monica was trying to tell him. Moreover, right now he was not going to pursue it further. "Email me some pictures. You do have pictures?"

"Straight out of a catalog...pictures and specifications. Your tracks were made by the Overland Model twenty-one," proclaimed Monica obviously thrilled at the results *Ralph* her computer had been able to find.

Knight decided to wait for the photos before trying to sort it all out. The morning would be soon enough. "You did a good job babe," said Knight wearily. "But I need you to check on something else when you get a chance."

Monica knew that that meant right away. Knight had very little distinction between; rush, ASAP, and when you get a chance. To him they all meant yesterday. "What is it?"

Knight sounded like he was already drifting off to sleep. "I need you to find out about diamonds in Las Vegas."

Now it was Monica's turn to be confused, "You mean diamonds…like the rich old farts give to their mistresses when they sneak out of town to Vegas?"

"No! Not those diamonds…real diamonds. You know…like…right out of the ground."

"You mean *uncut* diamonds?"

"Yeah!" said Knight impatiently. He would have come up with that word also if he were not so damned tired.

"What exactly do you want to know?"

"I need to know if anyone around here has ever found diamonds and if they did…where…and how many. You know that kind of thing." Knight longed for his bed.

"Does this have anything to do with the kidnapping?" asked Monica, her unquenchable curiosity getting the better of her.

Monica was a source of boundless energy and when she had the bit in her teeth, time meant little to her. She would talk for hours but Knight was finished. "I don't think so. I'm just curious about a guy that cut off his leg with his pocket knife."

"What . . .?"

Knight ignored the question and firmly ended the conversation, "Good night. Call me in the morning."

———.———

Isis Flynn whimpered pathetically as the tranquilizer again started to wear off. Her throat was on fire and she could not force it to make any kind of intelligible words.

The near total darkness was making her seasick as her brain attempted to establish equilibrium against a visual image.

She struggled weakly as suddenly a massive claw cradled her head and bent it forward. Then a wonderful cool liquid was poured across her chapped lips and down her inflamed throat. She coughed as the water attempted to go down the wrong way. She drank and drank, gulping as much as she could of the life restoring fluid. Finally, when she could drink no more, she turned on to her side and vomited the excess. Her head was spinning from the effects of the drug. She was only vaguely aware of her blouse being ripped open. Massive coarse lips started rudely suckling and biting her breasts.

Then as before, a menacing hiss and the smell of rotten eggs filled her nostrils. The slobbering lips left her body and the now familiar prick in the cradle of her arm again sent her into the world of psychedelic dreams. As she drifted off, she barely heard the screeching sound of the electric meat saw as it tore through the human bone.

———.———

Bulldog Basham was definitely not living up to his name. He was naked except for a black latex thong. He had a bright orange rubber gag ball in his mouth attached to a leather harness that went around the top of his head. His hands were handcuffed and he had been hoisted up, using a block and tackle, to where he was standing on his tiptoes.

The brunette in the black leather bustier was filling an eyedropper full of honey from a jar. Using a candle, she heated the honey in the dropper until it was bubbling. She then held the eyedropper up to the shackled victim so that he could get a good look at her work. Very carefully, she squeezed the bulb on the eyedropper and a drop of the burning liquid landed on Bulldog's right nipple.

He thrashed about as the pain hit his brain. After letting him suffer for a few seconds, the brunette reached into a nearby ice bucket and extracted a cube of ice. She sucked on it momentarily before moving to the pinkish red burn. With her cold tongue, she licked the honey from the nipple.

Bulldog Basham was having the time of his life! He loved every minute of the painful humiliation. If the gag had been removed, he could have been heard calling for more.

The session lasted for hours and the brunette was an absolute master of extending the delicious agony.

Bulldog had become so addicted to this sensual torture that he would have physical withdrawal systems when his mistress refused to accommodate him.

No one knows how they will react under torture. Some people can be tortured to death without revealing secrets. Bulldog might have been one of those. However, this kind of torture was different and he would spill his guts about anything for some more of this cruel punishment.

The brunette unbuckled the rubber gag from her victim. Then she asked, "What does the FBI think about the kidnapping?"

"I told you. I'm not supposed to talk about it and Flynn will have my balls if he found out what I already told you."

"Slave, in case you haven't noticed I already have your balls," she said as she reached down and gave them a hard squeeze.

"Ow!" he cried as the painful pressure made him feel as if he would vomit. "You promised me you would keep it secret!" he protested, realizing for the first time that she really was in charge and that the slave master charade had stopped being a game.

"Tell me slave!" she ordered as she squeezed again.

He struggled fruitlessly, gasping for air and trying to talk through the wave of pain, "I don't know…there is a briefing tomorrow…I'll find out then."

"You will tell me if they have any suspects…right?" threatened the inquisitor as she released him, took up the eyedropper and again dropped scalding honey onto his left nipple.

He moaned, "They claim they're looking at everyone. Then he pleaded, "Oh…please do the other one again."

———·———

CHAPTER 6

Knight would have sworn he had not gotten a wink of sleep and yet he was startled when Steve had thrown back the blinds and shaken him awake. He was grateful for consciousness after enduring a night of terrible nightmares. Susan Strong, the alien in snowshoes, and the honey-haired blonde on the motorcycle, were all having their way with him. Contrary to what he might have thought, it had been highly uncomfortable. The alien especially, had seemed to be insatiable. Once awake, Knight was famished and Steve had to make two trips to the suite's kitchen before the chef began to gain ground on his appetite.

———·———

The early morning call for Senator Devlin from the White House was completely unexpected. The youthful aide that answered the phone stammered, "Yes…Yes. I understand. I will get the Senator immediately."

The aide put the call on hold and quickly moved across the high roller's suite to the bathroom. A quiet knock on the door provoked an impatient response.

"What do you want?"

"Sir…the President is on line one and wants to speak to you immediately. The secretary said it was important."

"Thanks. I've got it," came the answer from behind the closed door. The Senator reached over to the telephone on the marble wall, and as he punched the lit button for line one he muttered, "I can't even take a crap in peace anymore."

The pleasant but no-nonsense voice on the phone inquired, "Senator Devlin?"

"Yes!"

"Please hold for the President of the United States," replied the official voice followed by a brief silence.

"Hi Joe," greeted the familiar and distinctive voice with the Southern drawl.

"Mr. President."

"I need you to take a meeting with General Guts Grant this afternoon at the NTS north of Las Vegas. He says it might take a couple of hours."

"What's up Mr. President?" inquired the Senator with thinly disguised annoyance in his voice.

"Guts will fill you in," the President answered in a tone that left no doubt his request was definitely to be considered an order. "The boys over at FBI have been keeping me up to speed on the situation with your daughter, but this meeting can't wait. Do you need any more resources?"

"No. Thanks. There is a literal army out here already and they're tripping all over themselves."

"My people tell me Thomas Knight is helping out."

"Yes," answered the Senator surprised that the President knew that Knight was involved. "He arrived here yesterday and we're waiting to see if he comes up with something."

"Well he's a good man to have around in a crisis. You know...now that I think about it some more, I think we need to bring him into the loop on this new situation. I'll call Guts and tell him that's what I want. Take him with you to the meeting."

"Yes, Mr. President."

"This business with your daughter is certainly unfortunate and the First Lady and I are praying that it all works out. If you find you need anything call me. Good luck to you all." Then the line went dead.

The cold efficiency of the call was almost as unsettling as having to attend some mysterious meeting with some pompous General. "Are you still out there?" the Senator shouted at his aide through the closed door. He knew he was, probably with his ear glued to the keyhole.

"Yes sir."

"I'm going to get a call from a General Grant to go to a meeting. Tell him I'm going to be bringing Thomas Knight." He hoped he could move the meeting along, he hated the idea of being to far away in case something were to break with Isis.

"Yes sir!" replied the aide with unbridled enthusiasm.

"That kid is going to be severely disappointed when I don't make him Chief of Staff after I win the election," mumbled the Senator to himself. But, for now the kid's youthful naiveté was serving him well. Plus, the kid's father's significant fortune and subsequent contributions had been helpful in getting his candidacy off the ground.

———·———

Knight had chosen to forgo the small lap pool adjacent to his suite for his daily exercise. There were three major pools at the Colossus. The giant wave pool attracted the fun-in-the-surf crowd, the jungle adventure pool meandered over three acres and its little coves were perfect for drinking, sunbathing and relaxing. While the two large pools were open to any guest, the Olympic-sized lap pool was restricted. It was perfect for his morning regime of three miles. Besides, the scenery was better. Flynn had ringed the pool with private cabanas and their use was reserved for the high rollers and VIPs. Within the cabanas, anything went and any request was indulged. Unwanted press was kept at bay by security. Sports stars, Hollywood celebrities and rock stars found the place irresistible. A private cabana by the Colossus's lap pool was the hottest coup in town.

The pool boys were still preparing everything for the midmorning rush when Knight dived in. He had only half a mile to go when one of the pool boys called to him. He did not like having his exercise interrupted, and especially the last part. That part did the most good.

The heavily tanned attendant apologized as he handed Knight the cordless phone. "Sorry…but they said it was urgent."

"Hello," said Knight.

"You're up early. I thought you might like to join me for breakfast," said a sultry voice.

Knight had heard that voice before but he was having trouble placing it. "I'm just trying to stay in tune," he answered cautiously. "Is this some sort of an emergency?" he asked, still trying to put a face to the voice.

"I told them to say that," replied the voice. "You can go swimming any old-time but you can only have breakfast now."

Knight was now thoroughly upset that his routine had been interrupted by such a trivial request. "I'm sorry I already ate," he said, not bothering to disguise his displeasure.

"Then you can watch me," the voice persisted.

"Well I don't know who you are, and I'm not dressed for eating out. I'm in the pool."

"I know you're in the pool silly, I'm right in front of you."

Knight looked up into the nearest private cabana. The brunette with the cell phone waved and then added a come hither motion. From what he could see, she filled out her gold bikini just right. "What the heck," he said to himself. His exercise program was already ruined. He laid the phone on the pool apron and in a single fluid motion pulled himself out of water. He picked up his towel and dried himself as he walked toward the cabana.

"You look marvelous!" exclaimed the brunette as she pulled down her dark glasses and peeked over them. His natural athletic build had been enhanced by extensive exercise and his well-defined muscles rippled as he walked.

This peeking thing must be all the rage thought Knight. First, the band members last night and now this vixen by the pool. "Do I know you?" he asked.

"Why darling…I thought I made a strong impression on you last night."

Knight touched his cheek; she was the woman from the highway and the lounge. "You did," he answered. His cheek had still been sore when he had shaved earlier. "You were a blonde."

"I am a blonde darling. I just wear this silly old wig so that my thousands of adoring fans will leave me alone." Her voice dripped with fake sarcasm. "I'm Honey of Honey and Her Bears," she announced, as she extended her hand as if she expected Knight to kiss it.

Knight shook the hand weakly and said, "Thomas Knight."

"I know who you are. I've been checking…sit down." She was used to having her way.

Knight wearily obliged. "You hit me pretty hard."

"You deserved it! My lawyers tell me that that numb nuts cop's ticket will cost me a grand." Her exaggerated ladylike demeanor had vanished.

"You shouldn't be drag racing," mocked Knight.

"Well it still wasn't very chivalrous!" she spat. Then as she tempered her anger, "But let's let bygones be bygones. Are you sure you don't want some breakfast?"

Knight looked at the table. There were four squeeze bottles of pure honey, nearly a half a loaf of toast, and a silver coffee carafe.

She poured a half a cup of coffee from the carafe and then held it up as if to offer Knight some.

He waved it off with the back of his hand.

She picked up one of the honey bottles and squeezed it into the cup until it was full. Sensing Knight's curiosity she said, "I love the stuff. I can't seem to get enough." She stirred the bizarre concoction and then instead of sipping it, she began to eat it with a spoon.

Knight watched in disgust as she wolfed down the thick brew. When the cup was empty, she took a slice of toast from the pile and squeezed a pool of honey in the middle. Then using her index finger, she spread it out carefully over the toast. She looked up and stared at Knight as she placed her finger in her mouth and slowly sucked away the excess of the golden liquid.

Knight's face began to feel warm.

Honey continued to stare as she devoured the toast in four crunchy bites. With her appetite temporarily satisfied, she pushed back her chair and looked into Knight's eyes. "I would have won you know," she said.

"No doubt," he came back, his face still warm. "My antique car really isn't up to the latest motorcycle technology."

She laughed, "Your car is hardly an antique."

"It's a 1996," answered Knight. "In the world of high performance *that's* an antique."

She laughed again, "Of course there is no way you could have known that I had them tweak my Suzuki a bit. From the factory it will do 190 but mine is at 210 now."

It was Knight's turn to laugh. "And you go around picking on gullible guys in Ferraris."

"Your Testarossa should do 195."

"Maybe, under ideal conditions. But about 170 is what I would expect."

"Life begins at 200," she taunted as she stood up and stretched. "I only have one show tonight so I'll let you make it up to me by buying me dinner."

Knight stared, he did not want to, but he could not help himself. She was absolutely beautiful. She was nearly six feet tall and except for her oversized breasts, was perfectly proportioned. Her two-piece bikini left nothing to the imagination. The deep dark tan of her body and the gold of the suit made her look naked.

Her eyes were dark and dangerous. There was no warmth, only lust. She circled behind Knight's chair and leaned over him. Her soft natural breasts bracketed his head. She draped her well-toned arms over his shoulders and softly scraped his chest with her fingernails as she whispered in his ear, "I hope you are not very fast in bed either."

Knight shuttered involuntarily as she traced the inner ridges of his ear with her still sticky tongue.

They both jumped when the phone rang.

It was the pool boy; he interrupted their conversation with a message that a call was waiting for Knight.

The instructions given by the phone had been to the point and Knight hung up after only a few seconds of conversation.

"I have to go," he stated as he slid back his chair from the table. "Business."

"I'll expect you around ten," said Honey reconfirming their scheduled rendezvous.

Knight only nodded. He knew any assignation with Honey was a dangerous endeavor. However, she was incredibly attractive and certainly seemed willing.

Back in his suite, Knight quickly exchanged his swimsuit for another of Victor Cherenko's outfits. He smiled as he gave himself the once over in the mirror. Not bad he thought. Everything fit perfectly. He made a mental note to complement the frail Russian when he got a chance.

He arrived right on time at Flynn's office. He was surprised when the blonde receptionist guided him to a nearby conference room, instead of the office.

As Knight entered the room, Flynn looked up quickly from his conversation with the FBI Deputy Director. "We were wondering," he said with an annoyed tone.

Knight checked his Rolex. "I thought you said ten o'clock." The hands on the white watch face were in the correct position.

"I expected everyone to be ready to go by ten," Flynn corrected, not willing to admit he had started prematurely.

A small group was seated around the boat shaped bird's-eye maple conference table. Two insulated, gold carafes of water and coffee acted as a centerpiece.

"You know everyone of course," said Flynn as he gestured for Knight to take one of the two remaining dark gray leather chairs on the left side of the table.

Knight looked down the table and nodded in acknowledgment.

In addition to the FBI Deputy Director, there was Bulldog, the barrel-chested Clark County Sheriff, Senator Devlin and his young aide. Knight and Flynn made it seven. Only one chair was still empty.

Knight sat down and poured himself a cup of coffee. As he took his first sip, he almost gagged. The coffee was the consistency of espresso. He had been anticipating a well-brewed coffee, but this was either a very exotic and unrecognizable blend or two-day-old dregs from a previous pot. He suspected the latter. At least it was hot. He reached over to the small gold plate by the carafes and selected a packet of artificial sweetener. He was tearing the corner off the packet when the voice startled him.

"I'm sorry I'm late!"

Knight turned quickly to find the source of the familiar voice and in doing so inadvertently tore the top completely off the package of sweetener. The small white granules sprayed across the table. He felt his face grow red as he fruitlessly tried to sweep the particles into his hand. It seemed that every time he encountered Susan Strong he was blushing.

Susan moved to the open chair beside Knight and sat down. Her familiar floral scent perfume with the top note of jasmine seemed to target Knights nose. She looked at the still blushing Knight and winked!

Between the mess he had made at the table, Susan's unexpected presence, the unexpected and unexplained wink, Knight was only vaguely aware of Flynn's opening.

"I have asked you all here this morning for an update." Flynn was all business. "I'm not expecting to hear from the kidnappers before this evening, but I want to know if any of you have come up with anything or where you're at." He turned to Bulldog and ordered, "You're up!"

Bulldog Basham was thoroughly enjoying every minute of being the cock of the walk. He was the master marionette and he was having the time of his life pulling the strings of the FBI, the Sheriff's Department and the Secret Service. He had early on established what was sure to be a winning strategy.

He would shoot down every theory that was advanced about the kidnapping while carefully avoiding presenting any of his own ideas. Then when the situation began to resolve itself he would quickly jump on the winning team and claim the credit. If he could pull it off, he would be out from underneath Thomas Knight's shadow forever. Of course, the only possible flaw in his plan was that Knight might actually solve the case. However, he would just have to gamble on that not happening. The odds were against it. After all, Knight was only one person and the combined resources of all the other players were formidable. The risk was worth it. Even if he lost, he would still be right where he was.

He had always considered himself lucky and the fact that Isis Flynn had been kidnapped from the golf course, rather than the Colossus, was a great piece of luck. Flynn would definitely have had his hide if it had happened at the hotel. However, Isis's refusal to let his security accompany her on the fateful morning ride had effectively let him off the hook. Even Flynn was saying that no one was responsible but Isis herself.

"I have the entire security staff probing every lead and I called in some personal favors to keep the lid on the press. We are ready to move immediately if something breaks," he answered. He would let the others stick their necks out with their theories first.

Flynn looked at Bulldog with disgust and shook his head. He had gotten exactly what he had expected from his V.P. of Security. He turned to the Deputy Director. "How about the FBI?" he asked hopefully.

The FBI Deputy Director was all business. His high and tight haircut, the out-of-place class ring, all indicated he had come out of one of the military academies. He was the type that would do very well as a career bureaucrat.

He opened an artificial leather folder in front of him. "I'm here because it's Senator Devlin's daughter that is missing. The Director got a call from the President asking us to do what we can. As you may know, we are not officially on the case. We can't do anything officially unless we have knowledge of or at least reason to believe that the victim has been moved across state lines. Unofficially, I have put everything in place so that if we acquire evidence that will allow us to investigate, we can do it immediately."

Flynn stared daggers at the Deputy. "That's it! That's all the FBI, the supposedly best police department in the world, can come up with." The veins in his forehead were starting to pulsate with anger.

The Deputy looked down at the folio, sheepishly and said, "I did have our best profiler look at the case, unofficially of course, and he came up with a conclusion."

"Dammit man," swore Flynn. "Spit it out!"

The Deputy was still tentative, "He…he thinks it is an inside job."

Flynn exploded and pounded the table with his fist. Everyone at the table jumped at the sudden outburst. Susan reached across and stabilized the carafes that nearly tipped over. Knight's coffee sloshed over the rim and into his saucer.

Flynn slumped back into his chair and tried to recover his composure. "I don't suppose your so-called profiler has any idea who it might be?"

The Deputy was still smarting from the outburst. "No.but, we're sure it has to be someone who knew your wife's schedule. So, it is probably someone close to her." He glanced quickly around the table hoping to see some sign of agreement.

Knight could not make up his mind whether the Deputy was looking for a confirmation about his theory or a suspect.

"Anybody else got anything?" asked Flynn in exasperation. Then not waiting for an answer, he turned to the Sheriff. "Well?" he asked impatiently.

The Clark County Sheriff was nearly as fond of Flynn as he was of Knight. "We're looking at everything," he answered. "There was almost no physical evidence and then the crime scene was comprised by everyone just having to have a look." He stared at Knight as he finished his statement.

"Do you have any theories or not?" Flynn asked impatiently.

"I agree with the FBI," answered the Sheriff. "If someone was planning an abduction, that would be the place to do it, away from everything."

Flynn looked at Susan, "Ms. Strong?"

"I agree. Someone had to know she was going out there alone. It is most likely then that someone at the golf course or the hotel did the kidnapping or tipped off the one who did."

This time, the Senator interrupted, "Do you have any suspects?"

"No!" answered Susan emphatically. "Not yet."

Flynn turned in his chair, lowered his head and ran his manicured fingers through his hair. "Thomas, please...please, tell me you've got something," he pleaded.

Knight was in a quandary! He knew exactly what had happened, an eight-foot alien wearing plastic snowshoes had abducted Isis! Realizing that nobody was going to believe such a preposterous idea he chose to keep his theory to himself. "I'm not sure it was an inside job," he said. "But since no one appears to have anything tangible, probably the best thing is to wait and see if the kidnappers make a mistake when they tells us how to make the exchange." He had barely finished speaking when he suddenly jerked upright, banging his knee on the bottom of the table.

"Are you all right?" Flynn asked, as Knight winced in pain.

"Yes...yes I'm okay. Just a cramp from my morning workout," Knight lied, feeling his face getting warm. He certainly had not expected the nylon-clad foot under the table to raise his pant leg and rub up against his calf. He reached down under the table as if to massage the phantom cramp and pinched the offending foot.

Susan smiled and ignoring the pain, retaliated by kicking him in the shin.

Again, Knight's knee banged the table. Everyone stared at him. His face was now fully flushed and he was praying the game of footsie had ended. "I'll be fine now."

Flynn ended the meeting without saying a word; he simply stood up and walked out, slamming the door behind him.

The participants looked at each other as if to confirm the fact that the meeting was indeed over.

Knight stood up turned to Susan and whispered, "What kind of a sophomoric stunt was that?"

Susan did not back down, "I was trying to scratch my foot. And, besides what makes you think I care if you make an ass of yourself?"

Knight calmed down, "Well you rushed off last night and I simply wanted to explain…"

"Oh…there's nothing to explain. It was obvious that you prefer the overly endowed."

"There's nothing wrong with your…" Only the Senator coming up behind him and putting his hand on his shoulder saved Knight from total disaster.

"Thomas, I need to talk you," he commanded.

Susan took the hint, "Well Mr. Knight I see you are very busy. It was nice to meet you." Even in her highly miffed state, she knew not to let anyone else in on their relationship. She turned and left.

"The President called me and asked me to ask you to attend a meeting," said the Senator.

"Who?" asked Knight, he had not been paying attention. He was still watching the gorgeous blonde as she shut the door behind her.

"The President," answered the Senator, annoyed at Knight's reaction.

"The President?" repeated Knight, distractedly still staring at the door.

"The President of the United States. Dammit man what's wrong with you?"

Knight recovered, "What meeting?"

The Senator spent the next ten minutes explaining to a protesting Knight why he was being asked to leave the Colossus and take the meeting the President had requested. "And you know I'm more anxious than you are about leaving the hotel. I don't want to be very far away if something breaks about Isis."

"I understand," apologized Knight. After all, he was only helping out friends, but Isis was the Senator's daughter. "Do you have any idea about what's up?"

"No…not a clue, but it must be important. The President doesn't micro-manage and so to ask us both to take time away from finding Isis is significant," answered the Senator with a worried look.

Susan had made a decision. Seeing Knight again in Flynn's meeting had made it perfectly clear what she had to do. It was amazing how quickly things could change. Only an hour before, there was no way in her wildest dreams that she could have imagined what she was about to do.

Knight left Flynn's office and was surprised to see Susan waiting by the elevators. He approached her with apprehension.

"We need to talk," she announced matter-of-factly.

"About what?" he asked warily.

"I don't want to talk here there are too many cameras and inquisitive ears," she cautioned.

Knight checked his watch. "Well it is a little early, but we could go for lunch," he suggested as he searched Susan's blue eyes for some hint of what she was up to.

Susan thought for a second, "My Company has a membership in the nearby country club." Then she ordered, "I'll meet you there in an hour."

"Your treat?" teased Knight hoping for some reaction. He did not get one.

The elevator door opened and Susan stepped in. As the door started to close, she said suggestively, "I want to proposition you!"

The door closed before Knight could reply. "Now, what in the world is that all about," he muttered to himself as he took the next elevator.

Flynn was beside himself. He had assembled the best team in the world to help him find Isis and they had absolutely nothing to show for their efforts. It did not matter to him that most of them had only been involved for less than twenty-four hours. He was used to getting results, he wanted to lash out at someone and vent his frustrations. He chose Bulldog.

He had been berating his hapless victim for nearly twenty minutes. The secretaries on the other side of the massive door leading to his office were having no trouble picking up the conversation.

"What kind of a V.P. of Security are you anyway?" He shouted rhetorically. "Ever since I gave you the job, I've had nothing but trouble. First, someone steals my bathtubs, then someone kidnaps my wife and then I come to find out that Thomas Knight caught a cheat in the casino that got by your crew."

Bulldog looked away sheepishly. He knew better than to interrupt Flynn when he was like this.

"Now get out of my sight and stay out until you have something constructive to add!" ordered Flynn as he dismissed the fully cowered Bulldog with a wave of the back of his hand. He walked to the bar and poured himself a triple vodka, not bothering to mix it with anything. He moved back to the windows in his office and stared down the Strip. He longed for the good old days when all he had to do was screw someone in a business deal.

When Knight returned to his suite Steve greeted him. "You have a fax and a small package. I put them in your bedroom."

"Thanks," answered Knight. The fax would be from Monica but he had not been expecting a package. When he got to the bedroom, he ignored the folder with the fax on the antique table and instead looked at the shipping label on the box. He had no sooner read the label than he eagerly tore at the package like a child on his birthday. It was from Tony Amato in L.A.

When the reinforcing packaging tape proved to be obstinate, Knight took the small, engraved, combination knife, nail file and money clip from his pocket. He removed the money and opened the knife. He smiled. It was the last thing his father had given him before he and his mother had been killed in the plane crash. He was amazed at how often it had been useful.

He sliced through the reinforced packing tape and eagerly pulled back the cardboard flaps. He plunged both hands into the foam packaging peanuts. Several of them were still sticking to his arm when he retrieved the treasure, his Glock 18 pistol in its well-worn shoulder holster!

He slid the pistol out, released the magazine, saw it was empty, and then snapped the slide back to confirm the chamber was also empty. He toggled the laser sight and held the gun in a two-handed combat stance. He sighted the laser on one of the pictures of an apple tree on the wall and the pinpoint red dot froze on an apple. It wobbled slightly. "Well it will probably take me a couple of hours to get my hand back," he said aloud. He switched off the laser sight and again rummaged through the box. There were eight more things in the box. Two seventeen shot magazines, two thirty-three round magazines and three boxes of fifty rounds of 9mm Winchester 115 grain J H P + P + ammunition.

Knight smiled, Tony had extended the magazines' capacity by adding +2 floor plates. The floor plates allowed two extra rounds to be available if needed.

The last thing in the box was a folded twenty-five yard slow-fire pistol target. There were five neat holes inside the eight ring.

Tony had written in the margin of the target, *Best I could do using a bench rest.*

Knight took out a fifty-cent piece from his pocket and placed it in the center of the target. The group was only slightly larger. If Tony could get a group that tight, Knight knew he could do better. Tony was the best gunsmith in the country but he was far from the best marksman.

On the back of the target was scrawled a terse message.

Thomas, I put my blood sweat and tears into my work and you insisted on tearing it up. I had to replace the entire receiver, that somehow you had managed to melt, and those are damn hard to come by for the Model 18. Please, please see if you can make this one last at least a little while! I can't vouch for the fully automatic fire accuracy. There are only a handful of people other than you that could tame that beast. My staff and I went through nearly five hundred rounds and managed to hit the target five times.

Knight laughed aloud, Tony was right. It took a special trigger technique to keep the Glock 18 under control on full auto. At 1,300 rounds-a-minute, it took real talent to squeeze off a short burst.

Knight loaded the magazine, jacked a shell into the chamber, and put the Glock into its holster. He slid his arm through the holster and adjusted it over his shoulder. The familiar weight gave him confidence but he also soberly realized that there was both life and death close at hand. He slipped one extra magazine into the pouch on the shoulder strap and snapped it shut. He would put the other magazine in the Ferrari. For the first time since Palm Springs, he felt fully dressed.

With Tony's present disposed of, he picked up Monica's fax. It was about diamonds.

When the earth was young, between twenty million to one hundred and fifty million years ago, it was the time of the beginning of the continental drift. This was when Africa and South America separated and the Atlantic Ocean was formed. It was then, during the creation of the Atlantic Ocean that violent volcanic activity erupted. The kind necessary to create enough heat and pressure to produce diamonds.

The only place on the planet where enough heat and the pressure can be achieved to produce diamonds is roughly a hundred and twenty miles deep into the earth. When a volcano erupts, it allows small rock or magma to flow to the surface from deep cracks and fissures called dikes. As these dikes near the surface, they develop a carrot shape. The diamonds ride these carrot shaped flows or pipes, like an elevator to the surface. The rock in these pipes is called kimberlite, after the city of Kimberley in South Africa where these types of pipes were first discovered in the 1870's.

The volcanic cone formed above the kimberlite pipes is very small compared with volcanoes like Mount St. Helens.

Unlike most volcanoes, which are created by relatively low-pressure expulsions of shallow magma, kimberlite pipes are formed when deep magma is forced upward by high-pressure eruptions, comparable to gunshots. These columns of kimberlite magma erupt into the air, then fall back and solidify. This activity does not produce easily identifiable cones or other discernible features.

Kimberlite pipes are very narrow below ground and they broaden at the surface. The diameter of the pipes may vary from just a hundred yards to more than a mile.

Upon exposure to the elements, kimberlite weathers into a clay-like material. It erodes easily, and after only a short time can leave no visible trace that a pipe exists just below the surface.

Worldwide, there are four thousand known kimberlite pipes, but only about ten percent contained diamonds. Of those, only thirty are rich enough to provide a basis for commercial mining.

Knight was disappointed. He had asked Monica about uncut diamonds in Nevada and she given him a general encyclopedia response. But, he continued to read on.

In 1996, a producer of African diamonds announced that they had found a twenty-eight carat, gem-quality yellow diamond at its Kelsey Lake mine. The news media had been all over the story. It was neither the size nor the quality of the diamond that was so impressive. It was where it was found. The Kelsey Lake mine was not in South Africa, but in Colorado only eight hundred miles from Vegas! The diamond reserves were estimated at one million carats worth over a quarter billion dollars. The quality of the diamonds was equal to those from South Africa and about sixty-five percent were anticipated to be of gem quality.

Monica had added a handwritten note on the fax.

Boss, I talked to a professor at the Colorado School of Mines. He told me kimberlite pipes could be anywhere. However, unless one finds a surface indication, usually a diamond, no one knows they are there. He said diamonds could easily exist in Nevada because of the abundant evidence of previous volcanic activity.

She had also added a postscript, *Boss if you find any diamonds I would like to have a nice twenty-five carat or so as a bonus!*

Knight smiled, Monica, bless her, was always angling for a raise. He located a paper shredder in the suite's office and disposed of the fax. No sense in anyone knowing he had been inquiring about diamonds.

He checked his watch and headed for the mysterious luncheon meeting with Susan. He had come to Vegas to help his friend get his kidnapped wife back. Yet, here he was chasing aliens, dealing with amputations, diamonds, a meeting with an Army General, and that unfathomable blonde. What else could possibly be added to his overflowing plate?

———·———

The golf course restaurant that Susan had recommended for lunch was located about two miles from the Strip.

"Good afternoon sir. May I help you?" inquired the restaurant's maitre d' in a patronizing tone.

"Ms. Strong?" asked Knight.

"Oh…yes sir," came the reply, obviously impressed by the question. "She is waiting for you on the patio." The maitre d' snapped his fingers and a young waiter appeared quickly. "Take this gentleman to Ms. Strong's table."

Knight smiled and nodded his head but ignored the maitre d's posturing for a tip.

Susan was sitting under an umbrella at obviously the prime table. She did not rise when Knight came up; she only smiled and gestured to the chair next to hers.

Whew! She is gorgeous, thought Knight. She was dressed in shades of yellow with an oversized white straw hat sporting a yellow ribbon that ran down her back. Even though she was sitting in the shade of the umbrella, she had kept her hat on.

"Nice place," admired Knight as he looked out over the palm trees and toward the pond that surrounded the eighteenth green. "Do you golf?" he asked as he sat down, removed the napkin from the wine glass and put it in his lap.

"I used to. However, I don't seem to have the time these days. How about you?"

"Same problem. Golf takes a lot of time if you're hoping to maintain any kind of proficiency."

"Are you any good?" she asked.

"Not really. I did get my handicap down to a six a few years ago," said Knight with obvious false modesty.

"That's impressive," said Susan nodding her head up and down.

"How about you?" asked Knight.

"Oh…I won a few amateur tournaments a while back before my father died and I took up this job," she replied, quite aware she had trumped Knight's boasting.

The young waiter interrupted the banter by handing them overly large menus. "Would either of you care for something to drink?"

"Iced tea with lemon, thank you," answered Susan.

"The same but without the lemon," Knight added. He hated lemon. He knew it would probably not make any difference. Rarely did restaurants fail to put the offensive tart citrus wedge on the glass anyway. But, sometimes he got lucky. "I'm surprised you didn't opt for a Piute Bill," he teased.

"I've had enough of those," she answered with a frown.

"What's up?" he asked.

"I was surprised to see you and I are working on the same case," she answered.

"Small world," he said.

"Smaller than I thought," she countered. "Anyway…I am a stranger here and you know things I don't know and couldn't find out soon enough. So I figured why not offer you a contract to help my company."

Knight looked into her soft blue eyes and noticed for the first time since he sat down that her pale lipstick was glistening in the sunlight. "You want me to work for you?"

"Just temporarily," she corrected quickly.

"I'm already working for Jack Flynn."

"I know that!" she said impatiently. "You and I both want the same thing. We both want Isis Flynn back alive. It so happens I need something more."

"And that is?"

"Well I want her back, but without paying the twenty million dollar ransom."

Knight suddenly realized what Susan's real stake in the game was. "You're on the hook for the twenty mil through a kidnap insurance policy."

"Exactly!" She acknowledged. "Find the victim and save my company the money, and I'll pay you a handsome fee for your services."

The waiter silently placed the drinks in front of them and retreated before Knight could object to the yellow wedge clipped onto the rim of his glass.

"Fifteen percent," announced Knight quickly, hoping to catch her off guard.

"Seven," she countered, without a hint of a smile.

"Twelve," he bid. "Like I said, I am already engaged."

"Ten…and you can keep working for Flynn also." She stared into his cool blue eyes made even more noticeable when set off by his tanned face. She thought she saw a hint of a twinkle. "Final offer!"

Knight smiled, took the confounded lemon off his glass and placed it on a saucer. He sipped slowly from the opposite side of the glass and nodded.

Suddenly a honeybee, attracted to the color of the lemon, buzzed by Susan's head. She instinctively jerked back. Then she reached into her lap, retrieved her napkin and swatted at the insect.

"Freeze!" shouted Knight. He grabbed her wrist to stop the flailing. "Don't move!"

Susan looked at him with surprise, but obeyed his command.

Evidently satisfied that the lemon was not a viable source of sugar, the bee flew away.

Knight loosened his grasp on Susan, "Whew! That was close."

Susan reached over and massaged her wrist. Knight's powerful grip had left a red handprint on her skin. "What was that all about?" she asked defensively.

"That…was an Africanized honeybee," said Knight. "Nasty little buggers."

Susan looked into his eyes as if she wanted more explanation for his bizarre behavior.

Knight wiped the rim of his glass with his napkin, took another sip of his tea, and leaned back in his chair. "Back in the '50s some do-gooder Brazilian geneticist came up with this harebrained idea to breed high producing but aggressive African honeybees with passive Brazilian bees. The idea was to come up with a bee that would produce more honey and help stimulate the Brazilian economy. Of course, as with most of these schemes, something went wrong. About twenty-nine of the bees escaped and started breeding with the local bee population outside of the laboratory."

Knight looked at her to be sure that she was still following his story. "Anyway, it seems that these hybrid bees, while producing lots of honey, also developed a very bad attitude. It wasn't very long before they started to take over everything. By the '90s, they had moved all the way north to Texas. Since then they have killed a number of people, including one just a few years ago right here in Vegas. If you kill one, their buddies find out about it and then they take retribution. It's not a good idea to antagonize them."

Susan looked into Knight's eyes for the hint of a lie, "Is this the truth?" she asked. "You're not just pulling my leg?"

Knight flashed a broad smile. The prospect of running his hands over Susan's legs was definitely appealing, but he kept the thought to himself. "Yeah, you can check it out in the library."

Susan, still not convinced that he was not telling her a wild tale, changed the subject. "Well, now that disaster has apparently been avoided. What have you got on the kidnapping?" she asked matter-of-factly.

"You first," he countered.

"Like I said in the meeting in this morning, I think it is an inside job. Of course, I can't prove it. It's just my gut telling me that."

"Who have you talked to?" he pressed.

"Just the head parking valet. They always seem to know all the comings and goings."

"Johnny?" asked Knight.

"Yes, that was the name on his badge. I got the feeling he thought the Russians were somehow involved."

Knight chuckled; Johnny was always mad at the Russians. "I doubt it... it's not their style. But I can check it out."

"Okay…it's your turn. Who do you think did it?"

Knight, satisfied he had removed all but the faintest trace of the lemon, took a substantial drink of his tea. Deliberately ignoring her question, he opened his menu and glanced at the offerings. He spotted his choice: the chef's salad and closed the menu. He looked up at her nonchalantly and said, "Well...from what I have been able to find…Isis was abducted by an green eyed, eight-foot tall, giant alien wearing plastic snowshoes."

———·———

CHAPTER 7

The house, if you could call it a house, had once been a mobile home. There was nothing mobile about it now, however. The wheels and axles had been removed and now rested in a rusty pile nearby.

It was half buried into the slope of a small hill. A jury-rigged pile of concrete blocks provided what only loosely could be defined as a foundation. The whole thing looked like a metal building had been in a landslide leaving only a faded metal facade. The house, once an off white color, had faded and weathered leaving a bleached bones look about the place. The nearest neighbor was over five miles away.

It looked abandoned except for a new eight-foot high perimeter fence. The industrial grade fence ran across the desert and up the sides of the hill and across, enclosing nearly five acres. A decrepit wooden tool shed held a large diesel generator. The large, commercial sized air-conditioner mounted on the roof of the house was producing an oscillating screech from one of its out of balance fan blades.

Beyond the remote-controlled electric gate was a pile of debris. It was as if someone had fenced off a garbage dump. A brand new, refrigerated, ice cream truck was parked in front of the only door.

The electric gate opened suddenly, apparently without reason. The gold motorcycle appeared on the horizon leaving behind a rooster tail of white dust. The gate was fully open when the motorcycle sped through without hesitation. Deftly maneuvering its way around the piles of debris it turned quickly and came to a sliding stop. The wheels had thrown pea sized gravel into the air. The gravel rained down on the top of the metal roof and made a sound like the payoff on a nickel slot machine.

The dust cloud was still hanging in the air like smoke when the rider dismounted and without removing the helmet burst into the door of the house with a bang.

Upon entering the decrepit house, it was hard to tell which struck you first—the cold or the smell. After the heat of the desert, the house felt absolutely freezing. The large air conditioner had the interior at least sixty degrees cooler. You could not see your breath but it felt that way.

The smell was something else. It was the sickening sweet smell of rotting flesh. Overlaying the stench was the unmistakable odor of rotten eggs. Anyone entering the house would be both shivering and gagging at the same time.

The house had been set against a volcanic hill and then a large cave dug behind it. The rear side of the mobile home had been removed and it was difficult to see where the house stopped and the cave began. The cave penetrated nearly thirty yards into the volcanic rock.

In obvious contrast to the rest of the filthy house, the middle of the cave was extraordinary. There, under bright fluorescent lights, was the shiny stainless steel apparatus of a modern slaughterhouse.

A stainless steel table nearly twenty feet long ran down the center of the room. Above the table was a conveyor system from which hung meat hooks.

On the top of the table and in various stages of butchering where piles of decaying meat stacked in precise sized piles. A butcher's scale was mounted on the top of the table on the right end. Each pile weighed precisely twenty pounds. Blood and other assorted fluids oozed from the piles and flowed into a small gutter that ran the length of the table. This gutter dripped into an open fifty-five gallon drum at the left end of the table. There were two barrels of the fetid liquid already full, along the wall.

In the remnants of the mobile home, in what had been one of the bedrooms was a pathetic figure chained to an old iron army barracks cot. At irregular intervals, a loud hissing sound would emerge from the walls of the cave and the rotten egg smell would temporarily overcome the stench from the blood and rotting flesh.

———·———

Knight thought he knew all of the employees of Luciano's but he did not recognize the young salesman who approached him as he walked into the elegant clothing store.

"Can I help you?" The youth asked politely trying his best to hide his thick Russian accent.

"I would like to see Victor Cherenko. I am Thomas Knight."

"The clerk suddenly paled as he struggled with what to do with the request. "I…I vill have to call and see if he is available."

Knight followed him to the cash register and waited while the obviously new employee fumbled through the company's telephone book. With slightly trembling fingers, he dialed. "I have a Mr. Thomas Knight who wishes to see Mr. Cherenko." He listened for a second and then hung up, grateful for the exchange to be behind him. "Mr. Cherenko will be right out," he said and then cautiously added, "Vood you like some refreshment?"

"No, I'm fine," replied Knight realizing that this very well might have been the first time this new clerk had ever interacted with his boss.

"Thomas!" exclaimed a heavily Russian accented voice.

Knight turned to see the familiar short frail man.

Victor Cherenko looked every one of his seventy-seven years. His face was deeply lined and his once full head of hair was now just unruly gray wisps. He smiled as he walked up to Knight and extended his heavily nicotine stained hand. He used only his fingers to return Knight's handshake, very much an Eastern tradition.

"Good to see you again, Thomas," he said in a raspy voice, the product of far too many cigarettes. He then walked around Knight tugging at his clothes occasionally. Finally, he ran his hands over Knight's shoulders smoothing the fabric then he turned to the clerk and said in an emphatic tone, "Dis is how all my customers are to look."

The clerk shook his head in acknowledgement.

"The fit is perfect," smiled Knight.

As the two of them turned and strode toward the Russian's office, the clerk finally remembered he had been holding his breath and let it out with an audible sigh.

"Sit, sit,'" ordered the Russian.

Knight obliged but waved away the proffered cigarettes in the gold case.

Victor selected one for himself, lit it and tossed the disposable cigarette lighter back on to the top of his cluttered desk. "Yah…I know, I know," he protested holding up his hand, anticipating Knight's likely complaint. "Dey are Russian and probably da vorsed cigarettes ever made, but I have developed a complete reliance upon dem." He cradled the offensive object between his thumb and his forefinger with his palm upturned. Again, it was an Eastern style. He exhaled the acrid smoke, coughed gently and asked, "I suppose dat you are here about Mrs. Flynn?"

Knight frowned; the word had gotten around sooner than he had hoped. "I figured if anyone knew anything about her it would be you," he answered.

Victor smiled, "You give me vay too much credit." He took another drag without taking the dangling cigarette from his lips. "But I can assure you dat my organization had nothing to do vit it."

Knight studied the Russian's stone-cold, pale blue eyes. "I was hoping you weren't involved." He had first encountered Victor when he was setting up the Colossus's security system. There was no doubt about it; Victor was definitely a hard case criminal. He had not become the godfather of the Vegas Russian mob because he was less than ruthless. Yet, in spite of his fearsome reputation, his old world manners gave him a certain charm.

Victor coughed again, "Beneath dis big city exterior Las Vegas is a small village and everyone pretty much knows everyone else's business. It is hard to keep a secret here. Besides, Jack Flynn and I have an arrangement."

Victor's grandson had needed a visa to immigrate to America from Russia. At Flynn's request, Knight had pulled some strings and made it happen. In return, Victor had put the Colossus off limits to his mob except for the parking valets. Knight had always assumed that Flynn allowed that transgression because Victor needed somewhere to put his new recruits. And it was better to have them doing something semi-productive rather than trying to make their bones by rousting Flynn's guests. "You mean the valets?"

Victor smiled, "Yah dat's an another arrangement."

Knight looked puzzled. "Another arrangement?"

"Ven he was first getting started I helped him vith…how you say? Some bridge financing…and he is a very goot customer."

Knight waited patiently for the Russian to take another drag.

"You know I'm in the lending business, but I do not ask him to pay me back. I take out da interest he owes in free rent for my stores in his hotels."

"A very good arrangement," Knight acknowledged.

"Yah…it vorks out fine."

"Of course he still owes the principle."

"Of course," smiled the sly Russian. "Vodka?"

"It is too early for me," protested Knight.

"My friend, it is never too early or too late to drink vodka," laughed Victor, as he poured himself a small glass from the open bottle on his desk. He downed the fiery liquid in a single gulp. "I am still indebted to you for helping my grandson get his green card. You know he is now a senior in college." He reached across the desk and handed Knight a small silver framed picture.

The photo showed the frail Russian in a golf shirt towered over by a huge, black-haired giant in a body-builder's, posing thong.

"He is quite a hunk," admired Knight. "I certainly would not have recognized him as the skinny little teenager I remembered."

"Yah he is quite healthy. I don't know how he got so big. He eats nothing but the tuna fish." The Russian was beaming with pride. "He is a little spoiled perhaps, but a goot kid. You know he vorks right here at the hotel part time?"

Knight looked up quizzically.

"He parks the cars," answered the Russian, anticipating the question. "He is going into computers. After school, he helps me keep track of my accounts." He smiled slyly, "But of course, certain things should never be written down."

Knight smiled, "Of course."

Victor carefully replaced the picture. “Back to vhat brings you here. If I had to look for someone who may have been involved, I vood look at your former protégé.”

“Bulldog?” frowned Knight, amazed at the accusation.

“Vit out you keeping him on course he is like a ship vithout a rudder. Las Vegas has many distractions und it has been easy for him to succumb to them.”

“Do you know if he is involved?”

“No, but he is…how you say? Up to his neck in some strange activities.”

“Like what?”

“Vell let me yust say he has developed a need for large amounts of money. He has even tried to cut into some of my action.”

Knight shook his head, Bulldog had not only been his protégé but his friend and he had forgiven him for his betrayal when he had left Knight Security and gone to work at the Colossus.

“I know he is your friend, but he has changed since he vurked for you. He is clever und stays in the background but my people tell me he is in vay over his head. Maybe da pressure is the reason he also is starting to indulge in some unusual sex habits.”

Knight shook his head in disbelief.

———·———

The helicopter flight from the VIP terminal at McCarran Airport had been uneventful and the pilots had not offered a clue as to their destination. The chopper turned north and crossed over what Knight knew to be restricted airspace. It was obvious they were headed deep into the highly restricted Nevada Test Site area. The desert floor below was heavily pockmarked with craters left over from some the nine hundred nuclear tests conducted during the Cold War. The desolate area reminded Knight of pictures he had seen of the moon.

The helicopter started a steep descent and came in low over a large complex of unmarked beige buildings. The skids had barely touched down when two white Chevy SUVs emerged from one of the large hangar-like buildings and headed for the chopper.

No one said a word as Knight and the Senator were herded into the first vehicle. The interior of the SUV was cold and the air-conditioner was still turned on for maximum cooling. No sooner had they been seated than the doors were slammed shut and locked by attendants who had exited from the other SUV. They were all dressed in desert camouflage.

With everyone aboard, the SUV drove toward a low, single-story administration-looking building. As they passed by the nearest of the hangars Knight could see into the interior through the slowly closing doors. The hangar was full of ominous looking unmarked black helicopters.

———·———

Knight looked around at the other participants around the table in the meeting room. The only one he knew was the Senator. Everyone had been courteous enough but unless you had significant braid on your hat, you were only wallpaper in a meeting like this.

Army General, *Guts* Grant, entered the room as if he were taking a hill in battle. He had spent his whole career trying to be as colorful as his idol, General George Patton, the famous World War II hero. Guts approached everything as if it was as a military objective, to be taken regardless of the cost. George was his given name but he much preferred his nickname of Guts. He had earned it not for heroism as one might guess, but instead for a favorite expression he was always invoking. "Shoot 'em in the guts and let the hogs eat'em." It was supposed to be a battle cry, but in reality, it provoked ridicule among his troops whenever his back was turned. The press, of course, thought it was a great nickname and had adopted him as a hero of the Vietnam War. It made no difference to them that he had only been an administrator, located far behind the front lines, and had never fired a shot at the enemy. He was colorful, and that made for great copy.

Knight smirked ironically as Guts, the single General Officer's star glistening on his lapel, marched to the podium. Strapped around his now ample midsection were a pair of pearl handled nickel-plated Colt .45 Model 1911 pistols. The real General Patton would never have been caught dead with such vulgar firearms. Patton always carried a brace of .45s but his had real ivory grips. "Only a pimp in a New Orleans whorehouse has pearl handles on his pistols," he was often quoted.

Guts either had not heard the quote or thought that ivory or pearl, it made no difference. His grips were not even real pearl, they were plastic. They were as phony as everything else about Guts was.

"A week ago the President called me personally and asked me to spearhead this mission," Guts opened, his ferret-like eyes darting around the table. He was being sure everyone was appreciating his relationship with his Commander-in-Chief.

It took all his discipline for Knight not to whistle sarcastically.

"The name of the mission is Operation Big Deal!" Guts announced proudly.

Knight tried desperately to avoid laughing but could not keep a smile from leaking through.

"I thought the words Big Deal and the proximity to Vegas were a natural," stated Guts, obviously enamored with the brilliance of his choice.

The others at the table looked down, turned their heads or bit their tongues; trying everything they could not be the one that laughed first.

However, *Operation Big Deal* was in fact a big deal!

"Gentleman," said Guts. "The reason we're here today is because of the work of Professor Eric Aronson of Iceland and Jason Fulmar of the University of Nevada at Las Vegas. These two scientists have made a discovery that could have a significant impact upon the Nevada Test Site and its surroundings. I have asked Professor Aronson to bring you all up to speed on his findings, the possible consequences of them and the steps that we are taking to avoid the consequences." Guts waved his hand toward the table. "Professor Aronson." With that curt introduction, he took a seat.

The elderly gentleman that stood up and approached the lectern looked every bit the college professor. His thinning white hair was disheveled and his suit and shirt looked as if they had been retrieved directly from the suitcase without the benefit of a pressing. He walked to the podium, laid his notes down and reached inside his coat pocket to retrieve his reading glasses. Carefully bending the wires of the fragile glasses over his ears, he cleared his throat. "Approximately four months ago I received a report from Assistant Professor Fulmar. As a part of his doctoral thesis, he was studying earthquakes in southern Nevada and the surrounding area. In the process of conducting his study, he came across some anomalies that he could not account for. He sent me these findings and I was shocked. I had seen these conditions before. What impressed me about them was that in every case they were followed by a violent volcanic eruption."

Everyone at the table looked at each other to be sure that they had heard correctly.

The Professor continued to explain that starting in 1951 more than nine hundred and twenty-eight nuclear bombs had been detonated on and under the area of the desert now known as the Nevada Test Site. Originally, the blasts had been set off above ground, but due to the unpredictability of the direction of the fallout, the tests had eventually been moved underground.

In July of 1962, a bomb nicknamed the *Sedan* was detonated. Sedan was a nuclear bomb slightly smaller than a basketball. Its size gave little indication as to its potency however. It was detonated in a shaft 635 feet underground with a force equivalent to 104,000 tons of TNT. Scientists had hoped to find a peaceful use for atomic explosives, including the excavation of harbors, reservoirs and even a new Panama Canal.

The Sedan explosion released seismic energy equivalent to a 4.75 Richter scale earthquake. It displaced twelve million tons of earth, leaving a huge cone-shaped surface crater nearly thirteen hundred feet across and three hundred and twenty feet deep. The destruction to the surrounding geological strata also created an immense underground void or cavern. This cavern created by the forty-year old blast was now causing the instability that was threatening the area.

The Professor continued, explaining that according to Fulmar's studies, over the last year there had been a series of shifts in the Earth's subterranean plates along the San Andreas Fault in the Mojave Desert. Earthquakes in this area were common events and the residents accepted and even joked about their inevitability.

So, when Fulmar had tried to raise the alarm about the possible implications of the most recent quakes, he had been met with ho-hum apathy.

Deep in the bowels of the earth, decaying radioactive elements create heat so high it melts rocks. These molten rocks are called magma. The gases released when these rocks melt, collect in underground chambers like giant holding tanks, building up pressure like the pressure in a shaken can of carbonated soda. If the gas pressure builds too high, the pressure causes the magma to rise toward the earth's surface. If the pressure is not relived slowly a sudden venting, or volcano, can erupt.

According to Fulmar's theory, recent earthquakes in the area had created a plug of sorts that sealed off the normal gas venting from the Sedan chamber under the Nevada Test Site.

The Professor paused and poured himself a glass of water from the carafe on the side table. He returned to the podium and adjusted his glasses again.

"Yesterday, Fulmar and I found the critical piece of evidence confirming that gases have indeed built up in the large void created by the Sedan bomb. According to the seismic instruments the pressure in this void is so high that it could suddenly vent at any time."

The Senator could hold back his question no longer. "Professor Aronson, are you telling us that there is about to be a volcanic eruption right under our feet?"

"Yes, that's precisely what is about to happen," answered the Professor flatly.

There was an audible gasp from the audience.

The Senator was visibly shaken. "Is there anything we can do about it?"

The Professor stared at the Senator over the tops of the wire-rimmed glasses. "That's why you're here. And, that's what Operation Big Deal is all about. We plan to detonate a nuclear bomb of approximately ten kilotons, underground, over the top of the cavern created by the Sedan blast!"

Once again, everybody around the table looked at each other incredulously and whispered.

The Professor waited for the murmuring to die down and then continued. "If everything goes as planned, this blast will create a series of small fissures, allowing the built-up gases in the major chamber to slowly escape. This will hopefully prevent a major sudden venting or volcanic eruption." The Professor peeled the fragile glasses from his face and carefully placed them in his eyeglass holder. He stepped away from the podium and took a seat across the table from the General.

Guts moved to the lectern. "That's it gentlemen. Day after tomorrow at 1500 hours we will have detonation."

The Senator raised his hand. "General, as you well know, we have significant test ban treaties in force that bar the use of nuclear tests both underground and in the atmosphere. This explosion could certainly be construed as a violation of those treaties."

"I certainly am aware of that Senator," said Guts impatiently. "The President has been fully apprised of the situation and because of the compressed time frames necessary to take action, he has issued a Presidential Finding allowing us to proceed."

Knight had sat quietly, utterly in awe of what he was hearing. He would not have believed it if he was not hearing it firsthand. It had taken the Professor and Guts twenty minutes to explain the broad scope of the operation. The meeting had now turned into a progression of experts who were filling in the details from the makeshift podium.

The Senator nudged Knight and whispered, "Do you believe this is happening?"

Knight did not reply he merely shook his head slightly in a manner that left no doubt that he also thought it incredulous.

The final speaker sat down and again Guts took the floor. He looked sharply at Knight. "The explosion should be contained within the boundaries of the NTS but since the Colossus's golf course is private property and is close enough to the NTS to theoretically be in danger, we want you to evacuate it as a precaution."

Knight's mind was racing. He paused a second, surprised at the order. "Let me understand this! The Army is going to set off an underground nuclear explosion that is supposed to prevent a potential volcanic eruption that may come about because we weakened the Earth's crust with nuclear explosions in the past! You want me to evacuate the two hundred employees and guests of the Colossus's golf course in case something goes haywire! For crying out loud General!" admonished Knight. "You're talking about setting off an underground nuclear explosion!"

"In violation of any number of treaties ratified by the Senate, I might add!" interrupted the Senator.

"We are trying to head off a volcanic eruption!" said Guts impatiently.

Knight continued, "If what the Professor said is true, there is a risk that something could go wrong and that the area north of Vegas could be caught in a volcanic eruption. If that happens, then chaos in Vegas could quickly set in and there would be widespread panic. And, we have already seen how Vegas patrons react to a disaster. When the old MGM Hotel caught on fire back in 1980, some people were still grabbing everything they could get their hands on, even as they were succumbing to the deadly smoke. People are people and there will be idiots, criminals and heroes all panicked together." He paused. "If the situation has the potential to be as bad as you people think, I think the people of Vegas, not just the people in this room, need to know what you are planning."

"As you heard from the experts, there is little chance that Vegas would be directly affected. We want to evacuate the golf course only as a precaution," said Guts impatiently. "The Army knows what they are doing."

"Our priorities need to be the families that live in Vegas," Knight argued.

"You're not here to set priorities Mr. Knight! In fact, you wouldn't be here, if I hadn't been told by the President personally, to include you." Guts lectured. "And I would appreciate you keeping your negative comments to yourself."

Knight's mouth was slightly open as if he were about to add something. Thinking better of it, he closed his mouth and slumped back in his seat. He had made his point, but it was obvious that the outcome of this meeting was predetermined. Any further protest would be futile. Besides, he needed some time to study the problem. This was not a situation that required an off-the-cuff response.

The Senator reached over and touched Knight's arm as if to acknowledge his frustration.

The rest of the meeting was uneventful, if you could call planning for one of the biggest potential natural disasters in U.S. history uneventful!

To the relief of everyone, the meeting finally ended and Guts retired in full military fashion. The General's aide, a Major with an overly starched uniform and an attitude to match, came up behind Knight and whispered in his ear. "Sir, the General would like to see you privately."

Knight nodded and looked quizzically at the Senator who waved his hand casually as if to give permission.

With the tight-assed Major leading the way, Knight followed him through a labyrinth of corridors. The General's outer office secretary was a very attractive brunette female with Captain's bars on her obviously non-regulation, tightly fitted uniform. She motioned to the Major to go immediately into the General's office.

The office, even by military standards was Spartan, only a small metal desk, four, wooden side chairs and a couple of file cabinets made up the furniture. Obviously, whomever Guts was replacing had not been happy. He had taken all the office's creature comforts with him, leaving only the barest necessities for his successor. Guts had removed his uniform jacket and it hung on a hanger suspended from a coat rack. He was seated behind the desk in a small swivel chair frowning at an open red file folder. He barely looked up as Knight and the Major entered. With a wave of the hand, he gestured for only Knight to sit. Without further command, the Major exited the office and the door was pulled shut quickly by the brunette Captain.

Guts looked up. "Knight I don't like civilians in general and I don't like you in particular."

Knight looked at the source of the insult with his best poker face.

Guts continued, "I don't think civilians have any business in military affairs, but I follow orders. I don't have a clue why the President instructed me to include you in any of this." He paused. "But, he has.

I understand the Senator's daughter has been kidnapped and you are supposed to be the hot shot in charge of finding her."

Knight winced. The word about the kidnapping was really getting around. He had had enough of Guts' attitude. "I'm trying to get her back and all this hush hush stuff is taking me away from doing that."

Guts frowned. He was not used to being back talked, especially by a civilian. But, he let the retort slide. "We have been working around the clock trying to get this thing under control. The tech boys tell me we don't have much time left. Then for some unknown reason Fulmar chose last night to take a powder."

"Fulmar, the Professor?" asked Knight.

"Assistant Professor," corrected Guts. "No matter, Professor Aronson is the main man anyway." Guts sounded like he was trying to convince himself that it did not make a difference. "A few days ago, there was a minor earthquake near Palm Springs California and they tell me that was an early warning."

Knight's expression turned incredulous. He had been in that earthquake! Only good luck and a faulty fuse had prevented him from being buried alive in that fiasco. It had destroyed a large resort and all the water in Palm Springs had nearly ended up in the hands of a madman! He had ended up in the hospital with a concussion. He instinctively touched his right temple and ran his fingers back and forth softly confirming that there was no residual swelling. It had never occurred to him that there might be a connection with that event and the operation Guts was talking about.

Guts continued, "Anyway, as much as I hate to admit it, you probably can help."

"How's that?" Knight asked as he pushed the painful memories away.

"For one thing, we have a security system all around this place that allows us to pinpoint trespassers and then discourage them from returning.

"The camo dudes!" added Knight.

"You know about them?" asked Guts with surprise in his voice.

"Let's just say I've seen them around."

"Well, no matter what you civilians call them, they are Army security!" Guts thrust his finger at Knight to emphasize his point. When Knight did not rise to the bait, he continued. "That damned kidnapping out by the Colossus's golf course has had all sorts of civilians out there tramping around and I needed it to stop. We have very delicate sensors out there that hopefully will help us predict when and if this seismic event will occur."

Knight marveled at the way the General had spun an imminent volcanic eruption into a "seismic event". He was not about to give in to Guts. "Like you said, the golf course is private property and the Army shouldn't be messing around over there anyway."

The General ignored the admonishment. "Just get the people out of there." He then pressed a button on the phone on the edge of the desk. The office door opened and the brunette Captain entered.

"Take Mr. Knight down to TSG and have Sergeant Conway bring him up to speed and show him why we can't have civilians running around that damned golf course."

Knight had gotten up to follow the Captain but turned around as Guts spoke.

"Mr. Knight this operation is serious and the Army would appreciate your help. You have two days!"

For the first time since he met him, Knight hoped this pompous General was going to be capable of pulling off Operation Big Deal.

The shapely Captain led the way along the well-lit corridors to an elevator.

Knight followed her, admiring how her gait made her hips sway seductively. He smiled to himself. The swaying was definitely non-military and he wondered if it was strictly for his benefit or for any male, she might choose to tease. At the elevator, she pushed a button and as the door closed, she smiled flirtatiously.

Sometime between when she had shown him into Guts' office and now, she had put on a heavily cinnamon scented perfume. It filled the elevator and Knight knew the swaying had been for him. He looked at her chest and pointed to her nametag. "Captain Benteen? You wouldn't happen to be related to the famous Captain Benteen that was with Custer at the Battle of Little Big Horn?"

"He was my great, great grandfather," she beamed, obviously impressed with his knowledge of history. "You can call me Diane," she whispered suggestively.

"Well Diane, for both our sakes I'm glad he survived," he said trying not to stare obviously at her body. Suddenly aware that she was watching him, he tried his best to act nonchalant. He glanced around the elevator. "You don't get much sunlight in here."

She smiled at his feeble attempt to change the subject. "I know, on my days off I have to make up for it going topside and putting on my bikini."

Knight smiled as the vision of her without her uniform flashed into his brain.

When Knight failed to pursue with the obvious question as to when she took days off, she tried another gambit. "Do you live around here?"

"No, I'm from L.A. I'm here on business."

"Oh..." she answered; obviously disappointed that he would not be within convenient reach. She persisted, "Are you going to be here long?"

"It all depends upon what happens here."

She gathered hope and gave it another shot. "Where are you staying in Vegas?"

The elevator stopped just as Knight replied. "The Colossus."

The elevator opened into a bullpen area with cubicles, rows of florescent lights and no windows. The activity of the area prevented anymore immediate pursuit.

"This way," she ordered as she once again took up her suggestive sway.

They crossed the bullpen area and entered a door marked *Technology Security Group* without knocking. Sergeant Conway, his feet propped on his desk, was chewing on the remnants of a cigar. The Captain and Knight had obviously caught him off guard and he struggled awkwardly to get to his feet to attention.

"At ease Sergeant," she ordered. "Sergeant, this is Mr. Knight and the General wants you to show him our security system and answer any questions he might have.

"The whole system Ma'am?" The Sergeant asked with a frown.

"No, just the surface monitoring system will be enough," she answered.

She turned to Knight and extended her hand. Knight grasped it and was surprised that she had a man's handshake.

"I'll leave you here Mr. Knight." She continued to hold his hand as she followed up. "Sergeant please call me when you're finished." She gave Knight's hand a final squeeze and said; "I'll see you later."

Knight nodded with a smile, knowing it would give her some hope. He watched her departing sway and once again gave thanks that her famous relative had not shared Custer's fate.

The Sergeant interrupted in a voice dripping with disgust. "Are you looking for anything in particular?"

Knight turned to him, all business, "Just show me what you've got."

The Sergeant spent the next twenty minutes going over the security system. It was remarkably simple. Seismic sensors located in twenty-yard grids crisscrossed the entire surface area of the site and even beyond the borders. Infrared cameras had been strategically placed to give a visual check of large areas of the site. The system extended several miles into the desert with only a few pockets of private property escaping the monitoring. Flynn's golf course was nearly encircled by the system.

"How come you monitor activities beyond your perimeter?" Knight asked.

"Well…nobody knows this system is operating outside the boundaries of the site and we feel it can give us the heads up before a serious breach can occur," answered the Sergeant patronizingly.

"So when your sensors pick up an anomaly then you send out the camo dudes?"

The surprised expression on the Sergeant's face confirmed that Knight had caught him off-guard. He recovered quickly. "You must have been searching the Internet. That's where that term came from. All the conspiracy theorists, UFO junkies and kooks in general, started calling our contactor surface patrols that after we had a bunch of run-ins over on the other side of the Test Site near Groom Lake."

"You mean Area 51?" Knight corrected.

The Sergeant smiled slyly. He had caught onto the trap. "Why Mr. Knight, you know Area 51 doesn't exist."

"Actually I didn't find out about your surface security from the Internet, but rather from the County Sheriff."

A frown quickly replaced the smile on the Sergeant's face. "He talks too much!"

Knight changed the subject. "Do you track everything that shows up on your monitors?"

"The hard part is to figure out how to differentiate between a trespasser and animals that roam around the site. However, we have it pretty well refined by now, with the exception of the Spooks."

"Spooks?" asked Knight.

"It's a name we give to those hits we can't confirm. Officially, we call them machine anomalies but around here, we chalk them up to a Spook. We don't get a lot of them but they are annoying. We check them all out of course, but there is nothing there."

Knight's mind was racing, "Do you have a record of these contacts?"

The Sergeant was curious as to why Knight wanted to know, but he had orders to cover the surface security system, "We have them all plotted on the computer."

"Can I see them?"

"What the hell…I guess my orders cover that," rationalized the Sergeant thinking, even if he screwed up and said something wrong, he could claim he was following orders.

Sergeant Conway motioned for Knight to follow him to an empty computer terminal. A few deft keystrokes brought up an outline of the entire NTS site. Flynn's golf course was clearly visible. A few clicks of the mouse and a whole constellation of small X's and O's was superimposed over the outline.

"The X's are the security breaches we have picked up and have been resolved. The O's are "Spooks" the ones where our sensors indicated a breech, but the camo dudes couldn't find anything," explained the Sergeant.

Knight studied the screen and pointed to where the majority of the X's were concentrated toward the northeast corner of the site. "Area 51?"

The Sergeant grinned, "It seems everybody wants to see a UFO."

"Your Spooks seem to make up a corridor running north and south along both sides of Highway 95.

"They had a few over on the north side of the site also," said the Sergeant defensively, obviously resenting any implication that this side of the site was less secure.

"So you are responsible for the southern end of the site?" asked Knight, sensing the Sergeants' discomfort.

"You can see they have a lot more activity over there so they have better monitoring equipment. But, everything still has to be cleared through here," replied the Sergeant. He was not about to let a lowly civilian put him down.

"How long have you been tracking the Spooks?" asked Knight, concentrating on the monitor.

"As long as we've had this system. Why?"

"Can you sort your data to show when the hits have occurred?"

The Sergeant put his tongue in his cheek, thought for a second, and nodded affirmatively.

"I like to see the last hits first if possible," said Knight.

The Sergeant moved the mouse quickly, clicking on menu options as fast as they were displayed.

Both men watched intently as the screen twinkled with small O's moving from south to north along the west side of the NTS.

"That's interesting," remarked the Sergeant with a quizzical expression.

"It sure is," added Knight. "Can you slow that same display down?"

The Sergeant clicked the mouse deftly and the same information displayed using twice the time. He said, "There is a definite pattern there."

"Can you make up a grid to superimpose over the area?" asked Knight.

"We already have one," answered the Sergeant as he clicked away.

With the new grid on the screen, it was easy to see that the hits would fill one grid completely before moving to the next.

"Do your people have anything going on that is consistent with that pattern?" asked Knight.

"No…nothing," came the reply.

"It sure looks like your Spook has been covering your site very methodically."

"We would've never guessed there was a pattern," confessed the Sergeant. "They appeared to be simply random hits."

Knight stared at the monitor, an idea formulating in his head. "When were the most recent hits?"

The screen flashed in response to the Sergeant's new mouse clicks. "There were two of them yesterday, one at seven twenty-four P.M. civilian time," confirmed the Sergeant quickly doing the conversion from military time in his head. "And one about an hour later at eight twenty-seven."

Knight's brain was racing! "And the one before that?"

"Two days ago at ten forty-three A.M."

Knight pounded his right fist into his left palm and shouted, "I knew it!"

"What is it?" the Sergeant asked, totally confused as to the relevance of any of his mouse clicking.

"Sergeant, believe it not, your Spook is real and I've seen it!"

CHAPTER 8

Knight had drawn the short stick. He and the Senator had decided he would be the one to break the news to Flynn about the golf course.

The Senator had stayed behind at the site to coordinate public relations strategy with the Army brass.

As the chopper positioned itself for a landing at the VIP terminal at McCarran, Knight looked at his watch. The familiar white face showed that the whole meeting had taken only two hours. But, what an eventful two hours they had been.

Flynn was beside himself. It had been hours since he had heard anything about the progress in finding

Isis. "Where in the hell is Thomas Knight," he yelled into the intercom on his desk.

"He went with the Senator to attend a meeting," answered the box apologetically.

"What meeting?" Flynn demanded.

"I don't know sir," the box replied. "They said they would be gone about two hours and that was two hours ago."

Flynn did not like the idea of Knight and the Senator meeting together. What in the hell are they up to, he wondered as he keyed the intercom again. "Dammit…try his cell phone. But get a hold of him now!" he ordered as he hung up the intercom. He slumped back into his chair, wadded the printout of the email into a ball and threw it into his wastebasket. He was not having a good day, but it had to get better. He had no idea how wrong he could be!

———.———

Knight left the chopper, doing the obligatory crouch to avoid the rotor blades, and went directly into the waiting Colossus's limousine. He reached into his coat pocket, pulled out his cell phone, turned it on and dialed. By the time the limo was leaving the airport, he had Monica on the line. "I need some help," he opened.

"Yeah, but I'm not sure I can get you into a sanitarium before tomorrow," teased Monica.

"Smart ass," replied Knight. "But speaking of sanitariums, I do need a list of private sanitariums in the Vegas area."

Monica paused. "Boss…I was just kidding," she apologized; worried that she had been taken seriously.

"It's not for me," shot back Knight with a chuckle. "It has to do with this case."

Relieved that her tease had not hit home after all, Monica said, "I'll get right on it."

Knight ended the call and then punched another button on the cell phone and waited for an answer.

"Susan Strong," said the familiar sexy voice.

"Susan…Thomas…I've got some news. Meet me by the lap pool in about fifteen minutes."

"What's the news?" asked Susan impatiently.

"Just meet me by the pool," answered Knight curtly as he pushed a button and ended the call. He would practice his bad news speech on her before he confronted Flynn.

When Knight arrived at the pool, Susan was standing by the check-in counter wearing the same yellow pantsuit that she had worn at lunch having foregone the hat. Her short blonde hair literally sparkled in the Vegas Sun.

She is gorgeous, admired Knight to himself. "Hi," he said.

"What's going on?" Susan ordered.

He did not answer but grabbed her by the left arm.

Susan winced as he pressed on the still tender bullet wound.

"Oh…I'm sorry, I forgot," he apologized seeing her pain. He then took her right arm, steered her into an unoccupied cabana and motioned to her to sit. "I've got good news and bad news."

"What's the good news?" she asked hesitantly, fearing from the tone of his voice that the bad news was going to be really bad.

"I found out who kidnapped Isis," he said flatly.

"Is she…all right?" Susan asked tentatively, fearing the answer.

"I don't know," he answered.

Susan looked into his eyes hoping for a clue as to what was really going on. "Where is she?"

"I don't know that either," answered Knight.

"Well, what do you know?" demanded Susan impatiently, feeling that he had lied about having information he did not have.

"I only know who took her," he answered. "The rest I still have to figure out."

"Well?" she asked impatiently hoping that he had something.

"She was abducted by Spook," he answered.

"Who?" she was not sure that she had heard what she thought she had heard.

Knight explained at length what had happened at the meeting with TSG sergeant at the NTS and how he had discovered the connection between the Spook sightings and Isis's disappearance. "I also found that Spook had shown up on their sensors at the exact time that I spotted him at the golf course."

Susan looked at him incredulously, "You want me to believe that Isis was abducted by an eight foot alien, wearing plastic snowshoes, named Spook?"

"That's about it."

"Have you been drinking?" she asked.

"That brings me to Piute Bill," he answered flatly.

Susan could not believe that she was actually listening to this preposterous story.

Knight's cell phone rang before she could say anything. He took the phone from his coat pocket, punched a button and said, "Hello."

It was Monica. "Boss, I found two private sanitariums in Vegas. One is a rehab center and the other is a fancy, smancy, extended care facility."

"That's the one! Fax me what you have…just a minute I'll give you the number." He got up and went over to the message center in the cabana. Flynn had equipped each of them with the very latest in technology. At five thousand dollars a day rental, one had the right to expect the latest and greatest. "Fax it to this number," Knight ordered as he read it off from the fax machine. He punched a button on the cell phone, ending the call, and put it back in his pocket. The fax machine started spewing forth its document almost immediately. Knight read it as it appeared. When it was finished, he took the copy and walked over to Susan. "This is from my secretary Monica," he explained, handing the fax to Susan. "I think she found Buck Anders."

"Who?" asked Susan, completely confused.

"Buck Anders," repeated Knight impatiently. "He's the guy Piute Bill shot and who was rescued by Bugsy Siegel, the gangster.

Susan looked at Knight, he was remarkably handsome and there was no doubt she was attracted to him. Now here he was obviously completely insane.

"Anyway I need your help," said Knight oblivious to Susan's concerns. "I need you to meet me at the front entrance to the hotel in a hour and a half, dressed for a hike in the desert.

Susan stared at him blankly.

"I've got to go bring Flynn up to speed. After that you and I will drive out to the golf course and see if we can find Isis!"

Susan smiled, she had heard a raving lunatic responded well to kindness.

"I need you to get copies of the topographical maps for a thirty mile radius around the golf course." he ordered. Then not waiting for an acknowledgement, he again took out his phone. This time he talked to Steve his butler. "I need you to call the…," he paused, took the fax back from Susan and read the name, "The Pleasant View Sanitarium and ask if they have an eighty year-old man with one leg and then call me back on my cell."

"One leg?" Susan asked overhearing the conversation.

Knight ended the call and said, "Yeah…he cut off the other one with his pocket knife."

"His pocket knife?"

Knight ignored the question. "I'll pick you up in front of the main entrance in an hour and a half." He repeated and started to walk away. Then he paused, turned and said, "I almost forgot the bad news."

Susan looked at the poor pathetic creature and smiled patronizingly. Perhaps she could persuade him to take a long supervised vacation in the sanitarium until he was sane again.

"I assume you have Flynn's golf course insured?" he asked.

"Yes…why?" she answered with a frown.

"Well I'm afraid that you might have to cover his fifty million dollar loss when the volcano blows."

———·———

Jack Flynn was pacing the floor impatiently when Knight was shown into his office. "Where in the world have you been?" he demanded. Before Knight could answer he continued, "While you were out gallivanting around I got another extortion note."

Knight was shocked. The kidnappers had indicated they would not make contact again until tomorrow. In his experience, it was highly unusual for kidnappers not to keep to their timetable. "What did they say?"

Flynn went over to the wastebasket under his desk and rummaged around. He retrieved the wadded ball of paper and tossed it to Knight. "Here read it yourself."

Knight caught the paper missile in mid-air and sat down in one of the side chairs, unfolded the document and smoothed it out on the arm of the chair. It was a copy of an email. It read,

If you want your three hundred bathtubs back, pay us three hundred thousand dollars by midnight. Small bills in a metal suitcase, leave in second dumpster marked with an X behind the souvenir shop at Paradise and Flamingo. We will call you with the location of the tubs after we get the money.

"You scared the hell out of me!" said Knight in an annoyed tone. "I thought this was a note from Isis's kidnappers."

"Well they kidnapped my bathtubs!" Flynn exclaimed with a scowl.

"What are you going to do?" asked Knight in a tone that implied Flynn should be handling the problem. He laid the crumpled email on the desk.

"I told Bulldog to pay off. I need those bathtubs like yesterday. Bulldog is as worthless as tits on a boar hog, but even he should be able to put a suitcase in a dumpster."

Knight chuckled to himself; every time Flynn was really upset, he always reverted to the colorful expressions used in the rural Kansas of his youth.

"I've got that techno nerd convention starting tomorrow and have already rented those rooms."

"Can't you get some bathtubs from somewhere else?" asked Knight.

"Like I haven't already thought of that!" Flynn exclaimed sarcastically. "It would take two weeks to get that many here from somewhere else. I'm losing three hundred thousand dollars a day. I'm going to pay, just to cut my losses. Maybe Bulldog can run down the punk that took them later. Right now, I just want the frigging tubs back!"

Knight was relieved that Bulldog had been chosen to run the errand. He felt he was so close to having an answer about Isis that he did not want to have any more distractions. "Have you got the money?" he asked.

"Yeah, one of my assistants is down buying a metal suitcase in the shopping arcade. I'll have it ready in an hour."

Knight stood up. There was no reason to bring up the mess about the golf course. Flynn was in no mood to listen rationally to the concept that he could lose fifty million on top of the three hundred thousand.

Flynn asked, "Anything on Isis?"

"Not yet," replied Knight, "but I'm hoping something will come up soon." He was trying to sound reassuring.

"I miss her."

"We'll get her back," said Knight, secretly praying from his mouth to God's ears.

Flynn nodded and then added casually, "Oh, by the way, I paid that eighty thousand dollar marker you ran up at the craps table last night."

"That's generous," said Knight. He certainly had not expected that.

Flynn smirked mischievously, "Not so generous when you consider that we had to tell the IRS. It used to be that we could handle markers like that off the books, but now the IRS watches everything. They are everywhere and just looking for any excuse to put my balls in a vise. Anyway, according to the accountants, the IRS is going to treat it as income to you and they want you to pay the taxes."

"That will teach me not to gamble," said Knight shaking his head. The memory was still fresh of how Susan had beaten his brains out in the test of wills at the crap table.

———·———

Steve had called the sanitarium, confirmed that Buck Anders was indeed a patient, and on Knight's further instruction arranged a visit.

The sanitarium looked more like a large Italian villa than an institution. It was obvious that it was an expensive place to convalesce.

Knight announced himself at the gate and then maneuvered the Ferrari up the winding drive. The grounds were impeccable and it would take a small army of gardeners to keep them looking that way. There were no other cars in the visitor's parking spaces next to the covered portico. He picked up a package from the passenger's seat, exited the car and then locked the doors with the keyless entry pad on the key chain. Every time he used the clever device, he smiled. A purist would have gone ballistic at the thought of adding such a gauche accessory to a classic car.

A small fountain to the left of the entrance doors burbled pleasantly, further adding to the image of tranquility that the facility was trying to project. On the front door a small sign lettered in gold proclaimed, *Visitors by Appointment Only*. Knight ignored the sign and walked through the beveled glass and oak doors into the exquisitely furnished lobby area.

There was a small antique desk just inside the door. A small man in a dark tailored suit stood up as Knight entered, "I am the sanitarium's Director. May I help you?" He asked with a tone of annoyance as he pressed the tips of his fingers together.

He reminded Knight of an over eager mortician. "Yes. My name is Thomas Knight and I have an appointment to see Mr. Buck Anders."

The Director studied the tall, dark haired interloper thoroughly, "Oh yes. Your office called. You understand, of course, that we normally only allow our guests to be inconvenienced upon a doctor's recommendation."

Knight drew himself up to his full six-foot three height and looked down at the diminutive Director. "I appreciate your making an exception," he said forcefully.

The Director pondered his options for a second and then, like electricity, took the path of least resistance. "I will have you escorted to Mr. Anders." He took a small walkie-talkie from inside his suit coat pocket and turning away from Knight spoke quietly. Satisfied that he had forwarded his instructions he turned back, returned the walkie-talkie to his coat and said. "It will be just a minute. Please be seated. Would you like some refreshment?"

Knight shook off the offer and chose a chair where he could see both the outside door and the back of the lobby. It was pleasantly cool in the lobby and other than the hum of the air conditioner; there was no other sound. The Director silently walked across the double padded carpet and exited through a rear door.

Knight was pondering what this meeting might reveal when the rear door opened and a large, swarthy looking, male nurse in a heavily starched, white uniform approached. He was a full head taller than Knight was. "This way sir," he ordered.

Knight got up and followed him, noticing that exiting through the door required a code entered on an electronic keypad. Once inside, the interior of the facility was startlingly stark compared to the sumptuous lobby. It was well lit and the tile floors glistened from their overnight wax and buff. They walked down several corridors before the nurse stopped at a door and keyed in another code. The electronic lock snapped and the door opened automatically. It led into a large day room and there were several guests, as the Director had referred to them, sitting quietly throughout the room. The nurse checked to be sure Knight was following him and led him to a small alcove with potted plants. A large picture window offered a magnificent view of Mount Charleston. Obviously, the view had provided the inspiration for the sanitarium's name. A small, emaciated man with the lower part of his body covered with a wool blanket was seated in a wheelchair.

"Good luck," snickered the nurse sarcastically as he left without making an introduction.

Knight moved around in front of the figure and looked into the pale but deeply lined face. "Mr. Anders?" Knight asked. There was no reply only a catatonic stare. Knight put his hand on the man's shoulder and shook him gently. "Mr. Anders?" he asked again.

"He can't tell you anything," said a voice with obvious authority. Knight turned and was surprised to see a very elderly woman in a motorized wheelchair. "His mind has been gone for sixty years," she proclaimed.

Knight looked at the petite, white haired lady with amazement. She looked as if she could be easily a hundred years old, but her voice was crisp and concise. "Who are you?" he asked.

"I'm Vera, his nurse, Sonny! Who in Hades are you?"

"Thomas Knight. Did you say you were his nurse?" he asked incredulously.

"Jeez…I'm ninety three years old and my hearing is perfect. Evidently you need to have yours checked!" she answered defiantly, shaking her head in disgust.

Knight smiled, his grandmother had called him Sonny and had the same proper aversion to swearing. The frail lady reminded him of her. She had the same feisty attitude. "I was surprised to hear you were his nurse that's all," he said trying to clarify why he was not a candidate for a hearing aid.

"Well…I'm waiting," Vera said impatiently. "What do you want?"

Knight looked closely at his interrogator, in spite of her weak appearance and advanced years she was no pushover. "I found something in the desert and when I found out Buck was still alive, I thought he might want it back."

Vera looked at the package under Knight's arm. "I don't suppose you'd happen to have a quart of bourbon in the sack?" she asked hopefully. "I do like my bourbon."

"I'm afraid not," apologized Knight with a smile, his grandmother had been equally fond of the potent brown elixir. He carefully unwrapped the package and took out the ancient boot, spur and leg bone.

"Jeez…Louise!" exclaimed Vera, her eyes dancing. "Where did you find that?"

"In the desert north of town. I was told it was Buck's."

Vera guided her chair expertly over to Knight and gingerly took the artifact and examined it closely. "It's Buck's all right!" she exclaimed. "People have been looking for this for sixty years."

"So I understand."

Vera ran her bony fingers along the weathered polished bone. "I thought I would never see this."

"Well it doesn't look like Buck will know he got his leg back."

"I'm afraid not," said Vera, still stroking the bone.

"I was hoping he might be able to tell me something about a diamond he supposedly found," said Knight.

Vera snapped her head up and angrily shook the white bone at him. Her eyes were flashing. "That darned diamond has caused more grief than you'll ever know, Sonny," she swore.

"How so?"

"Well for one thing it's the only reason that Buck here has not been allowed to die. He should have passed on years ago. He certainly hasn't had any quality of life."

"What do you mean he hasn't been allowed die?"

"Every time that he was about to leave us, this place would pull out all stops to prevent it. It wasn't pleasant to watch." Vera put the bone back in her lap and her anger subsided.

"Who and why did they want to keep him alive?" asked Knight.

"The who is that abomination known as Baby Doc," she answered. "The why is because Buck is the only one that knows where that confounded diamond came from."

"If he has been like this for years then he couldn't tell anyone anything, including this Baby Doc," observed Knight.

Vera's eyes started flashing again with anger. "It didn't stop Baby Doc from trying." She maneuvered her wheelchair in front of Buck and using the bone, gingerly parted Buck's gown to expose his stomach. Knight looked on in horror. There were obvious burn scars covering Buck's entire lower body. "My Gosh!" he said softly.

"They worked on him for years and all they ever got was the ravings of a lunatic."

"They?" asked Knight.

"Baby Doc and the so-called doctors he hired."

Knight shook his head. He never ceased to be amazed at how human beings could be so cruel to one another. "Who exactly is Baby Doc?"

"Are you sure you don't have any bourbon?" Vera asked again, hoping against hope.

"I'm afraid not," apologized Knight. "I would've brought some if I would have known I would run into you."

Vera looked disappointed. "I haven't had a good drink in years. I used to have a nurse that I could bribe now and then to sneak in a bottle, but he retired. This asshole I've got now constantly teases me but never comes through."

Knight smiled, her ladylike demeanor had gone out the window. "About Baby Doc," he reminded her.

Vera looked out the window at the mountains and said softly. "It all started back in 1946. I was employed by a doctor in Indian Springs by the name of Prentice. He was the one that saved Buck after he cut his leg off."

She looked back at Knight to see if he was paying attention. Seeing he was, she continued the story by telling how Old Doc Prentice had found the rock that Buck had dropped in the emergency room. How years later he found it to be a diamond. She told how Old

Doc's wife had fallen into the bottle and then ended up pregnant by an unknown someone. She described the birth and the injury done to the first baby by the application of the forceps.

Knight interrupted, "There were twins?"

"Totally unexpected," answered Vera. "Old Doc's wife, finding the one baby was horribly damaged and would never improve, rejected both of them, even though the second one was perfect. The babies never formed an emotional bond with their mother. It wasn't surprising that both developed severe detachment disorders."

Knight shook his head.

Vera continued, "Old Doc felt sympathy for the children but also was unable to muster any real attachment. The first born, the forceps baby, developed into a huge, misshapen creature with a bad attitude. The locals gave him the name Baby Doc. Over the years, in spite of special attention from the well-meaning women of the town, he turned into a dangerous sociopath. He takes immense pleasure in terrorizing everyone in town. They're all afraid of what he might do next."

"What happened to the Doctor?" asked Knight trying to move the story along.

Vera was not about to be rushed; it was not often she had someone sane to talk to, "His wife quickly returned to the bottle after the births and proceeded over the next three years to drink herself to death. Old Doc withdrew from his practice, moved into an old trailer in the desert, and retreated into a world of his own, consumed with his hunt for the source of the diamond."

"Didn't the townspeople catch on?" asked Knight.

"To disguise his search for the treasure he told everyone he had an interest in desert flora. Indeed, he became a leading expert on the plants in the area. He was so convincing that when he went out to prospect, nobody questioned his intent. Everyone simply assumed that it was his way of dealing with his wife's addiction. Somehow, he caught pneumonia and it proved to be too much for his system. He was worn down by years of self-neglect. He died coughing himself to death in his trailer, unable to even check himself into the small clinic he founded.

"How does this Baby Doc afford to keep you two in this place?" asked Knight, glancing around the sparkling facility.

"Old Doc was a strong believer in insurance and when he died, he was the most insured person in Clark County. Thus, his children, as the only surviving beneficiaries, each inherited a small fortune when they turned twenty-one. Take two screwed up kids and give them money and you've got a recipe for trouble. The money removed any need for them to pursue any socially redeeming activities. Baby Doc, in particular, indulges himself to excess, not caring in the least about the consequences of his actions. He only cares about himself."

"If Old Doc was as paranoid as you say, how did Baby Doc find out about the diamond?" asked Knight.

"The locals claim that Old Doc, as he scoured the desert, kept a journal documenting his search. It was his best-kept secret and while several had seen the book, no one had ever seen its contents. Supposedly, the only witness to his final words was his first-born, sociopathic monster of a son. According to the story, on his death bed, Old Doc finally revealed the contents of his long kept secret journal and passed it and Buck's diamond onto the creature."

"Why didn't the locals try to find the treasure?" Knight wondered aloud.

"Oh some did and a few even disappeared while looking. But then the Army came in and turned most of the area into the Nevada Test Site and the locals found other diversions."

Knight asked, "Baby Doc kept on looking?"

Vera nodded, "Old Doc was fixated on finding the treasure, but Baby Doc is totally consumed by the thought of riches beyond measure. Eventually the story about the diamond just kind of faded away. Anyway, the locals were both surprised and relieved when Baby Doc suddenly started keeping to the desert. They prayed that whatever was keeping him so preoccupied would continue."

"How did he end up in here?" asked Knight nodding at Buck.

"Old Doc realized that Buck was the only one who actually knew the source of the diamond and so he had him removed from the State Home and put in here. He hoped that somehow Buck's mind would return long enough to reveal the source. Unfortunately, as you can see he has never recovered."

"How about you?"

"Using some of his share of the inheritance, Baby Doc had taken over the cost of Buck's confinement and hired me to look in on him. Where Old Doc had hoped to get a few lucid moments from Buck, Baby Doc took the more proactive approach of torture."

Knight looked at Vera, her eyes were full of sadness. She continued, "After a while I couldn't look after myself, let alone Buck, so Baby Doc paid for me to move in here full time. It was not really to keep an eye on Buck, but more to prevent me from doing anything about how he was being treated. I am as much a prisoner as Buck."

"Does Baby Doc still mistreat Buck?" Knight asked.

"No…not for years now. He finally gave up after getting nothing but Buck's ditty for all his efforts and money."

"Buck's ditty?"

"Yeah…he has been singing the same goldurned refrain for sixty years. It is all he has ever said."

Knight's curiosity was piqued. "Does he still sing it?"

"Yes. I can get him to sing it." Suddenly, Vera's guard went up, "Look Sonny, I don't know you. All I know is you are someone who waltzed in here with Buck's old leg and started asking a bunch of questions. And besides, you don't have anything to drink."

Knight realized that in spite of her frail appearance, her mind was still razor sharp and she was no pushover. He showed his hand. "I represent the owner of one of the Strip's hotels. His wife was kidnapped from his golf course north of Indian Springs and I'm trying to find her."

Vera shook her head in disbelief, "Sonny that's a load of horse puckey. There is no golf course north of Indian Springs."

Knight realized that he had wrongly assumed that she was up on current affairs. "How long have you been in here?" he asked.

"Twenty years. What's it to you?" she challenged.

"The golf course that I'm talking about was built within the last year. Maybe that's why you didn't know about it."

Vera looked at him, trying to decide if he was telling the truth. He had a strong, but honest face and he had not threatened her. "It's true about the kidnapping?" she asked cautiously.

"It's true," he answered.

"How does Buck fit in?"

"I'm not sure. The only thing I do know is that every way I turn it seems to end up back at Buck's diamond. Someone or something has been methodically searching the desert around the golf course and I'm assuming whatever it is, it must be looking for the source of the diamond. My instincts tell me that there is probably a connection between that hunt and the kidnapping."

Vera softened. "Would it really help if Buck sang his ditty?"

"I don't know. What's it say?"

"Nobody has been able to make heads or tails out of it for sixty years so I guess it wouldn't do any harm if you heard it too," said Vera. "But, I must warn you it isn't pleasant to watch what I have to do to get him to sing it."

Knight looked concerned, "I don't want to do anything to hurt him."

"Oh, he doesn't really feel anything one way or the other, but it is the only way to get him to sing." Not waiting for Knight's approval she moved her chair directly in front of Buck, leaned over and again lifted the front of his gown with her left hand. With her right hand, she reached over and pinched the heavily scarred pale flesh on Buck's abdomen.

Buck jerked involuntarily and then whispered in a singsong voice, "The lizard stared at me and winked. The shadows played the flute...but I plucked its eye and he blinked."

Vera looked at a puzzled Knight, "I told you. Nobody has been able to make any sense out of it."

Knight shook his head and gently placed his hand on Buck's arm and said, "I'm sorry, Pardner."

Vera smoothed out Buck's gown and pulled up the wool blanket. There were tears in her eyes.

They were interrupted by the large male nurse, "Are you two done playing with the veggie?"

Knight stood up suddenly and with a roundhouse uppercut punched the source of the offensive remark in the solar plexus.

With a loud "Uh," the big nurse doubled over and fell to his knees gasping, trying to catch his breath.

Vera clapped her bony hands together in delight at seeing her tormentor in pain.

"I'll have someone bring you a bottle," said Knight over his shoulder as he strode across the day room.

Buck's refrain was still going around in his head as he squealed the tires on the Ferrari down the sanitarium's drive.

CHAPTER 9

Susan was waiting impatiently at the Colossus's porte cochere. She checked her three-dialed Patek Philippe watch. Thomas Knight was already nine and a half minutes late. Susan had a thing about punctuality. Her father had been maniacal about being on time. Evidently, it was an inherited gene.

She had just glanced at the watch again when the bright red, wedge shaped car skidded to a stop in front of her. She opened the door and slid into the tan, smooth leather seat.

"I'm sorry I'm late," apologized Knight seeing the frustration on her face. Without waiting for a response, he accelerated around the other cars under the canopy. He was carrying too much speed over the drainage curb next to the street and the car bounced and bottomed, momentarily leaving a shower of sparks.

"You'll get us killed before we get two blocks at this rate!" exclaimed Susan as she tightened the aircraft style seat belt.

"Sorry," said Knight sheepishly as he slowed to match the traffic. She was right, there was no sense in having an accident, not when he was this close to having Isis's case resolved. "Incidentally, you look great," he admired as he gave the gorgeous blonde next to him the once over. She always looked good even when she was wearing, as he had requested, appropriate desert attire, good solid hiking boots, long sleeve blouse and jeans. She was holding a large straw hat and a pocket type purse in her lap.

She peeked at him over the top of her designer dark glasses. "Just watch the road," she chided.

"I picked up a good lead over at the sanitarium," he announced proudly.

"They didn't want to keep you for observation?" she teased, half serious. After the ridiculous conversation by the pool, she was still convinced he was completely insane.

Knight ignored her comment. "I found out a ton of info from Buck Anders's nurse."

"He's the one that cut off his own leg with his pocketknife, right?" she asked sarcastically.

Knight glanced at her trying to figure out what she meant by her tone of voice. "The same," he answered. "It turns out that I found the name of someone who might be connected to Isis's kidnapping."

"I thought his name was Spook."

Knight looked at her disgustedly. "That's the Army's term. I'm talking about Baby Doc."

"The ex-Haitian dictator!" exclaimed Susan praying that this was not going to be another one of his lunatic ravings.

Knight looked at her utterly confused. He was making perfect sense and she was acting as if he was out of his mind. "No not the ex-Dictator!" he spat out impatiently. "Darn it Susan this is serious," he lectured. He was in no mood for her games. "Did you bring the maps I asked for?"

Susan sensed he was getting angry. For some inexplicable reason she felt herself caring about how he felt. "Yes, they're in my purse."

The thirty-minute trip to the golf course went by quickly. Knight turned the Ferrari loose once they were out of the city traffic. And in spite of Susan's constant interruptions, by the time they turned onto the golf course road he was convinced that she was up to speed with what was going on.

———·———

Back in Las Vegas, the loud scream coming out of the stuccoed home overlooking the 13th green of the golf course broke the concentration of the player putting out.

The plasma screen television showed the NBA power forward in the yellow jersey making his patented no look pass. The trailing guard caught the ball in mid-stride and pulled up for the three point jump shot. The entire arena was transfixed following the flight of the ball. The ball hit the inside back of the rim and bounced almost vertically into the air. Finally yielding to the inimitable laws of gravity, it fell back through the net. The final buzzer sounded. The most knowledgeable fans did not yield to the immediate temptation to cheer, but instead shifted their eyes to the referee, who with an exaggerated stutter step motioned up and down with his hand that the basket counted.

Dwight Basham aka Bulldog threw the television remote control across the room and again screamed at the top of his voice, "No!" It was not possible he had lost the bet on the game. He had taken every dime he still had and had lost it all. Now, there was no alternative, he would have to have the big score to salvage his life.

He could not control his anger as he backed the black, the salesman had insisted upon calling the color obsidian, Hummer H2 with the tinted windows out of the four-car garage. He pounded on the leather wrapped steering wheel and shouted. "No! No!"

Bulldog, thanks to Knight's tutelage, was reasonably competent at his job and everything would have probably turned out well except for one major thing. Bulldog possessed one very bad flaw. He was envious. He did not have just a little envy he had a lot of envy. He envied Knight's reputation and Flynn's power. He envied the big shooter gamblers that could blow fortunes at the Colossus. His nice six-figure salary and all the comps that his job provided were more than adequate to properly pay him for what Flynn asked him to do. In fact, he spent so much time at the hotel that it allowed him to bank almost his entire salary. The house on the golf course and the intimidating black Hummer had been his only real indulgences. However, Bulldog had not banked his money. Any money he made, he tried to leverage by the worst of all processes in Vegas. He gambled and he lost.

He had an anti-gambling clause in his contract that forbade him from gambling in any form at the Colossus or anywhere. To all outward appearances, he appeared to be complying with the contract. However, he was gambling: primarily on the sports books.

The really big-time subsistence gamblers in Vegas played either the sports books or poker. When you gambled at the table games or the slots you played against the casino. There was always the chance that the casino could lose, even though they had all the odds in their favor. Contrary to their massive public relations programs that claimed they were happy when their patrons won, the casinos hated to lose. If you were somehow able to defy the odds and win, you were immediately suspected of cheating. If you beat them consistently, they made sure that you knew that they were unhappy about it. If they decided you were too lucky, they simply banned you from playing in their casino. The pros, whose livelihood depended on their winning, could find themselves behind the eight ball with no place to play. To overcome this problem, the casinos had made a place for the pros by letting them play poker and the sports books. In those games, you were not playing against the house but instead, against other players. Regardless of who won or lost, the casino collected a rake or commission from the amount bet. It was classic Vegas, the casino won and the pros won, both at the expense of the hapless amateur gambler who could only dream of winning.

Gambling professionally, using the sports books, involved an elaborate system to escape the prying eyes of the IRS. Someone with a large amount of money to wager placed it with one of the major sports books by using a series of runners to take the bets to the casinos. This was illegal of course, but the casinos cast a blind eye to the practice because it was a way for them to indulge the big bettors while increasing their cut of the action. Occasionally just to make it appear that things were on the up and up they would throw a small fish to the authorities.

Bulldog had found one of these runners working the Colossus and rather than sacrifice him, had converted him to his own use. The two had never met. The system worked by having the runner paged and then he responded to the page by calling an unlisted 800 number. Bulldog then gave him his instructions as to what bet was to be placed, where to pick up the money to be wagered and where to deliver the winnings, if any. For his services, the runner received an envelope full of cash every week. The legend of welchers being buried alive in the *Gambler's Graveyard* kept the runners in line.

———·———

Knight and Susan had usurped the best table in the dining room of the Colossus's golf course clubhouse. Topographical maps covered the entire surface and Knight was studying them intently.

"What are you doing now?" asked Susan.

"I'm trying to find how someone could have taken Isis from the golf course without being seen," he answered. "I've marked the spot where she was abducted." He pointed to a small red x on the first map. He flipped over to the second map and pointed to another x. "That's where I saw Spook."

"What's that mean?" asked Susan pointing to a black x on the same map.

"Well I don't know if it means anything. But using the landmarks I identified and referencing them with hands on my watch I was able to triangulate where I found Buck's leg."

Susan looked at the map, "Well if I had just kidnapped someone I would probably want to make the shortest getaway."

"That's what I figure also," agreed Knight. "Using that theory they would have probably escaped by the highway and the shortest route to the highway would have brought them out about here." He pointed to a spot on the road about three miles south of the entrance to the golf course.

"Even if we find where they came out, how will we pick up their trail once they're on the highway?" Susan asked.

Knight shook his head, "I don't know. But, I suspect that he has used that spot to park his vehicle many times. Maybe someone will have seen it."

Susan shrugged resignedly, "It's pretty thin, but is probably the best option to look at."

"I want to go out to the spot where she was taken," said Knight. "I still haven't figured out how the kidnapper managed to surprise her. You can see for miles out there."

"Well I brought my hiking boots," said Susan holding up one of her legs so Knight could see.

"Let's go," said Knight as he gathered up the maps. "How are you on horseback? It's the best way to get out there."

"I can hold my own," she answered. "You didn't forget how we rode together in Palm Springs did you?"

Knight chuckled; he was remembering how he had rescued her by flinging her across his saddle during that fiasco.

"By the way," she asked. "What exactly did you mean when you said I might have to pay off this place when the volcano blows?"

"I'll explain it on the way. C'mon, Pardner we're burning daylight!" He congratulated himself for working in his favorite expression from his summer job in college, working as a Colorado cowboy.

The afternoon shadows were lengthening by the time the two of them reached the kidnap site.

"It's lovely out here," said Susan as she dismounted. She was grateful the ride had not been longer. She definitely was not acclimated to horseback riding.

"It would be if it weren't a crime scene," agreed Knight. He had adjusted the length of the stirrups on his saddle twice during the ride but his butt told him that they were still not right. He dismounted and took both horses' reins and tied them to sagebrush with a half hitch. While Susan looked around, he reached into his saddlebag and took out one of the topographical maps. He pointed to the southeast. "They probably went that way," he said with a casual wave of his hand. When he turned around Susan had vanished. "What the…" he exclaimed.

A faint voice called, "Help! I'm over here!"

Knight still could not see her, but ran in the direction of the voice. He was nearly on top of her before he saw the hole she fallen into. He peered over the edge. "Are you okay?"

"Does it look like I am?" Susan asked angrily, dusting off her clothes.

Knight grabbed her hand and pulled her out of the hole, surprised at how little she weighed.

"Why didn't you tell me about that?" she questioned. Her accusatory tone left little doubt that she thought it was Knight's fault that she had fallen into the hole.

"I didn't know it was there," he answered, shocked that he had not seen it on his previous examination of the site. "Didn't you see it?"

"Now would I have stepped in it, if I had?" she answered rhetorically. "It was covered over with that sheet or whatever it is."

Knight went to the edge of hole and pulled out what indeed looked like a sand colored tarp.

"It's a camouflage cover," he said as he lifted it completely out of the hole.

The hole was about four feet deep and about five feet square. A large man could sit down in it and his head would be below the desert surface.

Knight remarked, "So that's how is done."

Susan looked at him quizzically, "How's what done?"

"How Spook has been able to avoid being seen by the camo dudes. He must have holes like this all over the place," he said gesturing around him. "I wouldn't be surprised if he wasn't sitting in the hole and Isis simply fell in on top of him, just like you did."

"You mean she wasn't kidnapped?"

"Oh, she was kidnapped all right. Only now I think it was just an accident. I don't think it was planned."

Susan shook her head skeptically, "How do you explain the ransom note?"

"Simple," clarified Knight. "Whoever was in the hole and took Isis decided to make the best out of the accident."

"I guess it could have happened that way," agreed Susan reluctantly. She hated to admit that his theory made sense. "But, we still need to find out exactly who took her and where."

"The tracks lead that way," said Knight studying the ground and pointing.

Susan looked where he was pointing. "I don't see anything."

"That's because he was wearing snowshoes," said Knight definitively. "In fact," he said as he got down on one knee and squinted at the ground, "I'm positive that the tracks were made by the Overland Model twenty-one." It was all he could do to not laugh aloud at the look of amazement on Susan's face. "Let's turn the horses back into the stable and drive down the highway to the spot we picked. Who knows what we might find."

Susan was still stiff from the ride out but gamely smiled as she mounted her horse. There was no way she would let Knight see she was hurting.

"Hi-Yo, Silver! Away!" shouted Knight remembering the refrain his father had told him that the Lone Ranger, the famous radio lawman, had used. He spurred his horse toward the clubhouse. He had forgotten how much fun it was to be a cowboy.

The desert was producing another spectacular sunset by the time Knight and Susan turned in their horses to the stable's groom. Susan was glad that little escapade was over. Her butt was thoroughly sore from the ride. She hoped Knight had not noticed her slightly bowlegged gait. "Do you really think that a volcano could destroy this place?" she asked as the Ferrari proceeded down the drive to the entrance. That would be a shame she thought. Flynn's wife had done an outstanding job of decorating the place. It was a first-class facility. To think of the beautifully manicured golf course and clubhouse covered in volcanic lava and ash was inconceivable.

"Who knows," answered Knight. "The Army hasn't had the best record of being right on things like this. After all, it was their own miscalculations about the effects of their atomic tests that made the whole incredible scenario possible. I would hate to see it happen," he added.

Susan looked at him. He frustrated her, but to be fair she had to admit that she brought on most of it herself. She had not been in a relationship for a long time. Her skills of dealing with intimacy had severely atrophied, but given time she would be back to her old self.

Knight looked at her and smiled. There was no motive behind it; he just felt a sudden warmth toward her. It was remarkable given how she was constantly goading him.

Susan smiled back. She had to admit that this tall, tanned; strong specimen was definitely her type. They had kissed before in Palm Springs and each time she felt as if a million volts of electricity had shot through her. No one had ever affected her that way.

Knight pulled the Ferrari off the highway onto a turnout cut into the desert. "This is where Spook probably intersects the highway," he announced. He stopped the car and exited without waiting for a reply from Susan.

"What do you hope to find?" she asked as she wiggled her way out of the confining seat of the low-slung car.

"I'll know it when I find it," he answered sarcastically, he was in no mood for sparring.

An examination of the area revealed nothing but the expected highway litter. Knight hated to accept it, but there did not appear to be anything of value to investigate.

"Hi," said Susan unexpectedly.

Knight turned quickly to see to whom she was talking.

It was a bicyclist in full road racing attire riding down the shoulder of the highway. "Hi," he answered breathlessly, not interrupting his practiced pedaling stroke.

Knight moved toward him. "Excuse me. Can I ask you a question?"

The cyclist unclipped his cycling shoes from his pedals, squeezed the handlebar brakes and stopped. "What do you want?" he asked impatiently, obviously miffed at having his exercise routine interrupted.

"Do you ride by here often?" Knight answered the question with a question.

"Almost every day," said the cyclist. "Weather permitting. It's part of my daily twenty miles. Why?"

"Whew!" said Knight admiringly. "You have to be in serious shape to maintain a routine like that." Then he asked, "Have you ever seen anything strange around here?"

"Sorry, I just watch the road. Rattlesnakes, you know," answered the cyclist as he clipped into the pedals again and started peddling. He went about fifty feet before he unclipped and stopped. He turned back over his shoulder. "There is an ice cream truck parked here frequently."

"An ice cream truck?" repeated Knight.

"Yeah, you know, like the kind the kids run after." Then the cyclist clipped in again and pedaled off into the enveloping darkness.

"An ice cream truck?" repeated Susan.

"Maybe Spook likes pralines 'n cream," answered Knight sarcastically as he crawled back into the Ferrari.

———.———

The shapely, brunette Captain knocked on the General Guts Grant's door.

"Come!" barked Guts, trying to mimic the military characters he had seen on television

The brunette entered, stood at attention and announced, "Sir, the latest seismologist's report."

Guts did not look up, but instead extended his hand.

The brunette placed the document in his right hand and returned to attention.

Guts ignored her and skimmed the fax. "Damn!" he exclaimed as he slapped the paper with the back of his left hand.

The brunette Captain jumped slightly at the sudden outburst. "Sir?" she asked tentatively.

Guts read the fax again, carefully this time. "Have the staff in Conference Room B in fifteen minutes," he barked and waved his hand toward the door as if to shoo her away.

"Yes, Sir," replied the Captain as she turned smartly toward the door. She was nearly there when she was called back.

"Wait!" ordered Guts.

She turned, "Sir?"

"You better get a hold of that smart mouthed guy with the golf course. What's his name?"

"Thomas Knight?" asked the brunette with a hopeful sparkle in her eye.

"Yeah, that's the one," spit Guts, not trying to hide the contempt in his voice. "Tell him I want the place cleared by 1400 hours day after tomorrow. It would allow for a three-hour margin. Things could easily get FUBAR when civilians were involved.

"Yes Sir!" exclaimed the Captain, eager to have an excuse to talk to the handsome hunk again.

"Oh...and by the way, get Senator Devlin on the phone ASAP."

The brunette Captain left and Guts had barely finished reading the fax again when his intercom announced. "Sir, Senator Devlin is on line one."

Guts picked up the phone, "Joe," he said with an out of place familiarity, "Operation Big Deal is a go at 1700 hours day after tomorrow."

———·———

Darkness had final engulfed the desert. Susan looked at the handsome driver illuminated by the dashboard's lights. She had not felt what she was feeling since Palm Springs. There was no explaining it and she was helpless when it over came her. It always lurked in the background just below the surface. Her brain knew it was emotionally dangerous to ever let it loose. But, her heart betrayed her and let the evil demon of feelings overtake her. She did what she always did when it happened. She flirted shamelessly.

Susan leaned across to Knight and gently cradling his chin in her right hand kissed him behind the right ear.

Knight shuddered violently; it was the only spot on his entire body that was ticklish. He scrunched his shoulder up toward his ear in a fruitless attempt to ward off the soft pecking of her lips. It was driving him crazy! The car drifted back and forth across the inky black highway as he fought to keep the involuntary shudders under control. "Dammit Susan, I can't drive with you doing that!"

She ignored his plea and instead supplemented her ear kisses by dropping her hand down from his chin to his crotch. She started to gently rub him through his 501 Levis.

Knight bolted upright at her touch and this time the car swerved violently. "I'm going to have a wreck!" he scolded as he reached up to push her velvet like lips away from his ear. It was impossible to fight this war on two fronts!

"Well…pull over!" she ordered as she tightened her grip on his crotch.

Knight braked hard and turned the car off the highway and onto a gravel access. He was going too fast to make a smooth transition and the Ferrari bounced wildly as it started careening along the rough gravel road. Actually, it was more of a trail than a road. The bright red car was throwing up a rooster tail of light gray dust.

Susan's head hit the headliner. "Are you trying to kill us?"

Knight did not answer, instead he stepped on the brakes, and the vented discs responded with authority.

The car skidded on the gravel before coming to a stop, completely engulfed in a cloud of dust. Knight turned off the engine, threw his arms around Susan, and found her mouth with his. Their tongues fought each other like serpents.

With their mouths still pressed together, they clawed at each other's clothes. Susan grabbed the collars of Knight's shirt with both hands and ripped downward. The buttons popped and flew around the interior tinkling against the inside of the windshield like the payoff on a quarter video poker machine.

Knight slid his hands up under Susan's silk blouse and fondled her soft warm breasts. He tickled her hardening nipples with his thumbs.

"I…I don't think…there is enough room," protested Susan between kisses.

Knight grunted and shifted his body to get above her. Susan lifted her left leg and slid it over the tan colored leather console. Knight reached down and unbuttoned his pants to free himself.

"Oh…my gosh!" she exclaimed. "You're huge!" Susan's hand had found the erect appendage between her legs. She fondled it and then with a start asked, "What's that?"

"What's what?"

"You're deformed!" shouted Susan, her lust making her oblivious to Knight's feelings.

Knight looked down and then laughed. "That's not me! That's the gear shift!"

Susan yanked her hand back as if it had been scalded. "Who buys a car with the gear shift on the floor anyway?" she asked as her face blushed with embarrassment.

Knight kissed her again and mumbled, "They don't make Testarossas with automatics."

The console was a real impediment to their passion and the two of them shifted repeatedly to try to get into a more promising position.

Susan scraped her manicured nails across Knight's chest and then tried to peel his now buttonless shirt from his shoulders. His shoulder holster was proving to be an obstacle and the shirt was soon hopelessly tangled. "You could help," she pleaded sarcastically, between Knight's kisses.

"Don't drop my Glock," mumbled Knight, moving his kisses from her lips to her neck.

"Oh yuck!" she exclaimed. "You have a name for it!"

"What?"

"You...you know."

Knight looked up quizzically into her soft blue eyes, "My Glock?"

"Why didn't you name it...you know...Willie...or something like that?"

Knight giggled, "My pistol is a Glock, not my manhood!"

Susan was not amused by her faux pas. She just knew she was too uncomfortable to make love. She reached back over her head and opened the door.

They were both huffing and puffing from exertion and anticipation when they finally untangled themselves and rolled out onto the coarse gravel of the desert. Free of the confines of the car, their lust returned and they grabbed for each other again.

Knight picked her up and held her in a bear hug as he carried her to the rear of the car. He soul kissed her as he reached down, unzipped her jeans and pulled them down to her knees. With both hands under her hips, he lifted her and placed her naked butt on the rear deck lid.

"Ow!" Susan screamed in pain as she jumped from the car into Knight's arms. "That's hot!"

Knight momentarily congratulated himself on his lovemaking technique before he realized that Susan was talking about the deck lid being hot from the rear-mounted engine. Disappointed that the rear of the car was out of the question Knight carried Susan, still locked in his bear hug, to the front of the car. They looked like some weird half-dressed four-legged animal. The gently sloping hood of the Italian machine proved more appropriate for lovemaking.

Carefully laying Susan on the hood between the still extended pop-up headlights Knight undid his belt and his pants fell free. He pulled her jeans off over her hiking boots. He grabbed Susan's knees in both hands, spread her legs wide, and then pulled them up behind him and around his own butt.

Susan was powerless as he drove himself between her thighs. "Oh," she moaned. "Yes."

Even in the harsh reflection of the headlights, Knight could see her blue eyes were flashing with passion. He kissed her deeply again and their bodies began to thrust against each other in unison.

The lingering heat of the desert and the physical energy they were expending soon had both of them covered in sweat and their bodies glistened in the headlights. They took turns maneuvering for the perfect position. They were completely unselfish with each other and finally they both fell back at the same time fully satiated.

Knight rose first. He pulled up his pants, buttoned the fly and buckled his belt. Susan found her jeans on the ground and leaning against the car for support wiggled into them. She stuffed her blouse into the waistband and zipped them up.

Knight found the remnants of his shirt inside the car and untangled the shoulder holster. He struggled to slide the shirt over his sweaty body and then walked back around to Susan. He stood directly in front of her. She had moisture in the corners of her eyes. He tilted her head back with his finger under her chin and leaned over to kiss her again.

His eyes were nearly closed in anticipation of the kiss when a sudden movement in the darkness behind the car made him freeze. He recovered instantly, pushed Susan aside, scrambled to the open driver's door, and dove for the Glock. In less than two seconds, the handgun was at the ready and the laser sight's red beam was sweeping the darkness.

Susan's eyes had been closed to receive Knight's kiss. His unexpected dash for the car surprised her and she turned to see what had happened. She saw Knight frantically digging for something in the car. When he popped up, he was waving his pistol at the darkness. She stepped around from in front of the headlights. It took a second before her eyes adjusted to the darkness. She sensed at first, rather than saw what Knight was pointing at with his pistol. Something was shuffling through the darkness away from them. Without warning, the apparition turned and looked at her. Even her hardened investigator's brain betrayed her. She screamed! Whatever it was, was staring at her with huge green phosphorescent eyes. She watched in frozen horror as a small red dot appeared between them. It was from Knight's laser sight!

The creature turned and vanished into the darkness. Susan was angry at having been so scared. "Why didn't you shoot?" she demanded.

"He wasn't a threat," replied Knight calmly. I don't think he was armed. I didn't see a weapon."

"I would've shot him anyway, just for scaring the hell out of me." Susan was shaking.

"I think he's gone," said Knight still staring into the night.

"What the hell was that?" Susan asked, her voice trembling.

"My dear, you have just been Spooked," answered Knight, hoping his own voice did not betray the presence of the adrenaline coursing through his body.

Susan was still frozen. "Those…those eyes, they weren't human," she stammered.

Knight moved over to her and put his arms around her shaking body.

She looked up into his eyes for reassurance. "I'm sorry," she said softly.

"For what?"

"For thinking you were insane. There really is an eight-foot alien."

Knight hugged her again and continued to hold her tight. "I don't think he was eight feet tall," he said.

She pulled back from him and looked into his eyes quizzically.

"Now that I've gotten a better look. I think he's only seven eleven," he said with a twinkle.

———·———

Isis Flynn emerged from her fog. The hallucinogenic drug had started wearing off. Each injection lasted less than the previous one. Her body was adjusting; it demanded more to maintain the same state of euphoria.

She looked around. It had not been a dream after all. She really was in hell, or so it smelled and looked. She tried to move, but her shackles held her back. She looked at them; they were sturdy enough to hold back a very large animal let alone a petite woman.

Only a small florescent light fixture in the rear of the cavernous room illuminated her dungeon. A bottle of water stood upright on the floor next to the leg of her cot. She turned on to her left side and with the tips of her fingers reached for the bottle. She had to work at it but she was able to stretch just far enough to coax the bottle into her hand. She laid back and unscrewed the cap. She raised her head and by tilting it to the side was able to pour the water down her inflamed throat. Nothing had ever tasted so good! She screwed the cap back on the bottle and laid back again. It was all coming back to her.

She had ridden out to the corner of the golf course property and dismounted. As she reached for a small cactus, she had mysteriously lost her footing. In an instant, she had fallen headfirst into a large hole that she had not seen. The fall had temporarily knocked the wind out of her. As she struggled to gain her breath and her equilibrium, she had heard a scream. It was hers! She was still gasping for air when she realized she was tangled in the tentacles of a giant, gray skinned monster. She screamed and the creature starred at her with giant phosphorescent green eyes. Before she could scream again, the monster placed its claws across her mouth and nostrils, blocking her air. She had struggled furiously, but she was no match for the monster's superhuman strength. She felt herself lapsing into unconsciousness. It had all taken only a few minutes but it seemed as if it took eons.

She maneuvered around; fighting her shackles, and took another drink. "How long as I've been here?" she asked herself trying to distinguish between what had been real and what had been a bad dream. She looked down, her blouse was unbuttoned and she could see but not feel the light pink bite marks on her breasts. That hideous experience had been real. She tried to cover herself with the remnants of her blouse but with her hands restrained, it was hopeless.

Suddenly the cave was illuminated completely. Someone had turned on the lights. She quietly lowered the water bottle over the side of the cot with her fingertips. She closed her eyes; she would feign being asleep until she could find out more about her captor.

The creature walked over to the helpless captive on the bed. He bent over and lifted the victim's left eyelid. The eye was dilated.

Isis summoned all her remaining strength to remain motionless and not to vomit at the putrid stench of his breath.

The beast ran a claw over the nipple of her left breast. He smiled, as the nipple involuntarily grew erect. The sudden sound of an approaching vehicle prevented him from moving his examination lower.

Isis shuddered. She struggled with all her might to avoid screaming. She wanted to be free. Free to cover herself. Barely opening her eye, she could see that the creature was having an animated conversation with another person that she could not make out. Although she could not hear what the pair was saying, there was something vaguely familiar about the voice of the unknown stranger. It was obvious that there was a substantial difference of opinion between the two.

Finally, the large creature threw up his arms in disgust turned and walked away. Evidently, he had lost the argument.

Isis found herself in the unusual position of praying that her tormentor had been lobbying to keep her alive. Then, without warning, the lights went out leaving her once again in near darkness. Her only companion was a solitary fluorescent light at the end of the cave. She listened intently, but there was nothing but complete silence. As she finally gave into exhaustion and the remnants of the drug injection, she thought she heard the bells of an ice cream truck. She must have been hallucinating.

———·———

CHAPTER 10

The Ferrari pulled off the highway and into the gas station in Indian Springs just past the entrance to the airbase.

Knight climbed out and headed for the pump just as a trucker highballing south into Vegas sounded a salute from his air horns. Knight smiled and waved. The red sports car seemed to attract admirers wherever he went. He swiped his credit card through the reader on the pump and felt the familiar pressure as the high-octane gas flowed through the hose as he squeezed the handle.

While the pump pinged the amount of the sale, he looked down at his button-less shirt. It was a warm night and he guessed it would not look too far out of place. He smiled, thinking about how Susan had torn into him. She was fantastic.

The pump handle clicked and the pressure in the hose relaxed. He gave the handle an extra squeeze to top off the tank. He replaced the pump handle, tore off the receipt and shook his head as he read the bill. If gas continued going up at this rate the Ferrari was going to be relegated to special occasions. But, somehow, he could not quite see himself putting around in some electric powered mini car.

He looked at Susan as he opened the door and slid into the slick leather seat. She was putting on lipstick using a small mirror from her purse. He could just see the butt of the nickel-plated .380 automatic pistol in the purse. “Not taking any chances I see,” he said.

Susan looked at him, then at the partially open purse, put the mirror away and snapped the purse shut. “It seems every time I’m with you I’m in need of protection,” she sparred.

Knight pointed to the brown, stuccoed building adjacent to the gas station. A sign flashed *CASINO* in large neon letters. In smaller letters, a backlit sign said *Restaurant.* “Let’s get a cup of coffee,” he said. “Maybe I can get a line on this Baby Doc. This is his hometown.”

Susan felt grimy from their tryst in the desert and she really wanted a bath but she reluctantly agreed.

The casino was like every small town casino in Nevada. A slot pit was in the middle surrounded by a low mezzanine of blackjack tables. There were no craps or roulette tables: those games were too manpower intensive for the revenue generated. The place, filled with a blue haze of smoke, appeared to be the local’s favorite. Nearly every machine and table was occupied. A sign at the rear, next to the cashier's cage, indicated that the restrooms were to the left and the restaurant was to the right.

They both headed left simultaneously.

Refreshed from their pit stops they walked together into the restaurant. After the dark, smoky casino the almost institutional interior of the restaurant was refreshing. They took a booth along the wall.

"What'll ya have?" asked the hardened, gum-popping waitress with the plastic nametag showing her name was Janice.

"Coffee?" asked Knight looking at Susan.

She nodded.

"Two coffees…black," he saw his needed sweetener was already on the table. "It's too bad there wasn't a craps table in there," he said gesturing with his head toward the casino.

"You really are a glutton for punishment," smiled Susan.

The waitress appeared with the coffee in the heavy white crockery cups that were the de rigueur of all small towns.

Knight looked up at her. "Have you been in this town long?"

"All my life," answered the waitress cautiously with a loud crack of her well-chewed gum. "Why?"

"Do you know a fellow that goes by the name of Baby Doc?"

A sudden look of terror came over the waitress's face. "I…I…don't know anything about anyone with that name," she stammered as she quickly departed.

"Seems I hit a nerve," said Knight, carefully adding only half a packet of sweetener to the steaming brown liquid.

Susan nodded toward the cash register at the end of the lunch counter. The waitress was talking to the counter waitress and a customer sitting on a stool. She was gesturing back toward them. All eyes in the restaurant were now on them.

The customer that had been sitting at the counter approached their booth. He was about fifty, husky and his clothes indicated he spent a great deal of time outdoors. He was wearing a sweat stained ball cap embroidered with Colossus Slot Club in gold letters. "Jan says you wanna know about Baby Doc."

"You know him?" asked Knight calmly.

The customer looked the couple in the booth over carefully. Their expensive clothes and watches were certainly not from any of the local stores. "Are you a friend of his?" he asked.

"Never met him," answered Knight. "I'm from the Colossus hotel and he won a motorcycle in a raffle he entered. He didn't put an exact address on his entry form. It just said Indian Springs." From the expression on the customer's face, he could see the lie was working.

"What kind of motorcycle?" asked the customer.

"A Harley-Davidson 1200 Sportster," answered Knight confidently, continuing to embellish the deception.

The customer took the bait. "Well, he doesn't exactly live in town. He lives about ten miles northwest in the foothills."

"Has he got a phone? His entry card didn't list one."

"No phone. He doesn't come around here often," answered the customer with growing suspicion. "I'm surprised you drove all the way out here to see him."

"Why's that?" asked Knight, suddenly sensing he might have overdone the ruse.

"He works for the Colossus, and I'd be surprised that the hotel would allow employees to enter a raffle like that."

Susan kicked Knight under the table. She knew the jig was up.

Knight took the hint. He stood up, fished his money clip from his pocket and laid a five-dollar bill on the table. He offered Susan his hand as she slid across the green plastic seat on the booth. "If you see Baby Doc tell him to contact the Human Resources Department at the hotel," ordered Knight over his shoulder as he and Susan left the restaurant.

Back in the car, he said sheepishly, "I guess that wasn't the best lie I ever told."

"I'm surprised you didn't do better," chided Susan. "You certainly have had enough experience." She was still convinced that there was more to his relationship with the overly endowed blonde that had slapped him in the lounge of the Colossus than he had admitted.

———·———

Johnny, the head parking valet at the VIP entrance, opened the passenger's door of the Ferrari with trepidation. The blonde insurance investigator who had questioned him earlier stepped out.

"Thank you," Susan said politely, coldly looking him in the eye.

Johnny had not expected that she would be aligned with Thomas Knight. He did not know anything about the blonde, but he knew that Knight was definitely nobody to trifle with.

Knight and Susan had barely entered the hotel before Johnny was on his cell phone. "That insurance investigator showed up again and this time with Thomas Knight," he said with obvious consternation in his voice. He listened for a minute and then said, "They must have been out in the desert somewhere because their car is covered with dust." He listened again. "OK, but I don't like what is happening. You said there wouldn't be any trouble."

The other party hung up and Johnny put the cell phone back in its holster on his belt. He jumped at the tap on his shoulder.

"Boss, should I have this car washed?" asked the big Russian valet pointing to the Ferrari.

Johnny recovered, "No, I'll take care of it myself. You take care of parking the others," he pointed to the small line of cars that had backed up behind the valet parking sign. There was no way in hell he was going to trust the Russian behind the wheel of Knight's car. Hopefully, he would not have to put up with the big Russian much longer.

———·———

Knight looked at his watch. It was nearly eight o'clock.

"You want to get something to eat?" asked Susan as she and Knight entered the hotel.

"I think I'd better find out what is going on with Operation Big Deal, whether or not it is going to be a big deal," he said. "By the way, I must say you are certainly taking it calmly that your company might have to pay out fifty million dollars."

She smiled slyly, "Not really. You see, we buy what is called reinsurance. Basically, we have a policy with another company to insure us if we have to pay out."

Knight chuckled, "You people in the insurance business don't miss a trick."

"We try to cover all our bases. Our stockholders wouldn't have it any other way," she said with a twinkle in her soft blue eyes.

Knight grabbed her left hand and pulled her toward him. They stared at each other for moment and then kissed. It was a kiss of passion. If they had not been in the lobby, surrounded by hundreds of guests and observed by the eye in the sky, things could have gotten out of hand.

They kissed again. Knight tried to pull her tighter to him but she pushed him back with her hands on his shoulders. "Not here," she said with a hint of a blush.

Knight acquiesced; desperately fighting his urge to throw her on the garish carpet of the lobby and jump her bones, damn the consequences. "I'd better go check in with Flynn. I'll call you later?"

"Okay," she said, trying to turn off the wave of passion he stirred in her.

He watched her walk away. No doubt about it, she was drop dead gorgeous! An elderly couple walking by looked at him strangely and shook their heads. Knight, caught their look out of the corner of his eye. He looked down and realized that he was less than presentable in his buttonless shirt, although anything went in Vegas. He recalled one of Flynn's favorite expressions. Vegas is a town with way too many freaks and not enough circuses.

Knight called Flynn's secretary to see if he was in. He usually was. Other than a couple of trips a year to see the powers that be on Wall Street, Flynn rarely left the Colossus. He worked nearly round the clock, stealing a nap here and there during the day. His schedule would have killed a lesser man, but Flynn thrived on action. He wanted to always be in the game. Knight told the secretary he would be up to the office just as soon as he could shower and shave.

Knight requested Steve to throw together a simple ham and cheese sandwich to hold his hunger at bay. He shaved and showered between bites. He had just finished toweling off when Steve walked in with a gift-wrapped box.

"It just arrived," he announced.

The package was from Lucianos. Knight looked at the card, it read: *For the good times*. It was not signed. He removed the wrapping, still trying to decipher the card's meaning. Inside the box neatly wrapped in tissue paper were six silk shirts of different patterns and colors. He laughed. Susan had wasted no time in replacing the shirt she had torn off him. He called her suite. Gary, her butler, answered and told him that she was bathing and could not be disturbed. "Take a message," he ordered.

"Yes sir."

"Tell her T K got her gift and can't wait to try them out with her."

Knight selected a dark blue shirt from the box and found it fit perfectly. "Good old Victor," he said as he added a pair of dark gray slacks and a navy blue sport coat.

He was nearly out the door when Steve called to him, "Some gal who says she's from the Army wants to talk you on the phone. She says it's urgent."

Knight picked up the phone on the table by the door. "Hello."

"Mr. Knight," the voice was instantly recognizable. "This is Captain Benteen from General Grant's office.

The image of the brunette with the suggestive sway to her hips shot through his mind. "You're working late," he said.

"No rest for the wicked," she teased, hoping he would pickup on the hint.

"What's going on?" Obviously, he had missed the clue.

"The General told me to tell you that Operation Big Deal is a go, day after tomorrow. You are supposed have the country club and the golf course cleared by fourteen hundred hours."

"You mean two P.M.?" Knight asked, making the conversion from military time.

"Yes," the Captain said sheepishly, she had forgotten that most civilians did not know how to use the twenty-four hour military clock.

"I'll take care of it," he said.

"Call me if I can do anything for you," she hinted again.

"Thanks," he said as he hung up. Flynn definitely was not going to like this piece of news.

———·———

Flynn was seated at his desk intently studying the computer monitor built into its top. He was talking on the phone and occasionally clicking a wireless mouse. He motioned to Knight to have a seat without interrupting his phone call. It was from the blackjack floor supervisor. "Who is he and what's he into us for?" he asked. He wrote the answer on a notepad and once again clicked the mouse. "Call me if he gets to three hundred thousand," he ordered the other party on the line. Then he hung up and turned off the computer. "What's up?" he asked distractedly, still thinking about the call.

"I've got some bad news, Jack," said Knight, with trepidation.

"Is it Isis?" Flynn's face suddenly turned pale and he held his breath.

"No. I'm sure she is still fine," said Knight trying to sound reassuring. He had taken the wrong approach. "It's about the meeting the Senator and I had with the Army this afternoon."

Flynn slowly exhaled, "So nothing's happened to Isis?" he asked with obvious relief in his voice.

"I haven't found her yet. So, the situation hasn't changed. But I'm working on a lead."

"I need her back!" Flynn looked desperate.

"I know…I know," Knight repeated. "I've got to talk to you about the meeting with the Senator."

"Well what is it? Dammit man I'm busy." Flynn's relief had been replaced with hostility.

"The Senator and I had a meeting with the Army at the NTS site," said Knight still trying to find a way to make his news palatable.

"Yeah…look you've told me that. Spit it out man!"

There was not a good way to say it. "Jack, the Army's going to set off an underground nuclear explosion day after tomorrow."

"That's it!" Flynn's patience was growing thin. "So what's that got to do with me?"

"The reason the Army is going to set off the blast is to relieve seismic pressure that has build up in an underground cavern caused by their nuclear testing in the past. They're trying to prevent a volcano from erupting."

Flynn squinted and looked at Knight skeptically, "A volcano?"

Knight nodded. "Anyway the Army thinks that there is an outside chance that a volcano could erupt in spite of the explosion and if it does it would likely impact your golf course."

Flynn jumped up from his chair, shouting, "The frigging Army is going to blow up my golf course?"

"They hope not, but it could happen. They want us to evacuate the place by two P.M. day after tomorrow. They don't want anyone to get hurt."

Flynn's face turned red and he exploded, "Nobody is to get hurt! How about me…I've got fifty million invested in that place and because of some Army screw up I'm going to lose it?"

"Jack, it's just a precaution. You know how the government always exaggerates this stuff," Knight was hoping to prevent Flynn from killing the messenger.

The phone rang before Flynn could erupt again. "What is it?" he demanded angrily. "He's what?" he shouted at the top of his voice in response to the answer to his question. He screamed into the phone. "I told you to call me if he got to three hundred thousand and now you tell me he's at six ninety-six!" He banged on the keys to bring the desktop computer to life. He starred at the screen. "Yeah…I see it! Dammit I'm not blind!" He listened to the voice on the phone. "I don't want to hear about how lucky he is! Your job is to change his luck!"

Knight smirked. Only in Vegas could you be fired for being unlucky. The whole gaming industry was built on the laws of probabilities and as long as the house was winning, everyone in the business was convinced that it was all mathematics. But let the house start to lose and suddenly the laws did not apply. The gaming industry was run by gamblers and in their souls they all believed in luck.

Knight knew that the Casino Manager, floor supervisor, and dealers were pulling out all the tricks to change the momentum of the game. They probably had already tried the free drinks to impair the player's judgment. They had slowed the game to provoke frustration. They had offered free front row show tickets to Honey and Her Bears, but the show started in ten minutes. They had changed decks. They tried different dealers hoping to get a lucky one. They had put a stacked blonde on one side of the player and a brunette on the other side. The women were playing footsie, hoping to distract the player into making a mistake. They needed him to leave the table, let his luck cool down. They did not want him to walk out of the casino with their money. They would comp him to everything; a suite, food, drinks, even one of the girls or both of them, anything to keep the money in the house. They wanted him to continue to play but at a different time, hopefully when his luck had run out.

Flynn continued to vent at the phone, "I don't want any excuses and I don't care what you have to do. Get my money back!" He slammed down the receiver and slumped into his chair. He was having a crappy day. Someone wanted twenty million for his wife and the Army was going to blow up his fifty million dollar golf course. He was paying some jerk three hundred thousand to get his own bathtubs back. Now, there was some cowboy, from Wyoming of all places, down in the casino at the blackjack table, kicking him in the nuts for nearly seven hundred thousand!

The phone rang again on Flynn desk and he picked it up. "What?" he demanded impatiently. "Uh huh…uh huh," he said, listening intently to the caller. "No, two nights are plenty," he said. He looked at Knight and smiled broadly, "It seems the cowboy went to the rodeo one too many times. He kept a hundred thousand and let the other five ninety-six ride. Unfortunately he busted when he came up with a twenty-two to the dealer's seventeen." He walked to the bar. "You want a drink?" he asked over his shoulder.

"Yeah…sure," answered Knight, relieved that Flynn was calming down.

Flynn handed Knight his drink and sat down next to him in one of the side chairs. "To the cowboy's lonely lament," he said as he clicked Knight's glass in a toast.

Knight smiled, the cowboy had won enough to drive home in a new four by four, extended cab, dually diesel pulling a new six horse trailer with a couple of new horses.

Flynn smiled, he had comped the cowboy two nights free room because he had won only one hundred thousand of the house's money instead of the million three he was going for. That only rated a junior suite with a mini bar instead of the big shooter suite with its open bar. Instead of unlimited room service, he got meal chits and, of course, the girls disappeared the minute he busted. Who knows, thought Flynn, maybe the cowboy would try again and lose back the hundred thousand. "They will never learn it is mathematically impossible to beat the house," he said taking a large swallow.

Knight snickered and shook his head. Only a few minutes before, Flynn had been pleading with his crew to change the players luck.

The phone rang and Flynn got up and answered it. "Send him in," he said.

The door opened and Bulldog walked in. He tried to conceal his surprise at seeing Knight sitting there. "Thomas," he said politely.

"Dwight," answered Knight, deliberately ignoring his chosen nickname.

Flynn reached under the desk, lifted up a shiny new metal suitcase and placed it on the top. He clicked open the locks. He lifted the lid, inside, neatly wrapped were bundles of five thousand dollars. "Just drop off the case like I told you," ordered Flynn. "I don't need any heroics, I need my bathtubs back."

"Yes Sir," acknowledged Bulldog as he closed the case. "I'll be back after midnight." He looked at Knight and then left without a word.

"Do you suppose he can put a suitcase in a dumpster without screwing it up?" Flynn asked, stirring his drink with his fingers.

"So you really are going to pay?" Knight was surprised to see Flynn actually give in.

"Like I told you before, it's pure economics. I need the bathtubs," Flynn answered taking a drink. "You know this is the damnedest business. The Corporation is always trying to limit my authority to make these kind of seat-of-the-pants decisions. To them everything needs to be analyzed to death before anything gets done."

Knight nodded, he was surprised to hear Flynn's authority was not absolute. He thought that Flynn was accountable to no one.

The liquor was having its desired effect and Flynn was starting to lighten up. "Running a place like this is a real trip," he said.

"Well it is the size of a small city."

"Yeah, the logistics are something else, but the real challenge is trying to find competent people."

"You've got a good staff from what I've seen," said Knight. He wanted to make an exception for Bulldog but decided against it.

"I pay them enough," added Flynn. He suddenly jumped up and ran to his desk. "I almost forgot!" he said excitedly. "Oh, you've got to see this. I've been saving it for you." He opened his desk drawer, took out a small gold presentation folder and handed it over.

Knight opened the folder and read the synopsis sheet. He started laughing as he read. "This *is* precious!" he said between laughs.

"Isn't it? One of the interns came up with it. This numb nut of a kid spent all summer working on a computer model showing that if I reduce the size of the twelve inch pizza in the restaurants to eleven and a quarter inches nobody will notice and I'll make another twenty-five thousand!" Now Flynn was laughing. "Wait you haven't read the best part." He rushed over to the report and flipped to page twenty.

Knight read the page and again started laughing.

Flynn was laughing at Knight. "It only applies to the twelve inch pizza and not the ten and sixteen inch because we don't sell enough of them," he howled. He reached into his desk drawer, took out a tissue and between peals of laughter, wiped the tears from his eyes. "To cowboys, bathtubs and pizzas," he toasted, lifting his drink up and then draining the glass.

Knight held his drink up in a confirming salute.

"Want another?" asked Flynn walking to the bar still chuckling.

"Sure," answered Knight polishing off his first one. Two was always his limit, but it had been a long time, college in fact, since the two of them had laughed together.

Flynn handed Knight his refill. "So, what's up with you and the blonde?"

Knight almost choked, the question had caught him in mid swallow. "Blonde?"

"Yeah the one that was playing footsie with you in the meeting this morning."

Knight blushed, "You saw that?"

"Everyone did."

"I met her out in Palm Springs. We got caught up in a helluva mess together."

Flynn stirred his drink and studied the swirling ice cubes. "That's what you need, you know."

"What's that?"

"You need to settle down. Find someone and get a life. From what I've heard about the blonde, she would make a perfect catch. She's certainly a good looker, smart, and I understand, one of the richest women in the world."

"She's just a friend," Knight protested, he always felt uncomfortable discussing his private life.

Flynn shook his head, "You never could see when you were having a run of luck. That's why I used to pluck you like a pigeon in the old dormitory card games."

"You did that, all right," Knight nodded. Flynn had perfected his card playing at Knight's and all the other dorm's residents' expense.

Talking about the past had mellowed Flynn's mood. "You said you had a lead on Isis?"

Knight was grateful for a chance to change the subject. He told Flynn the whole story.

Flynn stared at him, "I don't appreciate you dumping a load of bull shit like that on me." The drink was making him belligerent.

"I swear it's true," said Knight.

"An eight-foot alien with snowshoes looking for a diamond?"

Knight protested, "Susan saw it too."

"The blonde? When?"

"This evening. We went out to the golf course to look around, stopped on the way back and there it was."

Flynn looked at Knight closely, searching for the liar's tell. "You're not shitting me, are you?"

"I'm dead serious. In fact, he may even be an employee here."

"I don't have any aliens working here!" Flynn was getting angry.

"I think his name is Baby Doc Prentice. Ask Personnel."

Flynn picked up the phone, "Get me someone in Personnel." He waited impatiently. "Dammit I know what time it is. Isn't there someone down there?" He did not like the answer. "I need some information now. Find someone who knows what goes on down there and have them give me a call." He slammed down the receiver. "Idiots!" he said as he moved to the bar again.

Knight could see Flynn was on his way to a bender. He also knew Flynn was a bad drunk. It was time to leave. "Call me if you find anything," he said as he put down his empty glass and walked to the door.

Flynn poured himself another double. "Screw you!" He said caustically.

———.———

It was ten o'clock before Knight left Flynn's office. The drinks had relaxed him, but now he was hungry. He was on his way across the casino to the ice-cream store in the shopping arcade, when he heard the familiar sound. It was coming from the lounge of the casino. Like the pied piper's tune, he was drawn toward it.

Inside the darkened lounge he could see Captain Jack and the Shark Attack were hard at work. The place was jumping and the small dance floor was packed with gyrating steaming bodies. Whenever

Captain Jack was in town, it was where all the beautiful people went to play. Every table was occupied, so Knight headed for the bar. There were two unoccupied stools. The bartender put the obligatory paper coaster in front of him and leaned over to hear his order.

Knight hollered over the music, "A banana split, with three cherries." It was his favorite.

The bartender looked like he had not understood. "A banana split?" he asked.

"Yeah, with three cherries," confirmed Knight as he placed a fifty dollar bill on the bar

The bartender looked at the bill, shrugged, picked it up and went to the house phone. He nodded to Knight confirming the order had been placed.

The banana split hit the spot and there were only two bites left when he felt the tap on the shoulder. He turned to see a stacked vixen in a brunette wig starring at him with a pouty expression.

"Stood me up I see?"

Knight swallowed the cherry he was sucking on and wiped his mouth with the bar napkin. He had forgotten about the date he made that morning by the pool. "We had a date?" he asked, feigning surprise. He took a drink of water, trying to buy time to figure out what his excuse was going to be.

"I thought so," the brunette answered, sliding onto the vacant stool next to him.

The bartender leaned over to hear her order.

"Three fingers of your best Russian vodka and a bottle of honey."

The bartender looked at her and then shouted over the music. "The usual!"

She smiled at him flirtatiously.

"That's an unusual drink. What is it called?" asked Knight.

"Why Honey and the Three Bears of course," answered Honey, as she rubbed her shoulder against his seductively. "It's a house specialty."

The bartender put the awful looking concoction in front of her and laid a plastic spoon next to it.

She stirred the thick yellow brown mixture with a swizzle stick and then dipped out a spoonful. She held it up to Knight as if to offer him a bite.

He put up his hand in protest.

She shrugged and placed the spoon in her mouth. She closed her eyes in ecstasy at the taste and then licked the spoon suggestively. "Your loss," she said, continuing to run her tongue over the spoon.

Knight had to admit that she had a way about her. It was obvious she had perfected the art of turning men on.

"Want to go for a swim or a drag race or something?" she asked in a sultry voice. She rubbed her thigh against his.

Knight's cell phone rang before he could answer. It was Susan.

He held the phone against his right ear and put his index finger in his left ear to help drown out the band. "I'm down in the lounge," he answered and then listened. "Actually I'm eating a banana split." He listened again. "No! I'm not kidding you. I'm eating a banana split!" he protested. He continued to defend himself. "I know they don't make banana splits in the bar. They ordered it from room service." He listened and looked at Honey. "I wanted to listen to Captain

Jack and I was hungry that's why." He listened again. "Yes, I'm alone," he lied. There was no way Susan was ever going to believe that Honey had just shown up. "I'm going to listen to one more song and then turn in. I'll call you in the morning." He listened. "I had a good time too." He folded the phone up and put it back in his coat pocket.

"Your blonde girlfriend?" asked Honey.

"She's really not my girlfriend. More like a business partner."

"I don't think a business partner would care why you're sitting in a bar eating a banana split."

Knight smiled sheepishly.

"Buy me another drink," she ordered as she licked the last of the foul concoction off the spoon with her moist red lips.

Knight nodded at the bartender and then tilted his head toward Honey.

"You used to work here, didn't you?" she asked.

"A couple of years ago. Why?"

"I thought I recognized you. You were the big gun in security."

The bartender brought Honey's drink before Knight could answer.

Honey put a spoonful of the golden liquid into her mouth. "Yummy," she said. "You really should give it a try."

Knight wrinkled his nose. "I'll pass."

"You know ancient Greeks claimed honey was an aphrodisiac."

"I hadn't heard that."

Honey dropped her hand to Knight's crotch. "Want to try it out and see if it's true?"

Knight's body screamed, go for it! But, he said, "I'll have to take a rain check, I have a big day tomorrow." He gulped down the last two bites of the sundae.

She rubbed her hand against the growing bulge in his pants. "It feels like you're having a big day already."

He wanted to give in, and any other time he would have, but he could not shake the fresh memory of Susan in the desert. He stood up and said, "Not tonight. I have a headache." He slid off the stool and walked away without looking back.

In the elevator, Knight massaged his forehead with his fingers. He had eaten the last spoonfuls of the banana split too fast and now really had a cold induced headache. Today he had had a salad for lunch, sex in the desert, a ham sandwich, two whiskeys and a banana split. He shook his head and smirked, by any measure a well-rounded diet.

———·———

Bulldog placed the shiny new metal suitcase on the passenger seat of his black Hummer. Flynn's instructions had been explicit. There was no doubt as to what he was supposed to do. The green digital clock display on the dashboard showed 11:47. It would take no more than ten minutes to drive to the designated alley behind the souvenir store at Paradise and Flamingo Road.

As he steered the big black all-terrain vehicle out of the VIP parking garage, he reached behind the passenger seat and picked up a large black gym bag.

He unzipped the bag and took out the five smaller bags inside. He snapped open the metal suitcase and started transferring the bundles of bills into the smaller bags. By the time he turned into the alley, the metal suitcase was empty. He placed the now full, smaller bags back into the large gym bag and zipped it shut.

He slowed the vehicle to a walk as he approached a row of dumpsters. The second dumpster had a large X spray-painted in red on the front. The lid was open. Without coming to a complete stop he picked up the metal suitcase and tossed it out the driver's window and into the waiting dumpster. The drop made, he accelerated and at the end of the alley turned onto Paradise Road.

He laughed to himself. He had done exactly what Flynn had told him. Put the suitcase in the second dumpster, the one marked with an X. Flynn had not really said anything about leaving the money in the case!

He looked up into his rearview mirror and saw the large garbage truck turn into the alley. It had been timed perfectly. The garbage truck would empty the dumpster before anyone might accidentally find the case.

Bulldog knew better than to completely trust Flynn. It was entirely possible that Flynn had had him followed. If that were the case, the observer would have seen that he had followed Flynn's instructions to the letter. Anyone seeing the drop would now be following the garbage truck as it completed its rounds. It could be hours before the case made its way to its final resting place, the Las Vegas City Dump!

If anyone followed the truck and eventually recovered the case, they would find it empty. They would, of course, figure that somehow the money disappeared somewhere along the route.

Bulldog reached into the glove box, pulled out a Cuban Cohiba Esplendidos cigar and snipped off the tip with the clipper on his key chain. He used a match to expertly spread the flame across the end of the cigar as he puffed it to life. He blew a smoke ring and watched as it wafted against the windshield. With his right hand, he reached over and patted the gym bag. Three hundred thousand for less than ten minutes work! What a town!

He returned to the Colossus and carrying the large gym bag headed to the spa. Inside the men's locker room, he placed the five smaller bags in five different lockers. He then took the nearest elevator to his office. It took only a minute to open his computer, encrypt and send the email. Still enjoying the cigar, he continued to blow smoke rings as he walked down the hall to Flynn's office.

He had barely finished briefing Flynn on the evening's events when the secretary came in with the email.

Flynn read it quickly and shouted, "Yes!" He stood up and handed the document to Bulldog. It read: *Your bathtubs are in four orange shipping containers marked with red X's in the storage yard at Tamarus Street and Russell Road.*

Flynn dialed his V.P. of Operations and instructed him to retrieve the bathtubs. "Do whatever it takes to get those tubs installed by noon tomorrow," he ordered. He hung up the phone, sat down in his chair and looked at his V.P. of Security. "Good job," he said. "Now, I want you to pull out all the stops and find the jerk that caused me all this grief."

Bulldog nodded, he had already picked his patsy.

CHAPTER 11

Johnny Ford had driven to his usual street corner on his way home from work. He stopped, rolled down the window and handed five, crisp, one hundred dollar bills to the shirtless drug dealer. He looked at the small sandwich bag full of white powder he got in return. Feeling good was expensive; there was no doubt about that. After the day that he had had, he really needed to have a pick me up. First, there was the damned Russian wrecking the customers' cars, then the nosy investigator who was getting too close for comfort. Finally, he was not going to get his valet's paycheck for two days. He needed that money like yesterday.

He pushed the garage door opener and guided his '64 classic Mustang convertible into the left bay of his three-car garage. The '88 ZR1 Corvette and the customized, chopped-top '50 Mercury lead sled were where he had left them. He loved his cars. He loved how the women looked at him with hope and how the men looked at him with envy every time he drove them.

He lowered the garage door and walked into the house. He tossed his car keys on the hall stand, retrieved the sandwich bag from his pocket and headed directly to the bathroom.

The cocaine rush was just coming on when the phone rang. "Hello," he said rubbing his nose to stop the tickle. "Okay," he said to the caller as his head started spinning. He listened again to the caller, barely able to stay awake. "A loop of five numbered accounts," he slurred. "Look I've got it," he said defensively. He hung up the phone and headed to the bedroom. He stripped off his clothes and stepped through the double French doors and onto the patio. He set the timer and slowly lowered himself into the bubbly hot spa. Within minutes, he was nearly comatose.

The rider of the large gold Suzuki motorcycle down shifted and braked expertly, stopping the bike in front of the three-car garage. She then upshifted the transmission one notch with her left toe. With the bike in neutral, she turned off the key and used her left heel to lower the kickstand. She leaned the bike over, threw her leg over the machine and dismounted. She took off the gold helmet, walked to the front door and pushed the doorbell. When she got no answer, she used a key on her key ring to open the door. "Johnny," she called, opening the door. She went from room to room trying to find the house's occupant. In the bathroom, the small mirror and the razor blade with the remnants of the white power told her where he was.

Johnny was still passed out in the spa when she found him. "Oh no!" she cried. She put her arms under his shoulders and lifted him onto the pool apron. "You stupid kid," she said as she slapped his face to revive him.

He coughed twice and opened his eyes a crack. "Hi," he slurred.

She was really angry now. "I'm sick of this crap. You're going to kill yourself with that junk."

He shook his head and struggled to his feet only to fall back on a pool lounger. "I'm okay. Don't worry about it." He waved his hand as if to dismiss her complaint.

"Well, I am worried about it, you little twit. Everything is riding on you."

Now he was getting angry. "Look, I said I was fine. I'll do my job."

"You'd better," she threatened. She tossed him a towel. "Dry off." She sat down next to him and pulled his head down between her ample breasts. "I'll fix you some tea with honey."

He hugged her tightly and then looked up into her eyes. "It's going to be all right isn't it?"

"Of course darling. Mommy won't let anything happen to her little boy."

Knight had been sound asleep when Steve shook him awake. "Mr. Flynn is on the phone. He says it's urgent."

Knight looked at his Rolex. "It's three thirty in the morning," he said sleepily.

"He says it's urgent."

Knight nodded. Steve left the bedroom and forwarded the call to the bedside phone."

"Hello."

"Thomas, this is Jack, I found an address for your Baby Doc."

Knight shook his head, still trying to clear the cobwebs. "Huh?"

"I found that address you're looking for," Flynn repeated impatiently. "He lives out in the desert about ten miles southwest of Indian Springs. I'll have my secretary run a map over to you."

"Okay."

"You know, I thought that name Prentice was familiar. It took me awhile to remember where I'd seen it. I bought the land for the golf course from the estate of a D. R. Prentice."

"Is Baby Doc an employee?" asked Knight, finally getting up to speed.

"No, that's why it took so long. It turns out his real name is Bruce David Prentice. He's a subcontractor."

"What does he do?"

Flynn paused. "Are you ready for this? He feeds the bears!"

"The bears?"

"Yeah you know, Honey's bears, the ones she uses in her act."

Knight's mind was now racing. "Thanks," he said.

"Thomas get Isis back," pleaded Flynn. "Do whatever you need to."

"I'll do my best," promised Knight.

It was only minutes before one of Flynn's secretaries, a petite blonde barely out of her teens, showed up at Knight's suite. She handed him the map. Flynn's secretaries worked in shifts. There was no other way to accommodate his work hours. Evidently, this one was the new kid on the block because she was working the graveyard shift.

Knight spread the map across the antique dining table and studied it intently. There was a yellow highlighted line running southwest from Indian Springs and then turning north back toward the golf course. The line terminated with a circle about ten miles from the town and just beside the huge parcel of government owned Bureau of Land Management land.

The secretary, who had been waiting patiently while Knight perused the map, yawned. She had been on this damnable shift for nearly three months and still her body clock rebelled at the hours. "Is there anything else?" she asked, trying to stifle another yawn.

"No, thanks." Knight was barely able to stay awake himself. He opened the door to let the poor girl escape. He looked at Steve, "When's sun up?"

Steve shrugged his shoulders, "About six thirty. I guess."

Knight looked at his watch. He could still catch a couple of hours of sleep. "Call me at six," he said over his shoulder as he stretched and then shuffled off to the bedroom.

Steve awoke Knight by shaking his shoulder. "It's six o'clock," he said.

Knight opened his eyes reluctantly and nodded. After Flynn's nighttime interruption, he had had a terrible time going back to sleep. Now he felt he was unfairly being asked to wake-up long before his body desired. "I need a good breakfast," he ordered as he sat on the edge the bed and stretched. His pathetic diet of the day before demanded to be offset by solid nourishment. "Oh, and by the way go down and get the red duffle bag out of my car and bring it up while I shower."

The full-body, multi-head, temperature controlled shower was wonderful, but it was no substitute for his usual three-mile swim. He would have to pass on his exercise today; there was too much to do.

The extra thick, fluffy towel with the Colossus logo was almost too hot from the towel warmer rack attached to the bathroom wall. Flynn had included every possible indulgence in the big shooter's suites.

Steve walked in with the red duffel. "Breakfast is ready when you are," he announced and then left. He would have been happy to help Knight dress, but unlike many of his spoiled guests, Knight liked things simple. He was unpretentious and he dressed himself.

Knight opened the duffel, took out the matching sand colored, cotton pants, T-shirt and safari jacket and put them on. He stuffed his pants legs into the twelve-inch tall, waterproof boots from the duffel and bloused them over, military style. His well-worn shoulder holster with the Glock 18 was next. He snapped the slide back on the pistol and confirmed a round was in the chamber. He pushed the magazine release and examined the small inspection holes in the magazine to verify it was fully loaded. He took the floppy bush hat out of the duffle, rolled it up and put it into the left pocket of the jacket. His ensemble was complete. He was ready for Spook, Baby Doc or whoever or whatever it was.

Over breakfast, he again studied the map the secretary had given him.

———·———

Susan had slept fitfully. It was all Thomas Knight's fault. The sex in the desert had been great, if uncomfortable. No, it was not the sex but his confounded enigmatic attitude that had her tossing and turning. She could not figure out how he felt about her. Whenever they got close, he was always distracted by something. She did not want to admit it, but to be fair they never had really been together when they were not working a case. After this mess was over, she would present him with the proposition of taking some time off together. Maybe then she could figure out where she stood. She needed a massage even more than breakfast. She would just have a cup of coffee while she waited for Gary to have a masseuse sent up.

She moaned softly as the heavy set, Swedish masseuse expertly kneaded her back. The Swede ran her palms and thumbs up and down Susan's spine and then using her fingertips, pulled the flesh taut. After the wild love making fiasco in Knight's car, Susan's body ached all over. She could feel the muscles respond as the massage continued to her waist.

The masseuse gently lifted the warm towel covering her lower body and turning it back, she let out a small chuckle.

"What's so funny?" asked Susan impatiently, miffed at being left out of the seemingly inside joke.

"I yust never saw one of does," came the heavily accented reply.

Susan was surprised, after all, tattoos were more popular than ever and women today had them in every conceivable location. Hers was not that special—-just a small blue lightning strike on the left cheek of her butt. It had been an impetuous thing. Her father had been missing and she did it to remind her to take care of business. Elvis had invented the logo of the lightning strike with the letters TCB, which stood for "taking care of business", entwined and he had used it everywhere. Not wanting to be an out and out plagiarist Susan had adopted the lightning strike, but left out the letters. After all, it was a reminder to her and no one else. "I am sure you see tattoos all the time," she said.

"Dat's not vhat I am talking about. It's da burn!"

"The what?" shouted Susan as she pulled herself up from the table. Gathering a towel around her, she moved to one of the full-length mirrors around the table. She turned and lowered the towel to see her butt. "What the…?" she exclaimed. The fresh, red brand was unmistakable and even the mirror image was instantly recognizable. The inch and a half letters spelled out in neat block letters "Ferrari."

"Damn you Thomas," she cried as she tried fruitlessly to wipe away the welt.

———·———

Flynn had waited impatiently for his stockbroker to arrive in his New York office. He had very little sympathy for people who kept regular work hours. When you worked for Jack Flynn, he expected you to be available twenty-four seven, three sixty-five. The phone rang on his desk. His secretary had his stockbroker on the line. "I want to sell all or as much as you can of my Colossus stock. But, it has to be sold by closing today," he ordered.

The broker started arguing on the other end of the line.

Flynn did not like being second-guessed. "I know what the law says about disclosure. I guarantee there is nothing about the financials that is out of line. I just want to dump it as quickly as I can."

The broker continued to argue.

Flynn was getting exasperated. "I don't have time to file all that SEC crap. Sell the stock and I'll straighten it out later!" He listened again to the protesting broker. "Look you ungrateful twit, I've made you a frigging fortune. I'm the reason that you are the President of your firm. Without my accounts, you'd still have your phone growing out of your ear trying to screw some poor pathetic widow out of a life-insurance payoff! Now either you do what I tell you or you'll never see another dime from this town. And, don't think I can't make it happened!"

Evidently, the threat worked because the broker backed down.

"Just sell as much as you can," Flynn was calming down now that he had won. "Call me after the stock market closes!" He hung up without waiting for reply.

He smiled as he moved the mouse on the computer. The Army had dumped an opportunity to make a fortune in his lap and he was not about to squander it. The minute the story about the possible volcano came out, regardless of whether or not it really happened, all Vegas stocks would tank. He would then buy back his shares at a deep discount. He would end up with the same amount of shares and as the stock inevitably recovered, a huge gain in his net worth. Oh, there would be an investigation of sorts and much weeping and gnashing of teeth by the SEC regulators, who were always looking for inside traders, but that was the beauty of the plan. He could claim that he was a victim of a natural disaster and there was no way they could ever make it stick that somehow he could predict what nature would do. He had his bases covered. If he did happen to lose the golf course, his insurance would cover the loss. The gain he stood to make by his arbitrage was going to be a literal fortune. Money in Vegas was not made by scrounging every dime out of operations and certainly not by trimming pizzas by three quarters of an inch. No, the big money was made by buying and selling gaming stocks at the right time.

———·———

Knight had severely misjudged the road to Baby Doc's. On the map, it was classified as improved dirt. In reality, two miles out of Indian Springs the road turned little more than what looked like wagon wheel ruts, so deep that the sports car was constantly bottoming out. He certainly had brought the wrong vehicle. The Ferrari was definitely not made for this kind of off-roading. More than once he thought he was going to be permanently high centered. He hated the thought of having to retreat to the Colossus and use one of their shiny, new Hummers. It was only his stubbornness that kept him going.

"Dammit!" he shouted as the car bounced and bottomed out again. He stopped the car, crawled out, got down on his knees and inspected the bottom of the car for fluid leaks. Relieved when he did not find any, he retrieved the handheld GPS locator and checked his position. He still had three miles to go. He looked at his watch. It had taken nearly an hour to go seven miles on the terrible excuse for a road. The one good thing was that he was going so slow that he was not throwing up a dust cloud that would announce his coming.

Banging back along the road, he prayed that he would not have to beat a hasty retreat. With a mile to go, he stopped again and studied the map. It was obvious that there was only one road in. He pulled off the road and into a dry wash bed that the map showed ran near the circle Flynn had drawn. Carefully avoiding the occasional rock, he was able to follow the wash to within half a mile of his destination before he stopped. Since he could not see the house from his parked car, he felt confident that no one in the house could see him.

He slipped his cell phone and a small nylon duffel bag with his breaking and entering tools into his right jacket pocket. He looped the 7 X 50 Bausch and Lomb binoculars around his neck. Out of habit, he checked his Glock one last time

He climbed up the bank of the wash and half crouching snuck along the desert. The house, or whatever it was, was where the map said it would be. With a hundred yards to go, he lay down prone on the ground and glassed the house with the binoculars.

The place looked as if someone had put up an elaborate chain link fence around a pile of rusted trash. There was no sign of a vehicle. The place looked uninhabited.

Using little clumps of sagebrush for cover, he moved to the fence. He looked it over carefully to see if it was electrified. He was relieved to see that it was not.

He studied the inside of the fenced-in courtyard for any signs of a dog. Years ago, when he was learning his trade, he had been terrorized more than once by an unexpected guard dog with a bad attitude. There was no sign of one this time.

The fence was nearly new and the wire gauge was too much for the lightweight snips in his breaking and entering kit. He would have to find his way in by the front gate or by scaling the fence. The gate was the easiest option, so he decided to try it first.

The gate was unlocked but could only be opened with a remote control that would engage the power gate mechanism. He would have to scale the fence.

He ran and jumped on the fence. Using the diamond-shaped openings in the chain links, he was able to find enough hand and toeholds to get him over the top. He dropped down on the inside and paused, listening for any sign that he might have been detected. He approached the front door cautiously and had his hand on the doorknob when he heard the ice cream bells. He searched frantically for a place to hide. There was no time and precious little cover. Just as the gate opened automatically, he threw himself prone on the ground behind what looked like the rusted axle of the house trailer.

The ice cream truck skidded to a stop in a cloud of dust; the driver exited and went into the house before the dust settled.

Through the dust, Knight could not make out who the driver was. He looked up over the axle just in time to see the gate automatically shutting behind the truck. He could not make it in time. He was trapped!

———.———

Bulldog smiled. He had done a great job of manufacturing evidence that one of the Russian valets had stolen Flynn's bathtubs. It had been easy enough. He had forged a set of freight bills that did not show the three hundred bathtubs as being shipped or received. He had planted the originals and the copies of the forgeries in the employee locker of the valet.

The Russian was the perfect patsy. First, nobody in Vegas liked the Russians and it was easy to believe the worst about them. Second, with his thick accent it would be difficult to articulate his innocence. Third, it would send a subtle message to the other Russians to stay out of his territory.

To be absolutely sure there would be no doubt about the Russian's guilt and as the coup de grace, he had broken into the Russian's apartment and used his fax machine to send the ransom note.

All that was left was to announce to Flynn that the thief had been caught. Flynn would want to kill the Russian of course, but then Bulldog would intervene with the voice of reason. The local press would get hold of the story and Bulldog was sure to get plenty of airtime. The whole town would know what a brilliant V.P. of Security he was. The three hundred thousand would remain missing and insure that the D.A. did not cut a deal. Yes, the word would get around that you did not fool with Bulldog.

He could not wait to see the looks on Flynn and Knight's faces when they found out who had solved the case.

"A Russian valet?" asked Flynn with amazement.

"Yes, there is no doubt about it," said Bulldog as he laid a manila folder on Flynn's desk.

Flynn studied the contents of the folder. It was all there in black and white. The evidence was overwhelming. He was more shocked than angry. How could a lowly valet clip him, Jack Flynn, for three hundred thousand? "Did you find the money?" he asked.

"No, not yet. I've had the boys start to work on him. I'm sure he'll give it up."

Flynn shook his head in disbelief, "Where have you got him?"

"He's down in a storeroom off Maintenance Tunnel C."

"Let's go," said Flynn. "I want to see the size of the cojones on this bastard."

A labyrinth of maintenance tunnels ran for miles beneath the Colossus. It really was the bowels of a city.

"Where in the hell are we?" asked Flynn. It seemed that they had walked forever after getting off the elevator.

"Just around the corner," answered Bulldog, striding along with a military gait.

The pair rounded a corner and an armed Colossus security guard was standing in the corridor. "Sir," he said to Bulldog as he opened the door for them.

The cement walled room was dark except for a single floodlight in a metal reflector. It shown down on a huge, pathetic looking person slumped over and tied to a metal chair. The chair was bolted firmly to the floor. On either side of the victim were two guards also in Colossus uniforms. They came to attention at the site of Bulldog and Flynn.

"Has he said anything?" asked Bulldog.

The tallest of the guards answered, "Not yet. He claims he doesn't know what we're talking about."

The severely beaten wretch in the chair moaned softly.

Bulldog went over to the man and pulled back his head by his hair.

Flynn almost vomited. The man's face had been beaten to a bloody, swollen pulp. He was unrecognizable. Flynn talked and acted tough but the sight of blood made him queasy. He inhaled sharply, steeling himself against the horror of what he was looking at. He could not let the guards witness how revolted he was.

Crack! Bulldog slapped the man across the face with the back of his hand. He secretly enjoyed inflicting pain and sometimes he enjoyed it when the pain was his own. "Where's the money you son-of-a bitch?" he shouted. He was putting on a good tough guy act for Flynn.

The helpless man moaned and a small trickle of blood started to flow from his nostrils.

Flynn wanted to turn away. He was actually going to be sick at any minute. His mind was racing trying to find an excuse to leave the room and vomit.

Bulldog released the victim's hair and let his head fall down on his chest.

Flynn waved his hands toward the guards, "Get rid of them."

The guards had barely left the room when the man in the chair raised his head slowly by himself and opened his eyes. He looked at Flynn. "I'm sorry Mr. Flynn, I didn't steal any money." He mumbled with a thick accent through his swollen lips, before passing out.

Flynn recoiled in horror, barely able to breathe. "Oh no!" he shouted. He had recognized the creature. "It's…it's Victor Cherenko's grandson!"

Bulldog's face turned white with fear. His brain was racing with the implications of what Flynn had just said. "His name isn't Cherenko," he protested, hoping against hope that Flynn was wrong.

"Of course not you stupid dunce!" spat Flynn. "His father married Victor's daughter. His last name is Mikhailov or something like that."

"Georgie Mikhailov," Bulldog added. There was no way that he could have known the connection with Victor Cherenko.

Flynn was pacing, his heart pounding. "You've dumped both of us in the shit big time!" Flynn was all too familiar with the frail Russian émigrés reputation.

The Soviet Secret Police, the KGB, had tried to eliminate the influence of Russian Jews. Using trumped up charges to disguise their agenda, Victor Cherenko and others were arrested on trumped up charges. A rigged state court had sentenced him to seven years in a work camp in the Gulag, the Soviet's prison system.

In the Gulag, you survived because you were either strong or clever. Victor had been both. Originally, a strapping young lad, the terrible food and a hard labor had eventually broken his body. His mind however had only grown stronger. In the Gulag, the Jews banded together for protection from the other inmates. They called their organization the VOR V ZAKONYE. By the time Victor was released he was a full-fledged member of the VOR Brotherhood, the Russian version of an Italian Made Guy. By using the contacts he made in prison, he was able to cultivate these relationships after his release. After years of being degraded like a criminal on the inside, it was natural that he became a criminal on the outside.

Through his cleverness, Victor had finagled his way onto a list of Jewish gangsters that the K.G.B. wanted to deport. Israel had taken most of the exiles, but Victor was one of a small group that made it to New York.

Once in the U.S. the members of the exiled group, that were in the VOR, banded together and started a ruthless organization that extorted Russian communities and neighborhoods. Eventually the Italian Mafia and the Russians formed alliances. The Mafia supplied the political connections and the Russians supplied manpower and muscle.

Victor's health continued to decline in the humidity of the East Coast and he moved to Vegas for its dry, high desert climate. However, he maintained his Eastern contacts and set up a new VOR organization in Vegas. By pure muscle, he slowly gained control over many of the hotels' and casinos' human resource departments. He was now able, for a kickback, to dictate who got the best jobs. The kickbacks funded his loan sharking, which in turn provided the funds for his other businesses. Luciano's, his chain of upscale men's stores, provided the semblance of legitimacy needed to keep the IRS off his back.

Victor's advancing years had not diminished his ruthlessness, but instead had tempered it. He no longer went immediately to the knife and gun, preferring to negotiate. He now was a firm believer that if you scratched his back, he would scratch yours. It was a perfect philosophy for Vegas, because in Vegas everyone needed something.

He found that a low profile kept his organization out of the headlines and under the authorities radar. This coupled with his fearsome reputation for gruesome reprisals against those who antagonized him was sufficient for him to maintain control. Only an idiot would challenge him. The smart players simply stayed out of his way. As long as he got his way, everything was fine, but get in his way and it was a different story.

Flynn had seen the wisdom in not crossing swords with the wily Mafioso as long as he kept out of the Colossus's affairs.

Victor had also seen that little was to be gained by taking on an adversary like Flynn. After all, there were bigger fish to fry that did not require him to risk anything. The two of them had developed an accommodating attitude toward each other.

After Victor's wife had died from cancer, he had doted on his only child, a daughter. She turned out to be every bit as ruthless and clever as he was. In spite of Victor's objections, she had married a big, but dumb enforcer in Victor's organization. His new son-in-law's lack of cleverness, meant it was only a matter of time before he ended up on the government's shit list. They deported him to Israel. And, over Victor's protestations, his wife went with him. Georgie, their only child, had been born in Israel. He had inherited his father's size but not his mother's brains.

Georgie was only thirteen when his parents had been killed in a suicide bombing. Victor had moved his grandson to Vegas and tried as hard as he could to develop what little brainpower he had.

Georgie tried hard to please his grandfather and the two were very close. Georgie was the only thing in Victor's life that really mattered.

Bulldog was in a panic. One minute his plan had been working to perfection and the next everything had gone to hell in a hand basket. "What are we going to do?" he asked Flynn. His voice was hoarse with fear.

Flynn was thinking and pacing. There had to be something he could do to make this right with Victor. If they warred against each other, they would both lose big-time. There simply was no way to cover-up what happened. He would have to try to talk to Victor and appeal to his reason. He looked at Georgie slumped in the chair. "How badly is he hurt?" he asked.

Bulldog pulled Georgie's head back and examined him as closely as he could through the blood. "I think his nose is broken. The rest is just small cuts and bruises."

"Clean him up. Put him in a suite and have the house doctor patch him up," Flynn ordered, shaking his head. "No one and I mean no one, is to know what happened!" He needed time to talk to Victor.

"Yes Sir," answered Bulldog. He needed time to figure out how to get out of town.

CHAPTER 12

Thomas Knight waved away the remnants of the dust cloud the ice cream truck had thrown up. He cautiously raised his head and peered over the axle he was hiding behind. There was no one in sight. He rolled over onto his side and then snapped open one of the magazine pockets on the shoulder holster. He took out the Glock and replaced the nineteen round magazine with the one with thirty-five rounds. He snapped the Tenifer-coated slide back on the pistol to confirm one round was still in the chamber. If he got into more trouble than thirty-six rounds could handle he was probably going to be dead anyway.

He slowly stood up into a crouch, ran to the driver's side of the truck and peered cautiously through the window. The keys were still in the ignition. If he had to beat a hasty retreat, he could use the truck. At least he would be driving.

He jumped with surprise when suddenly the diesel generator started. He laughed to himself when he realized that he had instinctively pointed the Glock at the whirring machine. He wondered how many rounds it would take to dispatch a generator.

Having recovered from his fear of generators, he again approached the door of the house. He listened for a minute, his ear pressed against the surprisingly cool aluminum of the door. Over the noise of the generator, he could barely make out what sounded like a woman crying.

Everything pointed to the voice belonging to Isis: the ice cream truck, the story about Baby Doc's diamond hunting. Anyway, if it were Baby Doc inside, he would confront him and find out for sure. He slowly turned the handle with his left hand, the Glock at the ready in his right. He felt the latch give way and very slowly, he pushed open the door with his fingertips.

The interior was nearly dark and his eyes had not dilated enough to make out anything about the interior. His first instinct was to turn around and run. The overpowering smell of putrid flesh caused him to involuntarily gag. He forced himself to step inside, shutting the door behind him quietly. Now, except for a solitary light fixture at the end of what looked like a tunnel, he was in total darkness. The pupils of his eyes slowly opened and he began to make out shapes. He flipped on the laser sight of the Glock and pointed its reassuring red beam onto the floor. He shivered.

He had not noticed it before, so powerful was the stench, but the place was freezing.

A sudden shrill screech froze him. It sounded like the dying squeal of a banshee from hell. He starred desperately into the darkness trying to figure out where it was coming from. It sounded like it was above his head. Looking up, he saw the blades from the roof type air-conditioner spinning and casting intermittent shadows across the floor. The red dot of the laser was pointed directly at the offensive appliance. He had nearly shot a generator and now an air-conditioner. He needed to get his nerves under control! The screeching suddenly stopped, replaced by the steady whir of the air conditioner fan. "That could definitely use some WD40," he said softly to himself.

With his eyes nearly adjusted to the darkness, he snapped his head quickly to his left at the sound of a moan. He crept toward the source of the sound, the beam of the laser sight dancing in front of him.

There it was again! A low moan straight ahead! He could just make out a dark shape on the top of some sort of a bed. He cautiously moved closer. He shivered involuntarily. It could have been from the cold or from the adrenaline coursing through his body. Slowly raising the Glock, the red dot from the laser beam froze right between the eyes of the creature on the bed. It was Isis!

The little hairs on the back of his neck suddenly stood up! It was an early warning system that had saved his life more than once. He felt, not heard, the presence of something behind him. Whirling about quickly he peered into the darkness, the Glock at the ready. He watched for a minute checking for any movement. There was nothing, just a couple of large metal storage cabinets and other assorted piles of junk.

Isis let out another moan; he turned back to her and bent over the bed.

He heard a loud crack as his clavicle was smashed from behind with a heavy metal claw. The blow instantly paralyzed him and he only vaguely remembered the floor coming up to meet him as he passed out.

———·———

Susan had left two messages with Steve at Knight's suite and had tried his cell phone five times. Finally, in frustration she walked down the corridor and rang his doorbell.

Steve opened the door and Susan brushed him aside before he could protest.

"Where in the hell is he?" she demanded, quickly glancing around the palace-like suite.

"He left early this morning," answered Steve tentatively. Knight had not left instructions on how to deal with this angry blonde.

"Well…where did he go?" she demanded again.

Steve looked at her and could see she was not about to be put off. "He received a map last night. After breakfast he got dressed and left about 6:30."

"Did he say when he would be back?"

"No. But he was dressed like he was going hiking in the desert."

"He didn't happen to show you the map?"

"No. I'm sorry," Steve apologized.

Susan turned on her heel and walked to the door. "Tell him to call me the minute you hear from him."

"Yes Ma'am." Steve would be sure he got the message. He did not want to be accountable to this firebrand.

Susan walked to her suite and dialed Knight's cell phone again, only to be told again it was out of service. "Dammit, turn on your phone," she cursed. Anger was how she coped with her concern. She did not like it when she was angry with a man. It was the first sign she was getting involved emotionally. And, Thomas Knight was not the best one to pick for that honor. He was too enigmatic. She had no idea how he really felt about her. She prayed that he was not playing her. He was definitely a Boy Scout, there was no doubt about that, but when she needed him to do her a good deed, he was nowhere to be found.

———·———

Flynn walked into Victor's Cherenko's office in the rear of Luciano's men's store.

"Mr. Flynn," said the Russian feigning formality.

Flynn took his heavily nicotine stained hand and returned the lukewarm handshake. He looked into the small Russian's eyes. He had never noticed it before but there was nothing, not a trace of emotion, simply cold, expressionless eyes. "Victor," he replied.

"Vhat brings you down from your palace to my humble merchant's stall?" The Russian had cut right to the chase. He motioned to Flynn to have a seat.

Flynn sat down, avoiding making eye contact.

"Vodka?" asked the Russian pointing to the bottle on his desk. Something must be really wrong. Flynn had never approached him like this.

"Thanks," said Flynn, grateful to buy a little more time before the inevitable.

The Russian poured two straight drinks and handed one to his quest. "To your health," he toasted, clinking glasses.

Flynn did not acknowledge the toast, but downed the vodka in one swallow. He shook his head involuntarily as the potent liquid seared his throat.

Victor tossed down his own drink and then reached for a cigarette. He lit the disgusting object, inhaled deeply, and then let the smoke out simultaneously through his mouth and nostrils.

Flynn looked down at the floor, "There has been a situation involving your grandson."

"My Georgie?" asked Victor, fear spreading across his face. "Is he all right? He didn't get hurt parking da cars?"

Flynn shook his head and said, "He's all right. There was a misunderstanding." He got up and poured himself another drink from the bottle on the desk without asking permission.

"Vhat kind of a misunderstanding?"

"Someone stole some bathtubs from me and my V.P. of Security said it was Georgie." Flynn knocked back his drink quickly.

"Bulldog said my Georgie vas a thief?" asked Victor intently.

Flynn nodded.

"My Georgie is not a thief! He is a goot boy!" Victor stood up and looked down at Flynn.

Flynn looked up and nodded, “I know. It was…like I said. A misunderstanding.”

Victor sat down and poured himself another drink.

“Bulldog was convinced that Georgie had stolen three hundred bathtubs and then extorted three hundred thousand dollars from me to get them back. So, without my knowledge he put some pressure on Georgie to tell him what he had done with the money.”

The Russian did not say anything; he simply drained his glass again.

“By the time I found out what happened, Bulldog had slapped him around a little.” Flynn continued to look at the floor.

“Bulldog beat up my Georgie?”

Flynn looked up. He could see the anger building in the Russian. “Well he didn’t really beat him up, he just slapped him around.”

“Vhere is he now? I vant to see him right now!” The Russian stood up, his fists clenched.

“I put him in a suite and had the house doctor look at him. He’s okay. Of course, I’ll take care of whatever he needs.”

“I vant to see him now!” Victor was shaking with anger.

Flynn nodded, stood up and led the Russian to the elevator.

———·———

The house doctor pulled the blanket up to the chin of the patient on the bed. Being the house doctor for the Colossus brought no end of challenges. Vegas had a way of bringing out the worst in people. They drank too much and they stayed out too late. Many brought their problems from home hoping to find some kind of salvation among the mind-numbing distractions of the Vegas fantasy world. Usually it just made their problems worse.

He had treated every type of domestic disturbance injury and every known type of drug overdose. He was constantly patching up suicide attempts. He had seen things never shown in the medical books. He had removed all kinds of foreign objects from every body orifice.

He would have left and taken up a nice practice in a wholesome neighborhood long ago, if it were not for his own weakness. He gambled, and Flynn carried his substantial marker. It was a modern form of indentured servitude.

He handed Bulldog an orange vial full of painkillers. "I gave him one to keep him quiet for a few hours. When he wakes up, give him one every four hours for the pain. Keep the cold ice pack on the swelling. I put a stabilizing bandage on his nose but don't let him blow his nose for a few hours. I didn't see any evidence of concussion so it's all right if he wants to sleep. His lips are badly swollen so he probably won't feel like eating, but let him drink all the fluids he wants. I'll be back this afternoon to check on him." He snapped his black medical bag shut and let himself out of the suite.

Bulldog put the pill vial in his own pocket; there was no sense in wasting perfectly good drugs on a worthless Russian valet. He headed for the spa to retrieve his money. He was not going to stick around to see how Flynn had made out with the Russian godfather.

______·______

Thomas Knight slowly emerged out of the fog of unconsciousness. He was lying on a smooth floor. There was a sharp pain in his left shoulder. He moved to try to find a more comfortable position. As his senses began to come fully around, he started to recall what had happened. He shivered as he remembered the cold. The place was still dark except for a far light down a tunnel. He tried to stand only to find himself shackled by his left hand to some sort of a ring screwed into the floor. He no longer had his safari jacket, handgun and shoulder holster.

Suddenly off to his left there was a moan. "Isis?" he asked, remembering what he had seen before he was knocked out. He tried to reposition himself to see over the metal cot about three feet away from him. He could barely make out the restrained half naked person lying on the creaky iron bed. "Isis?" he asked again, finding he could not reach the bed because of his own shackle. Pain shot through his shoulder again and he used his right hand to tenderly probe the point of origin. He ran his fingers over his clavicle bone and found the source of the pain was next to his neck. He could not be sure but it felt as if the bone might be broken. Whoever or whatever hit him had certainly not pulled their punch.

With his free right hand, he tugged on the shackle around his left wrist. It was tightly secured to the floor ring. He pulled again but the result was the same. It would not budge. He stared around into the darkness and could not see anyone but Isis. They were alone.

Isis moaned again.

"Isis?" asked Knight.

She did not answer but suddenly started to cry and struggle against the restraints that held her against the metal cot.

"Isis, it's Thomas Knight," he said.

"Who?" The voice was barely audible.

"Thomas Knight. Jack sent me."

"Thomas…is that really you," she asked hoarsely. "Where are you?"

"I'm over here on the floor. I'm chained up."

Isis turned her head and as best as she could peered over the edge of the cot. "Thomas!"

"Hi kid," he said smiling. "You've been hard to find."

"What happened to me?" she croaked, her voice nearly gone.

"You were kidnapped."

"I don't remember very well," she whispered.

"Who did it?" he asked.

"I don't know. They must have drugged me with something. It's like a bad nightmare."

"How many of them are there?"

"I think there are two, although I've only seen one. Thomas, it is the most horrible creature you can imagine."

"Is it about eight feet tall, gray skin, lots of tentacles and big green eyes?" Knight asked.

"Yeah, that's the one I've seen. What is that thing?"

"I don't know for sure. You said there were two?" Knight suddenly remembered that Vera the nurse had mentioned that there were twins. He hadn't counted on double the trouble.

"I've only seen the one creature, but I've heard it talking to someone. I couldn't see who it was."

Knight looked around again trying to make sense out of the surroundings.

Isis raised her head from the cot and looked toward Knight. "Thomas there's a water bottle by the base of the bed. I can't reach it. Could you kick it over to me with your foot?"

Knight twisted as best he could, extended his foot and gently pushed the water bottle toward Isis's cot.

She reached over the edge and using the tips of her fingers was able to pick up the bottle. She unscrewed the top and poured the precious liquid down her throat. "I'd swear I'm in hell but it's too damn cold!"

"It sure stinks like hell," said Knight, wrinkling up his nose. "Isis?"

"Yes."

"Did they hurt you?"

She remembered the creature suckling her breasts and biting her. She recalled with horror how he had run his claw down the insides of her thighs. She did not want to tell anyone. "No…not really I guess. They've kept me pretty well drugged."

Knight was relieved. "When do they normally show up?"

"I don't know. I can't tell whether it's night or day. Do you know how long I've been here?"

"It's going on three days."

That explained her hunger. They had not fed her a thing. "I haven't had anything to eat."

"I'll buy you a banana split as soon as we get out of here."

The thought of the cold ice cream sliding down her inflamed throat was more than she could stand. She started to cry.

"Are you okay?" he asked hearing her sniffling.

She choked back her tears. "Thomas, I think there is a body of a man hanging from a conveyor or something over there."

Knight looked, but it was too dark to confirm her pronouncement.

She started sobbing again. "How are we going to get out of here?"

"Don't worry. I have a plan," he lied. He did not have a clue.

———·———

Victor looked at his grandson with tears in his eyes. He moved to the edge of the bed and gently brushed back a lock of black hair that had fallen down over his forehead. He carefully pulled back the bedcovers. His grandson's bodybuilder's physique appeared undamaged. However, his face was nothing more than adhesive tape and dark blue bruises. A small drop of blood appeared in his left nostril. Victor took a tissue from the box on the bed stand and carefully daubed it away.

Georgie slowly opened his eyes a crack. "Hi Grandfather," he whispered through his swollen lips.

"I vill take goot care of you," said Victor, patting his grandson's giant hand with his yellow stained fingers.

"I tried to tell them I didn't steal anything," he murmured.

"You're a good boy Georgie," answered Victor, bending over to kiss him on the forehead.

Flynn was sitting on the couch in the living room of the suite when Victor walked in from the bedroom. "How is he?" he asked.

"Beat to hell, dat's how he is." There was no mistaking the venom in Victor's voice. "Someone is going to pay for dis!"

"Bulldog got carried away," said Flynn, trying to compartmentalize the damage.

"This vould never have happened if Thomas Knight vere still in charge."

"Tell me about it!" agreed Flynn.

"Why did you hire such a man as dis Bulldog?"

"Because I had my head up my ass, that's why," confessed Flynn. This was not the first time he had regretted that decision.

Victor sat down in a side chair and starred at the bedroom door. "He is very strong. He vill recover but maybe not as handsome as before."

Flynn nodded.

Victor lit one of his offensive cigarettes. "You know of course I must do something." He really had no choice. "I have already put the word out dat I vant to talk to Bulldog." His entire organization was built on ruthlessness. If he let someone attack a member of his family without reprisal, he would be seen as too weak to run the organization. There was no shortage of young lions eager to make their reputations the minute any crack showed in Victor's armor.

"Do what you have to do," said Flynn. Bulldog would have to argue his own way out of this, if he could.

———·———

When Flynn returned to his office Susan was waiting for him in the reception area. She followed him into his office.

"Where's Thomas Knight?" she ordered, foregoing any pleasantries.

Flynn was definitely in a foul mood after the mess with Bulldog and Victor. "How in the hell should I know?"

"I understand you gave him a map this morning. Is that true?"

Flynn went to the bar, poured himself a vodka, and splashed it with water. He did not offer her one. "What's it to you?"

"He's out looking for your wife, you ungrateful jerk and no one can get a hold of him."

Flynn did not reply. He went over to his desk and picked up a copy of the map he had given Knight and handed it to her.

Susan studied it for a second and then left the office without saying another word. "Damn you Thomas!" she swore as she punched the button for the elevator. It seemed all she did anymore was swear at him. He obviously had gone off to locate Baby Doc without bothering to tell her he was going. She was angry because she was worried about him and he obviously could not care less.

Back in her suite, she quickly changed into her desert clothes. Before she pulled up her jeans, she looked in the mirror at the Ferrari welt on her butt. It was still bright pink. It would just have to fade with time. She put the .380 Colt Mustang automatic into her purse and called the LSI Las Vegas office. "I need a four-wheel-drive SUV ASAP," she ordered. "Have it delivered to the VIP entrance at the Colossus." She hung up the phone and then tried Knight's cell again. Once again, the now familiar message told her the phone was out of service.

She looked at her watch. It was nearly noon. She had a finite amount of time to find Knight and get back to the Colossus before the next email was to arrive from Isis's kidnappers. She ordered Gary to pack a quick lunch and three bottles of water. She would eat as she drove.

Susan blinked as she stepped out of the casino into the bright sunlight. She opened her purse and put on her vintage, aviator style, Ray Ban sunglasses.

"May I help you Miss Strong," Johnny asked tentatively

Susan did not smile. "I was supposed to pick up a rental SUV."

Johnny looked confused. "The only rental that has been dropped off here was a green Dodge Caravan for someone from LSI Insurance."

"Dammit," swore Susan. She did not have time to chew out her employees. The van would have to do. "Where is it? It's for me."

"I'll have it up in a minute," Johnny answered, quickly using his intercom. When the green van arrived, he opened the door.

"Thanks," said Susan politely out of habit. The van looked as if it would be okay in the desert. She turned onto the Strip and headed for the highway. She opened the small lunch sack Gary had given her and picked out an apple. Holding the apple in her teeth, she tried Knight's cell phone. Again, there was no answer. She had a sudden premonition that he was in trouble.

———·———

Bulldog emptied the five lockers in the spa where he had stashed the three hundred thousand he had gotten for the bathtubs. He put each bag full of cash into a larger bag. He had planned to let his sports book runner bet the money in six thousand dollar increments. He would have had it bet on the favorites. It was a typical subsistence gambler's scheme, by betting favorites he stood to increase his bankroll by perhaps twenty-five percent. If he had a winning streak, he might even double it.

It had been a good plan, but all that had changed. He needed to run. Put as much distance between him and the fearsome Russian as he could. He had been around long enough to know that there was not going to be any penance that Victor would accept. Victor would have to make an example of him. And, because it had been a member of his family that had been wronged, the retribution would have to be particularly gruesome. Bulldog shook his head. He did not want to dwell on it.

On his way out of the spa with the duffel, he placed a call using his cell phone. He needed someone he could trust to liquidate his Las Vegas assets and then send him the money, wherever he finally went to ground.

"Hello," he said when the familiar voice answered the phone. "I need to see you immediately," he ordered. "No, it can't be in the Hotel," he responded to the voice on the phone's suggestion. Bulldog listened, "Okay…Okay, but it has to be in fifteen minutes." He had given in to the other party's demands to meet in the hotel. He looked at his watch; only ten minutes had passed since he had left Victor's grandson in the suite. He doubted Flynn had met with Victor yet. He probably still had a few minutes before a contract could go out on him. It was dangerous to stick around, but he needed to be sure his assets would catch up to him. The three hundred thousand was not going to last long. He needed enough to stay deep undercover for at least two years. Who knows, by then maybe the frail Russian Don would die either from old age or from smoking those foul Russian cigarettes he preferred.

It was nearly completely dark in the prop area behind the main showroom's stage. It looked completely deserted. The stagehands and the technicians would not report to work for three more hours.

"What's up?" asked the voice in the dark.

"Thanks for coming," said Bulldog. He was grateful that the person had not wasted any time in getting there. "I need your help."

"What's going on?"

"Do you really love me?" Bulldog asked.

"What brings that up?" asked the sultry voice.

"I need to know. Do you really love me or was it all an act?"

"Of course I love you, silly."

"I mean do you love me enough that I can really count on you?"

"Yes, you can count on me." The voice was impatient. "What's going on?"

Bulldog relaxed. She had said what he had hoped he would hear. "I'm leaving town and I need you to sell my house and car and send me the money."

"Where are you going?"

"I don't know yet. I'll call you as soon as I figure it out."

"How long will you be gone?"

"I don't know that either. I just need to know I can trust you."

"You can trust me."

"I'll send you my power of attorney and a list of what I need you to do in a couple of days."

"This sounds serious," said the voice with apprehension.

"It is, but it is nothing I can't handle if you help me out."

Honey stepped out of the darkness, put her arms around his neck and kissed him.

Bulldog wrapped her in his arms and crushed her breasts against his chest. He kissed her and then said, "I do love you."

"I know," she said softly.

"Who's there?" demanded an authoritative male voice.

"Damn!" whispered Bulldog, he recognized the voice.

"Who is it?" asked Honey.

"It's one of my security guards. I don't want him to see me with you."

Honey quickly grabbed him by the hand and led him through the dark into a large box like object. "Quick, hide in here. I'll get rid of him."

Bulldog entered the box and cowered down in a corner.

Honey closed the opening to the box behind him and then called out to the security guard. "It's just me, Honey."

"Oh, hi Ms. Honey," said the guard with relief in his voice. "I thought I heard voices."

"I was just thinking about a new routine and I guess I was talking to myself."

The guard seemed satisfied. "You want me to turn on the lights or anything?"

"No, I'm just leaving. Thank you anyway."

"Okay," answered the guard. "I'm going to stick around for a while, until the stage hands show up.

Honey walked over to the box and whispered to Bulldog. "I'll be back in a little while, just sit tight."

"Okay," Bulldog whispered back. He really needed to get out of there as quickly as he could.

Honey left the show room and headed across the casino to the shopping arcade. She walked into Luciano's and ignoring the approaching salesman went directly into Victor's office. She towered over the diminutive figure sitting in a blue cloud of smoke behind the desk. "Word has it that you are looking for Bulldog."

The Russian nodded cautiously.

"What's in it for me if I can deliver your boy?" she demanded.

Victor lit a new cigarette and studied the stunning blonde. "My undying gratitude," he said matter-of-factly. "Vere is he?"

Honey poured herself a drink from the vodka bottle on the desk. She tilted her head back and let the fiery liquid slowly drain down her throat. "I've got him locked up in one of my bear cages."

———·———

Bulldog looked at the luminous hands on his watch. Honey had been gone nearly half an hour. He could not wait much longer. He stood up and felt his way in the dark to the door of the box. He put his ear to the door and listened. There was no sound; evidently, the guard had decided to take a leak or something. He put his hand on the doorknob and turned it. He pushed the door open slightly and poked his head around it.

He jumped with fright as the box was instantly illuminated by a bank of spotlights. He put up his hand to shield his eyes from the glare. "Honey is that you?" he asked. He took two steps ahead still trying to see beyond the lights. He banged into the bars before he saw them. He quickly looked behind him. He panicked as he realized that he had been in a box inside a barred cage.

Slowly a figure appeared out of the glare of lights. "Oh no!" he screamed as he recognized the familiar frail Russian. He panicked and shook the bars with all his strength. He clawed at the lock and chain holding the barred door shut. It was useless. He was hopelessly trapped in the cage.

Suddenly another figure stepped out of the lights and stood next to Victor. It was Honey! Panic tore at his stomach. His legs were weak and he fell to his knees still clutching the bars. "Why?" he sobbed. "I loved you."

Victor looked at the pathetic creature. He felt no compassion. "Vill your bears eat him?" he asked Honey matter-of-factly.

"They will eat almost anything," she answered. "Although I don't think they've ever eaten a bulldog."

Victor did not smile at the pun. He walked to the cage and looked down at the cowering creature. "In one of da work camps in da Gulag da camp commandant kept a bear in a cage. If you complained about da maggots and da roaches in the food, he vood have you stripped, then smeared with da food and put in da cage. Da bear vas even hungrier than we vere."

Bulldog was literally shaking with fear. "You are kidding…right?" He could not believe this was happening. He tried to tell himself that they were only trying to scare him. They could not possibly be serious about feeding him to a bear.

Victor starred at him with his cold eyes. "Sometimes da bear in the camp could not eat a whole man in one sitting. So, he would eat only part of him. One prisoner lived for three days before da bear had completely finished eating." He looked at Honey for confirmation. "I don't suppose your bears are as hungry as da commandant's. Dey might even take longer to enjoy their meal."

Honey went over to the cage and looked Bulldog in the eye. "Thor, my big brown Kodiak, is a remarkably light eater for his size."

"Please Honey…don't do this," Bulldog whimpered. "I've got money. You can have it all!"

Honey shook her head.

"Please Victor!" Bulldog moved his appeal to the Russian. "Georgie was not hurt that bad. I just left him…in fact I was on my way up to him to give him some pills the doctor ordered." He desperately fished into his pants pocket, pulled out the orange pill vial and held it up. "See!"

Victor walked over to the cage and took the pills. "These are for Georgie?"

"Yes…Yes!" stammered Bulldog, his ruse appeared to be working. "I was on my way to give them to him."

Victor looked at the vial and then asked flatly, "How much money do you have?"

"I've got one hundred thousand in cash," Bulldog lied. If he told Victor about the entire three hundred thousand there would be no doubt he was the one who framed his grandson. If the Russian found that out, he would be bear meat for sure.

"You said everything. I understand you have got three hundred thousand," added Victor matter-of-factly, "and some other assets. Honey had told him everything.

Bulldog felt the panic rising in his throat. The Russian had somehow found out he was the one! "Okay! Okay! All the cash, but not the house or the car," He cried, desperately trying to salvage something.

Victor smiled slyly. He had found how to punish Bulldog. "Everything. Including your house and car," he said. Leaving Bulldog penniless, watching all the material things he had sold his soul for disappear, would be a far worse punishment than a mere beating.

Victor gestured to Honey. “Unlock the cage.”

“But I…”

“Just do vhat I say.” Victor cut her off in mid-sentence.

“You’re a lucky bastard,” she whispered to Bulldog as she turned the key in the lock.

Victor motioned to his two huge enforcers. Each grabbed one of Bulldog’s arms in a vice like grip.

Victor looked up at the former V.P. of Security and snarled. “He leaves town with nothing but a headache.” The enforcers lifted Bulldog up on his toes and grunted in acknowledgement.

———.———

Honey walked toward her dressing room. She could not believe her luck. With Bulldog gone, her plan was even more secure. And, as an added bonus, the most powerful mobster in Vegas owed her whatever favor she wanted. She stared into the brightly illuminated makeup mirror and started smearing handfuls of cold cream on her face to remove her street makeup. As she removed the last of the cream with the little cotton balls, she opened up the small refrigerator under the dressing table and took out a plastic bottle of honey. She flipped the lid on the bottle, put it to her lips and squeezed. She continued to suck on the bottle periodically as she prepared the foundation for her stage makeup. The show had to go on as planned. It was her alibi.

CHAPTER 13

Flynn was exhausted when he returned to his office from his meeting with Victor. As he walked by, his secretary stopped him. "I was just writing you a note," she said. "The Casino Floor Manager needs to talk to you. He said it was urgent."

Flynn nodded, walked into his office and dialed the casino floor.

"The cowboy is back," said the Manager.

"Yeah, so?" Flynn was still preoccupied with how he had barely escaped ruin, or worse, at the hands of the Russian.

The Manager sounded concerned. "His luck picked up where he left off. He put the whole hundred thousand he won last night down and he's letting it ride. He is up eight hundred thousand now."

"What's wrong with this guy?" asked Flynn, the cowboy had to be nuts to tempt fate again.

"I checked him out as best I could. I couldn't get a hold of you or Bulldog so I approved his play." The Manager was praying that he would not have his hide nailed to the wall for exceeding his authority.

Flynn did not reply, he was thinking. Finally, he asked, "What did you find out about him?"

"He's from some small town in Wyoming. He's a rancher or something. Evidently, he hasn't played big here in Vegas recently. He doesn't have one of our big shooter's profiles in our database. Neither we nor any of the other casinos has a derog file on him."

Every casino in Vegas had built elaborate databases about known or possible cheats. In the early '80s, the emergence of standardized computer platforms had allowed the data to be shared freely among all the casinos.

Information about the big shooters and the whales was another matter. Each casino tried to find out as much as they could about those players. Any little thing could be used to create a competitive advantage in attracting them to play at their casino instead of the one next door. One whale's advance man had requested only brown M&M's be put in candy dishes throughout his suite. The player was highly superstitious and had to have everything just so. When the casino had put the standard packets of multi-colored ones out by mistake, the whale had packed up and moved his multi-million dollar play down the strip. This type of information was guarded as carefully as the combination to the casino's vault.

The Manager continued. "I had the head floor maid look around his suite. He drank up the mini-bar, but he still looks as sober as a judge."

"Don't let him press his bet," said Flynn matter-of-factly. He had made his decision. "Shut him down."

"You want to pull the plug?" the Manager asked, not believing that he had heard what he thought he had heard. Flynn had never backed up before from a bet.

"Yes dammit!" he cursed. "He is either the luckiest son-of-a-bitch alive or he's got something up his sleeve. Either way I'm not taking a chance."

"If he's on the square our reputation could take a dump," the Manager warned. Something had definitely changed in Flynn.

"Just get him off the table and send him up."

"Yes sir," replied the Manager reluctantly.

In less than ten minutes, the secretary escorted the cowboy into Flynn's office. He was tall and lanky with a deeply tanned face. Curls of dark hair, streaked with gray, poked out from beneath his triple-creased, light gray Stetson. He was wearing what looked like a crisply ironed, long sleeved, J.C. Penney shirt. A hand-tooled, wide, black belt with an oversized silver and turquoise buckle held up his well-washed, Wrangler jeans. The bottom of each pant leg was slightly frayed, just touching the carpet in back of the heels of his Luchesse, black roper boots.

He took off his hat as Flynn stood up and approached him. With his Stetson removed, his forehead was nearly white. His handshake was firm, his hand rough and calloused.

Flynn gestured to him to sit in one of the side chairs and then walked behind his desk and sat down. "Congratulations," he said.

The cowboy only nodded, his eyes looking around trying to take in the sumptuous office.

"You hit us pretty hard," said Flynn, trying to size him up. "You're obviously a betting man, so I'd like to make you a couple of propositions."

"What are they Sir?" the cowboy asked politely.

"I need a chance to get my money back. So, I'll give you half again as much as you've already won in chips, if you'll stay and play. Of course, everything will be a full boat comp, whatever you want."

The cowboy looked down at his Stetson and rolled the edges with his fingers. "You said there were two propositions."

"If you don't play, I'll give you a cashier's check for what you've won. But I never want to see your face again."

The cowboy, stood up, carefully put his hat on with both hands and walked to the door. Turning his head back over his shoulder he said, "Send the check to my room."

"Deliver me from Wyoming cowboys," said Flynn to himself as he dialed the phone on his desk. When the Casino Floor Manager answered, Flynn said, "Don't ever let anyone in a cowboy hat play above the table limits again!"

———·———

Susan was driving the Caravan down the increasingly eroded road and it had bottomed out several times. She was concerned; it would be necessary to turn around if it got much worse. She should have held out for the SUV. She would be sure that the employee who screwed up the order would definitely hear about it.

According to Flynn's map, there were still two miles to go. She was praying that she had taken the right road leading out of Indian Springs. Oh well, she would just continue to slug it out until she either found Baby Doc's place or she ran out of road entirely.

She approached a blind, steep rise and was nearly hit head-on by the big large ice-cream truck barreling down the road. She instinctively swerved to the right and just caught a glimpse of the other driver. He was a horrible looking man and showed no indication that he had seen her. She fought desperately to gain control, alternately braking and steering. She could not hold it. The van's tires caught in one of the road ruts and turned it sideways. Its momentum caused it to flip. It rolled and landed on its top. The energy in the van had not been fully dissipated and it slid down a steep embankment before stopping abruptly.

Susan looked out the shattered windshield and all she could see was dust. The odor of gasoline filled her nostrils. She was fighting the panic that was trying to grab her. A dull ache was making its way across her abdomen. She was upside down and her seat belt was nearly cutting her in two. She pushed frantically at the belt release and was instantly dumped on her head against the former roof of the van. She twisted and turned trying to get her feet below her head. She had barely managed to get her whole body on the same plane when suddenly an explosion nearly knocked her unconscious. The air bag had suddenly decided to inflate. It felt as if it would completely engulf and smother her. She clawed at the offensive balloon trying to push it away.

With a loud bang and a menacing hiss the air bag deflated, leaving her still pounding on the fabric with her fist.

Turning her head up she could see that the driver's side window was cracked but still intact. She reached over her head and pushed. It gave way suddenly and choking white dust rushed into the opening. She could not see a thing through the blinding white fog. Instinctively she snaked her body through the open window. She choked repeatedly as the fine dust tried to fill her lungs.

She wiggled and kicked as hard as she could and suddenly she was outside the van lying on the coarse stones of the desert floor.

A gentle breeze was finally blowing the dust away and she lay there sucking in the clean air. She ran her hand over her abdomen and found that the damage appeared to be nothing more than a bad bruise. She cautiously tried to stand, using the van to steady her. She let her legs stabilize, giving her a chance to establish equilibrium. Her body was shaking badly as the adrenaline released by the crash continued to run through her system. The whole crash had taken less than twenty seconds but it had seemed like a week.

Susan looked around, the giant's ice cream truck was nowhere in sight. Without the dust, there was no sign that an accident had just taken place except for the still spinning tires on the upturned van.

The shock of the accident started to wear off and her brain kicked into gear. She bent over, reached inside the van and recovered her purse. She opened it up and was reassured when it appeared that the .380 automatic had survived intact.

She looked back up the hill again but there still was no sign of the truck or its driver. If it had been Baby Doc, she was grateful to have a pistol in hand for their first meeting.

Everything still looked foggy for some reason. She tried to wipe her eyes and was shocked to find her Ray Bans were still in place. She peeled them off her face and looked at the lenses. They were caked with dust. Using the monogrammed, pure Irish linen handkerchief from her purse, she wiped them off and was surprised at how her outlook immediately improved.

Susan climbed up the bank to the road, the Colt Mustang in her right hand and her purse in the left. When she finally reached the top, there was nothing in sight. She was alone.

Her situation was bad, but it was not hopeless. She had options. She could either hike the eight miles back to Indian Springs, or the two more miles to Baby Doc's. She had water and the remnants of the lunch that Gary had made her back in the van. Both choices required a long hike in the desert. Storm clouds were starting to build off to the west and it looked as if it could rain in a couple of hours. The thought of hiking across the desert in a rainstorm was not appealing, so she decided to call for the cavalry. She found her cell phone in her purse.

The liquid crystal display on the phone lit up when she turned it on. "Thank goodness it's still working," she said aloud. Her relief quickly vanished when the display showed that she was out of range of a signal.

The ice cream truck pulled up in front of the brown-stuccoed casino in Indian Springs. The huge, misshapen driver in the filthy, bloodstained coveralls got out and walked inside.

The handful of local, midday gamblers suddenly stopped their play at the sight of the new visitor. They averted their eyes and looked away as the driver walked through the casino and into the restaurant.

Janice, the waitress looked up and with a look of pure terror dropped the coffee cup she was putting into the bus boy's tub. The crockery cup sounded like a gunshot as it hit the tile floor. The two patrons seated at the lunch counter looked up from their hamburgers at the sound and froze in mid-bite.

The driver did not acknowledge anyone. He walked around the counter and into the petitioned-off grill section.

The fry cook with the grease stained apron had been scraping the grill when the driver entered. He stopped in mid-scrape and cautiously moved aside as the huge man walked past him into the small office at the rear of the kitchen.

The office was empty. Baby Doc Prentice walked to the metal desk and picked up the telephone. He punched in a number and waited. When the phone was answered, he said in a deep guttural voice, "I caught another one." He listened. "I found him in the trailer. He was talking to the woman." He listened again. "No, I just have him chained. Should I cut him up?"

The voice on the other end of the line made a disparaging remark.

"I am not stupid! You're stupid!" he said, childishly defensive. He listened again. "No, I didn't see anyone else. Can I cut him up?" He paused then obviously not liking the other party's answer, said, "I am not stupid! You're stupid!" he repeated the childish refrain. "He wants to steal my diamond just like all the rest, so I want to cut him up."

The other party on the line was obviously angry.

"You're not the boss of me!" cried Baby Doc. "The doctors told me you weren't my boss! I'll cut him up if I want to!" he snarled defiantly.

The other party said something to calm him down.

"Okay. I'll wait until you get here. But, I want the woman, just like you promised." He hung up the phone and left the office.

The waitress, cook and patrons had armed themselves with a frying pan, meat cleaver and two steak knives. They had banded together in a small group, their backs to the wall.

Baby Doc stared at them. They were steeling themselves for a fight. "Boo!" he shouted as he feinted toward them. The group jumped with fright. Baby Doc turned and walked back into the casino laughing.

None of the players in the casino had gone back to their play. They were watching him intently. He walked to the nearest blackjack table, picked up the chips of the two players and rudely elbowed his way between them. He placed the pilfered chips in the small white circle in front of him and told the terrified dealer to deal the cards.

The dealer dealt the cards, peeked at his and without waiting flipped over his hand. He had the king of hearts and the ace of clubs. "Twenty one," he announced with trepidation.

Baby Doc did not bother to look at his cards. "I win!" he cried with delight.

The dealer did not protest. His hand was shaking as he slid over a large stack of chips without counting them.

Baby Doc picked them up and walked across the casino to the cashier's cage. He slid the chips through the slot in the bars to the frightened, gray haired, female cashier. She did not count the chips; she simply opened her cash drawer and stripped all the trays of their contents. She placed the stacks of bills on the well-worn marble surface and then slid them through the slot.

Baby Doc picked up the bills, stuffed them into the pockets of his filthy coveralls and headed for the door of the casino. "I'm not stupid! You're stupid!" he said to no one as he climbed behind the wheel of the ice cream truck. He backed the truck up, turned it around and with a squeal of the tires, headed back to his trailer.

———·———

Susan had a plan. It was not a very good one, but it was a plan nevertheless. She would walk the two miles to Baby Doc's place. If it were him, she had seen in the ice cream truck then perhaps his house would be deserted. As she walked, she would continue to try the recalcitrant cell phone to see if she could get service. If she did not, then perhaps she could find a car to steal. Who knows she might even stumble across Thomas Knight if she was lucky.

With the water and the lunch sack retrieved from the van, she started hiking. She looked at the sky with apprehension. The storm was approaching faster than she had anticipated. At her current gait, it would take her at least twenty-five minutes to cover the two miles. Suddenly her nostrils picked up the smell of moisture in the air. She started to jog hoping that the ominous rain cloud would hold off its water delivery for fifteen minutes.

Jogging as fast as she could she was surprised to find that she was going nearly as fast on foot as she had been in the van. After the first mile, she stopped and took a long drink from one of the water bottles. She was not thirsty, but she knew she had to stay hydrated and the secret was to drink before you were thirsty. She had just screwed the cap back onto the plastic water bottle when she heard the sound of a truck approaching. She had not counted on that!

She looked around for cover and finding precious little, threw herself prone on the ground behind a small sagebrush. She prayed. If the truck were indeed Baby Doc's, maybe he would not see her. After all, he had run her bright green Caravan off the road and apparently had not seen that.

The truck's dually wheels and high ground clearance was allowing it to move down the rutted road with ease. The driver was shifting expertly to maintain a consistently high rpm.

The truck roared by in a cloud of dust without so much as a pause. She had gotten away with it. The driver had not seen her!

Susan scrambled to her feet and waved at the remnants of the dust cloud. She had to clean her sunglasses again. A re-evaluation of the plan was in order. A quick check of the cell phone showed she was still outside of a service area. With all the satellites circling the Earth, it was amazing that somehow this little area, where she was located, had fallen through the cracks. "I'm going to call my Congressman about this crap when I get back," she said aloud, not letting her brain dwell on the fact that she might not return.

Another eight minutes of hard jogging brought her to a small rise in the road. As she crested the hill, she could finally see the object of her search.

The place was a real dump! She did not know what she had expected to see, but this was certainly not it. She crouched down and using the small rise as cover, slowly worked her way around to the right side of the compound. The ice cream truck was parked right in front of the door.

Susan took the .380 out of her purse and slid the slide back slowly, confirming that there was already a round in the chamber. She was still trying to figure out how to get inside when she felt the first raindrop on her cheek. She was going to get soaked, but maybe a dark sky and a good rain could give her the cover she needed!

General Guts Grant was livid. "What do you mean the situation is unstable and could blow at anytime?"

Professor Aronson had tried to explain for twenty minutes that predicting exactly when a volcano's venting would occur was nearly impossible. Even he, the world's foremost authority, could only give a ballpark guess.

"Dammit man," swore the General. "Everything is set up for tomorrow at 1700 hours!"

"I know, but I'm afraid the venting will occur earlier. Actually it could occur at any time," said the Professor matter-of-factly.

The red blush of anger covered Gut's face. "I just can't up and set off an underground nuclear explosion any old time I want. It has to be scheduled! There are thousands of people involved. They're all working as a team to pull this off. There simply is no way to move it up!"

The Professor nodded, "I understand, and the venting may hold off until we can release the pressure with the blast, but the only way to be sure is to do it now."

"I just told you, that it ain't gonna happen." The General stood up and started pacing. He took the .45 automatic out of his right holster and started spinning it around his right index finger. It was what he did every time he was nervous. "What is the worst that could happen without the explosion?"

The Professor peered over his reading glasses. "The dome of the underground chamber where the magma has been accumulating is like the crust on a freshly baked pie. The explosion would have the same effect as cutting venting holes in the crust with a knife. The pressure is released and vented where you want it. If you didn't cut the vent holes, then the pressure would seek the weakest area and vent through there. It could go anywhere!"

"Dammit we're not baking a pie!" Guts swore, still nervously spinning the automatic. "Isn't there anyway to tell?"

The Professor shook his head. "Not for sure, but the venting should start to show up on the ground sensors we've got all over the site."

Guts put the gun back in its holster. "Those sensors were to detect intruders, not to predict volcanoes!"

The Professor nodded, "I know, but they can do double duty. They can't tell us when the venting will occur, but they might help us predict where."

Guts picked up the phone. "Get someone up here from TSG immediately," he barked. If Operation Big Deal went south, his career would go with it.

The brunette Captain showed Sergeant Conway into the General's office.

"Sir," he said, coming to attention.

"At ease Sergeant," said Guts with a wave of his hand. "Do we have anything unusual on the site's security sensors?"

The Sergeant looked at him and the Professor quizzically, "No sir. Not that I'm aware of."

The General walked over to the Sergeant and looked him right in the eye. "Tell me immediately if you get any anomalies."

"Yes sir!" said the Sergeant snapping to attention again, obviously intimidated.

"Dismissed," waved the General. He sat down and put his head in his hands. Then he looked up at the

Professor. "I hope you know what in the hell you're doing."

———·———

Knight's eyes had finally adjusted to the nearly dark interior of the trailer. Isis had been right. There was no doubt about it. There definitely was a naked human corpse hanging from a meat hook.

"Thomas?" asked Isis weakly. "I was right wasn't I?"

"Yes kid, I'm afraid so."

"Who do you suppose it is?" she asked.

"If I had to guess. I'd say it is probably a young assistant professor from U.N.L.V." answered Knight. "He disappeared a couple of days ago."

"Why would the creature want to kill him?"

"I don't know. Maybe it was a fight over trespassing or something." Knight knew exactly why. Baby Doc was protecting his turf. So consumed was he with finding the source of Buck's diamond that he would kill to prevent anyone from finding it but him. He also knew there was no point in worrying Isis any more than she already was.

"Do you think he will kill us too?" Isis asked with apprehension.

"No of course not," he lied. "He's holding you for ransom. He wants Jack to pay twenty million dollars for you."

"Jack's going to pay twenty million for me?" she had real surprise in her voice.

"Yeah. It's all set up. He is supposed to find out where to deliver the money this afternoon. As soon as he gets the word he'll pay and you'll be back where you belong." Knight knew that given what he and Isis had seen, the odds on being left alive were worse than the twelve the hard way bet at a craps table.

The trailer was suddenly swayed by a small earth tremor and instantly there was a loud hiss followed by the smell of rotten eggs.

"What was that?" asked Isis.

"It's nothing. Just a small earthquake." Knight tried to sound reassuring.

"What's that smell?"

"The quake evidently opened up small fissures in the rocks under this place and the smell is sulfur." Knight had elected not to repeat what the Professor had told him about small ventings often being the precursor of a full-scale volcanic eruption. He continued to lie. "It's nothing to worry about. It happens all the time."

"Why is this place so damned cold?" asked Isis trying to control her shivering.

"My guess is that it's an attempt to slow down the decomposition of whatever he is butchering. Then he is probably using the refrigerated ice cream truck to transport it somewhere." He heard the sound of the approaching truck before he could speculate further.

"Oh no! He is coming back!" Isis cried with terror in her voice.

"He's just probably coming back to get you to take you to Jack so he can get his money." Knight was trying to prevent her from panicking.

Isis was shivering from fear and the cold so violently that the cot she was on was rattling.

"Stay calm kid, everything will be all right." Knight was fighting to keep the apprehension out of his voice.

They both jumped when instantly the entire place was brightly illuminated by a bank of florescent lights.

Knight held up his unshackled hand to fend off the glare. His eyes struggled to adjust to the bright light.

The giant walked over to Knight, starred down at him for a second then reached down and yanked on the floor ring to test whether or not it was still secure.

Knight had never seen anything like this creature! It was nearly eight feet tall and probably weighed four hundred pounds. It was dressed in a black T-shirt and filthy coveralls that had once been blue. They were caked in dry blood and were now almost black.

The creature's head was badly deformed and the whole left side of the face sagged. It was as if two different faces had been split down the middle and then fashioned together by some Dr. Frankenstein. Around his neck a large, hen's-egg, sized stone wrapped in a wire basket hung from a filthy, sweat encrusted leather thong.

The creature's right eye moved normally, but the left eye starred blindly straight ahead. A small drop of yellow pus-like fluid formed at the outer edge of the bad eye. He wiped at the discharge with the back of his enormous hand.

He walked over to the cot and starred down at the half naked Isis. His mouth was half open, his tongue partially extended. A drop of drool fell on Isis' left breast.

She tried not to scream.

The creature reached down and tested her chains with the same hard yank that he had given Knight's shackle. Finding the restraints satisfactorily secure, he moved over to a large butcher-block table next to the brightly polished stainless steel conveyor system. Knight's shoulder holster and Glock were lying on the table.

The creature took the handgun out of the holster and waved it around like a toy. "Bang! Bang!" he shouted in a deep voice as he pretended to shoot at something. "The doctors said I shouldn't play with guns."

He walked over to Knight and pointed the Glock at him.

"Be careful with that thing," admonished Knight. He had set the small lever on the left side of the slide for full automatic fire. If Baby Doc pulled the trigger, all thirty-six rounds would discharge before he could release it.

He was too late! The Glock went off with a deafening staccato! A bright flash of whitish orange flame shot from the barrel! The recoil yanked the pistol upward, pulling the arm of the unprepared shooter with it. The deadly, copper coated, 9mm bullets punched neat holes in the walls and the ceiling of the metal trailer. The spent, brass, shell casings danced around the floor with a sound like a slot machine payoff. It was over as quickly as it started.

Knight had ducked and covered his head instinctively with his good hand. It took a second before he realized he had not been hit.

Thin shafts of light crisscrossed the room from the scores of holes in the walls and the ceiling.

The creature stood frozen with his mouth wide open. When he suddenly realized the now, red-hot gun was burning his hand; he dropped it on the floor.

Knight's ears were ringing. "You stupid idiot!" he shouted.

"I'm not stupid. You're stupid!" shouted Baby Doc. He walked over to Knight and with one blow of his ham-like hand, knocked him unconscious.

———.———

Susan had scouted the perimeter of the fence around Baby Doc's house. The only way in or out was through the front gate. With Baby Doc in the house, any attempt she made to tinker with the gate would probably be detected. She did not relish the thought of being confronted by the giant creature. The Mustang automatic certainly could be deadly, but the .380 caliber bullet was not known for its stopping ability. Anyway, she did not want to try it out. She could wait and see what happened or she could scale the fence and steal the ice cream truck. Hot-wiring the truck would be a piece of cake for her. Her Grandfather had shown her how to do it when she was a teenager. Of course, he had been showing her how to prevent grand-theft auto, not how to perpetrate it.

Stealing the truck was one thing; scaling the eight-foot chain-link fence was another. She looked with sadness at her formerly, exquisitely manicured nails. "Oh well, there's always a casualty in a war," she said to herself. She put the nickel-plated pistol into her waistband and then jumped on to the fence. She clawed her way up the side and swung her body over the top. She dropped down on the inside of the compound onto the ground now sprinkled with raindrops. She drew the handgun from her waist and ran to the side of the truck. She flattened herself against the cold aluminum and waited breathlessly. There was no noise from the house and she felt confident that she not been detected.

She slowly snuck around to the driver's side of the truck and opened the driver's door as quietly as she could. Her Grandfather had once told her that while most thieves knew how to hot-wire vehicles it was rare that they had to do it. Usually the owner left the keys in the vehicle. That was the case. The keys were still in the ignition of the truck. She was just about to slide into the driver's seat when she heard the roar of the machine gun from inside the trailer. She instinctively threw herself onto the ground thinking that somebody was firing at her. Once she realized that was not the case, she stood up and sprinted to the side of the trailer. The only one she knew that had a machine gun was Thomas Knight. Putting two and two together, he had to be inside the trailer. If he was, then what in the hell was he shooting at?

With the small automatic at the ready, she cautiously crept to the door of the trailer. She put her ear to the side of the door and listened. She could hear what sounded like scuffling. Trying the knob on the door, she found that it was unlocked. Cautiously, she pushed open the door to the trailer. The stench almost forced her back. It smelled as if something had died in there and then left to rot. As she glanced around the brightly lit, interior she could not believe what she saw. In the middle of the room was a large stainless steel table with a conveyor belt suspended from the ceiling running around it. Hanging from one of the hooks on the conveyor was the obvious corpse of a human, on the next hook, hung Thomas Knight! His hands were handcuffed together and the cuffs were looped over the hook. His feet were nearly four feet off the floor. In front of him, with his back toward Susan, was the most gigantic creature she had ever seen. In his right hand, he held a giant bowie knife. She watched mesmerized as he used the knife to effortlessly slice Knight's T-shirt from his neck to his navel. She slowly raised the .380 and took dead aim at the creature's head. "Don't move!" she shouted.

The startled creature ignored her warning and quickly spun around with the menacing knife in his hand. Even though she was holding her pistol on him, she had to fight the urge to scream when she saw his hideous face. The monster slowly raised the knife and took a step toward her.

"Stop! Don't take another step!" warned Susan. "I'll shoot if I have too!"

The creature lunged at her, the stainless blade of the knife glinting in the bright lights.

She fired! The giant froze in mid-stride and stared at her. Slowly a stream of blood started oozing from the smoking black hole that, an instant before, had been his left eye socket. With a loud guttural moan, he raised the knife again and stepped toward her. Then he toppled forward onto his face, with a loud thud, sticking the knife into the linoleum floor six inches from the toe of her hiking boot.

A small pool of blood started to form around the giant's head. She could see a small hole in his skull above his left ear where evidently the bullet had exited. She walked slowly around the body, keeping the gun trained on the motionless hulk. She kicked him solidly in the ribs and got no reaction.

Susan ran over to the body of Thomas Knight hanging from the hook. She reached up and touched him carefully with her fingers on the side of his naked torso. He was still warm! She looked up at his face and suddenly his eyes opened!

He looked down at her. "Susan?" he whispered.

She looked around frantically trying to find something to stand on to get him down. She finally found a rickety chair and grasping him around his torso with both hands, she was able to lift him up the two inches necessary to slide his hands off the hook. She could not hold his weight and both of them toppled to the floor in a heap.

He moaned. "My shoulder," he whispered.

She ran over to the giant and using all her strength partially rolled him over onto his side. She reached into the front pocket of the filthy coveralls and found the handcuff key. She ran back to Knight and unlocked his shackles. She gently pulled his right arm down to his side without protest. However, when she touched his left arm he yelped in pain.

The shock of the pain in his left shoulder had the effect of instantly reviving him. He looked up at her "Susan?" he asked again, as if he was unsure that it was really her. He turned over onto his right side, gingerly holding his left arm with his right hand and sat up. He looked over at the huge body prone on the floor. "Is he dead?" he asked with a nod of his head.

"I'm afraid so," Susan said quietly. "There was no choice. I shot him in the eye."

Knight nodded and gestured to her to help him try to stand. Once on his feet, he asked, "Did you check on Isis?"

"Who?" asked Susan.

"Isis Flynn, she's chained up on a cot over there." He nodded again with his head. Together they walked over to the cot and looked down.

Isis was in a state of shock and stared at them with terrified eyes.

Thomas touched her gently on the right hand. She struggled violently at the touch. "Isis. It's Thomas," he said grasping her hand firmly.

Suddenly there was recognition in her eyes. "Thomas is it really you?"

"Yeah kid. You're all right." He turned and asked Susan, "Do you still have the handcuff key?"

She handed him the key and as he quickly worked the locks on Isis' restraints he said, "This is Susan Strong, and she was going to pay your ransom." Once he had removed the shackles, he walked behind Isis. Gently putting his good arm under her shoulder, he lifted her into a sitting position. "You're free," he said.

Realizing for the first time that she was not restrained, Isis reached down and tried to cover her naked breasts with the remnants of her tattered blouse. She carefully swung her legs over the edge of the rusty cot and put her feet on the floor. Then she started to sob uncontrollably.

Susan rushed to her side, put her arms gently around her shoulders and sat on the cot next to her.

She gently pressed Isis's face into her shoulder. Susan looked up at Knight and said, "See if you can find something for her to cover herself."

Knight looked around the interior of the trailer. There was junk everywhere. Baby Doc, in addition to being a sociopath was also a pack rat. Every conceivable desert picking seemed to have been piled along the walls in boxes and on makeshift shelving. The only sign of organization were the two, oversized, gray, metal, storage cabinets. Knight opened the one on the left and recoiled in horror! The cabinet was full of clothes, tattered and bloodstained. They were all carefully arranged on hangers. It appeared to be a kind of a bizarre trophy case of Baby doc's victims. There were a least a dozen outfits on the hangars. Knight's safari jacket was also hanging on the rack. Baby Doc had already assigned him a place in the case!

He pulled his coat off the hangar and quickly checked the pockets. Everything was there. He slipped on the coat and felt an immediate relief from the cold. If he did not find anything else, Isis could use the jacket.

Knight turned the chrome handle on the left door of the second cabinet and slowly opened it. Suddenly, the right side door flew open with a bang and Knight froze with fear. A huge monster with phosphorescent green eyes tumbled onto him. He did not have time to fight the panic. It seized him instantly and it felt like a huge hand was squeezing his heart!

The head of the thing thrust itself next to Knight's. It was literally eyeball to phosphorescent eyeball! The thing pressed against his chest. Slimy tentacles attached to the thing's shiny gray skin, draped over

Knight's shoulders and threatened to completely envelop him. He felt as if a tub of pythons had been dumped upon him.

With his one good arm and hand, he pushed, desperately trying to free himself. The weight of the thing was too much, he stumbled backwards and the thing fell on him, knocking the wind out of him. Knight clawed, pushed, kicked and twisted, doing everything he could to escape the morass of slimy tentacles that were entangling his body. The thing weighed a ton and his struggles were not producing results. He did the next best thing. He yelled for help!

Susan jumped at the cry, nearly knocking Isis to the floor. She looked across the room, horrified to see the gigantic thing on top of Knight. She pulled the .380 from her waistband and ran to the struggling shapes. The thing was so huge there was no way she could physically attack it. She pulled up the pistol and shaking with fright pulled the trigger twice. She could see two neat holes appear in the thing's head. The shots had no effect! Knight was still struggling with the demon!

Susan fired twice again, this time at the thing's torso. Instantly there was a loud hissing sound and white gas started enveloping the struggling pair. In less than a second, they were completely obscured by the gas. Desperately, Susan tried to position herself for another shot. She had only three rounds left. Slowly a shape started to emerge out of the gas cloud and she steadied herself for another shot. It was Knight!

He stumbled toward her, his right hand holding his injured left arm. He was shaking as he fell into Susan's arms.

Susan tried to catch him and still keep the automatic trained on the quickly dissipating white cloud.

Both of them looked at the huge dark shape lying on the floor. It was not moving.

"Thanks…" said Knight hoarsely; the adrenaline rush had left his throat feeling like a dry lakebed.

"What in the hell is that thing?" asked Susan, still keeping the pistol pointed in its direction.

Knight walked slowly over to the thing and kicked it soundly. The shape gave way at the kick. He could not believe what he was seeing! The thing on the floor was not a person or an alien, but instead it was simply a large, rubberized spacesuit! He picked up what had looked like its head. It was a crude, homemade space helmet with a large black contraption mounted where the eyes should have been. There were two phosphorescent green disks still glowing. "Nice shooting," he said as he put his hand into the helmet, stuck his fingers out through the bullet holes and wiggled them.

"Those eyes!" said Susan pointing with the barrel of the pistol.

"Night vision goggles," answered Knight. "Early Soviet I'd guess."

"What are those things? Susan asked, again pointing the pistol at the tentacles wrapped around the suit.

Knight lifted one up and traced its connection to the suit. "I see," he said authoritatively.

"What?" asked Susan.

He gestured to the two large black cylinders on the back of the suit. "Those are liquid nitrogen bottles and these tentacles are plastic tubes that allow the nitrogen to circulate around the body. Obviously, the object was to cool the exterior of the neoprene suit."

"What on earth for? Why did he need all that crap," asked Susan, relieved that Spook was only a suit and not an authentic alien. She put her pistol back in her waistband.

Knight bent over and inspected the suit carefully. "The NTS Security people have installed infrared heat imaging sensors in the desert. With this suit on, Baby Doc's natural body heat would not appear on any of their sensors. They wouldn't know he was there. One of your shots put a hole in one of the cylinders, that's what caused the gas cloud."

Knight went to the cabinet; "Baby Doc must have been hiding in here when I came in. That's how he got the jump on me." He gingerly touched his broken collarbone as he recalled the unexpected paralyzing blow. He reached into the darkened cabinet and retrieved two large plastic snowshoes. "With these on, his weight was spread around enough that the seismic sensors wouldn't pick him up. Wearing the cool suit and using the rest holes we found, he could move around the area pretty much undetected."

He looked back into the cabinet and withdrew what looked like a shovel handle, but with a huge metal claw attached to the end. "Evidently he used this to rake the desert for more diamonds, and for disemboweling, assistant professors." He gestured toward the remnants of the corpse still on the meat hook.

Isis whimpered and the two of them turned toward her. Knight gingerly took off his safari coat and handed it to Susan. She carefully spread it across Isis' shoulders and then buttoned it.

Knight walked over to the floor by the large butcher-block table. He bent over, retrieved the Glock 18 and picked up his shoulder holster from the table. He looped the familiar well-worn strap over his good shoulder and put the pistol in its proper place. He turned and started to walk back to Isis and Susan.

Suddenly there was a horrific boom! It sounded like a sonic boom only it was much closer. The whole building shook violently, sending everything that was on a shelf crashing onto the floor.

Instantly there was a large roar like the sound of a jet airplane engine on takeoff. Then without warning, the floor of the trailer split open and a cloud of yellow sulfuric gas started filling the building.

"What in the hell is happening?" screamed Susan over the noise. She was still holding the frightened Isis.

"It's the volcano!" shouted Knight, running toward them. "We have got to get out of here, now!"

CHAPTER 14

Johnny Ford was on his way home when he received the call he had been waiting for. Payday was finally at hand, no more nickel-and-dime time. In a few hours, he could have all cars, women and cocaine he wanted, not to mention finally being free of working with the stupid Russians.

The usual street corner where he bought his daily high was not active until after dark. Nevertheless, he thought he would give it a try. There was no reason why he should not start the party early.

He slowed the Mustang almost to a stop as he drove by the corner. The third time around the block the shirtless drug dealer was waiting.

"You're early today," he said taking a long look each way down the street. This could easily be a setup.

"I've got an appointment," said Johnny as he handed the four thousand dollars through the window.

"You must be having a party," said the dealer. Johnny's usual purchase was always five hundred.

"Just taking odds on my bet," said Johnny as he laid the eight small bags of white powder on the passenger's seat.

With the Mustang in the garage, Johnny went directly into his home office. It would only take a few buttons to bring the computer system to life. As the machines started their diagnostic programs, Johnny headed to the bathroom. By the time he had powdered his nose, the system was ready.

The multiple modems made their annoying sounds as they connected with their numerous servers. With everything online, each of the six computer monitors had a different bank's account displayed. In a few hours, those accounts that now showed thousands would show millions.

The phone startled him when it rang. "Everything is all set," he said. He listened. "Yes dammit, I'm sure!" he answered impatiently. He looked up at the six clocks, each set for a separate time zone, on the wall above the monitors. "I'll send the email in one hour." He hung up and started tapping in encryption codes with the keyboard. In spite of his cocaine high, he was able to type in seventeen nine-digit numbers without an input error. His previous employers had never appreciated his talent, they had only seen a coked-up kid instead of the 196 IQ computer whiz.

———·———

"Oh no! Sarge!" cried the Corporal. "You need to see this!"

Sergeant Conway laid down the men's magazine, the one he subscribed to for the articles, and rushed over to the corporal's station. His eyes darted across the monitor, his mouth opened and the well-chewed cigar fell out onto the floor. He picked up the phone in a panic. "This is Sergeant Conway in TSG I need to speak to the General immediately!"

"Look at this Sarge!" The Corporal had fear in his voice.

"Come on…Come on!" the Sergeant shouted at the phone. Suddenly there was a voice on the other end.

"General. Sergeant Conway TSG, Sir. I've got every ground sensor on the whole west side of the site going off!" He listened. "That's right sir! The whole west side!" He listened again. "Yes sir, we have the automatic recorders going." The General was giving instructions. "Yes sir, I understand. I'll have everything ready when you get here!" The Sergeant continued to stare at the monitor in disbelief as he absentmindedly hung up the phone. This was happening a whole day before it was supposed to!

Suddenly the monitor showed the sensors firing in waves. The pulses were moving from east to west. They would start about a mile east of the base site and move westward toward Indian Springs.

"What is it Sarge?" asked the Corporal, trying desperately to recall if he had been taught how to react to this situation in training class.

"This is definitely not good," said the Sergeant. "The pulses should be moving northwest and not southwest."

"Is this...FUBAR?" stammered the Corporal, obviously still trying to understand the term.

The burly Sergeant nodded, "Corporal, it doesn't get any more FUBAR than this!"

———·———

Knight, Susan and Isis ran and stumbled out the front door of the trailer. If they thought the inside of the trailer had been hell, the outside left no doubt.

The sky was nearly pitch black and it was raining hard. Off to the northeast there was a bright red glow on the horizon. There were small fissures in the ground of the compound and high-pressure gases were being released from the magma body below the surface. The gases, which to the nostrils had a sharp sulfuric smell, shot up through cracks with a roaring hiss.

Suddenly the air was filled with what sounded like a gigantic sonic boom. With a deafening roar, the ground opened up, exposing a brightly glowing yellow orange blob. The raindrops hit the molten rock and made a sound like someone frying bacon. Clouds of steam shot upward like from a thousand geysers. The ground was heaving and thrusting, making it difficult to stand. There was no ride in Vegas that could top this one.

Vulcan, the Roman God of Fire, supposedly lived deep in the earth. There at his underground forge, he made the weapons for the Gods. If legend was true, then he was busy as hell today.

Volcanic eruptions are driven by the explosive power of pent up gases. Like opening a well-shaken, soda can. The volcanoes with thick, pasty lava tend to hold in the gases and are the most dangerous. Those with a more fluid flow tend to be less gaseous and therefore are not as explosive. The lava simply flows from these eruptions like a river. This eruption had luckily produced the fluid type of lava. The first type could have destroyed everything within fifty miles with one mighty blast.

Knight struggled to recall what Professor Aronson and his experts had said about volcanoes in the meeting about Operation Big Deal.

They had been afraid that the pressure in the Sedan Chamber would simply build up and then blow with a cataclysmic force. Evidently, they had been wrong. Both about the time the volcano would blow and the type of eruption. What was happening now, although scary as hell, was more a gradual release of the pent-up gases. It was also obvious that the Army had predicted the wrong direction that the eruption would go. It was happening right under their feet at Baby Doc's, not as had been expected, ten miles north on Flynn's golf course!

"I think we better get the hell out of here!" shouted Susan over the roar of the venting and the hiss of the steam from the rain. It was coming down in buckets.

Isis was still in shock but her wits were catching up to her.

"Can you drive a truck?" Knight asked her.

Isis looked at the ice cream truck and nodded, "My dad owned a car and truck rental business while I was a teenager, and he used to make me wash them after school." Little did she know that that experience was going to save her life.

Knight pointed to an area behind the trailer, "My car is over there in a wash. I can't drive with my broken shoulder, so Susan will have to drive my car." He looked at Susan for confirmation.

She nodded.

"Isis you take the truck, get to Indian Springs, call Jack and tell him you're all right." Knight looked at her. "Are you sure you're okay."

"I'm still woozy as hell, but I'll do anything to get out of here!" Isis shouted over another loud hiss.

Suddenly, with another loud boom, the earth cracked open again. This time, not more than one hundred yards away from the trio. Glowing red lava started bubbling through the fissure. The lava started to puddle and then flow directly toward them.

"Go now!" shouted Knight, shoving Isis toward the truck with his good arm.

Isis jumped into the cab of the truck and it started immediately. She pushed the remote control for the power gate on the visor. By the time the gate was fully open she had the truck turned around. She ground the gears once, found the right one and gunned it through the opening.

Knight and Susan were already running hand-in-hand up the small rise beside the compound. When they reached the top Susan suddenly stopped. Knight turned and looked at her quizzically. She pointed to the trailer. The river of lava had already reached the fence and it was being melted and pushed over simultaneously.

"Oh!" she shouted as she put the back of her hand up to cover to her mouth as if to stifle a scream.

The door to the trailer had opened and Baby Doc had stumbled out. He looked around and then ran back inside.

"What the…?" asked Knight.

"I shot him in the eye!" cried Susan. "I know I did!"

"You might have hit his eye socket and it deflected the bullet out his temple without hitting his brain." Knight guessed recalling seeing the exit wound above Baby Doc's left ear.

"Well, he isn't going to survive this one," Susan said emphatically, pointing to the slow moving river of white-hot lava nearly to the steps of the trailer.

Again the door to the trailer flew open and Baby Doc stepped out, this time with his snowshoes under his arm. There were only a few square feet of desert left. He reached down and started to buckle them on.

"That ain't gonna work," said Knight, fascinated by the fact that Baby Doc was contemplating running across the lava flow to safety.

With the snowshoes firmly buckled on, Baby Doc backed up as far as he could against the trailer steps. Then he half shuffled, half skipped toward the creeping lava before jumping on top of it and starting to run.

Knight and Susan stared with their mouths open.

Baby Doc managed to make it over nearly fifteen feet of the molten rock before the snowshoes were reduced to gobs of formless melted plastic. On his next step, his right leg broke through the soft black crust and sunk up to his calf. He stared in disbelief at his leg before the other leg also broke through the crust and into the molten mass.

Between the continuous venting hiss of the gas and the sizzling of the rain on the lava, no one could hear Baby Doc's screams.

Knight and Susan looked on in horror as the nearly two thousand-degree lava reduced his feet to ash and melted body fat. His pants caught on fire and he flailed desperately with his hands trying to distinguish them. As the lava incinerated more of his legs, he slowly sank deeper into the white-hot morass. He continued to mouth fruitless screams. He looked like a flaming torch sticking out of the lava.

Suddenly a flaming arm shot up above what had been his head. Hanging from the arm was as small object that glinted brightly even from where Knight and Susan were standing. It was his diamond!

Then it was all gone and there was nothing to mark were only seconds before had stood the massive hulk of a human being.

Knight and Susan turned and continued running toward the Ferrari without saying a word. The memory of what they had just witnessed would be with them for a long time.

They were nearly to the Ferrari when suddenly Susan exclaimed breathlessly, "I've decided!"

"Decided what?" Knight asked, surprised at her sudden outburst.

"I've decided I'm getting a bigger gun," she replied.

If Knight had not been in such pain from his broken shoulder, he would have doubled over with laughter.

———·———

The Senator was in Flynn's office anxiously waiting for the email telling them where to pay the twenty million dollar ransom for Isis.

Flynn had been drinking heavily, desperately trying to cover his apprehension. He was now a bad drunk.

The Senator was doing his best to avoid provoking him into a physical fight.

Flynn could not win even though he thought he grew six inches with every drink he took. "That frigging insurance company better come through or I'll have that blonde's tits in a ringer," he threatened, using one of his rural Kansas expressions.

The Senator had had enough. "Dammit Jack. I'm sick and tired of you going on about the money. We're talking about my daughter!"

Flynn backed down and said apologetically, "I'm sorry, Joe. I really am worried about Isis. It's just that all this crap is catching up to me. I haven't had any luck but bad luck for days." Flynn was a gambler through and through and luck meant everything. "Why, I couldn't get over the top on a pass line six or eight bet." Next to throwing a seven with the dice, the odds of throwing a six or an eight were the best on the crap table. All true players thought they could make those throws every time.

Flynn walked over to the bar to freshen up his drink. As he reached into the refrigerator freezer to retrieve the ice-cold bottle of vodka, the whole building shook violently. "What the…?" he asked, ducking involuntarily.

A huge boom reverberated off the massive glass windows surrounding the office.

The Senator jumped up, looked out the window and pointed. "It looks like a lot of smoke off to the north."

"Was it an airplane crash or what?" asked Flynn, looking at the smoke cloud just visible beside the peak of Mount Charleston. "It looks like it's raining over there." It was not raining in Vegas.

"You don't suppose it was that nuclear thing you and Knight were talking about?"

The Senator shrugged his shoulders. "That wasn't supposed to happen until tomorrow afternoon."

Flynn walked to his desk and called his secretary. "Find out what in the hell that was all about," he ordered and then hung up.

"Whatever it was, it was a big sucker," said the Senator flatly.

General Guts Grant was studying the Corporal's monitor intently.

"Sir?" asked the Sergeant trying to rouse him from his concentration. The explosions had scared everyone, but at least they had finally gotten the annoying, whooping fire alarm turned off.

"Sir?" he asked again.

Guts looked at him blankly. His career had vanished in less than a second. The premature explosion would be seen as his fault. He had planned to spend the next week, being interviewed in front of television cameras. That would have been followed by at least a couple of weeks of Washington cocktail parties where everyone would have been dying to hear about how he had saved Las Vegas. He would have handled himself so brilliantly that they would have finally had to give him his second star. Now everything, just like the desert north of Indian Springs, had gone up in smoke.

He stood up and walked out the door of the TSG without saying anything or acknowledging his entourage that had gathered outside the office.

The shapely, brunette Captain stepped forward and put her hand on his arm. "I'm sorry Sir," she whispered.

Guts stared blankly at her as he continued walking. He reached into his left holster and took out the .45 automatic. He held it loosely at his side and thought about putting it to his head. Instead, he started spinning it on his finger. "If I find out who screwed this up, I'll shoot 'em in the guts and let the hogs eat 'em."

———·———

Isis was steering the big ice cream truck as best she could. But, the rutted road was twisting the front wheels violently. It was all she could do, in her emaciated state, to keep the truck on the road.

She suddenly started shaking again. The interior of the truck smelled like Baby Doc and she could not help replaying in her mind what he had done to her. She did not know how she would tell Jack. She really did not want him or anyone to know what had happened to her. She did not know if she could continue to live in Vegas. She wanted to just drive and drive, and get as far away as she could from that awful place.

She pulled the truck up to the convenience store next to the gas pumps beside the brown-stuccoed casino in Indian Springs

When she walked into the door of the convenience store, the young, pimply-faced clerk recoiled in terror. He had recognized the truck as Baby Doc's.

"I need to use a phone," she said.

The wide-eyed clerk did not answer, he merely pointed to the phone beside the cash register.

She dialed Flynn's private number. When he answered, she said, "Hi baby. I'm free." She listened. "Thomas Knight and some gal named Susan found me. I'm at a gas station at the main intersection of the highway in Indian Springs." She listened again. "I'm all right. I just need you to come and pick me up as soon as you can." She looked around at the convenience store's inventory. "Oh, and bring at least a couple of hundred bucks. I need to buy some things." She listened again. "I miss you too. Now hurry. I'll tell you all about it when I see you."

She hung up the phone and looked at the clerk. "I need some things." She checked the pockets on Knight's safari jacket. They were full of everything but money. "I can't pay right now, but someone is coming to pick me up and they will have money."

The clerk looked out the window at the ice cream truck. "Is Baby Doc with you?" He asked tentatively, straining to see if there was anyone inside the cab.

Isis sensed that he was deathly afraid of Baby Doc, so she lied. "Yeah he's in the back taking a nap. He told me to tell you to give me whatever I wanted."

The lie worked. The clerk nervously waved his hand toward the store's shelves.

Isis quickly did her shopping. She bought; six candy bars, a bag of cheese puffs, two ice-cream bars, three cold bottles of water, a lipstick, one comb, one toothbrush, one tube of toothpaste and one Souvenir of Indian Springs Nevada T-shirt. She made a pile on the counter. "I'll need the key to the women's restroom."

The clerk looked again out the window at the truck, grateful there still was no sign of Baby Doc. He reached beneath the counter and produced a ten-inch length of 2 X 4 with a key chained to it. There was obvious trepidation in his voice as he said, "It's around on the left side."

Isis took the key and unwrapped one of the ice cream bars. Her eyes filled with tears as she felt the ice cream slide down her parched throat. Nothing had ever tasted so good!

———·———

The Ferrari was sitting in the wash where Knight had left it. "I hope we can get out of here," he said. "I'm afraid that the Pirelli unidirectional tires aren't worth a damn in the mud."

Susan opened the driver's door and slid into the tan seat. Knight gingerly wiggled into the passenger's, trying not to move his injured shoulder anymore than necessary. They both neglected their seat belts.

"As I remember you are familiar with the gear shift," he chuckled.

"That wasn't funny," she protested. "I still owe you big time for what you did with your car to my butt."

Knight's mouth was open to ask her what in the world she meant, when suddenly there was another loud boom. He reprioritized his thoughts. "Let's get out of here!"

Susan turned on the windshield wipers and headlights and turned the car around. Knight had been right. The grooves in the tires loaded up with mud instantly and there was almost no traction. The Ferrari slid around violently as Susan started up the draw.

Suddenly there was a loud roar. Different from the booms the volcano had made. It sounded like a freight train was coming toward them. They both stared through the rain-covered windshield trying to see what was causing the sound.

"Oh no!" shouted Knight. He was the first one to see it. There was a six-foot high wall of foaming brown water roaring down the draw! A six-inch deep flash flood will knock a man off his feet. A two-foot deep flood can carry away a car.

The wave hit the Ferrari like a locomotive. The car rolled over onto its top and started bobbing along in the ice-cold murky water. The trapped occupants were being tossed around like clothes in a front-loading washing machine.

Susan grabbed her door handle and pushed with all her might. She had barely managed to crack open the door when with a loud bang, it was torn completely off the car. The interior instantly filled with frigid, filthy water. The pressure of the torrent on her body sucked her head under the flow. The roar of the flood was replaced by a loud gurgling as her ears filled with water. She flailed at the dark brown fluid, desperately trying to escape the watery coffin.

Then, suddenly she was free and her head broke the surface. She coughed and gagged, struggling to swim with the raging current, trying desperately to stay on top of the water. She looked around, but there was no sight of her passenger or the red sports car! Then she saw it! A large uprooted tree, tossed around like a toothpick in the flood, was headed directly for her! Before she could duck, it hit her a crazing blow on top of her head. Instantly she saw stars. Still dazed, she clawed at a root of the tree as it floated by, but her hand slipped uselessly off the slimy smooth surface.

Knight was semi-conscious. One minute he and Susan were in the car, in the next, he was face down submerged in ice water. He imagined he was holding his breath underwater in his pool and swimming toward the pool light. When he finally reached it, he was confused. There was no pool light. It was a headlight attached to a submerged red car! He was not dreaming! He was drowning! Instincts honed by his years of experience swimming and diving suddenly awoke. He had been spun around so violently he no idea which way was up! It took all of his discipline to fight the panic rising in his chest. Expelling what was left of the precious air in his burning lungs, he watched as the air bubbles floated down and to the left. He followed the bubbles, kicking as hard as he could, ignoring his confused equilibrium screaming that he was going the wrong way! It seemed like an eternity before he broke the surface, gasping for air. It took a few seconds before he could shake off the cobwebs and remember what had happened. His broken clavicle, feeling as if it was being stabbed with a red-hot poker, quickly cleared away any remaining confusion.

He looked for Susan, but she was nowhere to be seen. He called her name, but shouting against the roar of the muddy rapids was useless.

Ahead he could see the torrent was carrying him toward a small canyon with rock outcroppings. If he went in there, he would have no chance of crawling out of the raging flow. Trying to protect his injured shoulder, he kicked and swam using his strongest sidestroke, but the current was too powerful and it swept him into the chasm. The volcanic rock of the canyon walls tore at his body mercilessly as he was dragged along.

Then he saw it! A small sandbar-like shelf was sticking into the rapids! He turned his body and with two powerful kicks was able to make it to the edge of the shelf. He dug the fingers on his good hand into the wet sand desperately trying to pull his aching body onto the precarious refuge. Finally managing to crawl out of the filthy torrent, he collapsed onto his back. The canyon walls were spinning. The tossing and turning in the flood had made him seasick. He rolled over onto his right side and vomited.

Suddenly, above the roar, he heard a faint cry from upstream. Someone was calling his name!

He sat up and frantically looked up the canyon. There, among the white caps of the dark brown water, was a small flash of yellow. It was Susan!

Knight staggered to his feet and found there was barely enough room on the shelf to stand. Susan would be going by at a high rate of speed. He would get only one chance to grab her. He just had time to set himself before she went past. He plunged his good arm into the water and somehow found her wrist. He held on as tight as he could, but the weight of the rushing flood was pulling her from his grasp. Then from some unknown reserve, he found the strength to give her a huge yank. She popped out of the water and nearly flew onto the shelf beside him. He fell back in excruciating pain. He had dislocated his right shoulder from its socket when he pulled her out.

Susan was coughing violently and it took a few seconds before she could speak. "Thanks," she said hoarsely.

Knight was in terrific pain. "I think I dislocated my right shoulder," he moaned.

Susan rolled over and looked at him. He did look terrible. The remnants of his T-shirt hung loosely from his left arm. His finely chiseled body was covered with small cuts and bruises.

In between waves of pain, he said, "That's the last time I let you drive my car!"

Susan coughed again, when she tried to laugh.

"This…This isn't good," he stammered. The ice cold water had caused him to start to slip into hypothermia. His teeth were chattering uncontrollably.

Susan was shaking too. "One minute we're in danger of being barbecued alive and now we're going to freeze to death," she said.

"It's always something," said Knight weakly.

A pitch-black sky was suddenly bathed in a blinding flash of light. The lightning had hit only a few yards away. CRAAACK! The sonic boom from the strike echoed down the canyon. The smell of ozone filled the air.

"Buck's band!" shouted Knight, trying instinctively to raise his arm to point.

"What?" asked Susan.

"There! On the other side of the canyon wall, I saw Buck Ander's band!"

"What in the world…are you talking about?" she asked impatiently, her teeth also starting to chatter.

"When the lightning lit up the canyon, I saw some ancient petroglyphs on the opposite wall. They were dancing figures playing flutes! Buck has this ditty he sings, …the shadows played the flute."

Susan looked across the canyon. "I don't see anything," she said shivering. She could care less about the ranting of some old cowboy.

Suddenly from behind them, rocks started rolling off the canyon wall. Then the ground began to shake.

They both turned in unison and looked at the mud covered rock wall behind them. Without warning, a large car-sized chunk of the wall slowly caved off into the torrent.

The lightning flashed again and this time they both saw what it revealed.

"The lizard stared at me!" shouted Knight. There in the side of the canyon wall was the huge fossilized skull of a fierce meat-eating dinosaur. The white fossil showed up clearly against the dark brown rock.

They barely had time to contemplate their discovery. Another lightning strike landed nearby. Again, the wall and the dinosaur were bathed in bright white light. There, sprinkled among the skull and its ten-inch teeth were sparking reflections. The fossilized skull was encrusted with diamonds!

CRAAACK! Again, the sonic boom echoed, but this time the reverberations shook the canyon walls violently. Small rocks tumbled down the wall and then, as if in slow motion, the rocks holding the diamonds and fossils sloughed off, sliding toward the helpless duo on the shelf.

They, clawed, crawled and scrambled desperately trying to avoid being buried by the slide. It was hopeless and the massive rocks pushed them off their perch and into the frigid raging current.

They bobbed along like driftwood. Susan had managed to get her arm under Knight's chin and was holding his head above the torrent.

Suddenly the steep canyon walls changed into a riverbank, the muddy tide turning from a cascading rapid into a swift flowing stream.

They floated for nearly a mile before they were able to maneuver themselves up onto the riverbank.

Susan pulled her helpless partner out of the flow and onto the desert floor. She lay there exhausted, gasping for air.

Knight coughed repeatedly trying to clear his lungs of the putrid water. Each time he did, the pain from his injured shoulders caused him to moan.

Susan slowly struggled to her feet and looked around. The stream level was going down as she watched. In a few minutes, there would be no trace of the flood that had nearly killed them.

It was still raining, although not as hard and the storm clouds were already drifting away. Across the desert floor, lights were moving along the horizon. It was the highway.

"Can you walk?" she asked.

"I don't know. I think so but you'll have to help me up," answered Knight weakly.

He yelped involuntarily with pain as she lifted him up with her hands under his armpits. She steadied him against her.

Even in his semi-delirious state and intense agony, he could smell the remnants of her jasmine perfume.

They walked, stumbled and staggered nearly a mile and a half before they got to the highway.

Susan helped Knight sit down. "I'll flag someone down," she said as she walked onto the shoulder of the inky, black asphalt.

A car was approaching and she could see the flashing blue and red light bar on its roof. She ran onto the road waving her arms violently.

The police car braked and swerved, barely missing her. The barrel-chested driver got out of the car swearing. "Dammit what's wrong with you. You could have been killed."

Susan recognized him. It was the Clark County Sheriff!

"It's me, Susan Strong!" she cried

The Sheriff shined his flashlight on her. "Ms. Strong is that really you?" he asked skeptically. The mud-caked, pathetic creature in front of him bore no resemblance to the coiffed and manicured gorgeous blonde he remembered.

"I've got Thomas Knight over here by the side of the road. He is badly hurt!" She took the stunned Sheriff by the hand and pulled him with her.

"He's in bad shape," said Susan as the Sheriff bent over the half naked, mud encrusted, moaning man. "One shoulder is broken and the other is dislocated. Can you call for an ambulance?"

The Sheriff looked up at her. "There's a terrific traffic jam north of Vegas. Everyone wants to see the volcano. It would take the paramedics at least an hour to get here. Let's see if we can get him into my cruiser's back seat."

It was all the two of them could do to get the six foot, three inch, Knight into the car.

Finally, with their injured cargo as comfortable as possible, they sped toward Vegas, the bubble lights and siren announcing their coming.

"What in the hell happened back there?" asked the Sheriff.

Susan related the entire story of Isis's rescue and Baby Doc's demise.

"Baby Doc's dead?" asked the Sheriff

"Fried to a crisp," answered Susan.

The Sheriff smiled at the thought of the monster going up in flames. "Well I knew about Isis Flynn. She was picked up in Indian Springs by the Colossus's helicopter and flown back to Vegas."

"I was hoping she made it all right," said Susan. She then proceeded to fill in the Sheriff on what they had seen of the Assistant Professor's body.

"I had a hunch that Baby Doc had been involved in that. If what you say is true, that the son-of-a-bitch is toast, then I'll be leading the celebrating in Indian Springs tonight. Him and his twin caused us all no end of grief."

"His twin?" asked Susan. She vaguely remembered that Knight had said something about a twin.

"Well she's not as bad as he was. But, I'll bet you dollars to donuts she's involved in this somehow."

"She?" asked Susan.

"Yeah, his fraternal twin. Hell, you probably know her. She's the headliner at the Colossus."

"Honey?" asked Susan incredulously. There was no way she would have guessed that the horrible misshapen creature she had seen burned alive was related to the overly stacked blonde.

"Her actual name is Honeybee Prentice. She and Baby Doc were very close. In fact, the rumor was that they were so close that Baby Doc had knocked her up when they were teenagers."

"Honey had a baby?"

"Well he's not a baby now. In fact, he works at the Colossus too. He's the head parking valet."

Susan shook her head in disbelief. "Johnny is Honey and Baby Doc's son?"

"Johnny Ford Prentice, according to his rap sheet. Mostly minor drug stuff."

The cruiser pulled up to the emergency entrance at University Memorial hospital. The attendants carefully lifted Knight onto a gurney and started wheeling him down a corridor toward the emergency room.

Knight looked up at Susan. "My right hand," he said weakly.

She wrapped both her hands around his clenched fist.

"Come closer," he ordered.

She bent over and put her ear to his lips.

"I plucked its eye and he blinked," he whispered. He opened his fist and a rock fell into her hand.

"I am sorry Ma'am. You will have to wait outside," the white uniformed attendant ordered as he wheeled the rambling Knight through the swinging double doors.

Susan looked down at her hand. The egg-sized, uncut diamond sparkled brilliantly in the stark white interior of the emergency room.

CHAPTER 15

Johnny Ford had the ransom email ready to send. It instructed Jack Flynn to electronically transfer the twenty million dollar ransom to a bank in the Grand Cayman Islands. It was a simple but effective plan. Traditionally kidnappers had the ransom put in a suitcase and thrown over a bridge somewhere in the dead of night.

Of course, in the world of high-tech crime detection, the money would be marked, the drop site put under surveillance, and even a miniature homing device put in the money carrier. Even if a criminal where to pull off a successful abduction, the odds were overwhelming that the perpetrator would be caught when he tried to pick up the ransom money.

Johnny's system relied on the world of high-tech also, but he would never touch the money.

Once the ransom had been electronically transferred, it would be instantaneously transferred again, this time to a Channel Island bank. Then it would be moved again and again, to the Bahamas, to Hong Kong and finally to a numbered account in Switzerland. All these movements would be made at the speed of light. The money would vanish down the electronic pipeline before any authority could begin to track it.

It had only taken Johnny two days to set up the system. He had been able to put it together so that everything could be monitored and controlled right from his home office on the fairway of the golf course in Las Vegas!

The whole kidnapping had been an accident. Usually when someone discovered Baby Doc's diamond hunting, he simply killed the person, sawed them into pieces and fed them to Honey's bears. For years, he had gotten away with his murderous diamond hunt. Isis's kidnapping was different. When she literally stumbled upon him, he had taken her captive to fulfill his own twisted sexual fantasy. It was Honey, who, when she found out what happened, was able to see the profit potential.

Johnny put together the money transfer and Bulldog unwittingly supplied the inside information on what the law was doing. It was a perfect plan.

The email was typed, the encryption software loaded, and it was time to collect the money. Johnny was ready to press the button and send the email, when the doorbell rang.

It was probably the neighborhood kid he had hired to fluff up his flower beds. When he stood up from the computer, he was woozy. His high was already going away. At this rate, his quadruple order would be gone by the morning.

He unlocked the deadbolt on the front door only to have it violently kicked open.

The Ninja-suited policeman pointed his H & K 9mm machine gun at him and hollered, "On the floor now!"

When Johnny was slow in reacting, the officer moved to his side and kicked him behind the left knee. Paralyzed by the blow, his leg buckled and he fell down. Before he could say a word he was handcuffed and his house full of armed police officers.

———·———

Honey was as nervous as one of her female bears in heat. She had not been able to reach Johnny for over two hours and she had sucked three squeeze bottles of honey dry. She was in her dressing room, frantically taking off the stage makeup after the matinee. She would ride over and see if everything was all right. "If you screw this up kid, I swear you will live to regret it," she said to herself still scrubbing away with the cold cream.

She jumped when the phone rang. It was her private line and she rarely got calls. When she did, it was usually Baby Doc calling from a pay phone explaining why he had done something stupid. She prayed he had not killed Isis. They needed her in case

Flynn demanded some proof of life before he paid the ransom.

"Hello," she said.

It was Johnny. "Hello Mama," he cried. "I'm in jail!"

———·———

The Doctor told Susan that Knight would be in surgery for at least a couple of hours and then in recovery for another hour. Putting the dislocated shoulder back in place was straightforward. Fixing his broken collarbone was another matter. They would have to put him under general anesthesia and then put on an internal splint.

After much protesting, the Doctor had finally convinced her there was nothing she could do for a while and she should go back to the Colossus and rest.

The barrel-chested Sheriff drove her to the hotel. Gary almost fainted when he saw her. She looked as if she had lost the world's mud wrestling championship.

"Don't say a word. Not one word," she warned, seeing the shocked look in his eyes.

The shower, the antiseptic cream and the adhesive bandages had nearly put her back together. Her hair, nails and complexion would have to wait until she got back from the hospital. She had been amazed to find that her father's solid gold solidus was still around her neck. The prized .380 Colt Mustang however, was under six feet of mud somewhere in the Nevada desert.

She picked up the diamond Knight had given her and held it to the light. It looked flawless. She was much more familiar with the exquisitely cut and polished stones at Tiffany's. If this one was as good as she thought, it was worth a king's ransom. She had been trying desperately to understand what Knight meant when he gave it to her. "Damn you Thomas!" she swore. Even when he gave her a gift she could not figure out where she stood.

———·———

The volcano eruption, although it had no impact whatsoever on the city, had caused an enormous uproar. It seemed as if the whole population of the valley was on the Strip. Everyone seemed to want to take one more chance if the world was coming to an end.

The Colossus limo that was taking Susan back to the hospital had only gone a block before it was hopelessly bogged down in traffic. At this rate, Knight would be recovered, healed and back in L.A. before she saw him. Patience was not her best virtue.

The limo phone rang. It was an international operator from Singapore. Susan instructed her to put the call through. It was an English-speaking doctor. It was not good news. Her Grandfather had had a heart attack and the prognosis was not good. He was temporarily stable, but because of his advanced age, something could happen at any time. He had asked for her.

Susan was shaking as she jotted down the phone numbers and the particulars from the doctor. "Thank you," she said. "Tell my Grandfather I'll be there as soon as possible."

She buzzed the limo driver. "Turnaround and take me to the VIP terminal at McCarran.

She called her office and told them to have her pilots prepare her Lear Longhorn for immediate departure to Singapore. She would call Knight as soon as she could.

———·———

"You stupid little idiot," Honey swore into the phone. "What are you doing in jail?" She listened. "They what? They arrested you for possession of cocaine?" She could not believe her ears. "Did you send the email?" She listened again. "Are you sure they busted you before you sent it?"

That meant Flynn was still expecting it. The situation was not as bad as it could have been. At least the police were not onto Johnny about the kidnapping. According to the early news reports, the volcanic eruption occurred in the desert north of town. That would place it near Baby Doc's, but so far, no injuries had been reported. Evidently, Baby Doc and Isis were still alive. She could get Johnny out of jail and everything would still workout. It just meant she would have to wait one more day before she got the twenty million dollars.

Johnny was whimpering into the phone.

"Suck it up," said Honey. "I'll have my attorney come down and bail you out as soon as I can. Now stop your bawling and don't you dare say one word to anyone about anything...understand?" She hung up the phone praying he would keep his mouth shut.

Honey headed for the VIP parking garage, her gold motorcycle helmet under her arm. She would tell Baby Doc not to fool with Isis, just yet. When she walked out of the hotel entrance, she was shocked to see the crowd. Everyone was in the streets trying to see the volcano. There was no way she was going to be able to get to Baby Doc's until the traffic got under control.

———·———

Susan's Learjet climbed out from McCarran's runway. She had instructed her pilot when he was clear of the takeoff pattern to make a pass over Baby Doc's former abode.

On the scale of the great volcanic eruptions, the Vegas Volcano, as the press was referring to it, was insignificant. Small eruptions like this one happened a couple of times a month worldwide. It had been an inconsequential geological event. The only reason anyone had paid any attention to it was because of the proximity to Vegas.

The sleek white jet banked sharply over Indian Springs. Through her window, Susan could make out the mile long crack in the Earth's crust. There was only a small gray cloud of smoke hanging over the site. There was no sign of the white-hot lava that only hours before had incinerated Baby Doc. There was no sign whatever of the raging flood that had nearly consumed her and Knight.

She picked up the plane intercom. "Okay, light the fires for Singapore," she instructed the co-pilot. She smirked at the irony of her unintentional pun.

———·———

Honey had not slept well. She needed to be sure Baby Doc had not done anything stupid. She would have her breakfast by the pool and then ride out and check on everything.

The waiter had set up her usual. She was slathering her toast with honey and reading all about the volcano in the paper.

"I thought I might find you here!"

Honey peeked over the top of her paper, shocked to see a vivacious blonde, her hands on her hips, standing in front of her. Honey quickly glanced around the pool area for an escape route. The pool was completely surrounded by uniformed Colossus security guards. "What do you want?" she asked angrily.

Isis Flynn stared at her. "I thought it was your voice I recognized at Baby Doc's."

Honey tried to take the offensive. "I don't know what you are talking about."

"I'm talking about kidnapping and murder. That's what I'm talking about!" Isis exclaimed.

Honey was about to protest her innocence again when the Africanized honeybee landed on her left hand. She instinctively swatted at it. The now provoked bee, fearing another attack, launched a preemptive strike by plunging its barbed stinger into the sensitive flesh between her thumb and index finger. "Ow!" she cried in pain, slapping at the bee again. This time she connected, crushing the bee. She flicked it off her hand with her fingers and stared at the bite for a second. Unlike a wasp, that can sting repeatedly, a honeybee can sting only once and then it dies.

Using her professionally manicured nails as a tweezers, she plucked out the bee's stinger and its still pulsating venom sac. She put the increasingly painful bite to her mouth and sucked on it, trying to stop the spread of the poison.

The bee fell to the table, its body in its death throes, releasing a pheromone into the air. In seconds, other bees near the pool area picked up the scent and homed in on the dead bee's attacker.

Honey swatted furiously at the bees that were suddenly numbering in the hundreds. They focused on her face. Within seconds, her head was totally engulfed. She looked like a beehive with legs.

Isis and the guards looked on in horror.

Honey stood up and staggered around. She closed her eyes tightly trying to protect them, but the bees stung her eyeballs right through her eyelids. She tried to scream. Instantly the bees flew up her nostrils and entered her gaping mouth. Two thousand bees were attacking her. They stung her tongue and the lining of her mouth. They found their way down her windpipe and into her lungs, stinging as they went.

Hopelessly disoriented, Honey tripped on the pool apron and fell head first into the pool. The bees retreated as her head went under the water. Instantly she felt the water entering her lungs and she instinctively clawed for the surface. When her head finally emerged, the bees were again on her in an instant.

Her head started to slip below the surface of the water as the venom from the stings finally paralyzed her body, making it impossible for her to paddle to stay afloat. She gasped for air through her horribly distorted lips but her lungs only filled with pool water. It took nearly three minutes before she lost consciousness and drowned.

Isis and the guards ran from the pool. The bees retreated, leaving only hundreds of carcasses and a human corpse behind.

———·———

The new, Russian, head-parking valet with the flesh-colored adhesive bandage on his nose retrieved the classic red '76 Cadillac Eldorado convertible from the VIP parking garage.

The lanky cowboy in the triple creased Stetson tipped him with a crisp twenty-dollar bill.

"It's a thing of beauty," admired the valet, awkwardly trying to convert his Russian thoughts into English.

"I'm the original owner," smiled the cowboy, snugging down his Stetson with both hands.

The cowboy steered the big caddy onto the Strip. He reached into his front jeans pocket and pulled out the diamond-encrusted bracelet. He fastened the well-worn clasp with his left hand as he steered with his right. With the bracelet firmly secured, he twisted his wrist back-and-forth in the sunlight. He smiled as he read the words spelled out by the brilliant sparkle of the diamonds, *1976 World Champion of Black Jack.*

He headed east out of town and had driven about two miles when he saw the hitchhiker beside the road. The hitcher, with both an arm and a leg in casts, used his good arm to point his thumb at the caddy and then down the road. He was desperately trying to flag down a ride.

The cowboy braked and steered the big caddy on to the shoulder of the highway.

The hitchhiker shuffled quickly to the car, dragging the leg in the cast. "Thanks," he said, puffing from the exertion of the run. He opened the door, sat down on the warm leather seat and gingerly maneuvered his bad leg into the car.

The cowboy looked at him. Beyond the obvious broken bones, his face also looked as if he had taken a considerable beating. "Where are you headed?" he asked.

"Anywhere but back there," said the hitchhiker with a nod of his head toward Vegas. "By the way my name is Bulldog…I mean Dwight," he corrected.

"Well Pardner, I'm headed for Wyoming," said the cowboy.

"I've never been to Wyoming," said Dwight. "What's it like?"

The cowboy looked at him, smiled and said, "Well if you were born there, it's wonderful. If you weren't, well then it's a kind of an acquired taste."

"Do they have casinos there?" asked Dwight.

"Nope. Just wide open spaces," said the cowboy.

"It sounds perfect!" said Dwight aka Bulldog, Basham. If he never saw another casino again, it would be all right with him.

EPILOGUE

Jack Flynn had won his bet. The Colossus's stock and that of the other casinos had taken a dump after the eruption. But, as he had predicted, it had started to rise again within only days. He bought back his shares low and then sold them again high. He cashed out of the Colossus and Vegas and left town. Ostensibly, he had started a business enterprise consulting practice in the Bahamas. The rumor was that he had arrived there with a boatload of cash and was working on convincing investors to back his building of the world's newest, largest hotel and casino.

Isis was back to her beautiful self, but now did not go anywhere without a formidable team of bodyguards.

Flynn had called the Ferrari Company in Maranello, Italy to try to replace Knight's lost car. When the factory had found out what had happened they eagerly decided to send one of their new limited edition, six hundred and fifty thousand dollar, Ferrari Enzos to replace it. Because they were still grateful for Knight's cleaning up the fiasco in Italy, they made a get-well gift of the new super car. Some lesser Arab Sheik would find himself suddenly bumped from the prestigious waiting list.

Since the car was free, Flynn sent Knight a check for the money he would have spent instead. In keeping with his paranoia about the IRS, he withheld the appropriate taxes.

Senator Devlin had parlayed the worldwide publicity about the Vegas Volcano into a huge media bonanza. He was now firmly ahead in the polls in his race for the White House.

Johnny Ford was still awaiting trial. The DEA had gotten involved, smelling a slam-dunk case; they were doing everything they could to make an example of him. Because Johnny was a nobody without money, high-profile attorneys had shown no interest in taking his case. He was pretty much screwed.

Honey's dramatic demise had been a top news story for a couple of days. She had been immediately replaced in the show by her understudy, who was the spitting image of her. Not one performance had been canceled.

Dwight "Bulldog" Basham had simply disappeared.

Captain Benteen, the shapely brunette with the enticing sway had visited Knight in the hospital. Her job had been to persuade him to keep quiet about Operation Big Deal. The Army had decided to pretend the whole plan never existed. They also maintained that the volcano was strictly due to a natural phenomenon. There was no mention of the connection to the Sedan blast from the past or the plan to detonate an underground nuclear explosion.

General Guts Grant had unceremoniously retired.

Tony Amato had gone ballistic when he found out that the Glock 18 was toast. It took an hour of pleading by Knight before he agreed to put in an order for another one.

Monica had dutifully filed an insurance claim on the Ferrari. Knight had been surprised to hear that, purely by chance, she had insured it through LSI. Nevertheless, they had paid off without hesitation.

While Knight was still recovering in the hospital, he called Senator Devlin and asked him to exert some pressure on the board responsible for licensing the Pleasant View Sanitarium where Buck and Vera were held. Eager to avoid a scandal and an investigation, the owners unceremoniously fired the smarmy director and the abusive nurse and hired a new administrator.

The day he was released from the hospital Knight took a cab to the sanitarium.

Vera clapped her bony hands with joy as Knight walked into the day room with the obvious brown paper bag in his hand.

"Is that what I think it is?" she asked hopefully.

"I told you I'd take care of you," said Knight as he handed her the precious package.

Vera's eyes danced with joy as she slid the precious bottle of bourbon out of the sack. Her hands trembled with anticipation as she twisted off the lid, put the bottle to her lips and took a long hard swig. "It's been a long time!" she cried with joy. "I'd almost forgotten how good it is!"

Knight looked across the day room at the lonely person seated, in the wheelchair, in front of the picture window. "How's Buck doing?" he asked.

"Unfortunately, the same as always," answered Vera shaking her head.

Knight walked over to the helpless creature in the chair, leaned down and whispered into his ear, "I saw your band…the lizard stared at me…but, I plucked his other eye." He could have sworn that Buck smiled faintly.

Knight walked back over to Vera. "I've made sure that you and Buck are going to be getting much better care," he said as he leaned over and kissed her on the forehead. "And, I've made arrangements for you to have a steady supply of your tonic."

"Bless you Sonny," she said patting him on the hand. She dabbed at the tears in her eyes before she took another swallow.

———·———

It had been nearly two months since Knight had been released from the hospital. The longest two months of his life. Susan Strong had left a message that the doctor handed him as he came out of the recovery room. He had saved it and read it over a hundred times.

I have an emergency and I have to go to Singapore. I will catch up with you when I can. I hope everything went well.

brown elixir, he looked at his reflection in the mirrors. He ran his right index finger over the still pink four-inch scar along his collarbone. There was no pain, only a small bump of scar tissue under the skin.

He stroked his chin, trying to decide if he looked good in the full beard. The staff seemed to like it, but he had put that down to their training to tell him what he wanted to hear. "Aspen women are so used to sleeping with mountain men I doubt if they even noticed it," he grinned, as he stepped into the now steaming shower.

The shower perked him up and he wrapped himself in the luxurious, fluffy, white terry cloth robe without bothering to towel off. In the Rocky Mountains, the low humidity allowed you to air-dry in seconds anyway. Picking up the coffee, he crossed the suite, opened the French doors and stepped out on to the huge circular deck. The view was breathtaking. There were little hints of the seasonal change from green to gold in the aspen trees at higher elevations on the nearby mountain. In two months with a little help from Mother Nature, the mountains would open for skiing and the society season would start. During the last six weeks, he had seen, from the deck, increased activity around the neighborhood's houses. The staffs were preparing for the pending arrivals of their billionaire owners, their guests and entourages.

A sudden, loud, whooshing roar caused him to whirl to his left. There, not a hundred yards away was a large, red and yellow, hot air balloon. It had appeared from behind the eve of the house. The pilot, trying to increase the lift in the balloon to clear the tree covered ridgeline behind the house, tugged on a cord and the propane burners ignited again with another loud whoosh. Knight watched with fascination, when suddenly four more brightly colored balloons appeared. *Hare and Hounds*, he thought, as he watched the balloons drift past. It was a popular contest among balloonists. One balloon called the Hare would launch and after a short interval, others called the Hounds would leave. The Hound that came closest to landing next to the Hare was declared the winner.

He knew it was really not a serious competition, but it provided the successful Hound substantial bragging rights at the champagne brunch that followed.

Suddenly, a sharp pang of apprehension gripped Knight and he nearly dropped his coffee cup. It could not be! His brain raced to confirm it! He could not be positive given the distance, but there, in the wicker basket of the Hare balloon, was Susan!

———.———

Also by Richard Swanson

the GOLDEN OASIS

ISBN: #0-9673271-0-5

The first Thomas Knight, action, adventure novel is set in the glittering, desert playground of Palm Springs, California. Knight and the beautiful, but enigmatic, Susan Strong find themselves at the epicenter of a madman's monstrously evil plan.

Upcoming

Thomas Knight is recuperating in Aspen, Colorado, the favorite mountain retreat for the world's billionaires. Without warning, he is caught up in a diabolical scheme tied to a priceless treasure. Can he unravel the clues in time to thwart the scheme and head off a cataclysmic disaster?